# Die
# and Stay
# Dead

# Die and Stay Dead

**NICHOLAS KAUFMANN**

ST. MARTIN'S GRIFFIN
NEW YORK

DIE AND STAY DEAD. Copyright © 2014 by Nicholas Kaufmann. All rights reserved. Printed in the United States of America. For information, address St. Martin's Press, 175 Fifth Avenue, New York, N.Y. 10010.

www.stmartins.com

The Library of Congress Cataloging-in-Publication Data is available upon request.

ISBN 978-1-250-03612-4 (trade paperback)
ISBN 978-1-250-03611-7 (e-book)

St. Martin's Griffin books may be purchased for educational, business, or promotional use. For information on bulk purchases, please contact Macmillan Corporate and Premium Sales Department at 1-800-221-7945, extension 5442, or write specialmarkets@macmillan.com.

First Edition: October 2014

10  9  8  7  6  5  4  3  2  1

*For Richard Matheson, who left us with a lifetime of stories to cherish. And for Bob Booth, Rick Hautala, and Phil Nutman, who followed him, too soon, into the dark.*

# Acknowledgments

I owe a great deal of gratitude, as always, to Daniel Braum, M. M. De Voe, Ben Francisco, and David Wellington, all of whom helped hammer this novel into shape. Thanks also to Victor LaValle, Sarah Langan, and Christopher Golden for being inspirations. Thanks to Beverly Bambury for spreading the word. Big, big thanks to Richard Curtis, truly the best agent on East 74th Street, and to Michael Homler and Lauren Jablonski, the best editor and editorial assistant at St. Martin's Press. And, of course, my wife, Alexa, who deserves the biggest thanks of all for her kindness, patience, understanding, and love.

Every day is Halloween.
—Ministry


Do your demons
Do they ever let you go?
—Dio

# Die and Stay Dead

# One

There was nothing in the world like New York City at night. After the last of the sunlight faded and the sky turned black, there were parts of the city that remained as bright as day, shielded from the dark by neon signs and sodium streetlights, by the twinkling galaxies of headlights snaking across the bridge spans and the illuminated pinnacles of skyscrapers like burning spears. All three hundred and five square miles of the city raged with so much light that at times the night was no more than perpetual dusk. Yet no matter how brightly the city burned, there were secret places where darkness took root and flourished. Hidden, dark spots where New Yorkers never strayed, steered away by the whispers of some ancient and forgotten instinct. It was on one of those beautiful nights, in one of those secret places, that I was getting the crap beaten out of me by an infected magician named Biddy.

Joggers had been disappearing from Central Park at night, all of them women, and all of them vanishing from the same area: the dark, wooded, winding paths known as the Ramble. No clues had been left behind and no bodies had been found. The police and the newspapers thought there was a serial killer at work—"Invasion of the Hottie Snatcher!" shouted one *New York Post* headline—but we suspected something different was happening, something the police weren't equipped to handle. So that night, after the police patrol left the area, we sent Bethany out into the Ramble alone as bait. Isaac, Philip, and I hid at various points nearby, waiting. I watched Bethany through lightweight, high-definition binoculars whose special lenses boosted light transmission for nighttime use. They made her glow and look fuzzy around the edges, like a ghost haunting the park. It wasn't long before Biddy made his move, snatching Bethany up and dragging her into the woods. Isaac and Philip burst from their hiding spots and ran after him. I tucked the binoculars into my trench coat pocket and started running, but like an idiot I tripped one of Biddy's booby traps. A rope snare caught me by the ankle and hoisted me upside down into a tree. By the time I got myself loose and followed the trail of scuffed footprints and trampled plants to a camouflaged trapdoor at the base of the bronze *Alice in Wonderland* statue, I found myself locked out of Biddy's underground lair with the others already inside. It took me another ten minutes to break my way in. Frankly, the rescue part of our plan could have gone better.

Reeling from Biddy's punches, I stumbled backward, careful to stay away from the edge of the natural stone bridge we stood on. Below us, a wide pit extended farther down than I could see, a bottomless hole in the earth. The sides of the bridge had been lined with rows of black candles that burned with an eerie red flame. Everything about it screamed ritual to me. But what ritual? What the hell was Biddy doing down here?

I risked a quick glance at Bethany. She was dangling from a long, retractable metal contraption that held her over the yawning black pit, her wrists chained together over her head. Wet, slimy sounds echoed up from below, as if something were moving down there. Suddenly I had a pretty good idea what had happened to the missing women. Bethany struggled to free herself, twisting her diminutive, five-foot frame and pinwheeling her legs under her as she strained for any kind of leverage. But there was nothing beneath her, just a straight fall of untold hundreds of feet, all the way down to whatever was making those slithery noises.

"Trent!" she shouted. "Stop messing around and get me down from here!"

"What do you think I'm trying to do?" I shouted back. I hated when she got like this. Only Bethany Savory could micromanage her own rescue.

She nodded at the control panel of levers and knobs at the base of the retractable contraption. "Just get over there and press the damn button that gets me down from here!"

I turned back to Biddy and wiped blood from my lip. "Do yourself a favor. Let her go and I'll go easy on you."

Biddy laughed crazily. Crazy enough to remind me that he wasn't just bad, he was *infected*, which meant he was insane enough to see this through. He fully intended to feed Bethany to whatever was down there, just as he'd fed a dozen other women to it over the past few weeks. He would never let her go.

The infection had given Biddy's skin a rough, stonelike quality and a tumorous, misshapen head. At least he still looked somewhat human. I'd seen the infection do worse to people. Unfortunately, his fist felt as stony as it looked. As he landed another blow, it was like being punched by a boulder.

He smirked. He had good reason to. He was stronger than me, and I was weaponless. The grip of my chrome-plated Bersa semiautomatic pistol poked out of the waist of Biddy's pants. Though something told me that even if I had the gun, bullets wouldn't pierce that rocklike skin of his. It wouldn't be the first time I'd gone up against someone bullets couldn't harm, but I always felt better about the odds when I had the gun in my hand. No wonder Bethany had called it my totem.

"There must be some mistake," Biddy sneered, his voice as deep and hollow as the pit below us. "I thought you were the great and mighty Immortal Storm. I expected a challenge, at least." When he spoke, his lopsided mouth moved like a mudfish's.

"You're one to talk about funny names, Biddy," I said, spitting more blood onto the ground.

The Immortal Storm. I hated that name. It had been bestowed on me by the gargoyles as an honorary title after I freed them from their long history of slavery. I'd hoped to keep it private, but word had spread faster than I expected. Who knew gargoyles were such gossips? But it wasn't just modesty that made me uncomfortable with the title. The Immortal Storm was also a prophecy—a bad one, real end of the world stuff—and I didn't like being associated with that.

"My god and master, Mab-Akarr, will have His feast tonight, as He does every night," Biddy went on. "You cannot stop this, Immortal Storm. He craves flesh, and as His faithful servant, I willingly supply it."

"Tell me something, Biddy. Does Mab-Akarr insist on only eating women, or was that your idea?" He glared at me. "I thought so. What happened, you get rejected in high school too many times?"

Biddy sneered and feinted throwing another punch. I flinched. He laughed.

"Fool. Who are you to question the rites of Mab-Akarr? He does not protect you. He protects *me*." He thumped one stony hand on his chest for emphasis.

I looked up at him. "Protects you? You live under Central Park and kidnap women to throw in a pit. You're the one people need protection *from*."

He shook his head like he pitied my ignorance. "You do not feel it, do you? It is everywhere around you. It is in the air itself. Something dark and terrible is coming. Something no one can escape. No one but me. Mab-Akarr will protect me from it, as long as I keep Him fed."

Biddy strode toward the control panel, turning his back to me. I leapt to tackle him, but he was surprisingly fast. He spun and brought up one arm. His palm burst with a seething light, and a blast of something cold and painful caught me by surprise. I couldn't move. Every part of my body raged with agony. I gritted my teeth and bit back a scream.

Stupid of me. I should have expected a spell. Biddy was infected—of *course* he was carrying magic inside him.

He giggled insanely and inched closer. "Kneel."

"Go fuck yourself," I growled through the pain. You can take the ex-thief out of Brooklyn, but you can't take the Brooklyn out of the ex-thief.

"Kneel," Biddy repeated, louder.

The agony of the spell intensified. Magic. Sometimes I hated it. Okay, most of the time. I cried out and fell to my knees. I didn't mean to. I didn't want to give the bastard the satisfaction, but I didn't have a choice. The pain was too much.

"Trent!" Bethany yelled. Metal jangled loudly as she swung back and forth on the chain, struggling to get her legs high enough to wrap them around the retractable arm. But she was too small. Her legs wouldn't reach.

Biddy's spell dissipated. The pain subsided, albeit maddeningly slowly. Biddy picked up his sword from where he'd dropped it on the stone bridge. He loomed over me, putting the tip of the blade to my neck. It felt cold and sharp against my throat.

"The Immortal Storm," he scoffed. "They should have called you the Sniveling Worm instead."

I moved my fingers desperately along the ground, grasping for anything I could use as a weapon. All I got was a handful of loose dirt and pebbles. It would have to do. I tossed it in Biddy's face. He snarled and backed away, protecting his eyes with his free hand. I jumped to my feet, but Biddy recovered faster than I thought he would. He drove the sword deep into my stomach.

His lopsided mudfish mouth curled in a sneer. "Now die."

Hot blood spilled out of me, coursing down my shirt, my pants. I was dying, and I knew what that meant. With my last ounce of strength I grabbed Biddy's lapels, pulled him close, and didn't let go. A cold emptiness blossomed inside me, and I felt the dizzying sensation of falling even though I was still on my feet. The edges of my vision turned gray, then black, and everything went dark very quickly.

The last thing I heard before I died was Bethany's voice saying, "You shouldn't have done that, Biddy."

After the darkness came the mad rush back to life. I opened my eyes and greedily sucked air into my lungs. I was lying on a natural stone bridge, but I didn't remember where I was or why I was here. I never remembered anything after coming back from the dead, at least not right away. But as the fog began to clear, the memories edged in from the corners of my mind. Biddy was lying next to me, dead. He'd been drained of his life force, leaving behind a corpse as dry and wrinkled as old parchment. It looked like he'd been dead for years, even though I knew only a few minutes had passed. My hands were still clutching his lapels in an iron grip. I let go.

I'd held him close as I died because I knew what would happen. The terrible, nameless thing inside me would steal his life force and use it to bring me back. It had saved my life a dozen times over, but I still didn't know what it was or where it came from. All I knew was that it didn't care whose life force it stole. Friend or foe, innocent or guilty, everyone was fair game as far as it was concerned. I hated it. I hated it more than anything in the world. The fact that I'd just used it as a weapon, and not for the first time, didn't change that.

Biddy's sword lay beside me, expelled from my body. I looked down at the bloodstains that ringed the hole in my shirt where the blade had gone through. Another shirt ruined. Some things never changed. Underneath the shirt, the skin of my stomach was whole again, as if I'd never been stabbed. There wasn't even a scar. The thing inside me never just brought me back; it always brought me back completely healed.

I brushed myself off and stood up, mentally adding Biddy's name to the running tally in my head. His was the twelfth life I'd stolen. Every breath I took, every beat of my heart, was a reminder that I was just as much a killer as he was.

"Trent!" Bethany shouted, still hanging by her wrists from the metal contraption. "Get me down!"

"Working on it," I said. My voice was hoarse, my throat dry from being dead.

I squatted next to Biddy's corpse, retrieved my gun, and stuck it in the holster at the small of my back. Then I dug into his pants pocket. Through the cloth, his desiccated leg felt like a roll of old newspaper. I found what I was looking for, the long-necked key I'd seen him use to lock the padlock on Bethany's chains. I went to the control panel. I flipped the same switch Biddy had, only in the opposite direction. The contraption began to reel Bethany back toward the bridge. She looked down into the pit as she approached. Whatever she saw made her eyes bulge.

"Faster! Make it go faster!" she yelled, squirming.

I looked at the control panel in confusion. There were too many knobs and switches to choose from. How the hell was I supposed to work this thing? I turned the knob next to the switch I'd already flipped. The contraption ground to a sudden halt, leaving Bethany still dangling over the pit, ten feet from the edge of the bridge. Shit. Wrong knob.

"Trent, get me down from here! Hurry!"

I reached for another knob. A bestial roar came from the pit. A long, black tentacle snaked quickly upward from the depths and wrapped itself around one of Bethany's legs. Biddy's god, Mab-Akarr, wasn't about to let his dinner get away. Bethany kicked her leg, trying to dislodge the tentacle, but it held tight.

"Get it off me!"

I pulled my gun and squeezed off three rounds. The bullets punctured the leathery, reticulated hide of the tentacle and a foul-smelling green ichor welled up out of the wounds, but it wasn't enough. Undeterred, Mab-Akarr wrapped his tentacle around her leg more forcefully and started to pull. Bethany's arms strained in the chains above her head. If I didn't stop that thing, he would pull her in half.

I holstered the gun and snatched Biddy's sword off the ground. I would only have one shot at this. If I missed, Bethany would be Mab-Akarr's main course. Standing at the edge of the bridge, I threw the sword side-arm. It sailed out over the pit like a whirling helicopter rotor. It struck the tentacle, and then the sword went tumbling down into the darkness of the pit. At first I couldn't tell if it had done anything. Then the meat of Mab-Akarr's tentacle split apart in a long gash, releasing more of the foul-smelling green ichor. From somewhere deep below, Mab-Akarr screeched in pain. The tentacle stretched apart and snapped. The bleeding stump retreated into the pit. The severed tip remained wrapped around Bethany's boot, until it slowly uncoiled and fell into the pit after its larger half.

"Get me down from here!" Bethany shouted.

I turned the knob again, in the other direction this time. The contraption brought her back to dangle directly in front of me on the bridge. I wrapped one arm around her waist so she wouldn't fall, and with the other I used the key to unlock the chains around her wrists. She dropped against me, and I lowered her gently to the floor. Holding her close like that, something stirred inside me. I wondered if it made her feel something, too. If she'd changed her mind about us.

"Thanks, I'm fine now," she said, pulling away from me quickly.

I guess I had my answer.

We hurried to the far side of the stone bridge. There, a cave extended deep into the bedrock. Embedded in the cave wall was the thick, metal door of the cell where Biddy had locked up Isaac and Philip. I tried the same key I'd used to free Bethany, but it didn't fit the keyhole. From behind us, Mab-Akarr's low, angry growl echoed out of the pit. Crap. There was no time to search Biddy's lair for the proper key, so I put my shoulder to the door. I hit it two, three, four times, but the damn thing wouldn't budge. I heard movement on the other side. I took it as a good sign that they were still alive in there.

"Stand aside," Bethany said.

She reached into a pocket of her cargo vest and pulled out a charm. Charms were her specialty, and this one was a small, round object that looked like a brooch, only instead of a pin on the back it had four tiny metal clamps. She clamped it to the doorknob and twisted a tiny knob on top of the charm.

"Get back!" she shouted, not just for my sake but to warn the people on the other side of the door, too.

We ran clear to the other side of the cave. The charm erupted with a bright light. There was the sound of rending metal, and the smell of something burning. A moment later the light faded. The doorknob lay on the floor, leaving a smooth, perfectly round hole in the door. Bethany's hand was small enough to fit in the hole, so she reached in and pulled the door open.

Inside was a dark cell. The air smelled stale and terrible. I could only imagine how many women Biddy had kept in here, waiting in terror to be fed to his god. Bethany pulled out another charm, a small, mirrored disc that glowed in her hand like a flashlight. She cast its light on the two prisoners in front of us.

Isaac Keene, our leader, sat on the floor with his hands bound behind his back. He looked up at us, his lip and cheek bloody from when Biddy had beaten him into unconsciousness. His red, close-cropped hair and beard were matted with dirt and sweat.

"Where's Biddy?" he asked.

"Dead," Bethany replied, kneeling to untie him. "Unfortunately, the thing in the pit is still alive. And still hungry."

I turned my attention to the second person in the room: Philip Chen, our resident vampire. His skinny form was wrapped in so many silver chains he couldn't move. All that silver had to be sapping his strength and burning his skin like a branding iron, but his face didn't register any pain. Instead, he wore his usual scowl beneath the mirrored sunglasses he never took off.

"Get these chains off of me," he snarled.

Philip grimaced as I unwrapped the chains as gently as I could. The silver left angry red marks on his forearms, neck, and anywhere else his skin wasn't covered by his tight black T-shirt. I winced at how painful it looked. I didn't know how he did it. He should have been screaming.

When I finally got all the silver chains off of him, he said, "You should have left Biddy to me. The son of a bitch puts *me* in silver? I would have made him beg before he died. I would have made him wish he'd never met me." He rubbed at the red, blistered marks on his skin.

"I didn't exactly have a choice," I said.

Philip looked at the blood-rimmed hole in my shirt, noticing it for the first time. "So it happened again, huh?"

I didn't answer him. I didn't like talking about it.

"While you're at it, you might also want to look after our friend there," Philip added, nodding behind me.

I turned around. A woman crouched in the corner of the room, hidden in the shadows. I hadn't noticed her when I came in. She was trembling and holding a knife in my direction. I held my hands up and walked slowly toward her. She panicked. She started breathing heavily and jabbed the knife at the air between us.

"It's okay," I said. "We're here to help you. You're free now. Biddy's dead."

She gritted her teeth, her eyes darting quickly from me to the others and then back.

"Biddy's dead," I said again. I knelt in front of her.

Her face was streaked with dirt and sweat, but there was something striking about her, the way she looked both youthfully innocent and world-weary at the same time. There was a maturity to the lines of her face, but her cheeks were as full and round as a teenager's. She wore jeans that were torn at the knees, and a ratty old black sweater with holes in the cuffs and elbows. Her hair was cut into a messy black bob with a narrow band of blue running down one side. She had a diamond stud in the side of her nose.

I kept my hands where she could see them, one eye on the knife. It was a folding knife. I could see the groove in the handle where the blade fit inside. It was strange that Biddy had let her keep a knife, but I put the thought aside for now. I knew better than to touch her or try to take the knife away. She was so frightened she would slash me to ribbons before she knew what she was doing.

"My name is Trent," I said, keeping my voice calm and even. "What's your name?"

She looked at me for a long moment. She had two different-colored eyes, one blue and one a gold-flecked hazel. Like two people inhabiting the same body.

"C-Calliope," she stammered.

"Hi, Calliope," I said. "Would you like to go home now?"

Her eyes welled with tears. She nodded. She folded the knife and put it back in her jeans pocket. I helped her to her feet. She trembled in my hands like a frightened animal. As I introduced her to the others, she began to calm down.

"From what Bethany told me, the thing in the pit sounds like a trembler," Isaac said. "It's kind of like a land kraken. They don't have much in the way of intelligence or cunning, they mostly just eat and sleep. We can burn it out."

"Biddy said it was his—his god," Calliope said.

"It's true," I said. "He even had a name for it: Mab-Akarr."

"Biddy was insane from the infection," Isaac pointed out. "I have no doubt he really thought the trembler was speaking to him, ordering him to feed it, but I can assure you it wasn't."

"He also said it was protecting him from something," I said. "Something nasty that was coming our way."

"Likely more delusions," Isaac said. He tipped back suddenly, losing his balance and stumbling to regain it.

Philip rushed to his side to help him. "You all right, old man?"

"I'm fine, I'm fine," Isaac said. "Just still a little woozy. Now how about we get out of this damn cell?"

We walked out into the cave. Calliope gripped my arm like a vise, as if she thought letting go would bring all the horror back.

"Where'd you get that knife, Calliope?" I asked.

"I had it with me when he—when he brought me here." She looked around the cave nervously, as though she expected Biddy to jump out at any moment.

"And Biddy let you keep it?" I was skeptical.

Her jaw tightened at the mention of his name. "I tried to stab him with it. It didn't do anything. Didn't even break the skin. He thought it was funny that I tried to hurt him. That's why he let me keep it. It amused him."

We started back across the natural stone bridge.

"And yet he didn't feed you to the trembler, even though you attacked him?"

She shook her head. "I'm—I'm different. I can see the spirits of the dead, even talk to them sometimes. He liked that. He kept me around so I could tell him about the other women he fed to that thing. He made me watch. He got off on killing them, and he got off again on me telling him how angry or sad their spirits were. I guess for him it was like killing them twice. It amused him. Everything about me amused him."

"You're a necromancer?" I asked, surprised. I hadn't had good experiences with necromancers. Of course, maybe not all of them were like Reve Azrael. Calliope certainly seemed different.

She turned to me sharply. "Wait! What day is it?"

When I told her, she was stunned.

"Three days. I've been here three days. I—I've lost so much time!"

"What do you mean?" I asked.

I didn't get an answer. Calliope spied Biddy's desiccated husk on the bridge and clung to me with a shriek.

"It's okay," I said. "He's dead, just like I said. I killed him myself."

"But—but look at him . . ." She shook her head, her eyes wide with alarm. It was all too much for her. She choked back a sob, and then she wept, openly and unashamed. She buried her face in my shirt.

Not knowing what else to do, I put my arms around her awkwardly. "It's okay," I said. "It's over."

She looked up at me, wiped her eyes with her sweater sleeve, and nodded.

Philip went over to Biddy's body and brought his boot down hard on the misshapen skull, crushing it.

"Feel better?" I asked.

"Ask me again after I stomp the rest of this bastard into dust." He turned to Calliope. "You want a turn, kid?"

Calliope just shook her head and dug her fingernails into my arm. It occurred to me she wasn't just scared of Biddy. She was scared of Philip, too.

"Leave it, Philip," Isaac said. "We don't have time. The trembler is still down there, and it's awake and hungry."

"Fine," Philip sighed, disappointed. "Humans. No sense of priorities."

Isaac moved to the edge of the bridge, held up his hands, and chanted a few strange syllables that drew a chill up my spine. I didn't like the language of magic. It spooked me every time I heard it, like someone walking over my grave. When Isaac was finished, a huge fireball materialized in the air before him. Like Biddy, Isaac carried magic inside him. But Isaac was a mage, which meant he was immune to magic's infection.

He dropped the fireball into the abyss. It sailed down farther and farther, illuminating the walls of the pit as it descended, until it was nothing but a pinpoint of light in the darkness below. There was a flash as it burst, followed by a loud, bloodcurdling shriek. A moment later, the pit erupted with black tentacles, a veritable forest of lashing, groping, angry appendages.

"Damn it, the trembler's bigger than I thought," Isaac said.

I drew my gun, but Philip put out a hand to stop me. "I got this."

With a throaty battle cry, he threw himself off the bridge and into the squirming mass of tentacles. They coiled around him until he was lost inside the sheer multitude of limbs. Then Philip and the trembler fell into the darkness of the pit together.

I ran to the edge of the bridge. "Philip!"

Below us, the dark pit reverberated with the sound of shrieking and thrashing, and a wet, slimy sound that brought to mind handfuls of spaghetti being thrown against a wall. Finally, there was silence.

Next to me, Isaac called out, "Philip!"

No sound came from the depths.

Then we saw him, climbing up the wall of the pit toward us. He jumped and caught the side of the bridge, then pulled himself up. He was covered with gobs of the trembler's sticky, foul-smelling, green blood. Even his mirrored shades were coated. He wiped the lenses clean and grinned.

"Okay," he said. "*Now* I feel better."

# Two

We left Biddy's lair through the trapdoor at the base of the *Alice in Wonderland* statue. In the dark, the streetlights from Fifth Avenue half-illuminated Alice as she sat atop a toadstool, her arms spread in a welcoming gesture to her friends the White Rabbit, the Mad Hatter, and the Cheshire Cat. As someone who felt like he'd gone through the looking glass himself on a few occasions, I thought her expression was much too calm. But then, a hookah-smoking caterpillar was nothing compared to some of the things I'd seen.

Calliope still clung to me as we descended the steps from the statue. Gilded words had been etched into one of them: MARGARITA DELACORTE MEMORIAL. I didn't know who that was, but someone had cared enough about her to commission the *Alice* sculpture in her memory. That gave me pause. I couldn't imagine having someone in your life who would do that for you. It made me wonder again if I had a family or loved ones somewhere out there, and I cursed the amnesia that had taken my past from me. Everything was gone—my real name, where I lived, everything but the events of the past year. Statistically speaking, there had to be people out there who knew me, but so far no one had recognized me on the street or come looking for me. If they existed, where were they?

But until I knew the answer to that, I had another family, a new family. The Five-Pointed Star. For the first time, I felt like I belonged somewhere, with people I cared about, and who cared about me. I hadn't trusted them at first, but I didn't doubt their friendship anymore.

We passed the boat pond, a small, shallow pool where children sailed remote-controlled model boats during the day. It looked still and quiet now, reflecting the stars like a big mirror.

Calliope pulled my arm to get me to stop. "You said I can go home now?"

I nodded. "You're free to go."

But she continued to cling to me, nervously eyeing the dark woods around us. "I'm scared to go alone."

"I can take you home if you like," Bethany offered.

Calliope wrapped her hands tighter around my arm. "No, just Trent." She looked up at me with her different-colored eyes. She'd bonded with me as her rescuer, but after everything she'd been through it was clear she wasn't ready to trust anyone else yet. "Can you take me home?"

"Sure," I said. "Where do you live?"

"Downtown," she said. "In the Village."

Bethany shot me a glance that said be careful. She didn't fully trust Calliope yet. But there was something else in that glance, too. It was almost like she didn't want me and Calliope to be alone together. If I didn't know better, I'd think she was jealous. But of course, I did know better. Bethany had already made it clear we wouldn't be anything more than friends.

"It'll be all right," I told Bethany. "I'll meet you back at Citadel."

She studied Calliope's face. I knew Bethany well enough to know she wasn't entirely comfortable with this, but she nodded. "Fine. But be sure to come right back, and call me if there's any trouble. Okay?"

"Got it," I said.

"Thank you, all of you," Calliope said. "I don't know how to repay you. If you hadn't come, I—I think he would have eventually fed me to that creature, too."

"There's no need to repay us," Isaac said. "This is who we are. It's what we do."

He wasn't exaggerating. Biddy was the fifth Infected we'd put out of commission since the events of Fort Tryon Park last month, when we stepped out of the shadows as the Five-Pointed Star. There was a darkness growing out there, spreading with magic's infection, turning more and more people into dangerous creatures like Biddy. Someone had to take a stand. Someone had to fight back. That was us.

"Take care of yourself, kid," Philip said to Calliope. "Think of us the next time you order calamari."

She looked away from the vampire, down at her shoes. "Yeah, sure. It's going to be a while."

I escorted Calliope out of the park to the subway. At this hour of the night, the platform for the downtown 1 train was mostly empty, except for a couple of drunk twentysomethings passed out on a bench and a few mangy rats sniffing at the garbage cans. We waited in silence for a train to show up. Calliope didn't say a word. I figured if she didn't want to talk I would let her have some peace and quiet. But she jumped at every little sound and clutched my arm again. Eventually, a train came and we got on. The twentysomethings and the rats stayed behind.

The subway car rocked me gently back and forth in my seat as it sped through the tunnels, stopping occasionally at empty stations. The doors opened and closed, but no one got on or off, not at this hour. The only other person in our train car was a dirt-crusted man sleeping in the far corner seat. He was encased in two bulky down coats and surrounded by numerous garbage bags filled with what appeared to be everything he owned. His scent—a mix of body odor, cheap liquor, and a few other things I didn't want to think about—permeated the entire car. A matted, gray beard poked out of his drawn-up hood. I hoped he didn't wake up. There was a part of me that still liked not being seen. Of course, it was especially helpful to go unnoticed when I had this much blood on my shirt.

Calliope sat close to me, but not too close. "Your friend Philip, is he just a psycho, or . . . ?" They were the first words she'd said since we left the park.

"He's a vampire," I said. "Though maybe there isn't that much of a difference between the two."

"I've never seen a vampire work with humans before," she said. "Usually they stay with their own clans."

"Isaac saved Philip's life once," I explained.

"The, um, older guy with the red hair is Isaac?" she asked. I nodded. "I saw the way Philip ran over to help him. I've never seen a vampire act so concerned about humans, either."

"Philip owes Isaac a hundred years of servitude in return for saving his life," I explained. "I guess it's a custom among vampires. So Philip gave up being a predator and now he's—well, he's more than just part of the team. He's kind of like Isaac's bodyguard. Presumably he's not quite as psycho as he used to be, but sometimes it's hard to tell."

"So he's good now?"

I shrugged. "The jury's still out on that one."

She was quiet for a while as the train continued rocketing through the tunnels. Then she said, "You said you were the one who killed Biddy. What did you do to him? The way he looked . . . I've never seen anything like that before."

I looked away from her, at the sleeping man in the corner. "Biddy's dead. That's all that matters."

She nodded. "I guess we all have our secrets, huh? Like how your shirt's all bloody and torn but you seem to be fine."

"It's not my blood," I lied.

"Right," she said, unconvinced. "You're not human, either, are you?"

I didn't know how to answer that. There was still so much I didn't know about myself. "Jury's still out on that one, too," I said. I smiled at her, but it was even less convincing.

We got out at Houston Street just as the sun was starting to scale the horizon. Calliope led me uptown on Seventh Avenue a few blocks. She glanced nervously around the street.

"It's okay," I told her. "Biddy's dead. He won't come after you."

She looked at me and nodded, but her demeanor didn't change. Calliope was terrified.

We turned left onto Leroy Street, then St. Luke's Place, a quiet, leafy road of beautiful row houses. All the houses were lined up on one side of the street, facing a fenced-in playground and park on the other. It was like something out of a glossy magazine spread.

I had a sudden feeling of déjà vu, but this was no trick of the mind. I'd been on this street before, back in the bad old days when I was working for Underwood. He'd ordered me to break into one of these same row houses and steal a marble-and-gold urn that was supposed to be worth a fortune. I remembered the job vividly. I had walked from roof to roof and climbed into the house through the attic window. All these old row houses had attic windows with latches that turned brittle and easy to break after a few decades' exposure to the elements. The owners never knew how vulnerable their homes were because they never thought to check. Most people didn't go into their attics past the day they filled it with all the crap they never use. Out of sight, out of mind. One quick tug at the window was all it took, and I slipped right inside. The rest of the job didn't go so easily. The window wasn't alarmed, but the urn was, and as soon as I lifted it off its base a piercing electronic shriek permeated every corner of the house. I sprinted back up the stairs to the attic with the urn under my arm. Behind me, I heard a woman scream and a man threaten to wring my neck. Then I was outside and running into the cover of night.

I looked at the row houses in front of me again. I didn't remember anymore which house it had been, but suddenly I hoped like hell it wasn't Calliope's.

She stopped in front of 6 St. Luke's Place, a four-story, brick row house half hidden behind a wisteria vine rooted in the tiny, gated front courtyard. Next to the tree was an old-style gas streetlamp, though the tap had been replaced with an electric bulb. Well-manicured shrubs twined around the wrought iron banisters on either side of the stoop. At the top of the steps, a black-painted door stood inside a molded arch beneath a peaked cornice.

Calliope looked up and down the street nervously. I wanted to calm her, but it was clear there was nothing I could do. She was deeply traumatized. It would take time before she felt secure again. Her eyes met mine for a moment, and then she looked away quickly, focusing on her feet. She crossed her arms in front of her, her hands hidden inside her sweater sleeves like turtles withdrawn into their shells.

"Would you mind coming inside?" she asked. "Just for a second? Just until I feel safe?"

"Of course," I said.

"I'm not—I'm not keeping you up too late, am I?"

I shrugged. "I don't sleep." I wasn't just being polite. I didn't sleep. Not ever. The same thing that kept bringing me back to life also didn't let me sleep. It was as if my body no longer needed it.

Calliope looked past me suddenly, as if noticing someone on the sidewalk behind me. The hairs on my neck prickled. I turned around, but the sidewalk was empty.

"Let's go inside," she said.

I followed her up the stoop. She stopped at the door and fished in her jeans pocket for the key. She looked at me again, but only for a second before looking away once more. I got the impression she wasn't very comfortable around people. After being kidnapped and held in an underground lair for three days by a homicidal maniac, finding herself alone with a strange man, even one she'd asked to come with her, was likely putting her more on edge than she thought it would. I decided not to make it any worse. I would see her safely inside, and then be on my way.

"It's—it's funny," she stammered. "I don't normally let anyone inside without an appointment. I only ever see people by appointment. You know, for my job. I—I don't usually have guests over."

"What do you do?" I asked.

She pulled a key ring out of her pocket, slid a key into the lock. "I'm a medium. It's the logical career choice for a necromancer, I guess."

I looked up at the house again. If being a medium meant you could afford a beautiful home in a tony neighborhood like this, I was in the wrong line of work.

She opened the door. We stepped into a vestibule that smelled of dust and incense. No alarm sounded. She closed the door and turned the dead bolt.

"You should think about getting an alarm system," I said. "These old houses are surprisingly easy to break into."

She rubbed her sleeve-shrouded hands up and down her face. "Are you trying to scare me? Because I'm already plenty scared. What made you think I wanted to hear that right now?"

"Sorry," I said. I'd screwed up, spoken without thinking. It was hardly the first time, and it probably wouldn't be the last. "Maybe I should go—"

I was interrupted by a loud meowing. An orange-and-gray calico ran down the entrance hallway toward us and began twining itself around Calliope's feet. She squatted down and scratched the top of the cat's head. The cat purred happily.

"Oh, my poor Kali," Calliope said. "I've been gone so long. She needs to be fed. It'll only take a moment." She picked up the cat and started walking down the long hallway toward the kitchen. She nodded at an open archway on her left. "Make yourself comfortable in the living room."

"Are you sure?" I asked, but she just continued into the kitchen.

I walked into the living room, surprised to find myself amid more furniture for cats than humans. Cat toys, cat trees, and scratching posts took up most of the room. Definitely not the house I'd broken into back in the day. There was a fireplace against the far wall. Above it was a painting of a man in a gray overcoat and bowler cap, standing before the sea. The man's face was entirely obscured by a floating green apple. In one corner it was signed with the artist's name, René Magritte. I'd heard the name before, enough to know his paintings were enormously valuable. First the house, and now this. Calliope definitely wasn't hurting for cash. Still, in a room full of cat trees and scratching posts, an authentic Magritte seemed absurdly out of place.

I looked closer, noticing something in the brushstrokes of the cloudy sky over the sea. It was faint, but it was definitely the letter Y. Strange.

"Do you like it?" Calliope asked from the doorway. "It's new. I just bought it a couple of weeks ago. Cost me an arm and a leg, but it's worth it. It's my favorite painting. There's something about the way you can't see the man's face. The artist said everything we see hides something else, and we always want to see what's hidden. In the painting, he's not letting us. It's like he's saying sometimes it's better not to know."

Without warning, the cat ran into the room and darted under the couch.

"Don't mind Kali. She'll probably hide the whole time you're here." She gestured to the couch. "Please, take a seat. I hope you'll stay for a little while. I just need someone to be here while I decompress, you know? And maybe check all the closets, just to be sure." She laughed, but I had a feeling she wasn't kidding.

I sat down on the couch. The upholstery of the sofa's arms had been shredded to ribbons. So had much of the rug. Apparently, Kali was having no trouble living up to her namesake, the Hindu goddess of destruction.

"Sorry about all the stuff in here," Calliope said. "You know what they say, you own a dog, but you only rent space from a cat."

She sat all the way on the other end of the couch from me, still wary. If there'd been a chair on the other side of the room I was certain she would have sat there instead.

A spiral-bound, six-by-nine notebook sat open on the coffee table in front of us. The page it was open to showed an image sketched in pencil. An image I recognized immediately.

An eye inside a circle.

An electric charge went through me. In Ehrlendarr, the language of the Ancients, an eye inside a circle was the rune for magic. It also happened to be a big part of my earliest memory, coming to consciousness in front of a plain brick wall with that same rune etched into one of the bricks. I still didn't know where that wall was or why the rune had been there. Seeing it again now made me nearly jump out of my seat. Instead, I leaned forward for a better view.

"What is this?" I asked.

Calliope frowned at the notebook, as if she'd forgotten it was there. She closed it and pulled it away from me. "Sorry. This place is kind of messy. Like I said, I don't usually have people over without an appointment. Gives me a chance to tidy up."

"It's Ehrlendarr, isn't it?" I pressed. "The rune for magic."

Calliope studied me with her different-colored eyes, surprised I knew that. "It's not just magic. It also means change. Transcendence."

"Why do you have a drawing of it?"

"It's for a personal project," she said, growing defensive. "It's nothing that concerns you."

There was definitely more to Calliope than met the eye. I needed to know what it was.

"Does this personal project have something to do with why you were in the park the night Biddy kidnapped you?" I asked.

She hid behind her hair, not answering me.

"All the women Biddy kidnapped were joggers," I continued. "You're not dressed like a jogger. And you had a knife with you. So what were you doing there?"

"We all have our secrets, remember? Now, if you'll excuse me, it's been three days since I've seen a real bathroom."

She stood up and left the living room, taking the notebook with her. I waited a few seconds, then got up and followed her into the hallway. I watched her place the notebook on the kitchen counter and then go through a door into the bathroom. I started down the hallway toward the kitchen. I had to see what was in that notebook. What "project" was Calliope working on? What did it have to do with that damn rune?

I made it halfway to the kitchen before Kali appeared on the counter.

The little goddess of destruction sat right on top of the notebook. She stared at me with her tail swishing back and forth, as if daring me to risk the clawing of a lifetime if I tried to take it.

"Bad kitty," I muttered.

My smartphone chirped in my coat pocket. The screen showed me it was Bethany calling. I went back into the living room and answered it. "You know, if you keep calling me at other women's homes, people will get the wrong idea."

"I was just checking to see if everything was all right," she said. "I thought you'd be back by now."

"Everything's fine," I said. "Calliope is just freaked out and needs some company. I get the feeling she doesn't have a lot of friends."

"Well, while you two are becoming besties, see if you can find out why she was in the park," Bethany said. "Her clothes tell me she wasn't out jogging, and I can't stop thinking about that knife she had. Something's not adding up."

"Great minds think alike," I said. "I already asked, but so far she's not telling me anything."

"Do you think Calliope is dangerous?"

"No, I don't get the sense she wants to hurt anyone. I think she's telling the truth about why Biddy kept her alive and let her keep the knife. She's just scared and on edge."

At that moment, Kali jumped up on the couch and screeched at me. Not so much a hiss as a long moan of exasperation, as if my simply being there was making her crazy.

"By the way, there's a cat here you would really get along with," I said. "You have a lot in common."

"I'm going to pretend you meant that as a compliment, even though I suspect you didn't," she said. "Just see what you can find out. I'll meet you back at Citadel."

"Wouldn't you rather get some sleep? You've been up all night."

"I'll be fine," she said. "I'll see you later."

I ended the call. Kali watched me carefully from the sofa, in case I made any sudden moves. When Calliope came back into the living room, I noticed she wasn't carrying the notebook.

"I'm sorry about that," she said. "I didn't mean to get upset with you.

You've been so nice, and I'm grateful for everything you've done. Really, I am. It's just . . . there are some things I'd like to keep private."

"I understand," I said. "There are things I don't like to talk about, either. I just want to make sure you're all right."

She groaned and rubbed her face. "I'm not. I'm not all right. I don't even know where to start."

"Give it time, you've been through a lot," I said.

She shook her head. "It's not just what happened in the park. That was awful, but there's more. I think—I think someone has been watching me for a while now. At least a couple of weeks. Not Biddy, someone else. I know it sounds crazy, but I can't shake the feeling. I don't go outside very often, I don't like crowds, but when I have to go out I'm certain someone is following me."

"Did you get a look at them?" I asked.

She shook her head. "No. But before everything with Biddy happened, it was getting worse. I couldn't go anywhere without feeling like someone was following me. Watching me. I even started to feel like I wasn't safe in my own home. Which is ridiculous, right? If you're not safe in your own home, where *are* you safe?" She hid her hands in her sleeves again and hugged herself.

I'd misread her nervousness on the street. I thought she was scared that Biddy might still come for her. Instead, she was scared about something else entirely.

"Do you have any idea who it might be?"

She shrugged. "I hate to even ask, but do you think you could come back tomorrow? Just to check up on me? It's probably nothing, but it would make me feel a whole lot better if I knew you were coming back."

"Sure," I said. "I can do that."

She smiled, relieved that I didn't think she was crazy. She looked out the window at the brightening morning.

"Maybe I shouldn't say tomorrow. Tomorrow is already today," she said. Then she yawned, covering her mouth with her sleeve-shrouded hand. "God, I've barely slept for three days. I feel like I'm going to sleep for a week now. Maybe you should give me a couple of days to recuperate, and then come back."

"Okay," I said. "You'll be home?"

"I don't think I'll ever leave the house again." She smiled to show me she was joking. I suspected she wasn't.

Calliope led me back to the front door. Kali licked her nose and watched me go, satisfied that she'd successfully protected her territory from the invader. Before I stepped outside, I glanced down the hallway one last time at the notebook on the kitchen counter.

"Thank you, Trent," Calliope said. "Thank you for everything. I—I really don't know how to repay you." She paused a moment, then quickly kissed me on the cheek. She turned bright red.

"I'll see you in a couple of days," I said, stepping out onto the stoop.

I thought Calliope would say goodbye then, or even just close the door without a word, but instead she leaned against the doorframe, the blue band of hair hanging diagonally across her face like a painter's brushstroke.

"Hey, um, I don't know if you know this already, or if it matters to you, but you're being followed, too."

"What?" I turned around and scanned the sleepy little street, but all I saw were men and women in business attire walking down their stoops and heading for the subway station.

"It's a spirit from the other side," she said. "It came back across the dark for some reason, and it's following you."

I was skeptical, until I remembered the way she'd stared past me on the sidewalk earlier. "Who is it? What does it want?"

She shrugged. "I don't know, it's hard to say."

"But as a necromancer you can see it, right?" I asked. "At least tell me what it looks like. Male, female, tall, short, anything."

"That's the problem," Calliope said, rubbing her nose with her sleeve. "It's not a person. It's a wolf."

# Three

I didn't go back to Citadel right away. Instead, I walked around the Village to clear my head, occasionally looking over my shoulder. Calliope said I was being followed by a spirit in the form of a wolf. Why? What did it want from me? Part of me thought Calliope was out of her mind. She had to be, right? I mean, a ghost wolf? But another part of me thought—*hoped*—that maybe it was Thornton Redler.

I missed Thornton. Missed him like mad. He and Bethany had been the first members of the Five-Pointed Star I'd met. In fact, when I first met Thornton, he'd been a big, gray timber wolf. Only later did I learn he was a lycanthrope, able to change back and forth between human and wolf at will. Inherently good, heroically brave, and with a razor-sharp wit, he quickly became a good friend. And then he died. Right in front of me, with nothing I could do to save him. For reasons I would never understand, I could cheat death but someone like him, someone good and decent and with so much to live for, could not.

I glanced behind me again. If this ghost wolf really was following me, I couldn't see it.

On Hudson Street, I found a little neighborhood coffee shop and decided to grab a cup. I got in line behind an army of businessmen in identical London Fog trench coats and Kenneth Cole briefcases. They looked like clones who'd all walked off the same page of *Esquire,* as if they were here solely to rub it in that you couldn't afford to live in this neighborhood unless you made at least six figures. I was out of place among them. I was like a crack in an otherwise flawless piece of crystal.

A paper witch had been taped to the wall of the shop, wart-nosed and riding a broomstick. A Halloween decoration. I'd forgotten it was almost Halloween. There were other decorations taped up all over the shop: a black cat with its mouth open and its back arched, a groping mummy trailing strands of gauze, a knobby-kneed skeleton, and another witch, this one stirring a boiling cauldron, one crooked, green, outstretched finger shooting off a small lightning bolt. I shook my head. That was how most people thought of magic, as something out of fairy tales. They didn't know the truth. They didn't know how dangerous it really was.

Magic was a natural element, no different from any other. It could be manipulated, used as a tool or weapon if you knew how. But a thousand years ago the Shift had occurred, radically tipping the balance of light and dark. Ever since, magic had grown increasingly darker and more dangerous. If it got inside you, if you carried it within yourself instead of in a charm or an artifact, it corrupted you. Infected you. It twisted your mind and drove you mad. Often it mutated your body as well, transforming you into something deformed and horrible, like it did to Biddy. The only people who could carry magic inside themselves safely, without becoming infected, were mages like Isaac who had reached that level through decades of study and dedication. But the world was filled with greedy, impatient people who wanted power *now,* and the ranks of the Infected had quickly swollen to the point where there were a whole lot more of them than us.

Most people didn't know any of this, of course, because they didn't know magic was real. For the most part it was a willful ignorance, a strong desire to not *want* to know. Even after multiple witnesses had seen a giant, rampaging gargoyle turn the Cloisters into a pile of rubble, the news had chalked it up to a "freak seismic event." Everyone just kept on lying to themselves. Maybe that was how they stayed sane.

When the clones ahead of me in line were finished ordering their non-fat, no foam, six-pump chai lattes and whole wheat bagels with the insides scooped out, I bought myself a simple cup of coffee—black, one sugar. As I walked out of the shop, a cartoonish paper zombie taped to the door leered at me. I groaned. I'd already seen more than my share of reanimated corpses. If I never saw another one, it would be too soon.

Back outside, I walked down the sidewalk sipping my coffee and thinking about returning to Citadel. The urgency of what Calliope said about a ghost wolf had faded. It was probably a mistake anyway. She'd been through a lot. She said herself she hadn't slept much in three days. The wolf could have been a hallucination brought on by lack of sleep. That was probably it.

Something on the other side of the street caught my eye, something out of place. I stopped and turned. A man stood on the opposite sidewalk, facing me. He wore a black cloak with a hood that hung down low enough to hide most of his face. All I could see was his chin, as white as snow. A crow sat on his shoulder, cocking its head at me. People passed him on the sidewalk without seeing him. A bulky Pathfinder sped north on Hudson Street, distracting me with an angry blare of its horn. When I looked across the street again, the cloaked man was gone.

I turned to continue up the sidewalk, and nearly walked right into him. The cloaked man stood directly in front of me. As before, no one else on the sidewalk seemed to notice him. The crow on his shoulder tipped its head to one side, then the other, regarding me with both eyes.

"Immortal Storm," the man said. The snow-white flesh of his chin was run through with dark black veins. I still couldn't see the rest of his face under the hood.

"Who are you?" I demanded.

"Take my hand," he said. He held out one slender, pale hand. His fingernails were black. "Take my hand and see."

I didn't know what compelled me to do it. I grasped his hand like we were shaking on a deal. As soon as I did, the cloaked man turned his hand over. The skin on the back of his hand opened to reveal an eye. I felt like I was falling. Hudson Street was gone. Everything was gone.

Images rushed at me, changing constantly. I saw the burning ruins of New York City. I saw the dead lying everywhere—corpses on the sidewalks, corpses on the street. Ash rained from the sky, and so did human bodies. They fell slowly, so slowly, as if the laws of gravity didn't work anymore. I saw Isaac emerge from a bank of heavy smoke, only he was older, haggard-looking. One of his arms was missing, cut off below the elbow, the stump wrapped in a dirty cloth. I saw Bethany covered in blood and shouting at me, "What have you done? What have you done?" Then I was standing in an underground subway station. The platform was littered with bodies. The cloaked man stood before me.

"What is this?" I demanded through gritted teeth.

"The future. Your future," he said. He smiled. His teeth were yellow. His gums were as black as night.

A rumble came from deep within the subway tunnel, the sound of a train approaching the station. I turned and looked, but it wasn't a train. A tidal wave of blood poured out of the tunnel, flooding the station and catching the bodies in its current.

"Pave the way," the cloaked man said.

And then I was back on the sidewalk on Hudson Street, alone, with the still hot cup of coffee in my hand.

I didn't know what time it was when I finally got back to Citadel. Eight a.m.? Nine? The encounter with the cloaked man had shaken me, made me lose track of everything. The images he'd shown me were still reeling in my head when Citadel appeared before me out of the morning mist. Isaac's home and the Five-Pointed Star's headquarters, Citadel was a small castle that stood incongruously in a secluded glen in Central Park, hidden from prying eyes by a powerful ward. Only one person had ever breached the ward and broken into Citadel: Reve Azrael, the necromancer whose disturbing fascination with me I still didn't fully understand. But it had been over a month since she'd broken into Citadel, and she hadn't returned. I knew she'd survived the events of Fort Tryon Park, but there'd been no sign of her since. It made me nervous. I didn't like knowing she was still out there, still watching me. It made me wonder what she was waiting for.

I let myself in. The enormous main room on the first floor of Citadel was empty. After the night we'd had, Isaac was probably still sleeping. Philip was wherever Philip went when the sun was up. Bethany must have gotten tired of waiting for me and gone home to her own apartment. I wasn't used to Citadel being so quiet. I climbed the steps to the second floor and stopped halfway up to look at the new portrait of Thornton mounted on the wall. He was posing in a crisp suit, framed in ornately carved wood, and mounted on the wall with several other paintings. It made him look larger than life, just as his personality had been. His fiancée, Gabrielle Duchamp, had commissioned the portrait in his memory. None of us had objected when she asked to hang it in Citadel.

If Thornton hadn't died, they would be married by now. Gabrielle had taken a leave of absence to mourn. I missed her as much as I missed Thornton. The Five-Pointed Star with only four members didn't feel right.

*That's the problem. It's not a person. It's a wolf.*

I put Calliope's words from my mind. Whatever she'd seen, it wasn't Thornton. It couldn't be.

I continued up the stairs to the second floor. Down a hallway lined with marble busts and heavy red drapes, past Isaac's study and the storeroom where Bethany kept her arsenal of charms, was the room I now called home. With nowhere else for me to go, Isaac had allowed me to stay at Citadel in one of the many unused guest rooms. It was part of the deal we'd made. I worked for him, and in return he gave me a place to stay and helped me find out who I was. Mostly that help had come in the form of an artifact called the Janus Endeavor—essentially the magical equivalent of facial recognition software—but so far we weren't any closer to an answer. Isaac remained hopeful. I was skeptical but trying to keep an open mind. Sometimes I wondered if we would have better luck taping my picture to lampposts. HAVE YOU SEEN ME?

My room was small, but it was still a hell of a lot better than my old cement room in the fallout shelter. There was just enough space for a full-sized bed, a shallow closet, and a dresser. The adjoining bathroom had a shower. I didn't need much more than that. I opened the door and found Bethany asleep on my bed.

It wasn't unusual to find her in my room. Ever since she learned I didn't sleep, she'd been helping me pass the time at night, usually with a game of gin rummy. I was pretty good at reading people. For a thief, it came with the territory. But it was hard to get a read on her. Most of the time she was all business, as tough as a battle-axe and constantly berating me for not doing things by the book. Other times there was a deeper well of feeling between the two of us. But for all the times I caught her absently brushing her hair out of her face or knitting her brows in concentration and was stunned by how beautiful she was, she never gave any indication she felt anything but friendship for me. And yet, she came to my room every night just to keep me company. The signals were so mixed they made my head spin. Finding her curled up on my bed didn't help.

She stirred and blinked at me. She sat up and tucked her hair behind one pointed ear. Normally she was self-conscious about her ears and kept them hidden, but she didn't seem to care right now. I wondered if that meant she was growing more comfortable around me.

"How did it go?" she asked, still groggy with sleep. "Did she tell you anything?"

"No," I said. "You're tired. You should go home."

She rubbed her eyes. "No, I'm fine. Did you find out *anything*?"

"She thinks someone has been following her," I said. "Not Biddy, someone else, someone still out there. She asked me to go back and check on her in a couple of days."

"Are you going to?"

"Yeah." I shrugged. "Who knows, it might be nothing, but she seemed pretty worked up about it. It couldn't hurt just to make sure she's doing okay."

"I guess not," Bethany said. "But be careful. I feel like she's holding something back. Something important."

Bethany's instincts were usually spot-on. I had the same feeling. Calliope was hiding something, and it had to do with that notebook. I thought again about the Ehrlendarr rune sketched on one of the pages. I had to know why it was there. Did it hold the same importance to her that it did to me? Did we share a connection through the rune somehow? I planned to ask her when I went back. She'd asked for a couple of days to recuperate first, but I didn't know if I could wait that long. Maybe she wouldn't mind if I showed up a little sooner.

Bethany squinted at me. "You're holding something back, too. I can tell when you do that, you know."

"Oh yeah?"

She nodded. "Yeah. Your neck turns all red like you swallowed something bad. Right now your neck is about as red as a chili pepper. So what aren't you telling me?"

I sat down on the bed with a sigh. "Something happened. Something weird. A man in a cloak approached me on the street, only I'm not sure he was actually human. I don't think anyone else saw him, either. Just me."

I told her about the vision of a ruined city and dead bodies everywhere. I left out the part about Isaac missing an arm. I didn't tell her that I'd seen her, too, all covered in blood. I didn't want to scare her. It was foolish, I knew, but even after seeing time and again how strong Bethany was, there was still a part of me that wanted to protect her.

When I was finished, Bethany was quiet, taking it all in. Finally, she said, "The future isn't written in stone. Whoever this person was, what he showed you was *a* future, at best. Not *the* future. Not necessarily."

"He said it was *my* future," I said. "Why come to me? What does he want?"

"You're sure you've never seen him before?"

"Never," I said. "I would remember this guy."

"But there's a lot you don't remember," she pointed out. "He might know you, even if you don't remember him."

"You mean from my life before?" That piqued my interest. If I did know him from the time before I lost my memories, he might know who I was. He might know my real name. That made him someone I wanted to talk to again. "How do we find out who he is?"

"Isaac's database," she said.

The database was Isaac's pet project, a compilation of all known dark or infected magicians in the area. By his own admission it was far from complete, but if I wanted to know more about the cloaked man the database was the best place to start.

"I'll go set it up," she said. "Why don't you change out of those bloody clothes and meet me downstairs?"


I was in and out of the shower so fast it must have been a world record, but it still felt like it took forever for me to clean myself, dress in fresh, un-bloodied clothes, and get downstairs. At the big table in the main room, Bethany had connected Isaac's laptop to the bank of six video monitors on the wall. Two mugs of coffee sat steaming on the table.

"Look at you, you almost look human again," Bethany said.

I took one of the coffee mugs and sat down at the table. "Thanks. I almost feel human again."

She took a sip from the other mug. "Are you ready to start?"

"Let's do this."

She began typing on the laptop's keyboard, her face illuminated by the light from the screen. In that moment, it occurred to me she had no idea how beautiful she was. And in that same moment, I knew I had to let it go. I couldn't keep hoping she would change her mind about us. I had to move on.

The monitors on the wall flickered to life. Six different faces appeared, each on its own screen. I scanned them quickly, but none of them was the cloaked man. Only one of them looked remotely human, but she was a woman and her skin was green and scaly, not white with black veins. The other five looked like things that sprang from nightmares—lumpy, misshapen, inhuman faces. They disappeared and were replaced with six more.

"Just let me know if you recognize any of them as your mystery man and we'll see if the database has any information," she said.

"I know, I've done this before," I snapped. I immediately felt like a heel for talking to her that way. She was only trying to help. "Sorry. I'm just kind of wound up. I want to know who this guy is."

"It's okay, I get it," she said. "But if you hadn't apologized, I probably would have poured this hot coffee in your lap."

I sat there for thirty minutes watching faces flip past, human and non-human alike, but none of them was the cloaked man. I hadn't gotten a good look at his face. All I'd seen were his mouth and chin under the low-hanging hood of his cloak. But I figured that was a start, and if his face was in the database I would at least feel a twinge of recognition. Or if it showed his hands. How many people had eyes on the backs of their hands? But the longer it took, the more my frustration grew. By the time we exhausted the database, my frustration had turned to anger.

"Damn it, who is he?" I demanded. "What does he want? Why did he show me those things?"

"Don't worry, we'll figure it out," Bethany said.

She sounded confident, but I wasn't convinced. There was something not right about the cloaked man. Something that just felt off. No one else on the street had seen him. He wasn't in Isaac's database. What if—

I hung my head and rubbed my eyes with the heels of my hands. I didn't want to think it, but I had to face the possibility that the cloaked man didn't exist. That I was seeing things. That after everything I'd experienced over the past month my mind had simply had enough and *broken* somehow.

# Four

The way Isaac told it, the Janus Endeavor was an artifact that dated back to twelfth-century Italy, a time of pervasive superstition among the peasants of the countryside. They believed, among other things, that identical twins were an evil omen, a sure sign that the family would come to ruin. Routinely, twins were separated at birth, with one staying with the birth parents and the other usually sold into slavery, or if the kid were lucky, to a childless family that might give him or her a good home. The slavers paid better, of course, and soon word got around that there was money to be made. Children who weren't even twins were stolen from their homes and sold under false pretenses. Eventually, a law was passed that ended the practice altogether, but by then entire generations of families had been torn apart. The Janus Endeavor had been created to reunite them. It could match a subject's face to that of their identical twin, no matter how far away, provided the twin was still alive. Hundreds of adults who'd never even known they had a twin suddenly had undeniable proof that they hadn't been born alone, that the haunting feeling that some part of them was missing wasn't just their imagination. Of course, for our purposes, Isaac had altered the Janus Endeavor's scope to something quite different. There was a lot more visual media now than there was in twelfth-century Italy, and while I didn't have a twin—at least not that I knew of—the artifact could still search for my face.

"Comfortable?" Isaac asked. We were in a high room in the northeast tower of Citadel. Through one window, I could see Citadel's domed roof and the other three towers at the corners. Through another was a wide expanse of Central Park woodland.

I nodded, settling into the plush cushions of the wingback chair in the center of the room. "Let's do this. Maybe we'll find something this time."

He lifted the Janus Endeavor off the table by the window. It was a big, heavy, bronze helmet etched on both the front and the back with the identical, stylized face of a bearded man. Isaac opened the helmet along its hinged side seam, lowered it over my head, and then closed it again, sealing me into complete darkness. There were no eyeholes to let in the light, and no airholes, which made the inside of the mask dark, stuffy, and stale. I didn't like it, but the discomfort was a small price to pay if it gave me a chance to track down my past.

His voice came to me muffled by the heavy helmet. "Are you ready?"

"Hit it," I said, and braced myself.

Isaac began the incantation. I was glad I couldn't hear it clearly through the helmet. There was something eerie about the language of magic, even if no one else thought so. Something alien and cold that crept under my skin. A moment later, activated by the spell, the Janus Endeavor shrank around my head, molding itself to my features until the bronze was snug against my skin. The helmet caressed my face with invisible fingers like a blind man memorizing my features. Then, as it must have for all those Italian twins centuries ago, the darkness within the helmet burst to life with image after image, face after face. Only, these faces came from newspaper photos, magazine spreads, police reports, and obituaries. None of them was my face. Undeterred, the Janus Endeavor cast its net wider. Clips of TV news programs flashed by, followed by a Facebook timeline and a Twitter feed, then some newfangled Web site I didn't even recognize.

Then, suddenly, I saw myself in a grainy, black-and-white photo. My heart quickened. The Janus Endeavor caught the image and held it in place. The photo was from a page deep within an issue of the *Daily News*. My face was a blur of pixels and poor focusing, likely from a cell phone camera, but I recognized myself. I was standing on top of an overturned Ford Explorer while a man in a jet-black suit of armor approached on foot with his sword drawn. Damn. The Janus Endeavor had finally found something, but it wasn't from my forgotten past. It was from a month ago. The caption read, *YOUTUBE STUNT SPINS OUT OF CONTROL: Two unidentified actors tied up traffic in Times Square and injured several drivers.* Actors. I supposed that was easier for *Daily News* readers to swallow than calling us the Immortal Storm and the Black Knight. I shook my head, and the Janus Endeavor let the photo go. It continued zooming through more images, but it came up empty.

Eventually, the heat and airlessness inside the helmet got to be too much for me. I tapped the arm of the chair to let Isaac know I needed a break. He ended the session with another incantation. The images faded, and the Janus Endeavor loosened its hold on my face. Isaac pulled the helmet free.

"Still nothing," I said, sucking in a lungful of fresh, cool air. I wiped the sweat off my forehead with the back of my arm.

"We were close that time," Isaac said. "That photo from the newspaper."

"I don't get it," I said. "Somewhere out there, there *has* to be a record of me from before."

It wasn't the first time the mysteries of my own face had confounded me, but I thought by now the Janus Endeavor would have found something. Even if it was just me in the background of a photo. Even just a hint, a clue, anything but this big, terrible goose egg. It felt as much a waste of time as searching for the cloaked man in the database. But magic tended to act strangely around me, like a hose on full blast that couldn't be turned off. I'd broken a couple of Bethany's charms trying to use them. Maybe I'd broken the Janus Endeavor, too.

No, that wasn't it. The artifact was working fine, it just wasn't finding my face anywhere.

Isaac put the helmet down on the table and sighed, as disappointed as I was. "Let's take a break. We'll start again in five."

That night, I lay on my stomach on the bed, flipping through a volume of Bankoff's annotated *Libri Arcanum* from Isaac's library. It was part of my education in all things magic, but I was having trouble concentrating. After reading the same paragraph five times, I put the book down. I turned onto my back and stared up at the ceiling. In my head, I heard Calliope again.

*I think someone has been watching me for a while now. At least a couple of weeks. Not Biddy, someone else. I know it sounds crazy, but I can't shake the feeling.*

*I couldn't go anywhere without feeling like someone was following me.*

I'd asked her if she knew who it was. She'd shrugged. But she hadn't said no.

A knock sounded at my door. I sat up, swinging my feet onto the floor. "Come in."

Bethany opened the door. She was carrying a deck of playing cards, shuffling them idly as she walked into the room. "So," she said, "you ready for a rematch?"

I grinned and slid off the bed to sit on the floor. "Definitely. But I'm warning you, I'm becoming quite the gin rummy master."

"Prove it." She sat down across from me, shuffled the cards, and started dealing them out.

"You don't have to keep doing this, you know," I said.

She looked up at me. "But if I don't deal the cards, how am I supposed to beat you so bad that you cry like a baby?"

"Good luck with that. But that's not what I mean. You don't have to keep me company every night just because I don't sleep. Don't *you* want to get some sleep?"

"I don't mind doing this," she said. "Do you want me to stop?"

No. No, I didn't want her to stop. But part of me thought I should say yes. Seeing her in my room every night wasn't helping me move on.

"I can go if you want me to," she said.

"No, stay," I said, surprising myself. But what else was there to do to pass the time? Go back to slogging my way through the *Libri Arcanum*? "Besides, I'm feeling lucky this time."

She laughed as she finished the deal. "There's a first time for everything."

I raised my eyebrows. "Oh, that's how it's going to be, is it? You think you can take me?"

"I *know* I can take you," she said.

Bethany teased and ribbed me as we played, talking smack through the game the way we always did, but this time it was one-sided. The longer we played, the less I felt like laughing. After winning her fourth hand in a row, she scribbled our scores in the notepad next to her.

"All the pictures on the cards must be confusing you," she said. "The guy with the beard is the king."

I was lost in my thoughts again and didn't reply. She looked up at me sharply, her sky blue eyes flashing.

"What's wrong? You've barely said anything all night. It's not like you."

I sighed. "Let's just keep playing."

"No. Your neck is turning all red again."

It was my turn to deal. I took the deck out of her hands. My fingers brushed hers. I tried to ignore the feeling of her skin on mine and shuffled the deck.

She tucked her knees up under her chin and wrapped her arms around them. "I know you're not big on opening up, but you can talk to me. You know that, right?"

I started dealing the cards.

"Is it about Calliope?" she asked.

"Partially," I said. "I meant to go check on her today, even though she asked me to give her a couple of days. I had more questions for her, but more than that, I keep thinking about how scared she was. But then I got caught up with Isaac and the Janus Endeavor all day and lost track of time."

"I'm sure she's fine," Bethany said. "Let's go see her tomorrow. We'll go together."

I nodded. "Okay."

Bethany studied her cards. "You said it was only partially about Calliope. Is there something else?"

I thought back to the Janus Endeavor. I'd sat in that chair all damn day, enduring session after endless session, and all for nothing. The artifact's constant failure to find my face anywhere was crushing me. The search for my identity was starting to feel hopeless, but I didn't know how to confide in her. She was right, I wasn't good at opening up.

"No, it's nothing," I said. "I misspoke."

She looked at me skeptically, but she didn't press the matter. I could only imagine what color my neck was.

I looked at my cards. "Whose turn is it, again?"

"Mine." Bethany put her cards down on the floor, faceup. "Oh, look at that. Gin."

She beamed. I groaned.

At noon, Bethany and I climbed the front stoop of 6 St. Luke's Place. I rang the doorbell.

Beside me, Bethany adjusted her cargo vest. As usual, its plentiful pockets were filled with magic charms, most of which she'd engineered herself. I'd never seen Bethany as happy as when she was engineering charms. She'd taught herself to make them in order to stay sane and focused during her childhood. She'd been abandoned at a young age by parents she never knew, and shuttled from one foster home to another. Small, quiet, withdrawn, and with unusually pointed ears, no prospective parents had wanted her, so she'd stayed in the system until she turned eighteen. Then, no longer their responsibility, they'd kicked her out onto the street. I didn't know what happened to her in the ten years before Isaac found her and got her back on her feet. She never spoke of it. All I knew was that the only constant in her life had been engineering charms.

Calliope didn't answer the door. I rang the doorbell again.

"That's weird," I said. "She knew I was coming by today. She asked me to."

"Maybe she went out?"

Remembering her half-joke about never leaving the house again, I shook my head. "Not likely." I rang the bell a third time. Calliope didn't come.

I leaned over and peered into the window next to the door. It was too dark to see anything, especially with the glass reflecting the bright noontime daylight behind me. I got closer and cupped my hands around my face until I could make out the irregular shapes of Kali's cat furniture in the dark living room. I didn't see anyone inside. Then I noticed one of the taller cat trees had tipped over and was leaning against the couch. That was odd. Calliope didn't seem like the kind of person who would just leave it tipped over like that.

"I don't like this," I said. "Something's wrong."

Bethany tried the handle, but the door was locked from the inside. She rapped on it and called Calliope's name, but by then we both knew no one was coming to open the door.

Bethany looked at me. "It's your call. What do you want to do?"

I kicked the front door with all my strength. It crashed open, the locked dead bolt tearing out chunks of wood with it. Bethany glanced back at the street to make sure no one had seen us, then nodded at me. I pushed my trench coat back, drew my gun from the holster at the small of my back, and led the way inside. A broken front door hanging open would draw attention, so Bethany quietly closed it behind us.

We crept into the dimly lit living room. The springs and feathers attached to Kali's cat furniture swayed gently with the changes in the air. We moved deeper into the house, entering the large kitchen at the back. An island with a butcher-block countertop stood in the middle of the kitchen, arranged with vases, decorative bowls, and glass jars filled with sugar and flour. A rack of stainless steel pots and pans hung directly above it. The sink was set into a granite countertop, filled with a few dirty dishes and a wineglass. There were no signs of a struggle. Nothing seemed out of place. Even Kali's food and water bowls down by the baseboard hadn't been disturbed. We walked through a set of swinging doors and found the dining room, but there was nothing out of the ordinary here, either.

Bethany looked at me and shrugged.

I glanced around again, then backed out of the dining room. Everything was in its place, and yet my instincts wouldn't stop telling me something was wrong.

Something wailed loudly upstairs. We ran for the stairs and rattled up them two at a time. I noticed a bloodstain on the beige carpet runner, but I didn't stop running until I reached the second-floor landing.

A long, low moan came from behind a door to my right. The desperate sound raised goose bumps on my skin. I kicked open the door.

It was a bathroom. There were small spots of blood on the floor. Another moan, a truly miserable sound, came from behind the shower curtain. Bethany and I approached the tub cautiously. She gripped the edge of the curtain and looked at me. I lifted my gun and nodded at her. She yanked the shower curtain aside.

The cat sat curled against the wall of the bathtub, trying to make herself as small as possible. Kali's paws were red. She'd left a pattern of small, bloody paw prints all over the white porcelain. There was a splotch of red on the fur over her ribs, but she didn't appear to be injured. The blood was someone else's. Between pitiful mewls and wails, Kali desperately tried to lick herself clean.

"Oh, God," Bethany said. She picked Kali up out of the tub. To my surprise, the cat didn't fight her or try to run. Instead, she allowed Bethany to pick her up and immediately surrendered to her embrace.

"That's Kali," I said. "Calliope's cat."

She held Kali close and looked at me, her eyes brimming with worry. "Trent, all this blood . . ."

"I know."

I looked out through the open bathroom door. Blood drops and smears led from the stairs to about halfway down the hall before fading. Kali's little red paw prints filled in the missing information. They led out of a room at the far end of the hall and into the bathroom.

"Wait here," I said. I edged out of the bathroom, holding my gun ready.

"You can't be serious," she whispered.

"I mean it, stay there, Bethany," I said.

I walked as quietly as I could toward the door, trying not to step in the blood on the floor. I paused outside the door and put my ear to it. I didn't hear anyone inside. Of course, that didn't mean someone wasn't waiting for me with a weapon. I took a deep breath, turned the knob, and threw the door open, keeping the gun in front of me.

It was Calliope's bedroom. I scanned the room quickly, taking in the big, canopied, king-sized bed at the center of the far wall. A pool of blood stained the bedspread and dripped off the sides to the carpet below, where Kali's red paw prints tentatively circled the gore. A drop of blood fell from above, landing on the surface of the pool. I looked up. My stomach dropped. In my haste, I had mistaken the shape above the bed for a canopy. It wasn't.

"Oh, God," Bethany gasped in horror. She was standing behind me in the doorway, clutching Kali to her chest.

Calliope was on the ceiling, held there by long metal spikes that had been hammered through her arms and legs. Her different-colored eyes stared down at us unblinkingly. Her torso had been cut open in a single, long slit. Thick, ropy coils of something gray and glistening had been pulled out of the wound and spiked to the bedroom ceiling all around her, leaving her dangling over the bed in a web of her own innards.

# Five

"Damn it, I told you to stay in the other room," I barked at Bethany.

The tone of my voice startled Kali. The cat squirmed and mewled to be let down. Bethany released her, and the cat jumped to the floor. She ran out of the room as quickly as she could and down the stairs.

"Who would do something like this?" Bethany asked, looking up at the body.

"I don't know, but this wasn't random," I said. "This kind of brutality never is. This is something different."

"It's insane," Bethany said, shaking her head.

I looked up at Calliope's body again, at the spikes driven through her limbs and into the ceiling. "It takes more than one person to nail a full-grown adult to the ceiling. But there's no sign of a struggle. It doesn't make sense."

"It didn't have to be more than one person," Bethany said. "Not if they had magic."

I turned away from the body. I couldn't stand the way Calliope's open eyes were staring at me so accusingly.

"This is my fault," I said. "She told me someone was following her. She told me she didn't feel safe in her own home. I should have come back sooner. I meant to."

"It's not your fault," Bethany said. "It's no one's fault but whoever did this to her."

"I'm going to find them," I said. "I owe Calliope that, at least."

"*We're* going to find them," she corrected me. "You're not in this alone. You're going to need help."

I nodded. Whoever had cut Calliope open and spiked her to the ceiling was a sick bastard. No two ways about it. But they'd been following her before this. Stalking her for a couple of weeks, she'd said. Stalkers rarely chose random victims. They usually focused on people they knew.

I looked at Bethany. "The front door was still locked when we got here."

"You think she let her killer in?" Bethany asked.

"It's possible. She kept telling me how she never had social calls. She only saw people by appointment. If she did let him in, he would have to be someone she knew. Someone she trusted."

"Someone she was expecting," Bethany said. "You said she made a living as a medium. Maybe it was a disgruntled client."

"It's a place to start," I said, walking back out into the hallway. "If Calliope could afford a place like this, she must have had a lot of clients."

Bethany followed me into the hall. "She probably kept an appointment book that can tell us who came to see her."

Where would Calliope keep something like that? Probably in the same place where she met with her clients. Not here on this floor, this was her personal space. Not the parlor floor below, either. The living room was jam-packed with cat furniture and toys; it would put off her clients. But this was a row house. There was one more floor under us, at street level. The garden floor.

We went back downstairs. Under the staircase, we found a door that opened on another staircase that led down into the darkness. Bethany found a light switch and turned it on. A bulb flickered to life above the stairs, and we started down.

The garden floor was a single, large, open room that ran the length of the row house. Positioned in the center of the room was a big, round table covered with a black velvet cloth. In the middle of the table was a perfectly spherical crystal ball on a wooden stand. The walls were draped with more black velvet and decorated with framed prints of spirit photography—old-time pictures of transparent figures standing in abbey windows or walking through churchyards.

"Looks like something out of an old horror movie," I said.

"It's all set dressing," Bethany said. "Necromancers don't need all these bells and whistles to contact the dead, but her clients probably expected it."

I could see that. A black tablecloth and crystal ball would certainly draw more clients than a room full of cat toys.

"Most mediums are charlatans," Bethany said. "But Calliope was the real deal. Maybe that's why she was so successful. A medium doesn't live in a house like this without a lot of loyal clients. Loyal, and wealthy."

I peeked behind one of the black velvet drapes and found windows in the wall that looked out onto the sidewalk. In true New York City fashion, the windows were protected by metal security bars. No one could have broken in that way. More evidence she'd let her killer inside? Maybe. I moved on. Behind another drape, I found a bookshelf crammed full of paperbacks, all with covers featuring pale, voluptuous women in nightgowns surrendering to the embrace of well-built, shirtless vampires. They all had titles with some combination of the words *dark, eternal,* and *seduction.* Vampire romance novels. I wondered what Philip would think of them. I searched the shelves but didn't find Calliope's appointment book among them.

"Here!" Bethany called.

She was sitting at the séance table, the cloth pushed back from the edge, and rummaging through a drawer she'd found. She pulled out a small black appointment book. I went over to the table to look at it with her. A foil skull had been stamped on the cover. Bethany opened it. The appointment book was bookmarked to today's date with a rubber band that bound the preceding pages together in a clump. That was all the proof I needed that she had still been alive last night, maybe even this morning. But the morning slots on today's page were all empty.

"She didn't have *any* appointments this morning," I said.

"No, but she had one tonight. Look at this." Bethany pointed at the eight p.m. slot, where Calliope had written *Yrouel,* and beneath it, an address: *84A Bayard Street.*

"Bayard Street. That's in Chinatown," I said. "Who's Yrouel?"

"I don't know, but she was going to see him tonight." She looked up at me. "Maybe someone didn't want her to."

"Or maybe Yrouel came here instead, surprising her," I said. "She knows him, so she lets him inside. And then . . ."

"He kills her," Bethany finished.

I sighed. "It's a theory, anyway."

"We've got his address. It's a theory worth pursuing." Bethany tucked the appointment book into a pocket in her vest and stood up. "But first, I want to take another look at Calliope's body. We might have missed something."

We went back upstairs. Bethany continued up to the second floor and Calliope's bedroom. I told her I'd be up in a moment. In the living room, Calliope's notebook was back on the coffee table. I walked over to it. Kali peered out at me from inside the carpeted hutch of one of her cat trees and let out a low moan of warning. I ignored her. Somewhere inside that notebook was a drawing of the Ehrlendarr rune from my earliest memory. I picked it up and slid it into the inside pocket of my trench coat. Kali watched me do it, then turned around and disappeared into her hutch.

I went upstairs to Calliope's bedroom. Bethany had taken her boots off and was standing barefoot on the edge of the bed, careful to avoid the pool of blood on the bedspread. She was looking intently up at Calliope's body, studying the details. Somehow she managed to remain detached from the brutality of the scene. I couldn't. I had taken Calliope home from Biddy's lair. I'd stayed and talked with her until she felt safe again. I'd liked her. She was an odd one, but then, we all were. I'd made a promise to come back and check up on her, only I'd come back too late. I felt accountable. And angry. Very, very angry.

There were two nightstands flanking the bed. The one on the left held an alarm clock and a stack of paperback novels, their well-worn spines offering up names like Poppy Z. Brite, Anne Rice, and Laurell K. Hamilton. The other nightstand was bare except for a glass vase holding dried flowers and a jar full of seashells. I hadn't seen any photographs in the house, outside of the prints in the séance room. Even the shyest wallflower in the world would have pictures of her family, friends, or lovers *somewhere,* but Calliope didn't. Either she had a pathological fear of photographs or, more likely, she didn't have anyone in her life. The second nightstand was unused, purely ornamental. She lived alone. She slept alone. Calliope had died alone in the world.

But one very conspicuous thing was missing from the bedroom. There was no hammer or any other kind of tool here. Whoever had hammered those spikes into the ceiling had left with it. That told me this wasn't a crime of opportunity. This was planned. Calliope's killer had come prepared, bringing the spikes and hammer with him and taking the hammer when he was done. He must have also taken the knife he'd used to cut her open.

This wasn't the work of someone berserk with rage or jealousy. This was methodical.

Bethany stepped down from the bed. "Trent, you're taller than I am. Come take a closer look at this. I want to know if you see it, too."

"See what?"

"You tell me," she said.

I got up on the bed, standing right under Calliope's body. I wanted to tell her I was sorry this had happened to her, but communicating with the dead was her trick, not mine. She stared through me, both her blue eye and her gold-flecked hazel eye milky and unseeing. The diamond stud in her nose twinkled. There was very little blood on her face. Her sweater and the T-shirt beneath it, however, were soaked in it, both having been torn open by the knife. Her jeans were covered in blood, too. That made sense. She must have been standing when she was first gutted, and the blood had spilled down her body. But her hands, spread far apart on the ceiling, were positively red with gore. That stuck out for some reason. The more it itched at me as peculiar, the more it bothered me. Had she used her hands to try to stop the blood flow? No, she wouldn't have had time. She would have died within seconds from a wound this grave.

I looked closer. Her right hand had a strangely unbloodied patch, long and rectangular, running from one side of her palm to the other, as if she'd been holding something in her fist when the blood had run over her hand.

"Do you see it?" Bethany asked.

"The clean spot on her hand," I said. "What was she holding?"

"I don't know, but it's gone now," she said. "It makes me wonder if the killer took something from her."

"You mean, not just a killer but a thief?" I climbed down off the bed, careful to avoid stepping in the pool of blood under the body. Then I froze. A thief. Of course. How stupid of me. I'd had the answer all along. "I know how they got in the house," I said. I ran out of the room and up the stairs to the top floor.

Bethany followed behind me. "How? Trent, how do you know?"

At the top of the steps was a closed door. I tried the handle. As I expected, it was unlocked. I burst through into the attic. It was dark inside, the neglected, dust-caked windows filtering the sunlight down to practically nothing. I groped my way into the dark, bumped into the hard,

pointy corner of a sheet-covered table, and cursed. I heard Bethany mutter
a spell, and a bright light flared to life behind me.

"Slow down, Trent. Tell me what's going on." Bethany was holding her
small, mirrored charm aloft, using its bright light as a flashlight.

"Over here," I said, indicating the window at the rear of the attic. I
crouched down in front of it. Bethany knelt opposite me. I pointed at the
old, corroded window latch. It was snapped in half. "See? It's broken. This is
how they got in. I bet it's how they got back out again, too. That's why the
front door was still locked."

She looked at me incredulously. "How did you know about the window?"

"It's how I used to break into houses like this."

Her expression changed. She didn't like being reminded of what I used
to do. What I used to be. It reminded her that once upon a time I'd pulled
my gun on her. She turned away from me to inspect the latch, though I
suspected that wasn't her entire reason for turning away.

"So Calliope *didn't* let her killer into the house," she said.

"They still might have known each other," I said. "What he did to
her, you don't do that to a stranger. There's a motive behind that kind of
brutality."

She looked at me again. "But what does it all mean?"

"I don't know." I nodded at the appointment book poking out of her
vest pocket. "Let's ask someone who might."


But there were two things we had to do first.

Bethany refused to leave Kali in the house. She was convinced if we left
her, the cat would wind up taken to a pound and put down. While I found
that a tempting thought, in the end she persuaded me we should take the
little monster with us instead. It didn't take much effort to coax Kali into
the molded plastic carrier we found in one corner of the living room. As
soon as she was inside she began mewling, so I threw in a few of her smaller
toys to keep her quiet. In the kitchen I found a bag of her kibble, a bag of
cat litter, and her food and water bowls. I dumped out her litter box, and
then put everything in an oversized blue IKEA shopping bag I found under
the sink.

"We're going to have to find a new home for her," Bethany said.

"I thought you were taking her." I held the carrier out toward her.

She put up her hands and shook her head. "I can't. My landlord doesn't allow pets."

"Then what are we supposed to do with her?"

Bethany arched an eyebrow at me.

"No way," I said. "Forget it."

"Why not? She's just like you, Trent. All fierce on the outside, but just a big softie on the inside."

"Oh, I'm a big softie, am I?"

"You should focus on the fierce part, for your ego's sake," she said. "Now for the bad news."

"Did we skip the good news?"

"Isaac won't want Kali running loose around Citadel, not with so many fragile and irreplaceable artifacts in his collection," she said. "She'll have to stay with you in your room." I opened my mouth, but before whatever obscenity I was thinking of could spill out, she added quickly, "It would just be temporary, until we figure something else out."

"You've got to be kidding." I looked into the carrier through the small metal gate. Kali looked back at me with big eyes. "Fine. As long as it's only temporary."

Kali let out a throaty growl and swiped at me. I regretted my decision already.

Then there was the second thing we had to do. We waited until we were in the Houston Street subway station before calling 911. I used a pay phone on the platform and said I was a neighbor concerned about a strange smell coming from 6 St. Luke's Place. I hung up when the operator asked for my name.


Back in my room at Citadel, I closed the door, put Kali's carrier on the floor, and opened the gate at the front. The cat stayed where she was, glaring at me from the door of the carrier.

"Suit yourself," I told her.

I filled a bowl with her food and another with water, and set them against one wall. I set up her litter box in my adjoining bathroom. When

I walked back into the bedroom, Kali hadn't moved an inch. She continued to stare at me.

I pulled Calliope's notebook from inside my coat. I was about to open it when I heard Bethany calling for me. There was no time to look at it now. I slid it under my mattress, the same place I used to hide things from Underwood and his crew back in the fallout shelter. Old habits died hard.

I turned to see Kali still glaring at me.

"Here's the deal, cat. We're stuck with each other, at least for now, so what do you say we try to get along?"

Kali let out a long, low growl, hissed at me, and went back inside her carrier.

# Six

Chinatown at night wasn't any less crowded than Chinatown during the day. A living sea of pedestrians flowed along the narrow sidewalks and threatened to spill into the streets. As the Escalade idled at a red light, I watched people stream across Canal Street in front of us. Bethany and I had told Isaac we wanted to question Yrouel about Calliope's murder, and he'd insisted on sending Philip with us as protection in case things went south. Now, sitting in the driver's seat, Philip grunted and ran a hand through his thick black hair, restless. With the sun finally down, this was his first chance to be outside since last night, but he was spending it stuck in traffic.

Philip didn't cast a reflection in the rearview mirror. From where I sat in the backseat, all I could see in the mirror was the empty driver's seat. It was disconcerting. I could only imagine what the other drivers on the road thought, looking in their rearviews and seeing no one behind the wheel of the Escalade.

In the passenger seat, Bethany checked the stock of charms in her vest. She was keeping it together pretty well after what we'd seen at Calliope's house. Better than I was. It was eating me up inside. Calliope had told me she felt like someone was watching her. I should have trusted my instincts and gone back to check up on her yesterday instead of waiting. Maybe then she would still be alive. Maybe then she wouldn't have been gutted like a fish and spiked to the ceiling of her own bedroom.

I shook my head to get the image out. The clock on the dashboard read seven forty-five. Fifteen minutes until Calliope's scheduled appointment with Yrouel. An appointment we intended to keep in her place.

"So what's the point of this, anyway?" Philip asked. "What do you care what happened to that girl? Just because we rescued her from Biddy doesn't mean we're responsible for her. Why get involved? Why not just let the police handle it?"

I watched people walking by, talking, laughing, holding hands. Happy. "Because Calliope didn't have anyone," I said. "No friends, no family. All she had was her cat. There's no one out there who cares that she's dead. No one to make sure she gets justice. We're all she has. The police can't do what we can do."

I wasn't sure if he understood. Vampires lived in clans, loose associations of families governed by groups of elders, but at heart they were solitary creatures. They hunted alone. Solitude meant nothing to them. Philip was only a part of the team because of his duty to Isaac. I often got the feeling he would prefer to work alone. It came with the territory of being a predator.

But Philip didn't argue. The light turned green, and we navigated through the maze of short, curved streets just south of Canal. On either side of the road, narrow tenement buildings crowded shoulder to shoulder on top of restaurants, jewelry stores, storefronts selling knockoff perfumes and handbags, and the occasional Eastern medicine supply store with its bamboo shades drawn. Signs and banners hung from every fire escape and flagpole, printed with big *hanzi* characters I couldn't read. Every corner seemed to have its own fresh fish shop in the process of closing for the night. Men and women in white smocks retrieved buckets of shrimp and crab off the sidewalk and rolled down their metal gates. We turned the corner at a large restaurant with a string of red paper lanterns dangling from its eaves, and found Bayard Street. On the north side of the street were buildings marked 84 and 86, but there was no 84A. There was, however, a narrow alley between the two buildings. So, 84A Bayard Street was either the alley itself or, more likely, a building whose entrance was inside it. Philip managed to find parking on the street, which in Chinatown was nothing short of a miracle. We got out of the Escalade and crossed into the alley.

Clouds of steam billowed out of vents from the surrounding buildings and drifted like phantoms through the alley ahead of us. Beneath the rusted fire escapes, feral cats rummaged through overturned garbage cans and open Dumpsters. When they spotted Philip, they yowled in terror and ran off to their secret hiding places. Smart cats.

A wooden door was set in the brick wall at the far end of the alley. There was no number, but it had to be 84A Bayard Street. There was nothing else here. A strange glyph had been carved into the door. Not a *hanzi* character like the others, it was something else, a rune that reminded me of the magical symbols I'd seen etched along the tunnels to the Nethercity. Whoever Yrouel was, it was clear he was no stranger to magic.

Bethany traced the glyph with her finger. "It's a protection spell. It's supposed to keep out evil."

Philip tried the knob, found it unlocked, and pulled the door open. "Well, look at that, it let me right in. Guess the spell doesn't work."

Inside, we descended a plain cement ramp that came to an end about a dozen feet below street level. At the bottom of the ramp was a small, concrete antechamber. A circular, steel door with a big, wheel-shaped handle in its center stood in the wall. It was the kind of door you'd expect to see on a bank vault or in a submarine, not hidden under a Chinatown alley. I looked to either side of the door but didn't see a doorbell.

"I guess Yrouel doesn't like visitors," Philip said.

"Too bad. We're not leaving until we talk to him." I banged a few times on the steel door with my fist.

Philip chuckled. "Knocking. You humans are adorable. I could pull this door out of the wall in two seconds."

Bethany looked up at him. "Maybe you'd better let us take the lead. I think this situation is going to require some finesse. Tearing doors out of walls isn't liable to get Yrouel talking."

Philip shrugged. "Just say the word and I'll get him to talk."

Bethany rolled her eyes. "One of these days, I'm going to have to teach you about subtlety."

"Come on, open this damn door," I muttered. I raised my fist to pound on it again, but Bethany caught my arm, stopping me.

"I guess I'm going to have to teach you, too," she said. "He's expecting Calliope, right? I don't think she was the type to bang on his door like a maniac. Just give it a second."

I heard a lock disengage. The round handle in the middle of the door began to spin, turned from the other side.

"See?" Bethany said.

"Nobody likes a know-it-all," I grumbled.

The door swung inward, revealing a floating form on the other side. My jaw dropped. The first thing I noticed was the big, metal chair, which had no legs and hovered a good six inches above the floor. But as strange as the floating chair was, the creature inside it was even stranger. He was vaguely humanoid in form, but unbelievably obese, the swollen bulges of his body shrouded within a big, shapeless dashiki. Where it was exposed, his flabby, charcoal gray skin was creased with folds and stretch marks. While the chair looked wide enough for two people of average girth, he appeared to be stuffed into it, with rolls of flesh drooping over the edges and armrests. He didn't have any legs. His body was turnip shaped, flat on the bottom. He didn't have a neck, either. His head rested right on his shoulders. The sheer size of his cranium was astonishing. I'd never seen a head so big. It swelled up and back from his brow, extending halfway down the back of the chair. His wide, toothy mouth dropped open in surprise when he saw us. He tried to slam the door shut again.

Philip caught it with one arm and held it open. "Surprise."

"Yrouel, I presume?" I asked.

Unable to close the door, Yrouel retreated, his chair gliding quickly back from us. "Who are you? What do you want? This is private property!"

I stepped through the doorway. "We're here about Calliope."

"I don't know any Calliope!" Yrouel shouted.

His chair spun around and began gliding quickly down the well-lit foyer, away from me. A blur zoomed past him, and suddenly Philip was standing in his way.

Yrouel turned back to me, his eyes widening with panic. "I told you, I don't know who you're talking about!"

"You don't know Calliope?" I asked. "That's funny, because she was supposed to meet you here tonight. In fact, I'm pretty sure that's why you opened the door when I knocked. You thought it was her."

"It's okay, Yrouel," Bethany said, trying to calm him. "We're not here to hurt you. We just want to ask you some questions."

Yrouel glided back toward us. "I really must insist you leave immediately! You're trespassing!"

Philip caught Yrouel by the arm and held him in place. "Did you kill Calliope, Yrouel? Because right now you're acting guilty as hell."

Yrouel looked up at him in surprise. "Calliope is dead?"

"See? You know her after all. That wasn't so hard, was it?" Philip said. "Now, here's the thing. My friends here are good people. They're patient. They're willing to hear you out. But I'm not like them. I'm not a good person."

"You're a vampire," Yrouel said, swallowing nervously.

Philip nodded. "And I don't like when people lie to me. So how about we start over?"

Yrouel nodded, and Philip released his arm. "I didn't kill Calliope. But yes, I know her. *Knew* her. I—I didn't know she was dead. What happened?"

"Sometime between yesterday and today she was killed in her home," I said. "She was cut open and her body was nailed to the ceiling."

"Well, there you go," Yrouel said. "I couldn't have killed her, could I? Does it look like I could nail someone to the ceiling?"

"Depends," Philip said. "How high can that chair float?"

Yrouel scowled at him, then glided over to the door and closed it. "You'd better come inside."

He turned around and led the way into what appeared to be a large, luxury apartment directly beneath the alley. The foyer opened into a long, wide hallway. Hanging on the walls were paintings by Vermeer, Matisse, Cézanne, and artists even older than that—da Vinci, Raphael, Botticelli. Granted, I was no art expert, but the paintings looked authentic to me, right down to the wear and tear on the frames. The collection had to be worth a fortune.

"You're not police, are you?" Yrouel asked. "I won't talk to police."

"Do we look like cops?" I asked.

Yrouel laughed bitterly. "You force your way into my home, manhandle me, and accuse me of a crime I didn't commit. That sounds like cops to me. But if you're not, then who are you?"

"We're the Five-Pointed Star," Bethany said.

Yrouel paused a moment and glanced back at us. "*You're* the Five-Pointed Star? The ones who took out Stryge up in that park in the Bronx? Huh. So you're not police. You're *magic* police."

"Not exactly," I said. "But Calliope was a friend. We found your name and address in her appointment book."

"It stands to reason whoever killed her might have seen your name in the appointment book, too," Bethany said. "For all we know, he's coming for you next. Which means any help you give us would be helping your-self."

"That's the first smart thing any of you have said since forcing your way in here," Yrouel said. "Yes, if her killer knew about me, I could very well be next."

"Why? What were you two involved in?" I asked.

"I wasn't involved, exactly, but I was helping her," he said. "Calliope was researching a topic about which I happen to have a fair amount of knowledge."

Calliope hadn't let me look in her notebook. *It's a personal project. Nothing that concerns you.* Was the project what had gotten her killed? The answer could be waiting for me under my mattress.

"Have you heard of the Aeternis Tenebris?" Yrouel asked. "They were a doomsday cult here in New York City that believed the world would end when the clock struck midnight on January first, 2000."

"They weren't the only ones who thought that," Bethany pointed out.

"True, but unlike the other millennium doomsday cults, the Aeternis Tenebris didn't disband once they were proven wrong. They were much too stubborn for that. They decided that if the world wasn't going to end of its own accord, they would help it along. End it themselves."

"How?" I asked.

"They summoned a demon," Yrouel said. "A powerful, terrible demon. The worst of the lot. Nahash-Dred, the Destroyer of Worlds. But once they summoned him, the fools couldn't bind him."

"You mean like in ropes?" I asked, confused.

"No," Yrouel said. "Demons are dangerous creatures. You can't just summon them and expect they'll do your bidding. If you want to control a demon, you have to bind it to your will first. Otherwise, things can get ugly fast. That's what happened to the cult. Nahash-Dred slipped the leash, and instead of destroying the world he butchered them instead."

"Why was Calliope researching a doomsday cult?" Bethany asked.

He shrugged, his ample flesh jiggling beneath his dashiki. "She told me she'd heard things. Whispers from the other side. She was a necromancer, you know. She certainly seemed more comfortable around spirits than with the living."

That summed her up pretty well. For someone who had trouble looking people in the eye, the dead were probably a lot easier to deal with.

"But it's what the spirits told her that had her so frightened," Yrouel said. "They warned her that Nahash-Dred was coming back to New York. Coming back to finish the job."

We followed him as his floating chair glided into an adjoining hallway. Here, too, the walls were covered with priceless works of art—Dalí, Picasso, O'Keeffe. Yrouel glided through an open doorway into another room. There was no furniture here, just a mound of suitcases, a pile of dashikis, a heap of books, and various other personal items strewn about. Where the left-hand wall met the ceiling, a band of narrow, barred windows ran the length of the room. Through them, I could make out a snippet of the alley floor outside.

Philip eyed the suitcases. "You going somewhere?"

"To Tsotha Zin," Yrouel replied, gliding to a halt in the center of the room. "For years, there have been those who chose to live in the Nethercity to escape the growing darkness on the surface and enjoy the dragon's protection. But it was always a minority. Now, it's a full-fledged exodus. There are hundreds of us, *thousands* of us fleeing to Tsotha Zin before it's too late."

"Something scared you," Bethany said.

Yrouel nodded. "Surely you feel it as well? Something is coming. Something terrible. Worse than you can possibly imagine."

Bethany and I exchanged glances. Biddy had said the same thing. Something was coming, something he thought in his madness the trembler could protect him from so long as he fed it enough women.

"This thing that's coming," I said. "You think it's the demon. Nahash-Dred."

"After what Calliope told me, I have no doubt of it," Yrouel replied.

I remembered my vision—the ruined city, the bodies, the blood. Was this what the cloaked man had been trying to show me? Was this what would happen if Nahash-Dred returned? New York City in ruins? Countless dead?

Sometimes it felt like there were crosshairs over this city. Sometimes it felt like New York would never stop being a target.

"I plan to remain down in Tsotha Zin until this all blows over, or until the Destroyer of Worlds, well, destroys the world, whichever comes first,"

Yrouel said. He looked up at the ceiling. "Either way, I don't think I'll miss the constant stink of fish from those accursed shops outside."

I looked around the room again. None of his suitcases looked big enough to carry a painting. "What about your art collection? Aren't you taking that, too?"

Yrouel waved a hand dismissively. "Forgeries. I can always make more if I need to. Observe."

He gestured absently, and a thick stripe of blue appeared on the white wall. I went over to it. It looked like paint, right down to the brushstrokes. Painting by magic. I shook my head in amazement.

"It's easy for my kind to do," Yrouel said. "We were artists for millennia. Which more often than not meant we were starving and poor. I simply found a way to monetize my natural talent, that's all."

With another gesture, a small letter Y appeared in the paint. The same as I'd seen in the Magritte painting in Calliope's living room. Now I understood what it meant.

"That's how you and Calliope met," I said. "You sold her a painting."

"Quite right," Yrouel said. "She bought one of my paintings—a Magritte, if I recall—and we got to talking about our interests. When she found out I knew something about the Aeternis Tenebris cult, we made an appointment to talk some more. That's why she was coming here tonight."

"She told me the painting cost a fortune," I said, growing angry. "She didn't know it was a forgery, did she? How much did you bilk her for?"

"Come now, don't be so judgmental," Yrouel said. "Do I look like I can work in a Wall Street office, or slinging burgers at a restaurant? We all make a living how we can, and the information trade is feast or famine."

I shook my head in disgust. My past wasn't exactly squeaky clean and I wasn't one for throwing stones in glass houses, but the fact that Calliope had died without ever knowing this son of a bitch had cheated her out of her money infuriated me. My hands balled into fists, but luckily Bethany changed the subject before I did something I would have regretted.

"Calliope was coming here for information," she said. "What was it?"

Yrouel smirked, feeling smug that he knew something we didn't. I'd seen his type before, two-bit players who got a taste of money or power and thought it made them something. In the end, most of them had wound up floating facedown in the Gowanus Canal.

"Information is the most valuable commodity one can trade in, don't you think?" Yrouel said. "Every once in a while, something good comes my way. In this case, it was something *very* good. What would you say if I told you Nahash-Dred *didn't* kill all the cult members after all? One of them survived, a man who might just be planning to summon Nahash-Dred and try to end the world again. Calliope was coming here tonight so I could tell her how to find him."

"How about you tell us instead?" Bethany pressed.

Yrouel arched a fleshy, hairless eyebrow. "She was going to pay me twenty-five thousand dollars for the information. Are you prepared to meet that price?"

I glared at him.

"The more dangerous the information is, the more valuable it is," Yrouel explained, "and as you might imagine, this was a dangerous line of inquiry. The sole remaining cult member would no doubt kill anyone who got too close. Apparently he's already done so. Poor girl."

The urge to do grievous bodily harm to Yrouel resurfaced. It was all I could do not to follow through on it. Calliope had put her life on the line, but all this bastard cared about was getting paid.

"Calliope was convinced time was of the essence," Yrouel continued. "She believed Nahash-Dred would return soon. And when I say soon, understand I don't mean a matter of months, or even weeks. Calliope thought it was *days*."

"If she was right, we have to have that information," Bethany said. "We can stop the remaining cultist from summoning Nahash-Dred before it's too late."

"I told you my price," Yrouel said.

"But you're in danger, too," she insisted. "You said so yourself. If you know so much about him, he'll come after you just like he did Calliope."

"Twenty-five thousand dollars could buy me a lot of protection."

I'd had enough. "The way I see it, Calliope already paid for that information when you swindled her. Unless of course you'd like us to reach out to your other art customers and tell them they've been swindled, too?"

"You wouldn't," Yrouel said.

"You're right, it'll take too long," Philip said. "How about we just break your hands so you can't make any more forgeries?" He started toward Yrouel.

Yrouel nervously backed his floating chair away from him. "Okay, okay! The surviving member of the Aeternis Tenebris is a man by the name of Erickson Arkwright, though obviously that's not the name he uses anymore. That name came with a lifetime behind bars attached to it—racketeering, blackmail, murder. So after the rest of the cult was massacred, he allowed the world to think he was dead, too. He found a new name, a new identity that allowed him—"

One of the windows up by the ceiling exploded suddenly as something bright and crackling crashed through the glass. The blast struck Yrouel. He burst like a water balloon in an explosion of flesh and gore.

Blood and chunks of rubbery flesh rained over me. I stood frozen a moment, stunned. The floating chair dropped to the floor with a loud crash. Next to me, Bethany looked like Sissy Spacek at the end of *Carrie,* her hair, face, clothes, and cargo vest slick with blood. Her mouth hung open in shock.

"You have *got* to be kidding!" she cried.

I turned to run for the door, but Philip was already ahead of me, running like a blur to the alley outside, where the blast had come from.

# Seven

I raced up the ramp from Yrouel's apartment to the alley outside. Philip was already there, looking up at the buildings that surrounded us.

"It came from up there, on the rooftop," Philip said, pointing. He swept his finger down toward the shattered window at the base of the far wall. "A straight angle through the window to hit Yrouel. Whoever he is, he's a hell of a shot. And damn it, I had him for a moment, too. I could see his body heat up there, and then suddenly it was gone. He must be hiding behind something iron, or—wait, there!" He pointed up at a figure lurking on the roof of a five-story building that backed up onto the alley, little more than a dark silhouette against the night sky. I would have missed him if Philip hadn't pointed him out. But of course Philip was a vampire, a nocturnal predator. Night vision was natural to him, even through those mirrored shades he never took off.

The figure on the roof ducked away from the edge, disappearing from sight. Philip moved fast, effortlessly jumping ten feet onto the lowest landing of the building's fire escape. He didn't bother climbing the narrow iron staircase at its center. Instead, he began scaling the landings toward the roof, moving as quickly and smoothly as a jungle cat stalking its prey.

"Philip, wait!" I shouted, but it was too late, he was already halfway up. We needed Yrouel's assassin alive if we wanted any answers, but he was as good as dead if Philip caught him first. "Shit!"

I reached for my cell phone, only to find my pocket empty. The phone must have slipped out in the car on the way here. Just then, Bethany came bursting out of Yrouel's apartment.

"My cell phone is in the Escalade," I told her. "Get it and call Isaac. Tell him what happened."

She started to protest. "But—"

"Go!" I shouted.

I jumped for the ladder hanging off the fire escape and managed to grab hold of the bottom rung. Sharp flakes of rusted metal bit into my palms. While Bethany ran out of the alley toward the car, I started climbing up the ladder to the first landing, feeling a thousand times clumsier than Philip. I threw myself over the railing onto the landing, then ran up the narrow staircase to the roof.

By the time I got there, Philip was already in the distance, racing across the rooftops. In the glow of the streetlights, I could just barely make out the figure Philip was chasing. Philip closed the distance between them with his supernatural speed. Just as it looked like Philip was about to overtake him, the figure twisted around to point one hand at him. There was a high-pitched whine, building in tone and volume, and then a sudden explosion of light. A blast of crackling energy like the one that had killed Yrouel arced out of the assassin's hand. I smelled the bitter ozone of an electrical discharge on the wind. Philip dove aside as the roof exploded into rubble and smoke where he'd been standing a moment before. The assassin kept running, gaining ground before Philip was able to start chasing him again.

I kept running, too. A few moments later I found the charred, smoking hole the blast had put in the roof. Sprinting past it, I found myself on the last roof of the block, looking down onto Bayard Street. Philip and the assassin had turned the corner and were now racing across the rooftops of a side street. I took off after them.

They were both so far ahead of me that I had to push myself to run faster or risk losing them. I ran through an obstacle course of satellite dishes and heating vents, nearly got tangled in lines of drying laundry, skirted around boxed-in rooftop gardens, and hurdled over the low walls between adjoining rooftops. But each time I looked up, Philip and the assassin seemed farther away.

Another high-pitched whine hit my ears. Another bright blast erupted from the assassin's outstretched hand. Philip leapt aside, and a brick chimney behind him shattered to pieces. I ducked as I ran, protecting my head against the shower of mortar pebbles and brick chips. Before I could get my bearings, the whine came again. Another blast obliterated the edge of the roof under Philip's feet. He fell toward the street below, but at the last moment he managed to grab hold of a fire escape railing. The fire escape's bolts popped out of the brick and the whole structure pulled a few inches away from the building, but it held. Philip started scrambling back up.

I ran past him, taking the lead. I drew my gun and shouted, "Stop!" but the dark figure kept running. Every time I thought I had a clean shot, he would zig or zag and put a laundry line or chimney between us. I willed my protesting legs to keep moving.

And then, just like that, he was gone. I'd lost him. I slowed a bit, catching my breath. He couldn't have gone far. Probably, he was as tired as I was and needed a place to rest and plan his next move. I scanned the rooftop in front of me. If it were me, where would I hide? My gaze settled on the slanted concrete hutch of a roof access door, facing away from me. Bingo.

I climbed silently up the forty-five-degree incline of the back of the hutch. When I reached the top, I looked down. Sure enough, there he was, crouched in front of the access door, catching his breath and looking from side to side as if deciding where to run next. He was clad in black sweats, his face hidden behind a black ski mask. There were no holes for his mouth or nose, only one single, elongated opening for his eyes. He wore a plain black glove on his left hand, but on his right he wore an armored gauntlet, as if he'd taken it right off a suit of armor at the Metropolitan Museum of Art.

I holstered my gun and jumped off the hutch. I landed on top of him, knocking him to the floor. I tried to get my arms around him, but he wriggled away and punched a heavy, metal fist into my kidney. A streak of pain shot up my back. He scurried away, stood, and turned to face me. I found myself looking into two deep brown eyes that were almost black in the dark. He was lean, probably didn't weigh more than a buck twenty or thirty. No wonder he was so damn spry.

He raised the gauntlet toward me. It looked old, battered around the edges and discolored in spots. It didn't take a genius to figure out it was also a magical artifact, the source of those deadly blasts. The high-pitched whine started, coming from the gauntlet itself. The damn thing was powering up. But I still barely had my breath back from the kidney punch. There was no way I could get out of the way in time.

Philip came out of the dark so fast I didn't see him until he was standing right in front of me. The gauntlet sent out its blast, hitting Philip square in the chest. The force of it blew him backward, past me. He smashed straight through the roof access door like a wrecking ball and tumbled down the steps into the building below.

I wouldn't get another chance if I didn't act now. I leapt at the assassin and grabbed the gauntlet, trying to pry it off his hand. He swung hard with his other fist, connecting with my jaw and knocking me off my feet. I fell on my backside, empty-handed. He aimed the gauntlet at me again.

"I wouldn't do that if I were you," I said. "People have tried to kill me before. Bad things happened to them."

He didn't listen. They never did. I heard the whine of the gauntlet as it powered up again, saw the bright energy come bursting out of it—and then the blast seemed to hang in the air between us, crackling against a rounded, translucent green barrier that hadn't been there a moment before. A second later, the blast dissipated, absorbed into the barrier.

The assassin and I both looked over to see Bethany standing a few feet away. Her hand was out like she was a crossing guard stopping traffic. In her palm was a glowing emerald the size of a quarter, held in place by a leather strap around her fingers. Projecting out of the emerald was the translucent green barrier that had protected me.

She smirked at me. "Get back to the car, he says. Call Isaac, he says. But who is it who keeps saving your ass?" She walked closer, still holding out the charm, and addressed the assassin. "That's a Thracian Gauntlet you're wearing. The funny thing is, there are only four of them in the world and they're all supposed to be in England. So what are you doing with one?"

The assassin backed away, then turned and ran for the edge of the roof. I scrambled to my feet and ran after him. Before I could stop him, he jumped. The sidewalk was fifty feet down, there was no way he would survive that fall. But as he plummeted, he threw a small charm ahead of him. It exploded in midair right beneath him, opening up into a hole in space, a vortex of flickering blue light. He fell through it and it swallowed him, closing behind him.

Damn. A portal spell. He could be anywhere now—another block, another borough, another city. Like a lethal Boy Scout, the assassin had come prepared.

I cursed and kicked a nearby heating vent in frustration. The small, tinny clang it gave up wasn't satisfying at all.

"I take it the asshole got away," Philip said, stumbling out of the wreckage of the roof access door. He was covered in plaster dust and a few chunks of drywall. His clothes were charred and smoking, but he seemed unharmed. He brushed white dust out of his hair. "Anybody catch his name?"

# Eight

A wise man once said that when confronted with a mystery, the easiest and least complicated solution was usually the right one. The easiest and least complicated answer to the question of who attacked us in Chinatown was Erickson Arkwright. It made sense. Arkwright would want anyone dead who could reveal his secret or try to stop him from summoning the world-destroying demon Nahash-Dred again. Yrouel had figured out Arkwright's new identity, and Calliope had gotten too close to the truth. Arkwright had eliminated both of them.

Except we had no proof Erickson Arkwright was still alive, or that he existed at all. So far, the name was nothing more than a rumor perpetrated by a con man looking to make a quick twenty-five grand. For all we knew, Yrouel had made it up out of whole cloth. His murder might have nothing to do with Arkwright, or the doomsday cult, or Nahash-Dred. And yet, if that was the case, the timing of his death right after Calliope's was one hell of a coincidence.

There was something else nagging at me, too. The murders were completely different. Calliope's had been up-close and personal, with a brutality that didn't match the long-range sniper killing of Yrouel. If all signs pointed to Arkwright, surely it would have been a lot easier and faster for him to use the Thracian Gauntlet on Calliope, too. Why take the time to cut her open and spike her to the ceiling like that? I didn't know, and I didn't like not knowing. It felt like I was letting Calliope down again.

The only thing I knew for certain was that after tonight we'd added our own names to his kill list. I didn't doubt for a second he'd be back for us.

After showering off Yrouel's blood and changing into a fresh set of clothes, I sat with Philip and Bethany around the big, round table in Citadel's main room. Isaac paced the floor in front of us.

"If the killer has a Thracian Gauntlet, that makes him far more dangerous than we thought," he said. "What I want to know is, how the hell did he get ahold of it? Those gauntlets are supposed to be under lock and key in England. This is the first time one has been used in centuries. More than that, it's the first time one has *ever* been seen on this side of the Atlantic."

"Someone fill me in," I said. "What's the deal with these gauntlets?"

Isaac opened the laptop on the table and tapped a few keys. The bank of monitors on the wall flickered to life. Illustrations of two lavish suits of armor filled the screens. The breastplates were encrusted with gemstones and long tubelike formations that looked almost like the ribs of an animal. The helmets were flanked with golden wings.

"There are only four Thracian Gauntlets in existence. They're all that remain of these two suits of armor," Isaac said. "Have you ever heard the legend of Tulemkust and Sevastumi?"

"No," I said. "Who are they?"

"Not who, what," he said. "Tulemkust and Sevastumi were two of the hidden cities of southeast Europe, on the coast of the Black Sea in a region that was once known as Thrace. The two were constantly at war with each other. To defend themselves, Tulemkust created the Gemini Sentinels, two protectors who wore armored suits imbued with powerful magic, manufactured from armor fused with the bones of a grimleth."

I looked at the riblike tubing on the breastplates again. "What's a grimleth?" I asked, but Isaac didn't stop to answer.

"The suits granted the Gemini Sentinels the ability to fly, and access to a host of lethal weaponry, one of which was the gauntlets themselves. But the responsibility was so enormous that Tulemkust was forced to institute a lottery draft system. Every citizen was a Gemini Sentinel at some point, and none ever wore the suit more than once. Each morning, two new people would be chosen to guard their borders from invasion. But one day the suits were given to two brothers who used them against their own people.

"Whether the brothers were enemy agents or just insane, no one knows. Scores of innocent civilians were slaughtered in the ensuing carnage. The attack lasted well into the night. Tulemkust was brought to the brink of destruction. When the brothers finally took off the armor to sleep, they were killed. After that, the survivors of Tulemkust had learned their lesson. The suits were dismantled. A few centuries later the gauntlets found their way to a private museum in England. The Avalonian Collection, run by the same family of mages for ten generations. And there the Thracian Gauntlets stayed. Until now."

"But you can't just walk into the Avalonian Collection and steal a Thracian Gauntlet," Bethany said. "It's one of the most heavily guarded artifact collections in the world."

"And that's how we'll catch him," Isaac said. "The gauntlet can't have gone missing without being noticed. Nor can it have traveled across the Atlantic without someone seeing something. If we follow the gauntlet's trail, it'll lead us to our man, I'm sure of it. I'll contact the Avalonian Collection and see what they know. Philip, I need you to scour the black market message boards online for any mentions of the gauntlet."

"I'm on it," Philip said.

"Bethany, Trent, it's best for us to operate under the assumption that Calliope was right and this demon is about to make a return engagement. I'm going to see if I can find any information on Nahash-Dred, but we don't have a lot of time. We're going to need help, anything that can give us a leg up. Tomorrow, I want the two of you to go see the oracles."

After the meeting, I went back upstairs to my room for the night. I found Kali lying on my bed. She was sleeping on her back with each leg pointed in a different direction, her furry stomach exposed. Looking at her lying there so peacefully, I could almost forget I'd seen two murder victims today, one of them killed right in front of me. Suddenly I had an inkling why someone might actually want to live with one of these absurd little creatures. They made everything seem okay somehow.

Had I owned a cat once, back in the before time? Was I a cat person? Only one way to find out.

I reached out and gently petted Kali's stomach. Her eyes opened immediately. She hissed and swiped angrily at me, her claws drawing blood from the back of my hand. The scratch stung like I'd been burned. As I stood there cursing and shaking my hand in pain, Kali sprang off the bed and disappeared into her carrier.

Goddamn cat. I should have taken her to the pound myself. But at least now I had my answer. Definitely not a cat person.

I went into the bathroom, washed the wound clean, and returned to the bedroom. I knelt by the bed and pulled Calliope's spiral-bound notebook out from under the mattress. I glanced at the door, but no one was coming tonight. Bethany had offered to stop by for another game of gin rummy, but I told her I wasn't in the mood. She couldn't hide the surprise and disappointment in her eyes. It was the first time I'd ever turned her down. But tonight I had more important things to do.

I sat on the bed and opened the notebook. The urge to know why it included the same Ehrlendarr rune from my earliest memory spurred me on. Did Calliope know something about me? About my past?

I was surprised to find the first half of the notebook was filled with what appeared to be random words and phrases repeated over and over again. Some pages had only one or two on them, while others were cramped so tight that everything flowed together. Some phrases were circled emphatically. There were arrows pointing from one phrase to another, sometimes from one page to another. None of it made sense. It was like the scribblings of a madwoman. The only thing I recognized was the name Nahash-Dred. It was written over several pages, in letters both big and small, sometimes scrawled again over where it had been already written, as if for emphasis.

The second half of the book was filled with notes about the first half, as if she were trying to figure out what the hell she'd written. It felt like reading something by two different authors. Except both halves of the notebook were in the same handwriting. Calliope's.

There were pencil sketches throughout the notebook, too, rough drawings of people and animals and, in one instance, a woman with wings. And then, turning a page, I came across the Ehrlendarr rune. A jolt of adrenaline surged through me. I had woken up in front of a brick wall with this rune etched upon it. All around me the aftereffects of a spell had lingered in the air. Someone had been there with me but was gone when I woke. That was all I knew. Not knowing anything else was like an itch I couldn't scratch. Frustrating. Maddening.

Below the sketch of the rune, Calliope had written something, two short questions in a rushed, cramped script.

*Where is the eighth Guardian?*

*Did they meet?*

The Guardians. Bethany had told me about them. The story went that at the dawn of time eight beings had been granted immortality and dominion over each of the eight natural elements: air, water, fire, earth, metal, wood, time, and magic. Some called them gods; others thought they were something more than that, cosmic and unknowable entities. It was said they lived at the center of all things, in a place called the Radiant Lands, where their job was to watch over the world and maintain the balance of light and dark. Only, one of them had disappeared a long time ago—the eighth Guardian, the Guardian of Magic, who was represented by the same Ehrlendarr rune that appeared in both the notebook and my earliest memory. The eighth Guardian's absence had caused the Shift, throwing off the balance of magic, transforming it into something dark and dangerous.

Part of me was skeptical that the Guardians actually existed. There was so much pain, suffering, and injustice in the world they were supposed to be looking after that if they did exist, they must be unbelievably bad at their job. I would have been perfectly happy to call them a myth and nothing more, except after the battle in Fort Tryon Park I'd seen something. For just a moment, maybe even half a moment, I'd seen seven towering figures standing somehow *behind* the visible world, shrouded in a sizzling bright light that hid their features from me. Seven figures, and an empty space for the missing eighth. I'd only caught a glimpse, and then they were gone.

What did Calliope's investigation have to do with the Guardians? In particular, the AWOL eighth Guardian? It didn't seem to fit.

And then there was the second question she'd scrawled on the page, even more perplexing than the first.

*Did they meet?*

Did who meet, exactly? The eighth Guardian and . . . who?

I closed the notebook in frustration. It angered me that I couldn't figure this out. It also terrified me. Because suddenly the mystery of my identity felt much bigger than me. Much more complicated.

Something fluttered out from between the notebook pages and fell on the bed. It was a rectangular piece of heavy stock paper the size of a business card. I picked it up. It was an appointment card. Across the top it read: CALLIOPE GIANNOPOULOS, PSYCHIC MEDIUM. Beneath it, on the line marked DATE, was written an early morning appointment for just over a year ago. Below that was a line marked NAME.

The name written there was Ingrid Bannion.

I blinked in surprise.

The last time I'd seen Ingrid Bannion, she was lying dead in a pool of her own blood, murdered by the shadowborn after she tried to protect us. How did Calliope know Ingrid? I turned the card over and saw Calliope had scribbled the name Morbius on the back. I put the card back inside the notebook, piecing it together in my head. Ingrid must have gone to see Calliope in order to contact the spirit of Morbius, who had died years ago. Ingrid probably recognized Calliope as an authentic necromancer, and thus a true line of communication across the dark to the man she'd loved.

But her appointment had been over a year ago. Why had Calliope kept the card all this time? Why stash it with her notes? What did Ingrid have to do with any of this?

I tucked the notebook back under my mattress and lay down, staring at the ceiling. I was hoping for answers, but all I'd found were more questions. Yet I was sure of one thing now. Yrouel hadn't made up Nahash-Dred. If he hadn't invented that part of the story, did that mean the rest of it was true, too? Erickson Arkwright? The end of the world?

I met Bethany the next morning in front of the Provenzano Lanza Funeral Home on Second Avenue, in the East Village. She was waiting with a bird-cage. On the perch inside it sat two small, nearly identical finches. Our payment for the oracles' time, should they deign to see us. Birds were the oracles' favorite food.

Bethany didn't look any happier to be here than I was. We both had our issues with the oracles. The last time we were here, they'd made it abundantly clear that Bethany didn't matter to them in the slightest. As for me, they'd called me an abomination, among other choice words. I wished Philip could go in our place, but vampires weren't allowed inside the oracles' chamber. Not since long ago, when a vampire clan elder had tried to have the oracles killed after receiving some bad news. In retaliation, the oracles had wiped out the entire clan.

"Are you ready for this?" Bethany asked.

"Sure," I said. "I can't wait to hear what colorful new insults they have for me this time."

I took the birdcage from her. Using a key from her pocket, she unlocked the gate in a tall, wrought iron fence next to the funeral home. Beyond it was the New York Marble Cemetery, an enclosed yard of grass, shrubs, and the occasional small tree. There were no visible graves in this cemetery, only columns of tablets affixed to the walls to indicate who was buried in the vaults beneath the grass.

As she locked the gate behind us, I nodded at the key in her hand. "You went back to the Library of Keys without me?"

She put the key back in her pocket. "I didn't have to. I kept meaning to return the key after we were here last time, but it slipped my mind. I promise I'll bring you with me when I go back. You can pay my late fee."

"There are late fees for keys?" I asked.

She looked at me like I was a dolt, then shook her head. "You may be the most gullible person I know."

"I'm still new to all this, remember?"

"Trent, you stopped the Black Knight, released the gargoyles from slavery, and killed an unkillable Ancient. I don't think you get to call yourself new to this anymore."

Maybe she had a point, but it didn't feel that way to me. Every day some new revelation about magic and the world we lived in surprised me. I doubted I would ever stop feeling like the new kid in school.

At the back of the cemetery, what looked like the tower of a sunken castle jutted up from the grass, draped in moss and vines. I opened its heavy iron door to reveal a spiral staircase winding down into the darkness. With a muttered incantation, Bethany lit up her mirrored charm. Using it as a flashlight, she led the way down the staircase and through the subterranean tunnels below. I followed Bethany's glowing light. Everything else was pitch black.

"You want to talk about it?" Bethany asked as we walked.

"Talk about what?"

She glanced back at me over her shoulder. "I saw your face when we found Calliope, Trent. I'm not sure I've ever seen you like that. You knew her better than I did."

"But I *didn't* know her. I only met her the one time," I said. All I could see in my mind were her eyes, open and staring down at me from the ceiling, one blue and one hazel. It was like a mountain on my shoulders, crushing me under its weight. "I keep thinking about how she was so sure someone was watching her."

"You think it was the same person who killed Yrouel?" Bethany said.

"I think this project of hers got them both killed," I said. "I shouldn't have left her there alone. I should have gone back sooner. If I'd been there . . ."

"If you'd been there, what? You might have saved her?" Bethany stopped and turned to me. "Trent, you don't even know when it happened. Even if you'd gone back sooner, there's no way to know if it would have changed anything. Don't torture yourself like this. You can't save everyone."

Bethany didn't understand. I couldn't save Ingrid. I couldn't save Thornton. I couldn't save Calliope. I didn't know how to explain it to her, this sense that I'd failed somehow. But even if she was right that I couldn't save everyone, I could still find Calliope's killer and make him pay. I could give him a taste of the pain and terror he'd put her through. But in order to do that, I needed to find him first. I hoped the oracles could help me with that.

"Let's just keep moving, okay?" I said. "It isn't far now."

We walked the rest of the way in silence, until we reached the twenty-foot-tall doors to the oracles' chamber. I reached for one of the heavy bronze knockers. Bethany hissed my name, stopping me. I hadn't noticed that the doors were already slightly ajar.

"Something's wrong," Bethany said. She stepped closer with the light and shone it into the opening between the doors, but inside there was only darkness. "The oracles wouldn't leave the doors open like this."

I pushed them open the rest of the way. They swung inward without resistance, the loud creak of their hinges amplified by the silence. We walked into the chamber. The last time we'd been here, the doors had closed behind us of their own volition. This time they stayed open. Something was definitely off.

"Hello?" I called. No one answered.

"They're gone," Bethany said, her voice hollow with shock.

She shone her light around the chamber. Once, the darkness in this room had swallowed all light, but now Bethany's makeshift flashlight cut right through it, illuminating the bare brick walls and ceiling. Everything was right where I remembered it—the circle of tall candelabras, the dozens of birdcages hanging on long chains from the ceiling, the carpet of feathers and bones on the floor. Everything but the oracles themselves. They were gone, but they'd left everything behind.

Bethany looked at me, alarmed. "I don't understand. The oracles have been here for centuries. For as long as anyone can remember. Why would they just up and leave?"

Biddy and Yrouel had both sensed something terrible coming. *Something worse than you can imagine.* Biddy had sought protection from it. Yrouel had wanted to run away from it to the Nethercity.

The oracles would have sensed it, too. Foreseen it. And it had frightened them. The same oracles who had once wiped out an entire vampire clan in the blink of an eye. The same oracles no one threatened or questioned because no one dared.

They'd seen what was coming, and it had sent them running.

# Nine

Bethany paced back and forth on the sidewalk outside the gates of the New York Marble Cemetery, cradling my cell phone against her ear. She had Isaac on the other end. "I don't know where the oracles went. Back to wherever they came from, maybe, or down to the Nethercity. The point is, they're not here. They can't help. And if the oracles can't help, I don't know who can." It took a lot to make Bethany this nervous. She ran a hand through her hair, front to back, a nervous tic. I caught a glimpse of her unusually pointed ears, and then they were gone again, hidden behind her locks.

I put the birdcage down on the sidewalk. If we weren't going to give the finches to the oracles, I saw no reason to keep them. I opened the cage door to let them go. Both finches hopped off their perch and paused on the lip of the opening.

"What are you waiting for?" I said, tapping the side of the cage with my boot. They took off but didn't go far before perching on an air conditioner poking out of an apartment window above my head. "You better fly farther than that. Haven't you heard? Everyone's leaving. Even the oracles are gone." The birds ignored me, cocking their heads to one side in unison like creepy twins.

I wondered if the oracles had seen the same things I did in my vision— the city in ruins, the streets littered with bodies. Or had they seen something even worse, something about the demon himself? I wished we knew more about Nahash-Dred. If Calliope was right, time was running out, and we were still spinning our damn wheels.

I tried to put what I *did* know into order. Calliope was a necromancer, able to commune with the spirits. Those spirits had warned her about Nahash-Dred's return, presumably so she could stop it. But how was she supposed to do that? She couldn't have been planning to go after the demon herself. She was a necromancer, not a mage. She wouldn't be powerful enough to stop a demon they called the Destroyer of Worlds on her own. So what was her plan? Go to the cops? That was a laugh. She had to have something else in mind. She didn't seem the type to go into something like this half-cocked.

And then there was the appointment card I'd found tucked into her notebook . . .

Overhead, the finches took off, flying away side by side into the sky. My heart grew heavier as I watched them go. It wasn't that I wanted to leave, too. I wasn't one to run from a challenge. But watching them fly so gracefully, so effortlessly, tugged at something in me. These birds were doing what they were meant to do. They were being true to themselves in a way I never could be. My true self had been taken from me.

As the emotions swelled in my chest, my field of vision suddenly shifted. I didn't see the finches anymore, or buildings or the cars speeding past—instead I saw the elements they were made from, atoms that burned as brightly as stars. Running between those atoms, all around me, were the silken threads that bound everything together. Above, the finches flew like sparks into a sky where spheres patterned with mystical designs rotated around each other, the titanic gears of the universe.

I panicked, my breath coming in sharp rasps. How could this be happening? This was Stryge's power, the ability to see the inner workings of things. He had used it to unmake his victims, to take them apart like paper dolls. I had absorbed that power along with his life force at Fort Tryon Park, and it had nearly driven me mad. I'd almost killed Bethany and the others before getting a grip on myself. In the month since then, it hadn't come back. Why now? How was it even still inside me? Stryge's power had been inextricably tied to his life force, but I had died and absorbed a new life force since then—Biddy's. Stryge's power shouldn't still be with me. So why was it? What did it mean?

Just then everything broke apart. Behind it all, behind the skin of the world, I saw seven figures, seven towering, dazzling entities all looking at me, looking right at me—

I blinked, and just like that they were gone. Everything was back to normal. In the distance, the two finches were tiny dots against the clouds. The power receded inside me, shrinking down to a small flame at my core, out of my reach once again. I shook my head, trying to clear it. What just happened?

I sat down on the sidewalk and caught my breath. I looked over at Bethany. She was still on the phone.

"The only thing we can do is go back to Calliope's house and look for anything we missed," she was saying. "We can get around the police somehow, if we have to. But there must be something there we overlooked." She glanced at me. Something in my face froze her in her tracks. "Isaac, I'm going to have to call you back."

She ended the call and held my phone out to me. The screen was already flickering and emitting a low buzz, even though she hadn't been holding it for long. Prolonged exposure to the magic charms in Bethany's vest fried electronics for some reason. It shorted out their batteries or played havoc with their microchips. It was why Bethany couldn't carry her own cell phone, or any other electronic equipment. She couldn't even wear a watch.

I stared at the phone in her hand for a moment, still in shock.

"Earth to Trent," she said.

I snapped out of it and took the phone from her.

"What's wrong?" she asked. "You look like you've seen a ghost."

"It's still inside me," I croaked. My throat was dry.

"What is?"

"Stryge's power. Somehow, it's still there. I had some kind of flare-up just now. It was just like last time. I could—I could see the threads that bind everything together. If I'd wanted to, I could have unwound them, taken it all apart in the blink of an eye. Bethany, this power, it's—it's too much. Why do I still have it? It's like it won't let go."

She shook her head. "I don't know. Are you okay?"

I rubbed my hands over my face. "Everything would make sense if I just knew who the hell I am. *What* I am. I know it would."

"Right now I'd settle for an instruction manual," Bethany said.

I couldn't help it. I laughed. That, at least, felt good. Normal, even.

"Come on, we have to go back to Calliope's," Bethany said.

I stood up with a sigh. It was time to come clean. I wasn't looking forward to how she would take this. "I, um, heard what you said about there being something you missed at Calliope's house. You're right, there was, except it's not at her house anymore."

She knit her brow. "Where is it?"

"You're not going to like this," I said. "It's under my mattress."

I put Calliope's spiral-bound notebook on the round table in the main room of Citadel. Isaac, Philip, and Bethany looked down at the notebook, then up at me.

"Let me get this straight," Isaac said. "You took this from Calliope's home without telling anyone?"

I nodded. I hated how disappointed in me he sounded.

"I thought we'd earned your trust by now," he said. "I thought we were a team."

"We are, I just . . ." I trailed off miserably. I didn't know how to explain what I felt.

"Once a thief," Philip said. I glared at the vampire. He shrugged. "Why deny what you are? Embrace it."

"Guys, give him a chance to explain," Bethany said. "You do *have* an explanation, don't you?"

"I know I should have told you about it sooner, but there was a reason I kept it to myself," I said. "When I took Calliope home the other night, this notebook was lying open on her coffee table. I saw something in it, something I thought had to do with me. With who I was before." I opened the book to the sketch of the Ehrlendarr rune, the eye inside the circle, and showed it to them. "After I lost my memories, this was the first thing I saw. This rune, on a plain brick wall. It's the Ehrlendarr rune for magic. I know I shouldn't have kept the book from you, but I needed time to study it. I needed to know if there was anything else in here that sparked a memory. Anything else that might be about me."

"I don't understand," Isaac said. "Why couldn't you share that with us? We could have helped."

I sighed. "I didn't know what I would find."

"You were afraid of what it might say about you," Bethany said.

I nodded. "If it was something bad . . ."

"You thought we would reject you," Isaac said.

I nodded again. I felt like a kid called to the principal's office.

"You know we wouldn't do that," Bethany said.

"No, I don't know that," I said. "There haven't been a lot of clues about who I am, but so far what we *do* know isn't exactly encouraging."

"You're talking about the prophecy," Isaac said. "The one that says the Immortal Storm will bring about the end of everything. But we still don't know how valid the prophecy is, Trent, or if it means something other than what you think. Sometimes these things aren't what they seem."

I nodded, but I doubted the prophecy meant anything other than what it said. I was a threat to everyone—mortal, Ancient, and Guardian alike. Or so everyone kept telling me.

"So what did the notebook have to say about you?" Bethany asked.

"As far as I could tell, nothing. To be honest, I can't make heads or tails out of it. The whole notebook is gibberish. It's just page after page of random words and phrases, repeated over and over again." I turned to a page at random. "Here's a perfect example. On this page she only wrote one thing, and circled it about a hundred times. *Eternal voice and inward word.* I have no idea what that means. It almost sounds like part of a spell to me."

Isaac shook his head. "None that I've ever heard. May I?" I handed him the notebook. He flipped through the pages and frowned. "I see what you mean. She circled this phrase, too: *Hidden mariner lost at sea.* Could it be some kind of code, in case her notes fell into the wrong hands?"

"I thought the same thing," I said. "But how could it be a code if she didn't understand it herself? The whole back of the notebook is her trying to figure it out."

Isaac turned to the back of the notebook and started flipping through the pages.

"There's more," I said. "Calliope knew she was putting her life in danger. She probably felt like she couldn't confide in anyone, though ultimately she would have to. She couldn't handle this demon by herself. She would need help from someone who not only believed her story, but was powerful enough or connected enough to do something about it. I think once she had what she was looking for, she was going to ask Ingrid Bannion for help."

Isaac looked up at me from the notebook, surprised. "Ingrid?"

I showed them the appointment card I'd found inside the notebook. "According to this, Ingrid came to Calliope a little over a year ago, presumably to contact Morbius on the other side. Calliope must have known Ingrid was the last surviving member of the original Five-Pointed Star. She knew Ingrid was someone who could help her when the time came."

"But Ingrid is dead," Isaac pointed out.

"I don't think Calliope knew that. Right up until the end, she was still hoping Ingrid would help her. It's why she held onto the appointment card. But first she needed to crack this code."

"I'm not so sure it's *just* a code," Isaac said, scratching his beard as he flipped through the pages. "All this repetition, words written over words in a mad jumble. It reminds me of automatic writing."

"What's that?" I asked.

"It's a technique necromancers have been using for centuries. They go into a trance, allowing the spirits to take over their bodies for a short time. The spirits manipulate the necromancer's hand to write out messages. Looking at this notebook, I can't help wondering if that's what this is. If so, it's possible even Calliope hadn't deciphered it yet."

Now I understood why it looked like different people had written the notes, despite it all being in the same handwriting. In a way, it *had* been different people. Calliope and the spirits.

"I think that's what she was trying to work out in these back pages," Isaac said. "The meaning of it all."

"I don't know how far she got, but I'm pretty sure something in this notebook got her killed," I said. "Yrouel, too."

Bethany knit her brow the way she did whenever she was deep in thought. "Trent, where was the notebook when you took it?"

"It was still on the coffee table," I said, my cheeks starting to burn with embarrassment. "I, um, kind of waited until you weren't looking, and then . . ."

Bethany shook her head. "We'll have words about that later. But that's not why I asked. You're saying the notebook was out in the open. But if it was sitting right there, why didn't the killer take it with him? Wouldn't he want to know how much she'd discovered, or if she'd contacted anyone else beside Yrouel? Wouldn't he want to destroy it if it contained evidence against him?"

That hadn't occurred to me, but she was right. If the notebook was the repository of everything the spirits had warned Calliope about, everything she was subsequently investigating, then surely the killer would have turned the place upside down trying to find it. But there was no indication the house had been searched, and the notebook had been out in plain sight in the living room.

Isaac stood up and walked to the front of the table. "I spoke to a representative from the Avalonian Collection today. All she would tell me was that a recently hired custodian had stolen the Thracian Gauntlet from the gallery and sold it to a black market dealer in New York City for quick cash. Unfortunately, the custodian has since died, making it impossible to get any information out of him."

"He died?" I asked. "What happened to him?"

"The representative quite pointedly refused to elaborate," Isaac said.

"Ten to one the Avalonian Collection made his death look like an accident," Philip said.

Isaac sighed. "Regardless, we're going to have to take a different approach if we want to track the gauntlet down. Philip, what did you find on the black market message boards?"

"Guy named Langstrom was mouthing off on one of the boards about something that sounds like it could be the gauntlet," Philip said. "Langstrom's a fence, he buys and sells stolen goods. I know him, we've crossed paths before, back when I knew some people in the black market. Though *people* might not be the right word for these scumbags."

"See if you can set up a meeting with Langstrom this afternoon," Isaac said. He opened his laptop and tapped the keys. "In the meantime, there's something you need to see. All of you."

The bank of monitors on the wall flickered to life with a single, mosaic image spread across all six screens. It was a photograph of ruins in a jungle. Broken columns and crumbling stone domes were hidden amid the tall, verdant trees, choked by vines and thick vegetation. To one side, a colorful bird was perched on the fallen statue of a warrior in a helmet and cloak.

"I've been researching Nahash-Dred," Isaac said. "I found several instances in the past where the demon was summoned. Each resulted in the complete destruction of a civilization."

More pictures appeared on the monitors. Ruins in the desert, ruins in the jungle, ruins by the sea. Ghost cities under leagues of water and ancient, blasted cityscapes on the sides of mountains.

"Lost civilizations all around the world can be traced back to the presence of Nahash-Dred," he continued. "Mahendraparvata. Kuelanaku. Atlantis. Namib-Moremi. Korra-Zin. The Aksumite Empire. The Anasazi. The Olmec. It's no wonder they call him the Destroyer of Worlds."

"How does a demon destroy an entire civilization?" I asked. "It can't just be brute force."

"I wish I knew," Isaac said. "My library is woefully lacking in information about demons. I know they come from another dimension, someplace outside our world. I know they can be summoned, bound, and banished with the proper spells. But that's all I know. That's all most people know. But I'd say in order to achieve devastation on this scale, Nahash-Dred has to be using magic."

"But no spell can do *that*," Bethany said, pointing at the screens.

"No spell we know of," Isaac said. "Remember, demons aren't from here. Their magic would be different from ours." He tapped some keys on his laptop, and the monitors went black again. "There's one more thing I wanted to show you. Images of Nahash-Dred are almost impossible to come by. What few illustrations I found all contradict each other, as if no one can agree on what the demon looks like. But I did find one thing. It's a snippet of film an acquaintance of mine at the Pnakotic Archives in Montreal e-mailed me. It's from an expedition in the 1950s to a previously unexplored plateau in the heart of Africa. The footage has been kept under lock and key at the archives ever since. No one else has seen it in half a century. It's believed to contain the only existing photographic image of Nahash-Dred. You might want to brace yourselves."

He hit a key, and the film began to play. The bank of monitors lit up with the black-and-white image of a lush vista of trees, vines, and shrubbery. No sound accompanied it. The image jostled and shook as the cameraman climbed up an incline. Machetes chopped silently through thick under-brush, revealing what appeared to be a walled city, its buildings clustered around a towering castle of stone and clay brick. The image changed again, and now the cameraman was within those walls. Everywhere, buildings had been smashed to rubble and the streets were cluttered with overturned carts and debris. The camera moved through the streets, poked into buildings, but all was deathly still. And empty. There was no one to be found. There was a sudden jump cut, as if they'd turned off the camera for a bit, then turned it on again. The cameraman was outside the city once more, surrounded by a thick forest. The camera panned up to the sky, where a flock of birds suddenly took wing out of the trees. There were so many of them they looked like a huge, dark, roiling cloud. The camera whipped from side to side confusingly, and I realized the cameraman was running. A huge wave of something wet splashed over the trees. The camera stopped moving. Suddenly, a rain of big, bulky objects came down. Arms, legs, torsos, guts. The remains of the people who'd disappeared from the city. The camera whipped up again and caught a fleeting glimpse of something moving through the trees—an enormous figure that towered over the canopy. I couldn't make out any details, it all went by too fast, but something about that figure wormed its way under my skin and made me shiver. Then the screens went black.

I tried to swallow, but my throat was too tight and dry. "What *was* that thing?"

"Nahash-Dred," Isaac said. "I wasn't kidding when I told you to brace yourself."

He hit a key and the film began to play backward. He paused it right at the moment when the camera caught a glimpse of the demon. It was just a grainy image through the trees, but I could make out a wreath of horns around the demon's head, a dark, patterned hide, and a portion of the batlike wings that sprouted from his ridged spine. But it wasn't just his enormous size that made him so frightening. Even through a simple, blurry film-still like this, I could sense something infinitely terrible about Nahash-Dred, and infinitely powerful.

I couldn't help thinking again about the vision the cloaked man had given me. The city in ruins. Countless dead. Looking at the terrifying creature on the monitors, it could only have been about Nahash-Dred. We had to stop Arkwright from summoning the demon again, no matter what it took.

A familiar female voice from behind us said, "What the hell is that?"

I turned to see Gabrielle standing in the main room of Citadel as if no time had passed at all. She wore a red, ribbed sweater under her open black leather jacket, and a matching red silk scarf around her neck.

She stared at the demon on the monitors and tucked one long, braided dreadlock behind her ear. "Oh lord, what trouble have you gotten yourselves into now?"

We all got up from the table and hugged and kissed her, peppering her with questions about what she'd been up to and how she was feeling. She put up her hands in mock surrender.

"Whoa, whoa, one at a time." She gestured at the table. "Mind if I sit?"

"Please do," Isaac said. "You should have told us you were coming. We would have . . ." He turned off the computer. The monitors on the wall went black.

"You would have what, not shown the world's scariest filmstrip?" Gabrielle sat down. "Sorry to barge in. I had to get out of the apartment. I was going stir-crazy. If I don't keep busy, I'm going to lose my mind. I thought taking some time off after Thornton died would help, but there are reminders of him everywhere in that damn apartment. Don't get me wrong—sometimes, *most* of the time, that's a good thing, but other times . . ." She shook her head. "Other times it's more than I can bear."

She fiddled with something in her hands, a circular, brown object she turned over and over. It was Thornton's leather bracelet. She'd given it to him a long time ago as a token of her love. He'd cherished it so much he never took it off. He never even let anyone else touch it.

Gabrielle caught me looking at the bracelet and laughed, embarrassed. "I know, right? Here I am talking about too many reminders of Thornton, and I can't seem to leave this silly thing alone. I found it on my bedside table this morning. I must have taken it out of the drawer and put it there at some point, but I don't remember doing it." She smiled wistfully and shook her head. "See? Like I said, I'm going stir-crazy. If I don't find something to occupy my mind, I'm going to lose it entirely."

Isaac put his hand over hers. His pale skin looked like snow against hers. "It's all right. You know you're always welcome here."

She nodded. "I do know that. But sometimes it's good to hear it, too. Anyway, enough of this." She waved her hands like frantic birds, as if to clear the emotions out of the air. "Whatever that thing on the monitors was, it looked pretty damn nasty. What can I do to help?"

We brought Gabrielle up to speed. It felt good to have all five of us together again. We pored over Calliope's notebook, lifting out the phrases repeated throughout. Bethany brought out a whiteboard on a tripod and wrote them down in black marker. In the end, we had seven phrases in all:

*Eternal voice and inward word*
*Arching towers kirk*
*Hidden mariner lost at sea*
*Beneath the three monuments*
*Look to the Trefoil pieces*
*The Angel of the Waters*
*Codex Goetia*

"Arching towers kirk? What does that mean?" I asked. "Is it a place?"

Isaac studied the whiteboard. "I don't know, but I've heard of that last one. The Codex Goetia. It's a book for summoning demons. I'm guessing that's what the cult used to summon Nahash-Dred all those years ago. I wish I knew more about demonology, but it was never part of my studies."

Gabrielle leaned forward in her chair. "I may be able to help. I have a friend who's studying demonology. Her name is Jordana Pike. Do you know her?"

Isaac shook his head. "I'm afraid I don't. Can you put us in touch?"

"For something this important? Please. I can do better than that." Gabrielle pulled out her cell phone, scrolled to a number in her contacts, and put the phone to her ear. "I can get us a face-to-face with her today."

# Ten

I steered the Escalade across the Brooklyn Bridge toward Downtown Brooklyn, where Gabrielle's friend, Jordana Pike, worked in an office building near Borough Hall. As I pulled off the bridge onto Cadman Plaza West, I began to feel on edge. I didn't like being back in Brooklyn. The whole damn borough reminded me of the year I'd spent as Underwood's collector, and those were memories I didn't enjoy reliving. Funny, for a man with no past, I already had one I hated. I put it out of my mind by listening to Bethany and Gabrielle catching up with each other in the backseat.

"So you won't return my calls, but a *demonologist* you'll hang out with?" Bethany teased.

In the rearview mirror, I saw Gabrielle smile sheepishly. "Sorry about that. I met Jordana at the 92nd Street Y's grief support group. She lost both her mother *and* her brother recently, poor thing. We've been hanging out a little after the meetings, just going for coffee or a quick drink. I accidentally let it slip early on that I know about magic, and it turned out she did, too. I guess we bonded over that and became friends. I haven't been avoiding you, Bethany, I just haven't been feeling all that social lately."

"I remind you of him," Bethany said. "Of Thornton."

"You all do," Gabrielle said. "That's not a bad thing. It's just . . . sometimes it's overwhelming. It's so easy to forget that not much time has passed since he died. Some days it feels like yesterday. Other days it feels like *years* without him. The weird thing is, I—I keep seeing him. In the support group they say it's a perfectly natural form of wish fulfillment. 'A common state of bereavement' is how they put it. But sometimes it feels like something else to me. Like he's always in the corner of my eye. It's worse when I'm thinking about him, or thinking about all the plans we had. All the things we were still going to do. Then I see his face everywhere."

"I'm sure it'll pass in time," Bethany said.

"That's the thing," Gabrielle said. "I'm not sure I want it to."

Court Street was the major thoroughfare of Downtown Brooklyn, the artery of its business district, which made finding a parking space impossible. There were already cars, vans, and delivery trucks double- and triple-parked along the street. I turned onto a shaded, treelined side street. Court Street's fast-food joints and chain drugstores abruptly gave way to organic greengrocers and meticulously restored carriage houses. If Brooklyn did one thing well, it was making your head spin with its sudden pockets of upscale gentrification. Parking was impossible to find here, too, so I wound up pulling into a garage in a repurposed old factory warehouse. A sign on the wall informed us we would be paying through the nose for just one hour. Stenciled on the cement wall beside the sign was the illustration of a man with a monocle and top hat sitting in an old Model T. The smoke from the car's exhaust pipe spelled out WELCOME!

The attendant admired the car as we got out. "An Escalade, huh? Haven't seen one of these in a while. She's a beaut." He handed me a ticket stamped with today's date and time. "Don't worry, I'll take good care of her while she's with us."

This was definitely not the part of Brooklyn I knew from my criminal days.

Jordana Pike worked on a high floor of a towering brick-and-limestone office building overlooking the plaza of courthouses that gave Court Street its name. We took an old, brass-detailed elevator up. When the doors opened, Gabrielle led us into a glassed-in reception area. On the wall behind the receptionist's desk was one of those blandly nonspecific corporate names written in big, colorful, expensively designed letters—*Gamma Solutions, LLC.* The receptionist was also big, colorful, and expensively designed, a mannequin comprised of equal parts plastic surgery, hairspray, and too-tight clothing. She tore her eyes away from the open *New York Post* on her desk and looked up at us with undisguised disdain, annoyed that we'd interrupted her. The heavy black liner around her eyes made her look like an owl. Her sneering glare moved from Gabrielle to Bethany, and then to me, at which point the sneer left her face and was replaced by the look of someone who wished they were carrying a can of Mace.

"We're here to see Jordana Pike," Gabrielle told her. "She's expecting us."

The receptionist picked up the phone on her desk. She used one long, formidable nail to press a few buttons, and then spoke indifferently into the handset, "Visitors here to see you." In her thick Brooklyn accent, she pronounced it *visituhs*. She hung up. "Down the hall. Third door on the left." *Do-wah*. She blinked her owl eyes at us to tell us we weren't clearing out fast enough.

Down the hall and three doors in, we came to a sleek black door with a plaque beside it that read JORDANA PIKE, SYSTEMS ANALYST.

Gabrielle knocked on the door. "Jordana?"

The door opened. Standing behind it with an expectant smile was a woman I guessed to be in her mid-thirties, just a few years younger than me. Or younger than I appeared to be, anyway. When you've lost your memories and can't die, it's hard to know for sure how old you are. Jordana Pike was pretty, with thick brown hair that reached just past her shoulders, deep brown eyes, and an olive, Mediterranean complexion. Gabrielle introduced her to Bethany, and then to me. When Jordana looked at me, something seemed to change in her. It was small—a subtle, knowing look in her eye, a slight knitting of her brow, and then it was gone, replaced with impeccable composure as she shook my hand.

"It's nice to meet you . . . Trent, is it?"

"That's right," I said. "How's it going?"

She invited us into her office and closed the door. Then she turned the lock.

"Sorry for the dramatics," she said. "My boss already thinks I'm crazy because I actually do my job instead of hanging out on Facebook all day like everyone else here; he doesn't need to hear me talking about demons, too. I take it you met our friendly receptionist? I call her the Bay Ridge Harpy. She's the CEO's niece—surprise, surprise. Anyway, I'm guessing she didn't offer you anything to drink, so can I get you something? One of the vending machines in the break room actually still dispenses cans of soda and iced tea instead of just stealing your money."

"We're fine, thanks," Gabrielle said. "And thanks for taking the time to see us, too. I know they keep you pretty busy around here."

Jordana sat down in a black rolling chair behind her desk. "You asked me about the Codex Goetia on the phone. First of all, even though the word *codex* technically means *book*, it's not actually a book. I've never seen it myself, but according to what I've read it's more like a metal tablet or a disc. Written on its face are the names of all nine hundred and ninety-nine greater demons."

"What makes them so great?" I asked.

Jordana's gaze lingered on me. For the brief moment our eyes met, the air felt charged, like she was trying to communicate something to me.

"Greater demons are basically the nobility of demonkind," she said. "Lesser demons are their servants, their army. Most of the time, lesser demons aren't even given names. Greater demons, on the other hand, have names and titles. Sometimes their name *is* their title. It's fascinating, really. The pecking order is not all that different from the hierarchy of medieval nobility, and yet it's a completely different kind of culture from what we know, one where the peasants—or serfs might be a closer analogy—are so far beneath them that they're not even granted names." She couldn't hide her excitement as she spoke. Clearly, demonology was her passion and she didn't get the chance to share it with others often. "As for the Codex, it was created by the magicians of a city called Tulemkust specifically for the purpose of summoning, binding, and banishing greater demons. Do you know the story of Tulemkust and Sevastumi?"

I nodded. "It's come up."

"Good," Jordana said. "Then you know all about the two brothers who betrayed Tulemkust. There are a lot of scholars in my field who believe they were Sevastumi agents, and that the killings were only a distraction. Their real mission was to steal the Codex Goetia from Tulemkust's Great Library."

"Why do they think that?" Bethany asked.

"Because after the Tulemkust massacre, there are records of the Codex Goetia in the hands of Sevastumi clerics. Unfortunately for Sevastumi, it's much easier to summon a demon, or even banish one, than it is to bind one. They learned that the hard way. Whatever terror they brought upon Tulemkust was nothing compared to what they brought upon themselves. Thousands died. Even the mountain their city was built on was leveled."

"That's remarkably similar to what happened to the Aeternis Tenebris," Bethany said.

Jordana gave her a puzzled look. "Who?"

"A doomsday cult," Bethany explained. "They wanted to bring about the end of the world, so they summoned a demon named Nahash-Dred. But they couldn't bind him, and the demon killed them."

Jordana leaned forward, alarmed. "Did you say Nahash-Dred?"

"I take it you know the name," I said.

"Anyone who studies demonology would know that name," she said. "Nahash-Dred is not just a greater demon, he's *royalty*. He's the son of Leviathan, their king. He's a prince, and for demonkind that's not just a title. It means he's one of the most powerful demons there are. In his dimension, Nahash-Dred is charged with putting out dying stars when their time has come. He dismantles them, takes them apart somehow. In our dimension, he has dismantled—utterly wiped out—entire civilizations. Nahash-Dred has killed hundreds of thousands of people. Maybe millions."

"It gets worse," I told her. "There's a possibility Nahash-Dred didn't kill everyone in the cult. One of them may have survived, a man by the name of Erickson Arkwright. We have reason to believe he's going to try to summon Nahash-Dred again. Only now he's had over a decade to figure out what went wrong the first time. He'll be sure to bind the demon properly this time. And if he does . . ."

"Then we're all in danger," Jordana said. "Everyone. The whole world. Is this why you wanted to know about the Codex Goetia? Do you think Erickson Arkwright has found it?"

"What do you mean *found* it?" I said.

"The Codex is gone," she said. "I thought you knew that. It's been missing for years now. All anyone knows is that before it disappeared, the Codex was broken into three fragments, and the fragments were hidden in three secret locations. The Codex is the key to all of this. It's the only way Arkwright can summon and bind Nahash-Dred. You can't let him find it."

"How do we know he doesn't have it already?" Bethany asked.

"We don't, but the fact that we're still alive is a good indication," Jordana said. She sat forward again, clasping her hands on the desk before her. She gave me another funny look. A knowing look, as though she and I shared a secret. Something was going on behind her eyes, but before I could figure it out she broke eye contact and addressed the three of us.

"Find the three fragments of the Codex. Find them before Arkwright does. It's your only chance of stopping this."

"It sounds like he doesn't need all three fragments to summon Nahash-Dred," I said. "He just needs the one with Nahash-Dred's name on it."

"It doesn't work that way," Jordana said. "The Codex is a lot more complicated than that. It's more than just a list of names on a piece of metal. It's an artifact. It's got a spell inside it that opens a passage between dimensions, a doorway between our world and theirs. If Arkwright wants to open that doorway, he'll need all three fragments. The Codex has to be made whole again, or it won't work." She leaned back in her chair and sighed. "There's one more thing, and you're not going to like it. There are certain places and times of the year when it's easier to open the doorway. Most of the times align with the old, pagan calendars: the solstices, the New Year, certainly planetary alignments. The next one is midnight on All Hallows' Eve. That's when the skin between worlds is at its thinnest."

"Halloween," Bethany said. "That's just two days from now. That's not a lot of time to find all three fragments."

"I told you you wouldn't like it," Jordana said.

I wasn't following any of this. "The skin between worlds?"

Again Jordana looked at me funny. Was she flirting with me? I wasn't sure. I didn't have a lot of practice with flirting. Also, it seemed like an odd time for it. No, this was something else, something more. It was like she wanted me to see something, to acknowledge something right in front of me, but I had no idea what.

"Different dimensions exist side by side," she explained. "Think of them as apartments in a condo. They're separated by walls, only these walls can't be knocked down. All you can do is make a temporary doorway between them. At certain times of the year, the wall is thinnest and a doorway can be made more easily." She glanced at the watch on her wrist and groaned. "Shit. I'm sorry, I have to go. I have a meeting in five minutes, and I can't be late again. The coders say if I keep making them wait they're going to start calling me Zelda." She paused a moment, as if expecting us to laugh. "Not big video game players, huh? Tough crowd." She pushed her chair back and stood up, smoothing her skirt with her palms. "Anyway, I hope I was helpful."

"You were, absolutely," Gabrielle said, giving her a hug.

"Good luck finding the fragments," Jordana said. "Keep me in the loop and call me as soon as you find them."

Bethany shook Jordana's hand. "Thank you."

"Of course," she replied. "If you need anything else, just ask."

"If you come across any clues to where these fragments might be, let us know," I said. I shook her hand.

I tried to turn to leave, but Jordana refused to let go of my hand. "Can I talk to you for a second?" She pulled me over to the window, away from Bethany and Gabrielle, who waited by the door. "You don't recognize me, do you?" she whispered.

I frowned. "Should I?"

A mischievous grin grew on her face as if she thought I was joking. Still whispering, she asked, "What are you playing at? What's all this 'Trent' business?"

"Excuse me?" I said. The tone of my voice caught Bethany and Gabrielle's attention. They turned to see what was going on.

"It is you, isn't it? Lucas West?" Jordana sounded like she was on the verge of laughing, only I didn't know what the joke was.

I shook my head. "I don't know what you're talking about. Why are you calling me that?"

"It's your name." A moment of doubt flashed in her eyes. "Or . . . I thought . . . I'm sorry, I must have made a mistake."

I blinked at her. "Who is Lucas West?"

"What's going on?" Bethany asked, coming over.

Gabrielle followed her. "Is everything all right?"

"Yeah, no, it's fine," Jordana said. "I—I thought Trent was someone else, that's all. Someone I used to know." She studied my face. "I could have sworn you were Lucas. The likeness is uncanny. You could be twins."

No wonder she'd been giving me funny looks this whole time. She *recognized* me. I had to know more.

"Who is he?" I took an urgent, insistent step toward her. "Who is Lucas West?"

Alarmed, she stepped back. She looked nervously from me to Bethany to Gabrielle and back. "What—what exactly is going on here?"

I took a deep breath, trying to calm myself. "I'm sorry, I didn't mean to scare you. The truth is, I don't know who I am. I can't remember. I don't remember anything before about a year ago. Not my name, or where I lived, or the people I knew. It's all a blank."

"But you told me your name is Trent," she said, confused.

"It's a name someone gave me," I said. "I don't know my real name."

Her eyes softened with concern. "Then you *are* Lucas West. Oh, I knew it. I knew it the moment I saw you. I'd know that face anywhere. Oh God, you poor man, to lose yourself like that."

She put her hand on my chest. The phone on her desk buzzed loudly, and she yanked her hand back with a small, anguished cry. She rushed back to her desk and pressed a button on the phone. An irritated voice came through the speaker: *"Jordana, where are you? The meeting's about to start!"*

"I'll be right there." She hit the button to turn off the speakerphone. She opened a drawer in the desk and pulled out a business card. She quickly wrote something on it, then came over and put it in my hand. "Please call me. There's so much to tell you. Call anytime, okay? Whenever you want to talk."

I took the card from her. She put her hand on mine warmly. Familiarly.

"It's so good to see you again, Lucas. I always wondered what happened to you. I still think of you often."

"You . . . remember me?" I stammered. Then I winced at how much I sounded like Karloff doing his Frankenstein monster. I looked at the card. Under the bold, italicized letters of her name, *Jordana Pike*, was the address of the building we were in, her office phone number, and her work e-mail. Scrawled in her handwriting at the bottom was another phone number.

"That's my personal cell phone number," she said. "You'll call, won't you, Lucas?"

I nodded, unable to speak, and put the card in my pocket. Lucas West? Was that really my name?

Jordana opened her office door and walked quickly into the hallway. "I'm so sorry I have to go. You can show yourself out, can't you?" She paused and glanced back at me. "Call me, Lucas. I mean it." Then, like a tornado, she was gone, leaving everything in her path forever changed.

# Eleven

Gabrielle was standing by the doorway of Jordana's office, grinning at me. "Holy shit! Did she just tell you your real name?"

"I—I don't know," I said. I rubbed my forehead. This was a lot to take in.

Bethany, as usual, was more practical. "Do you think she's telling the truth?"

"You don't?" I asked.

"I don't know, she could be," she said. "But what are the odds that someone we've never heard of before, someone we're introduced to out of the blue, just happens to recognize you?"

"It was bound to happen at some point," I said. "Someone had to eventually recognize me."

"Maybe," she said. "But I would trust it a lot more if it had happened *before* word got around that you're the Immortal Storm. Now anyone can do a little digging, find out about your amnesia, and use it against you."

"Why would she?" I asked.

Bethany shook her head. "I'm not saying she did. I'm just saying be careful. You're famous now. Sometimes that's all the reason people need."

"I don't think Jordana's like that," Gabrielle said. "I've only known her a few weeks, but she seems pretty genuine to me. She wouldn't lead Trent on like that. Especially after taking the time to help us with information about the Codex Goetia." She turned to me with a smirk. "Besides, I think Trent was enjoying the attention she was giving him. She's pretty, isn't she?"

"What? No," I stammered, glancing quickly at Bethany. "I mean—I don't mean she's *not* pretty—I just mean that's got nothing to do with it."

"Mmm-hmm," Gabrielle said.

I rubbed my face, exasperated. "Look, you two take the Escalade and go back to Citadel. Tell Isaac about the Codex. Maybe he has an idea where the fragments are hidden. There isn't a lot of time." I handed the garage ticket to Gabrielle.

"What about you?" she asked.

"I'm not going anywhere," I said. "If Jordana really does know who I am, I have a lot of questions for her."

"Trent, this isn't the right place for it," Bethany said. "This is where she works—"

"I'm not going anywhere," I repeated.

She sighed and shook her head. She knew this was something she couldn't talk me out of. "Fine, just be careful, okay? You don't know her. You don't know anything about her."

"I can take care of myself," I said. "And I *might* know her. We might know *each other*. That's the whole point."

Gabrielle started steering Bethany toward the door. "Come on. Let's give them some time alone. For what it's worth, Trent, I think it would be great if it turned out you two know each other."

"Be careful," Bethany warned again.

"We'll see you back at Citadel," Gabrielle said. She took Bethany by the arm and pulled her down the hallway toward the elevators.

I felt like I was vibrating out of my skin. I closed the office door and went over to Jordana's desk. It was remarkably tidy, with only a few small piles of papers, a neatly trimmed spider plant in one corner, a white, porcelain coffee mug drained of its contents, a desktop computer, and a single framed photo. I picked up the photo. It showed Jordana and an older woman posing at the bottom of a ski slope. Jordana wore a puffy, light blue parka with the hood down to let the breeze blow her hair away from her face. The older woman wore a red parka with a matching red knit cap. Her yellow ski goggles made her eyes look almost buglike. Jordana's late mother, I presumed. Above them, a banner read OWMASS 2011. Only when I saw that partial word did I realize that the photo was oddly cropped, as if part of it had been cut out to fit inside the frame. There was even a sliver of the older woman missing, on the opposite side from where Jordana stood. It looked like the woman had her arm around someone else, too. Someone not in the picture. I put the photo down again.

I sat in front of the computer and wiggled the mouse until the monitor came to life. I launched the browser, went to an Internet search site, and typed in *Lucas West*. I paused with my finger hovering over the enter key, suddenly nervous. I'd always thought my real identity would be my salvation, my redemption, but what if I didn't like what I found? What if Lucas West was a thief? A con man? A killer?

What if Lucas West was no better than me?

But I had to know. After all this time, I had to know no matter what. It was the biggest question of my life, the question that had dogged me for as long as I could remember: Who was I?

I hit enter.

The results came up quickly, but the name Lucas West didn't get very many hits. There was a teenage cancer survivor who had started his own prosthetics company, a hypnotherapist offering online lessons on how to "get a woman every time" (a classic scam if I ever saw one), a high school–aged boy who'd died in a car crash in the 1990s, a project manager at a construction company in San Antonio, and a logistics operator—whatever that was—in the U.K. Judging by their photos, none of them was me. I spent the next thirty minutes scouring the Internet for any missing persons reports for Lucas West, but I didn't find any. I didn't find any articles, blogs, or Web sites by or about him, either. No wonder the Janus Endeavor had failed to find a match for me. If I really was Lucas West, I had disappeared without a trace.

What were the odds of that? How many people left absolutely no footprints online? It didn't seem possible. Either Lucas West had somehow erased all references to himself, or someone else had. There was a third possibility, of course, but I wasn't ready to doubt Jordana yet. Not when I might be so close to the answers I'd been looking for. I had to know what else she could tell me.

I cleared the history and closed the browser. I got up from the desk and walked to the window. Below, people moved through the plaza between the courthouses, tiny as ants. Each of them knew who they were. Each of them was secure in their name. Did they know how lucky that made them?

I heard Jordana's voice outside the door, chatting with a coworker on her way back from her meeting. A moment later, the door opened and Jordana came in. She stared at me in surprise.

"You're still here?" she asked. I thought she would be angry to find me waiting in her office, but she wasn't.

"I couldn't leave. I have to know more about Lucas West."

She smiled and closed the door. "I was kind of hoping you'd still be here when I got back. Seeing you again after all this time, Lucas, I—I almost can't believe it."

"So we've known each other a long time?" I asked.

She came over to stand beside me at the window. Her deep, brown eyes sparkled when the sun hit them. "You could say that."

"Tell me how you know me."

"You were a friend of my brother's when we were growing up, just a couple years above me in high school," she said. "You were this big, strapping football player, but you weren't like the others. You weren't a bully. You didn't pick on anyone or treat the girls like garbage. You were sweet and smart. I couldn't tell you at the time, but . . . I looked up to you so much."

She took my hand in hers. Her fingers felt cool as they wrapped around mine.

"If we grew up together, you must know my family," I said. "Can you tell me about them? Who are they?"

She nodded. "I met them more times than I can count. Your father was a chemistry teacher at the local community college. Your mother managed an organic grocery shop. They were both so proud of you, especially after you got into college."

"Was this in New York City?" I asked.

She shook her head. "Norristown." She saw the confusion in my face and clarified, "It's a small town outside Philadelphia."

I was from Pennsylvania? That was unexpected. I'd always imagined I was a native New Yorker. Apparently not. My home was Norristown. My parents were a teacher and a store manager. What were they like? Why hadn't they come looking for me? Or filed a missing persons report? There'd been nothing online. Did that mean . . . ?

"Are my parents still alive?" I asked.

"I assume so. I haven't been back to Norristown in years," she said. "What else can I tell you about your family? You didn't have any brothers or sisters. You were an only child, but you and Pete were like brothers in your own way. You went everywhere together. You were inseparable."

"Pete?" I asked.

"My brother." She sighed heavily. "You don't remember any of this, do you?"

I shook my head. Part of me had hoped hearing stories about Lucas West would awaken the memories I'd lost, but he still felt like a stranger to me. Was he really me? Lucas West sounded so normal. I liked that. I *wanted* to be normal. But there was nothing normal about me.

"What happened to me?" I asked. "How did I get like this? How did I lose my memories?"

"I wish I knew," she said. "I haven't seen you in so long. It's got to be, what, ten years? Anything could have happened."

Anything indeed. But nothing *normal* could have done this to me. That, at least, I was sure of. If I was Lucas West, something catastrophic must have happened. Something that not only took my memories but also erased me from public records. Damn it, how did I get this way? What the hell happened?

"Ah, there's that look," Jordana said. "I remember it well."

"What look?"

"Consternation. I saw it a lot when I was helping you with your math homework. You never did understand algebra. You were always much better with your hands." Her eyes widened suddenly and she quickly added, "On the football field, I mean! Not . . . not . . . oh, God!" She laughed, her face flushing with embarrassment. It was unbelievably charming.

So Lucas West was better with his hands than his head. That sounded like me, at least.

She rested both her hands on my chest and closed the distance between us. She looked up into my eyes. She spoke in a whisper. "I can't believe you're here, Lucas. I really thought I would never see you again." She kept her face tilted up toward me, and I realized she was waiting for me to kiss her.

"Did we . . . ? Were we ever . . . ?" I stammered.

My cell phone chirped suddenly in my coat pocket.

Jordana smirked and stepped back. "Saved by the bell."

"Sorry," I said, digging out my phone. It was Isaac's name on the display. "I have to take this." I hit the talk button and stuttered a hello.

"Philip was right about these black market types," Isaac said over the line. "Unsavory characters, all of them. Our legwork is paying off, though. We're getting information, even if I'm not entirely comfortable with the methods we're having to employ."

In the background I heard what sounded like cries of pain, then Philip's voice. "Quit being a baby, Langstrom. You still have three arms I *didn't* break."

"The Thracian Gauntlet was bought a couple of months ago at the Ghost Market, a black market auction specializing in magical artifacts," Isaac continued. "It was purchased by a man named Clarence Bergeron. Independently wealthy, worth billions. Apparently he's got a taste for expensive artifacts."

"Hold on," I said, walking away from Jordana. I tried to clear my head and focus. The Thracian Gauntlet had been the last thing on my mind just now. "You think Bergeron might be the one who attacked us in Chinatown?"

"That's what I need you, Bethany, and Gabrielle to find out," Isaac said.

"Bethany and Gabrielle aren't here," I said. "I sent them ahead. They should be back at Citadel by now."

"No, I was just at Citadel and didn't see them," Isaac said. "They haven't checked in with me, either."

"That's strange," I said.

"Go find them and wait for my next call," he told me. "We're working on locating Bergeron now. He doesn't have a public address or phone number."

"Sounds suspicious," I said.

"Maybe, but it's not unusual behavior for a billionaire interested in maintaining his privacy and security," Isaac said. "I'll call you back as soon as we've got something." In the background, Langstrom started screaming again. Isaac ended the call.

I turned back to Jordana. She was leaning against the wall by the window with her arms crossed, watching me. "Sorry," I said.

She uncrossed her arms and walked over to me. "You have to go, don't you? Just when things were getting interesting."

"Duty calls," I said. "Can we talk again soon? There's so much more I want to know. Maybe I can call you later?"

She stood on tiptoe and kissed me on the lips. "You damn well better call me."

I looked at her in surprise. I had thought she was pretty when I first saw her, but now, as she smiled at me and her eyes brightened, I thought pretty wasn't a strong enough word. Beautiful was more like it. Jordana Pike was beautiful. The feel of her against me was comfortable. Right. Familiar. I was certain then, without any doubt, that Jordana was telling me the truth.

"Um," I said, flustered and tongue-tied. I was worried that was all I'd be able to say from now on.

"I've been waiting a long time to find you again, Lucas West," she said. "I have no intention of letting you disappear on me a second time."

"Um," I said again. Damn it.

She smiled wider, clearly enjoying her effect on me. "You have my number. Use it. Besides, as I remember it, you still owe me a drink."

I couldn't stop grinning like an idiot in the elevator down to the lobby. Everyone who got in on the floors between must have thought I was a lunatic. I couldn't help it. I felt like I was soaring. I had just learned my name. More than that, I had met someone from my past. Someone who cared about me. Someone who missed me. I had started to think no one gave a damn. The feel of her kiss was still on my lips. And yet, the farther I got from Jordana, the more the questions started to creep back. Why hadn't the Internet search found anything? There should have been *something*.

I did my best to put it from my mind and focus on the task at hand. Bethany and Gabrielle hadn't shown up at Citadel. I needed to find them and await further instructions from Isaac. Back on the street, I went around the corner to the garage first. The attendant was leaning on the wall outside, smoking a cigarette. He nodded when he saw me.

"Mr. Escalade," he said. "You here to pick her up?"

"The car's still here?" I asked.

"Of course," he said, taken aback. "I told you I'd take good care of her, didn't I?"

"So my friends didn't come by to get it?" I pressed.

He shook his head. "Nope, no one's come for her. You want me to get the car for you?"

"Not yet," I said, looking up and down the street. Where the hell could they have gone?

I thanked the attendant and walked up the block. I tried Gabrielle's cell, but it went right to voice mail. I left a message telling her to call me back ASAP. Just this once I wished Bethany had taken a phone with her, but it wouldn't have done any good. The charms in her vest would have fried it by now.

Across the street I noticed an alley filled with a thick, roiling fog. I stopped. That was odd. The weather was wrong for fog. And what kind of fog only sat inside an alley, nowhere else? I looked at it, confused.

From somewhere within the fog, Gabrielle shouted, "Show yourself!"

Shit. I pulled the Bersa semiautomatic from its holster, ran across the street, and plunged into the gray fog of the alley. It was as thick as the smoke of a five-alarm fire. I couldn't see more than an inch in front of me. I moved slowly, one hand holding the gun, the other extended in front of me so I wouldn't run into a wall. Or worse.

"Gabrielle!" I shouted. "Bethany!"

My boot touched something. I stopped and looked down. Lying on the floor of the alley with her eyes closed, shrouded in tendrils of fog, was Bethany.

# Twelve

My chest squeezed tight. My breath caught in my throat. I begged whoever might be listening—God, the Guardians, the universe itself—to let Bethany be okay. I crouched down and touched two fingers to her neck. I felt a pulse and nearly crumpled with relief. She was alive, just unconscious.

What had happened to her? Who did this? Damn it, I should have been here.

Gabrielle's voice came again from farther within the fog-shrouded alley. "I said show yourself, you coward!"

I sprang to my feet. I was reluctant to leave Bethany, but clearly whatever was happening wasn't over yet. Holding my gun in front of me, I moved deeper into the swirling gray fog.

"Gabrielle!" I called again.

"Trent?" she called back. Her voice came from somewhere ahead of me, but how far ahead I couldn't tell. The fog was disorienting, and the close walls of the alley played tricks with sound.

Gabrielle cried out suddenly in alarm. I quickened my pace, shouting her name. I couldn't see a damn thing.

A shape appeared ahead. I stopped, lifting the gun. "Gabrielle?"

Gabrielle broke through the wall of mist, backing toward me, keeping her eyes on something I couldn't see through the thick fog.

"She's here," Gabrielle whispered.

"Who?" I demanded.

But Gabrielle was lost in her own fear and anger, staring into the fog. "She's here . . . in *his* body."

My pulse quickened. I knew what that meant. I gripped my gun tighter. "Reve Azrael is here?"

"She ambushed us," Gabrielle said. "Bethany—Bethany didn't even see her coming. I tried to warn her, but it was too late, and now . . ."

"Bethany's unconscious, but she's all right," I said.

"Oh, thank God," Gabrielle said, relieved. "This is all my fault. I—I hesitated. I couldn't help it. Reve Azrael knows what it does to me to see her using Thornton's body like that. She knows I can't stand it. It brings it all back, the pain of his death, the violation of that bitch stealing his body . . ."

A deep, derisive laugh echoed from farther ahead.

"It's her," Gabrielle whispered.

I raised my gun and moved into the fog. "Stay close."

She was right behind me, but the fog was so thick I could barely see her there. We moved another few yards into the belly of the alley. A silhouette appeared in the distance. I curled my finger around the trigger of my gun. As we got closer, the shape's features grew visible in the fog.

It was Thornton. He was still wearing the clothes he'd died in—the dark blue button-up shirt, jeans, and black sneakers, all much dirtier and worn now. His skin was pale and bloodless, but his body was still leanly muscled and undecayed, thanks to a spell that had rejuvenated his body but couldn't save his life. A red glow burned in his pupils, the telltale sign of Reve Azrael's necromancy, reminding me that what I was looking at was a revenant, nothing more. Reve Azrael had stolen Thornton's body after he died. Apparently she was still using it as her host body while her true form remained hidden in her lair, somewhere in the city.

"There you are," Reve Azrael said through Thornton's mouth. "I've been waiting for you."

"I wish I could say it's nice to see you again," I said. "It's not. So how about you tell me what you're doing here?"

She laughed again, then sank back into the fog until there was nothing left but the dim red glow of her eyes. Then even that was gone.

The fog parted suddenly, drawing back toward the depths of the alley as if it had a mind of its own. A tall figure stood before us. It wasn't Reve Azrael. There was no sign of her at all. There was only this eight-foot-tall figure in a billowing cloak. Its face was completely hidden in the darkness of its hood. My mind went immediately to the cloaked man I'd encountered in the Village, but this wasn't him. The figure reached up and pulled back its hood.

Instead of a face, there was only dark hair, as if its head was turned away from us. But that didn't make sense. The rest of its body was clearly facing us.

I aimed the Bersa at it. "Who are you?"

It didn't answer. Did this thing even have a mouth?

Bethany came running up behind us, pulling a small wooden rod from her vest. She pointed it at the creature and muttered a quick incantation. A spinning ball of green fire launched from the end of the rod, speeding across the alley. The creature put up one hand. The spell struck its palm.

And vanished harmlessly into it.

The creature thrust out its other hand then, and the spinning green ball of fire launched back toward us. We jumped out of the way, crashing through a row of metal garbage cans along the alley wall and landing amid the spilled refuse. The spell struck the ground where we'd stood and erupted in green flames, leaving a dark scorch mark on the bricks. Bethany and Gabrielle crawled behind a makeshift barricade of garbage cans, blockaded on the end by a pile of concrete cinder blocks. I brushed the trash off of me and followed them, coming up next to Bethany.

"Are you okay? You were out cold."

She nodded. "I'm fine, but I'm going to have a hell of a knot on the back of my head."

"So what is that thing?"

"It's a Fetch," she said. "Don't let it touch you. Whatever it touches, *whoever* it touches, it can mimic their power, just like it did with the spell from the charm."

"Got it," I said. "So if it touches me . . . ?"

She looked at me gravely. "Then whatever it is that doesn't let you stay dead, the Fetch would have it, too. We wouldn't be able to kill it. It would be twice as dangerous as it is now."

I didn't like the sound of that. Worse, if Stryge's power was still inside me, did that mean the Fetch could mimic that as well? That would be a disaster.

"What the hell is it doing here?" I demanded. "And where did Reve Azrael go?"

"It was a trap," Gabrielle said. "She led us right to the Fetch."

I peeked over the top of the garbage cans at the Fetch. Its hairy head began to slowly rotate on its neck, as if to finally reveal its face, but on the other side there was only more hair. It was creepy as hell, but what came next was even worse. The Fetch's hair-face split down the middle and cracked open into a vertical, toothy mouth. Inside the mouth wriggled a fleshy, twisting mass.

I'd seen enough. I aimed my gun at the Fetch. Before I could squeeze the trigger, a long, gray tentacle shot out from the mass in its mouth and struck the gun, knocking it out of my hand. The tentacle retracted into its mouth. My gun skittered across the alley floor away from me. I pulled my hand back quickly and dropped down behind the garbage cans again, my heart lurching against my ribs.

"It has a face tentacle?" I demanded. "You didn't say anything about face tentacles!"

Bethany shrugged apologetically at me. "What are we going to do?"

I risked a glance at the Fetch again. It stayed rooted where it was, waiting for us to make another move. How were we supposed to get away without it touching us? Especially with the long reach of its tentacle? I looked at the metal garbage cans in front of us and had an idea.

"We need a distraction," I said. "I'll keep it busy while you and Gabrielle get out of here."

Bethany stared at me. "Didn't you hear what I just said? You can't risk it touching you."

"It's the only way," I said. "That thing's not going to let us just walk out of here."

"Forget it, it's too dangerous," Bethany said.

"You're out of your mind," Gabrielle added.

"Probably," I said. "But when has that ever stopped me?"

I grabbed the closest metal garbage can lid by its top handle, jumped up, and started toward the Fetch. The tentacle lashed out of its mouth again. I held up the lid like a shield. The tentacle struck it, banging heavily against the thin metal. The force of the blow nearly knocked it out of my hand, but the makeshift shield held. I gripped the handle tighter and braced my feet.

Before the tentacle retracted, another shot out of the Fetch's vertical mouth. With my other hand I grabbed the lid off another garbage can and held it up as a shield. The second tentacle banged into it.

As the two tentacles began to retract, a third rocketed toward me between them, straight down the middle.

Shit. I pivoted and brought the first lid up again to block it. All three tentacles retracted into the Fetch's vertical maw. We regarded each other a moment, waiting to see what the other would do.

And then the Fetch's mouth exploded with tentacles.

One after another they lashed out at me, six tentacles in all. I backed away, swinging both garbage can lids again and again, blocking the tentacles as they came. It happened again, what always happened when I was in the thick of a fight. It was as though something took control of my body, some forgotten instinct that knew how to fight like I'd been doing it all my life. The Fetch's tentacles lashed at me harder and faster, nearly knocking the lids out of my hands.

"Go! Get out of here!" I shouted at Bethany and Gabrielle. I glanced their way and saw with some relief that they were already gone.

I'd only looked away for a moment, but that was all the time the Fetch needed. One tentacle wrapped itself around the lid in my right hand and yanked it out of my grip. The Fetch tossed the lid away, sending it sailing down the alley. I reached for another garbage can lid near me, but a second tentacle knocked it out of my reach. I only had one makeshift shield left against six lashing tentacles that I couldn't let touch me. It wouldn't be enough.

I backed away from the Fetch. "Look, pal, you don't want my power. Trust me, it comes with a lot of baggage. It's a real downer."

The Fetch didn't care. All six of its tentacles came flying at me. I raised the garbage can lid.

Something hit the Fetch from behind with a metallic clang. It stumbled forward from the impact, its tentacles missing me and retracting instantly. Gabrielle stood behind the Fetch, holding an empty metal garbage can with a big, new dent in its side. Before the creature could right itself,

Bethany came leaping out with a cinder block held over her head. She brought it down on the back of the Fetch's head. It fell to the ground at her feet. Bethany lifted the cinder block again, then dropped it as hard as she could on the Fetch's skull, smashing it into a puddle of gooey black ichor and bone. The Fetch's body melted into a thick black smoke that drifted harmlessly across the alley floor and eventually dissipated. All that was left of the Fetch was a dark stain where its crushed head had been.

"Thanks, but I had it under control," I said, catching my breath.

"Of course you did," Bethany said. "Garbage can lids, was it? *Great* idea."

"You suck at sarcasm," I said. I dropped the lid I was still holding.

Gabrielle put down the dented garbage can. "This was my fault," she said. "I should have known better than to follow Reve Azrael into an alley, but I didn't listen to my instincts. I was too angry. So I led us right into a trap. God, I'm such a fool. Reve Azrael is just going to keep using Thornton against me until I slip up even worse and someone gets killed."

"Anyone would have done the same thing in your position," Bethany pointed out. "There's no point blaming yourself."

Gabrielle glared at her. "No. She knew she could play me like that. And she was right." She shook her head. "I'm not ready for this. It's too soon. Or maybe I'm just not cut out for this anymore." She sank down against the wall until she was sitting on the alley floor with her knees up against her chest. "She's using Thornton against me. Against all of us. I just . . . I just want him back. I want everything to go back to the way it was."

I stood there, watching her. I didn't know what to say. I wasn't very good with words.

Bethany knelt down beside Gabrielle and spoke softly to her, doing a much better job of comforting and reassuring her than I could have. It made me wonder how many other times Bethany had had to do this. Back before my time they hadn't been the Five-Pointed Star, just a loose team of freelancers in Isaac's employ. Individuals he paid to locate and secure artifacts. I hadn't thought of it before, but given how dangerous this line of work was, it struck me as inevitable that Thornton wasn't the only one who'd died.

"There's something I never told you," Gabrielle said, wiping tears from her eyes. "After Thornton and I got engaged, I wanted to tell him not to take that last job for Isaac. I didn't want him to do it. I knew it would be dangerous. I also knew if I asked him not to do it, he would turn Isaac down. But I could see how proud Thornton was, how much he wanted the money so we could have a big wedding. I didn't need a big wedding to be happy. All I needed was him. But I didn't tell him that. I could have stopped him from going on that mission, but I didn't, and he died." Her breath hitched in her throat. New tears formed in her eyes. "Even when I had the chance, I couldn't save him. He died because of me."

Bethany shook her head. "You're wrong. The only one to blame is the gargoyle who killed him, and it's dead now. Thornton has been avenged."

"I don't want him avenged," Gabrielle said. "I want him back."

My cell phone went off. I pulled it out and saw Isaac's name on the caller ID. I got up and walked away from them, moving toward the mouth of the alley as I answered the call.

"I've got Bethany and Gabrielle, but there was a situation," I told Isaac. "Reve Azrael has finally crawled out of her hole. But the weird thing is, she didn't make a move herself. She sent some kind of creature after us instead. A Fetch."

"She must still want something from you," Isaac said.

"Yeah, revenge," I said. "She wanted to turn New York into her own personal city of the dead, remember? Just her and ten million revenants bowing to her will. She blames me for stopping it."

"But if she wanted to hurt you, why send a Fetch?" Isaac asked. "There are far more lethal creatures she could have sent, including her own revenants."

"Maybe she's shorthanded?"

"If only. There's no shortage of fresh corpses in New York City," Isaac pointed out.

I didn't like not knowing what Reve Azrael was up to. She'd been laying low for a month, and now this? She had something up her sleeve. I was sure of it.

"We found Clarence Bergeron's address," Isaac continued. "I'm sending it to your phone now. He's got a house up in Bronxville, about half an hour outside the city."

"A billionaire living in Westchester," I said. "Shocking."

"We also found out where the Ghost Market auction took place," he said. "It was a warehouse on the Brooklyn waterfront."

"Sounds a little seedy for a Bronxville type," I said.

"It's the black market, they don't go to Sotheby's," Isaac said. "I'm going to check out the warehouse now. I'm sending Philip to you."

I started to protest, but he stopped me.

"If Reve Azrael is gunning for you again, I want you to take Philip with you to Bronxville for protection. She's not just going to try once. She's going to *keep* trying."

A strong, sudden wind blew past me. I ignored it. "That's not necessary, Isaac. I can take care of myself. I don't need Philip."

I heard Philip's voice say, "Careful, you're gonna hurt my feelings." I turned around. He was standing behind me draped in the dark cloak and gloves that protected him from the sun. The gust of wind. I shook my head. Damn, Philip was fast when he wanted to be.

"Never mind," I said into the phone, "he's already here."

"Good luck," Isaac said. "And watch your back."

"You, too." I ended the call and turned to Philip. "Are you going to behave yourself, or do I need to bring bail money?"

He grinned, showing me his fangs. "Don't I always behave myself?"

I sighed and went back to the others. "A man named Clarence Bergeron bought the Thracian Gauntlet at the Ghost Market. Isaac just gave me his address. We should get moving. Oh, and Philip's here to help, in case we run into trouble."

"I don't run into trouble," Philip said. "Trouble runs into me."

I rolled my eyes.

Bethany helped Gabrielle to her feet. "We can drop you off at home first, if you want, Gabrielle."

"I'm sorry. I'm not ready. I'm just not ready for this," Gabrielle said. She looked up at Philip. "It was Reve Azrael. She was in Thornton's body again."

Philip grunted disdainfully. "If you walk away now, all you'll do is show her how weak you are."

"Philip, that's enough," I said.

"What's wrong with you? Why would you say that to her?" Bethany demanded.

Philip ignored us. "If you think Reve Azrael won't exploit that weakness, you're a fool. If you want to send her a message that you're not to be fucked with, you keep fighting. You take the fight to her. You don't stop until she's dead. Unless you really are as weak and foolish as she thinks. In which case, yeah, go home. You'll only slow us down."

Philip turned around and walked out of the alley, pulling the cloak's protective hood over his head. Gabrielle stared after him in silent shock.

# Thirteen

Isaac had said Clarence Bergeron owned a house in Bronxville, but *house* was an understatement. Mansion would be a better word. Or estate. I watched Bergeron's sprawling, three-story brick residence through the high-definition binoculars. In daylight, the special lenses that boosted light transmission for nighttime use gave everything a crisp vividness. The view was clear enough that I felt like I was standing right in front of the mansion, rather than lying on my belly in a grove of trees on a nearby hill. But at least here I could remain hidden from the house, the main road, and the great curving driveway in front. A marble fountain surrounded by meticulous hedges and spiraling topiaries stood at the center of the drive.

Bergeron had serious money. Casing the house of a wealthy man felt all too familiar to me. Like comfort food, in a way. I didn't like what that said about me.

In the back of my mind, a small but insistent voice kept reminding me that I didn't want to be here. I wanted to be with Jordana. I couldn't stop thinking about her and everything she'd told me. I felt alive, energized, and desperate to get back to her. Having to wait was unbearable.

Lucas West.

Lucas West.

The name had the rhythm of a drumbeat, one that wouldn't stop playing in my head. Calliope, the Thracian Gauntlet, Reve Azrael's latest ploy for my attention—they were the furthest things from my mind right now.

I pulled myself together and swept the binoculars along the mansion's front windows. There was no movement inside the house. Nothing moved in the enormous, columned portico that shaded the front door, either. I put down the binoculars and picked up my phone. I texted Philip: *I don't think he's home.*

Philip and Bethany had gone around to the back of the house to look for signs of life and find a way inside. Gabrielle wasn't with us. We'd dropped her off at her apartment before driving to Bronxville. She'd spent the whole car ride sitting in silence with her arms crossed, staring out the window. She was furious—at Reve Azrael, at Philip, at the world. I couldn't blame her. She had every right to be.

Philip texted back immediately. I could imagine his fingers moving lightning fast over the touch screen of his smartphone. *Agreed. Not seeing any body heat inside. Makes no sense. There should be staff in a house this big. Bethany says we have to remain cautious. Thousandth time she's said it. Thinking about tying her up in the trunk of the car just so I don't have to hear it again.*

I wasn't sure if Philip was joking, because you could never be sure when Philip was joking. I wrote back: *Please don't.* Then another message came through.

*This is Bethany. I've taken the phone from Philip, who clearly doesn't deserve to have it. Have to be quick before phone fries. Meet us in back. There's a storm cellar entrance. Bergeron won't notice signs of forced entry here.*

*On my way.* I put the phone in my pocket.

Something tapped me on the shoulder. Someone cleared his throat behind me. Damn. Like a fool, I'd been too caught up in my own thoughts about Jordana to hear him approach. I turned my head slowly and saw a man in his seventies standing behind me. He wore a pinstriped three-piece suit, complete with a watch chain looping from the vest. A horseshoe of short, white hair ringed his otherwise bald, age-spotted head. In his right hand he held an ivory-handled, wooden cane, which he used to poke my shoulder again.

"If you're going to skulk about my house, young man, you might try being less conspicuous," he said.

I twisted onto my back and saw two guards standing behind him in private security uniforms. They had their guns drawn and pointed at me. The tip of the old man's cane came down on my chest, as if to pin me to the grass.

"I assure you, I may be old but I'm not helpless," he said. He nodded over his shoulder at the two guards. "Nor am I alone, as you can see."

My eyes went to the old man's hands. He wasn't wearing the gauntlet. That was a relief. I didn't want to know what it felt like to get hit with the same blast that had popped Yrouel like a water balloon and knocked Philip down a couple flights of stairs.

"Clarence Bergeron, I presume?" I said.

He grunted with self-satisfaction, as if he'd outwitted me somehow. "So you know my name. That speaks to premeditation. Motive." He jabbed the cane into my chest again. "Now kindly get to your feet so my guards can take you into custody and call the police."

The two private security guards looked well trained. Their expressions were grim and their gun hands were steady. Still, I knew I could take them if I needed to. The one on the right was smaller, with a baby face. Probably a lot younger than his partner, which likely meant he wasn't as experienced. I could sweep his legs out from under him before he even knew what was happening, and while he was down I could draw my own weapon on the second guard . . .

Just then, Clarence Bergeron started coughing. Great hacking tremors shook his entire body, wet and deep and painful sounding. With his free hand he fished a handkerchief out of his vest pocket and put it over his mouth until the coughing fit passed.

This obviously wasn't Yrouel's killer. Clarence Bergeron was too old and sick to be the same man who'd led us on a chase across the rooftops of Chinatown. He didn't look like he could run more than a few feet before collapsing. Not that it let him entirely off the hook. We'd traced the gauntlet to him. He was involved somehow.

"Let's go, pal," the older guard barked, waggling his gun at me.

Bergeron tucked his handkerchief away. He pulled his cane off me and held out his hand. Against the protests of the guards, he helped me to my feet. His hand felt frail in mine, fragile enough that I wondered if his bones would break as he hefted me off the ground. When I was on my feet, I put my hands in the air.

"Are you alone?" Bergeron asked.

Philip's voice came from behind them, "No, he damn well isn't."

Bergeron and the two guards spun around. Philip was standing in his protective cloak a few feet away. Despite their surprise, the two guards fell back on their training with a speed I couldn't help admiring. The older guard turned back to me quickly, keeping his gun on me. Baby Face moved toward Philip, holding his weapon in front of him.

"You told me you didn't see anyone's body heat," I grumbled to Philip.

"I was looking in the house," he replied. "They must have already been outside, tracking you."

"Keep your hands up," Baby Face said. "I'm authorized to use deadly force if necessary."

"So am I," Philip said. "Care to make it interesting? How much do you want to bet I can take your head off your neck before you even pull the trigger?"

Baby Face glared at him. "Mister, you don't want to try me."

"Really? Let's see what you're made of, kid." Philip took one taunting step toward him.

Baby Face bristled at being called a kid, but he regained his composure quickly. He squared his shoulders and assumed a firing stance. "This is your last warning."

Philip smiled, baring his fangs. Baby Face's gun hand didn't so much as shake. Either he didn't know what he was looking at or he wasn't scared of vampires, which made him a fool. A fool with a gun. That was the most dangerous kind.

If something didn't change, this was going to spin out of control fast. "Tell your guard to back off," I warned Bergeron. "He's going to get himself killed."

"Is that so?" Bergeron said. "My private security firm is the best in the country. They've handled far worse than your friend here, I assure you. Besides, your friend is clearly bluffing."

"He doesn't bluff," I said. "He doesn't have to."

The older guard still had his gun trained on me. Suddenly, he went stiff. His eyes widened in surprise. Bethany peeked out from behind him.

"I don't expect you to recognize the shape of the object I'm pressing against your back," she told the guard, "but I assure you it can put a good-sized hole through you if I want it to. Drop the gun."

The guard lowered his gun. Bethany snatched it out of his hand. She pocketed the charm she was holding, the same one she'd used to put a hole in the door of Biddy's dungeon, and pointed the gun at Bergeron. The old man raised one hand. He kept the other on his cane.

"You'll excuse me for not raising both. If I let go of the cane, I'll fall," he said. He lowered his hand slowly and pulled on his left pant leg, lifting the cuff. Above his expensive leather shoe and crisp argyle sock, the skin of his leg was withered and discolored, black and purple like a nasty bruise. "An old injury that never quite healed right." He let go of his pants and raised his free hand again.

"Good enough. Just don't try anything," Bethany said.

"I wouldn't get very far if I ran," he replied.

Baby Face turned toward Bethany. Philip took another step toward him, drawing his attention back. The guard's jaw muscles clenched under the skin of his cheek. He was clearly torn, unsure what to do and unwilling to stand down without a direct order from his employer.

"That's far enough," Baby Face barked at Philip. "Come any closer and I will *drop* you!"

"That sounds fun," Philip said. "You promise?"

"Call off your guard," Bethany instructed Bergeron. "Do it."

Bergeron sighed. "That's enough, Francisco. Stand down. There's no need to make things worse than they already are."

Baby-faced Francisco lowered his gun reluctantly. He didn't take his eyes off Philip. The vampire snatched the gun out of his hand.

Bethany nodded at the second guard, who stood a few feet away with his hands up. "You, too. Get over here."

The second guard didn't move. He looked at Bergeron for instructions. The old man nodded. "It's all right, LaValle. Do as she says."

Keeping his hands up, LaValle moved to stand beside Bergeron. Philip herded Francisco over to join them. The three of them stood facing us angrily.

"Well, you've got us outnumbered and outgunned, so you might as well make your move," Bergeron said. "What's it going to be? Kidnapping? Blackmail? Petty theft?"

"None of the above," I said. "Let's start over. I'm Trent. This is Bethany and Philip. We're with the Five-Pointed Star."

Bergeron squinted at me. "The Five-Pointed Star. I see. So you're the ones everyone is talking about."

"You've heard of us?" I asked.

"Of course," he said. "You killed Stryge, and since then you've been taking out Infecteds all over the city. Even that lunatic kidnapping women in Central Park."

"Word travels fast."

"It's a small community," he said with a smile that was both mirthless and condescending. "I met them once, you know. The original Five-Pointed Star, Morbius and the rest of them, back in the day. I was living in the city then, in an apartment building on Amsterdam Avenue. We didn't know it, at least not right away, but an Infected was living in the basement. He'd mutated into something terrible. Something big and hungry. Let's just say he wasn't a vegetarian. The Five-Pointed Star came and . . ." He shook his head at the memory. "I never saw anything like it. Like *them*. They saved us. It's a pity what happened to them in the end." He sighed and composed himself. "So you're picking up where they left off, eh? A new Five-Pointed Star. I'll help however I can. I owe that much, if not to you then to your predecessors. But there's no reason to keep my guards here, is there? Whatever brought the Five-Pointed Star to my home, I suspect it should be discussed in private. Am I right?"

I looked at Bethany and Philip. Bethany nodded. Philip cracked his knuckles, his expression unreadable behind his mirrored shades.

"They can go," I told Bergeron.

Bergeron turned to his men. "Get back to your stations."

"But, sir," LaValle protested.

Bergeron didn't let him finish. "That's an order. I'll be fine."

The two guards began walking toward the house. Francisco stopped as he passed Philip. The baby-faced guard turned and glared at him, a silent challenge. His ego had been bruised, and the look on his face said he wasn't going to let it go. This guy was more muscle than brain.

"Go ahead and take a swing at me, kid," Philip said. "See how fast I put your face on a milk carton. Not a picture. Your actual face."

"We're not finished, you and me," Francisco snarled.

"Francisco, that's enough," Bergeron interrupted.

Francisco glared at Philip one last time. Then he and LaValle stalked back to the house.

"You must excuse my men. I pay them quite handsomely to protect me from trespassers," Bergeron said. The old billionaire sized up Philip like he was gauging how much he would go for on the open market. "A vampire, is it? Out in the daylight and working alongside humans? Well, I'll be damned. The times really are changing. Now, how about you tell me why the Five-Pointed Star is spying on my home?"

Bethany slipped LaValle's gun into her belt. "You bought a Thracian Gauntlet at the Ghost Market not long ago."

Bergeron narrowed his eyes at her. "I don't suppose there's any point in trying to lie to you," he said. "Yes, I bought the gauntlet. Please don't tell me the Five-Pointed Star is working with the customs department now."

"The gauntlet was used in the murder of an information broker named Yrouel," Bethany said. "Did you know him?"

"Yrouel? No, I'm afraid not," he answered, shaking his head. "But it's an interesting name. Yrouel was one of the Hebrew angels. Pregnant women wore his amulet for protection."

"This Yrouel was no angel," I said.

"Killed with the gauntlet, you say?" Bergeron tapped his chin. "Yes, it's quite possible. Quite possible."

"What does that mean?" I pressed.

"There's something you need to see." Bergeron began walking down the hill toward the house, the tip of his cane spearing into the grass alongside him. "If you've come to take the Thracian Gauntlet away from me, I'm afraid you're too late. Someone beat you to it."


Inside his mansion, Bergeron led us through a hallway adorned with portraits and lined with cabinets full of fine bone china and antique silver and brassware. Overhead, crystals dangled like raindrops from lavish chandeliers, refracting the light back onto the ceiling in tiny rainbows.

"What do you mean someone beat us to it?" I demanded, hurrying to keep up with Bergeron, who was walking surprisingly quickly for an old man with a bum leg.

"Stolen, my good man, what else could I mean?" he said. "And if you and your friends will follow me, I'll show you from where."

He led us deeper into the house. The hallway seemed to stretch on indefinitely, leading us past countless guest rooms, studies, bathrooms, kitchenettes, music rooms, even whole other wings of the house. The mansion was palatial. It was also empty. A house this size ought to have maids, cooks, gardeners to maintain the hedges and topiaries outside. So where was everybody?

Finally, we reached the end of the hallway. Bergeron opened a polished rosewood door, and we passed through into the bottom level of an indoor atrium three stories tall. The walls, from the floor all the way to the top of the atrium, were bookshelves, each filled to capacity. The two levels above us had wraparound balconies sporting several doorways leading to other parts of the house. In the ceiling at the top of the atrium was an enormous stained-glass window. The image of an angel holding a burning sword stared down at us.

"What is this place?" I asked, astonished.

"My library," Bergeron said, proudly spreading his arms. "The centerpiece of my home. These shelves represent lifetimes of book collecting, going back more generations than I can count. The sum total of centuries of knowledge, passed down from parent to child, from the very first members of my family down to me. Mathematics, history, philosophy, poetry, and yes, even some of the more arcane topics. Magic. Alchemy. Angelology, of course." He looked up admiringly at the stained-glass angel above us. "I'm fascinated by angels. You might say they're an obsession of mine. Did you know in early cultures angels and demons were the same? Twins, in a way. Both were terrible, unknowable forces that could either destroy or empower. And yet now we think of angels as our protectors, our personal guardians, and we think of demons as something to be feared and shunned. It's strange, don't you think? But of course angels and demons are merely aspects of our own nature. They always have been. It's remarkable, the dualities we carry within ourselves."

"Demons exist," Bethany said. "They're not just psychological archetypes."

"Then perhaps angels do, too," Bergeron said. "The universe is a vast place, full of infinite possibilities. Who am I to say otherwise?"

I looked up at the towering shelves of books again. Walls of hardcover spines stretched up to the stained-glass skylight. The angel reminded me of something I'd read in Calliope's notebook.

"Have you ever heard of the Angel of the Waters?" I asked.

"I can't say I'm familiar with the name," Bergeron said. "But it's rare for angels to be associated with a natural element like that. Usually angels represent emotions or states of being. Fear, loss, regret, anger."

"You collect more than just books, though, don't you?" Bethany said.

He nodded. "You mean artifacts. Yes, artifacts are something I've always been interested in. I have my genealogy to thank for that. Some distant great-great-grandfather was said to be a magician. Even though no one else in my family dabbled, his books were passed down with the others. The first time I read about artifacts, I was hooked instantly. Their beauty, the immense power hidden inside them, their very existence spoke to me on an aesthetic level. I was compelled to know more. To see one. To *hold* one. Now, if you'll come this way."

Bergeron walked to a door on the far side of the library. He took a key on a string from around his neck and unlocked the door.

"You're the first guests I've ever let back here," he said. "It's a private collection, for my enjoyment alone. Not everyone is ready to accept that the boundaries of the world extend farther than they thought. Until magic comes out of the shadows and is universally acknowledged, I'm afraid collections like mine will have to stay a secret."

Bergeron opened the door. On the other side was a small wing of the house that had been converted into a gallery. The walls were windowless, bare, unadorned slabs of marble. Along the floor, row after row of glass cases filled the room. In the aisles between the rows were plush leather couches, where Bergeron presumably sat and admired his collection on rainy days.

The rich weren't like other people. I knew that. Yet somehow their eccentricities never ceased to amaze me.

A lone painting had been mounted on the wall near the door, covered with a heavy curtain. My curiosity got the better of me. I lifted a corner of the curtain to see what was underneath. I caught a flash of aqua blue brushstrokes before Bergeron pushed the curtain back down.

"If you don't mind," he said. "It's a special piece I've commissioned, but it's not ready for viewing yet. If you'll follow me, I'll show you where I kept the Thracian Gauntlet."

He led us down one of the aisles. The items on display inside the glass cases reminded me of the artifacts in Isaac's vault. Bergeron's collection certainly rivaled his. Like most of the artifacts I'd seen, the majority of these were weapons—swords, daggers, axes, maces, a crossbow whose wooden stock was painted with the image of a fire-breathing dragon. They all had spells locked inside them that made them more powerful, more dangerous. There were other artifacts whose purposes I couldn't guess: a huge book with only four pages, each a thick stone slab etched with faded runes; a long, curving horn fashioned from a tea-stained ivory tusk and encircled with brass mounts; a clock in the shape of a pyramid that had strange, intricate symbols on its face instead of numbers.

Bethany stared wide-eyed at each artifact she passed. "My God, this isn't a collection, it's an armory," she whispered to me, horrified. She turned to Bergeron. "How many artifacts do you own?"

Bergeron mistook her horror for admiration and smiled with pride. "There are nearly seventy in my collection now. I've been acquiring artifacts for some time. Ah, here we are. This is where I kept the Thracian Gauntlet."

We stopped in front of the remains of a broken, empty case. Only the bottom and a small portion of its four glass walls remained, cracked and jagged at the edges.

Bergeron sighed. "I swear to you, I bought the Thracian Gauntlet as a rare curio, the crowning addition to my collection. Not as a weapon. I don't use any of these artifacts. I don't even know how. To me, they're works of art, nothing more. If I'd known any of them would fall into someone else's hands . . ." He shook his head. "I suppose it doesn't matter now. I only had the Thracian Gauntlet in my possession a few days before it was stolen. As you can see, the thief smashed the glass and took it."

"There must have been glass all over the floor," Bethany said. "Who cleaned it up?"

"I did," Bergeron said.

She raised her eyebrows. "You did it yourself?"

"Of course," he said, puffing up indignantly. "I wasn't born with a silver spoon in my mouth, miss. I can still sweep a floor when I need to."

"Sorry, it's just that with a house this big, I would have thought you had a staff to maintain it," she said.

"I do, of course, but they're not full-time," he said.

That struck me as odd. What kind of man lived in a house like this with no full-time staff other than security guards? That wasn't the only thing odd about Clarence Bergeron. What kind of man had a collection like this but never showed it to anyone? A misanthrope who couldn't stand other people? Bergeron certainly seemed eccentric enough. Or was it paranoia? He seemed eccentric enough for that, too.

"I have a cleaning service that comes twice a week, but they're not allowed back here," he continued. "I maintain the strictest security as far as this room is concerned. I know how dangerous artifacts can be. When this room needs cleaning, I do it myself and will continue to do so for as long as I can."

"I'm impressed," I said, glancing around. "It's pristine."

Bergeron sat down on the nearest couch, leaning the cane against the cushion beside him. "I come here every day, to sit and look at my treasures. And yes, I keep this place spotless. My treasures deserve no less."

"So if the cleaning service isn't allowed back here, who else has a key to that door?" Bethany asked.

"Only me," he said.

"What about your family?" I asked. "Do they have access to this room?"

He shook his head. "I don't have any family. I was married once, but . . ." He trailed off, sighing. "Time takes everything away from us, doesn't it? Our health. Our mobility. The things we cherish. Not these musty old artifacts, of course. They'll exist forever, until there's no one left to admire them. No, I mean the ephemeral things, the things we're only allowed to have for a short time." He began coughing again and put his handkerchief over his mouth. When he was finished, he put the handkerchief away. "The only residents of this house are me and the security guards, LaValle and Francisco. No one else. I value my privacy, and my solitude. You understand, even if I rarely leave this house I still need security. There are plenty of people out there who would love to have me out of the way. People who resent my wealth, my standing."

"Could any of those people have stolen the gauntlet?" Bethany asked.

He shook his head. "Impossible. They couldn't possibly know where to find me. Very few people do. I made sure of that. This house isn't even listed on any of the Internet mapping sites. No, if you want to know who I think stole the gauntlet from me, it's those hucksters and thieves at the Ghost Market. Sure, the auctions they run are all supposedly anonymous. The bidders use numbers instead of names. All transactions are in cash, with nonsequential bills. The winner is responsible for transporting the item home from the auction himself. The Ghost Market knows how to cover its tracks diligently. The only way you even hear when the auctions are scheduled is through word of mouth. But if you ask me, they knew how rare and valuable the Thracian Gauntlet is, and they came back for it. They're probably planning to sell it again once all the dust settles. Double their money. The only thing I don't understand is *how* they stole it from me. There was no break-in. The perimeter alarm wasn't even tripped."

"We've got someone checking out the warehouse in Brooklyn where the auction took place," I said, pulling out my phone. "I should call him, see if he's found anything."

Bergeron looked surprised. "How did you know about the warehouse?"

"Langstrom told us," Philip said. "Although he took some . . . convincing."

Bergeron shook his head. "Who?"

"Langstrom," Philip repeated. "He's a fence, a middleman for the Ghost Market. He buys stolen artifacts for the auctions. That's how we found you. Langstrom gave you up."

"But I don't know anyone named Langstrom," Bergeron said.

"You're sure? He's got four arms. Hard to miss."

"I tell you, I don't know him," Bergeron insisted, sitting bolt upright. "But that's proof, isn't it? The auctions aren't as anonymous as we were told. They keep records on us. You said it yourself, this Langstrom fellow knew my address! But how could he know it? I never gave it to anyone there." He shook his head. "I'm more convinced than ever. They *must* be the ones who took the gauntlet!"

I exchanged a skeptical glance with Bethany. If the Ghost Market really did steal the gauntlet back, why use it to kill Yrouel? What did any of this have to do with Calliope or Nahash-Dred? The pieces didn't fit. I stepped away and called Isaac.

When he picked up, I said, "It's me. Did you find anything?"

"No," he said. His voice had a strange echo, as if he were standing in a big, empty space. "The warehouse is completely cleaned out. The Ghost Market did a good job of it, too. Made the place look like no one's been here in years. They even replaced the dust on the floors. You'd never know anything happened here. But they couldn't disguise the traces of arcane energy left behind. I can feel it. It's everywhere, all around me, like the air before a thunderstorm. There were artifacts here. Hundreds of them." He grew quiet. "We made a terrible mistake, Trent. We should never have stopped securing artifacts. We took our eyes off the ball."

"We did what we had to do," I said. "We all made the same choice."

"You don't understand," he said. "These artifacts are dangerous in the wrong hands. Deadly. And there were *hundreds* of them here. Who knows where they are now, or what they're being used for? We never should have stopped."

"Quit beating yourself up," I said. "Believe me, I'm the king of beating myself up, but it doesn't get you anywhere. There's only so much we can do. There are only so many of us. Everyone else, all the magicians and mages out there, they're busy keeping their heads down. They're too scared to get involved. We're all there is."

"Sometimes it feels like we're fighting a losing battle, Trent. Whatever we do, it still isn't enough."

I looked down into the glass case in front of me. A serrated-edged sword rested on a metal stand. Rust covered the blade where it had tasted blood. Taken a life.

"I know," I said.

"You're right about one thing, though. We're all there is. And we're not enough." Isaac took a deep breath, centering himself. "I'll canvass the area and meet you back at Citadel. Did you make contact with Clarence Bergeron?"

"He's not our killer." I turned to look at the old man sitting on the couch. He was still talking with Bethany and Philip, occasionally coughing into his handkerchief. "For one thing, he's too old. For another, he only had the gauntlet for a few days before it was stolen. He's pointing the finger at the Ghost Market. He thinks they stole it back from him after the auction so they could sell it again sometime in the future."

"What do you think?"

"I'm not convinced, but it's the only lead we've got. I'll call you if we find anything else."

I ended the call and went back to the others. Bergeron looked up at me from the couch.

"The Ghost Market has already packed up and moved on," I reported.

"Of course they have," Bergeron said, shaking his head. "It's called the

Ghost Market for a reason. Ask about it and it doesn't exist. Look for it and it's gone. Blasted criminals, all of them."

"Yes, they are," Bethany said. "But you knew that already when you engaged in illegal activities with them."

He shot her a withering look. "What are you saying, that I deserved this?"

"No, but it does make you kind of a hypocrite, don't you think?" she replied.

Bergeron's mouth dropped open. "I don't have to listen to this," he said. "This is *my* home!"

He was angry, insulted in the way only the entitled bocame insulted when you point out that they've done something wrong. He was about two seconds away from throwing us out. I had to intervene quickly, so I distracted him with a question I'd been wanting to ask anyway.

"Mr. Bergeron, does the name Erickson Arkwright mean anything to you?"

"Hmm?" He looked up at me. "Arkwright? No, I'm not familiar with the name. But then, I tend to keep to myself. Why? Is he with the Ghost Market?"

"I don't know," I said. "He may not even be alive anymore. It's just a rumor."

Bergeron stood up, gripping his cane tightly. "Are you implying my gauntlet was stolen by a dead man?"

"I've seen dead men do stranger things," I said.

I took one last glance around the gallery. No windows. No skylights. No other doors besides the one we'd come through. Bergeron said there hadn't been any break-ins. So how had our mystery man gotten inside to steal the Thracian Gauntlet? I thought back to our encounter in Chinatown, the killer vanishing after jumping off the roof. Of course. It was so simple I could have kicked myself for not thinking of it immediately.

"He didn't need a key to get in here," I said. "He used a portal to get in and out."

Bethany nodded. "Teleportation. That makes sense. We know he has a portal charm."

"*Who* has a portal charm?" Bergeron demanded. "Who in blazes are you talking about?"

"That's what we're trying to determine." I pointed up at the tiny black objects that dotted the corners of the ceiling. There were more of them by the door and the far end of the room. I'd spotted them the moment we came in. Old habit. Always look for the security cameras. "Do you still have the footage?"

"I do, but I found it most unhelpful," Bergeron replied. "There's nothing on it."

"Can we see it anyway?" I asked.

He sighed. "Fine. Suit yourself. Maybe you'll see something I didn't."

We left the gallery, went back through the immense library, and eventually found ourselves in a small, dark room filled with electronic equipment and video monitors. Francisco the baby-faced guard was sitting at the desk in front of the monitors. He stood up and glared at Philip, but he left without an argument when Bergeron asked him to. On the wall, the monitors showed scenes from all over the house and grounds, including the hill where I'd been watching the house. No wonder they'd found me so easily.

Bergeron sat down behind the desk. He hit a few buttons on the control panel in front of him to call up the footage we wanted. On the monitors, the images of the gallery froze, then whizzed backward until we saw ourselves entering the gallery a few minutes earlier. Most of us, anyway. Philip, it turned out, didn't show up on video.

The vampire shrugged it off. "No reflections, no recorded images, and yet somehow I still manage to look damn good."

"Were there any protection spells the thief would have had to get through to reach the gauntlet?" Bethany asked.

"I'm afraid not," Bergeron said as he typed on the keyboard. "As I mentioned, I'm a collector of artifacts, but I'm no magician. I leave the handling of magic to the professionals. No, I'm afraid my security system is comprised of locks, alarms, and cameras, just like everyone else's. But believe me, I am now questioning the wisdom of that. Ah, here we go. This is it."

The monitors showed the gallery again, only this time the Thracian Gauntlet was there, inside its unbroken glass case. Bergeron let the feed play. About thirty seconds later, the screens went snowy with static. Ten seconds after that, the picture returned. The glass case was broken and the gauntlet was gone.

"The moment of the theft, completely obfuscated," Bergeron said, frustrated. "If whoever did this has a portal spell, then he's got other spells, too, including one that interfered with my security cameras."

"I take it you never called the police?" Bethany asked. Bergeron didn't answer. "No, of course you didn't. Reporting the crime would mean admitting you'd committed one yourself when you bought it on the black market. So there was no one here dusting for fingerprints or collecting fibers. In fact, I'm guessing no clues were collected at all before you cleaned up the mess."

Bergeron turned in his chair to face her. "You think you know all about me, don't you? You think you know everything. Well, you're right, I didn't call the police, but not for the reason you think. It's because the police wouldn't understand. They're not like us. They don't know the things we know. To them, this would merely be a stolen objet d'art, but you and I know differently. We understand the implications of its existence. We understand what it is, and what it can do."

"So does the man who took it," Bethany said. "There were seventy other artifacts in that room just as deadly, but he didn't take any of them. Only the Thracian Gauntlet. Why?"

"I don't care why, I just want it back." Bergeron stood up out of the chair. "Obviously, I want to help however I can. I know how dangerous the gauntlet is. I hate to think of it in the wrong hands."

"If you want to help, there are two things you can do for us," Bethany said. She took a pen and paper off the desk, wrote something down, and passed it to him. "The first is, you can e-mail the names and addresses of everyone who works in this house to this address. Everyone, no matter how part-time."

Bergeron looked at the piece of paper with mild annoyance. "You do understand that I employ several different service companies? This is a large estate, and it's quite a long list. It will take time to compile. That's if their company lawyers allow it, of course. Or mine. Quite frankly, they're going to hate the idea. They'll demand a warrant of some kind, but I'll see what I can do to convince them. Now, what's the second thing I can do for you?"

"You can stop," she said.

He raised an eyebrow. "I don't understand."

"No more Ghost Market," she said. "No more artifacts. Take every last one you have in that room and put it in a safe, or a vault, or better yet hand them over to someone who knows how to keep them safe. They're not toys. They're not art. They're dangerous. If you can't keep them safe, you shouldn't keep them at all."

"After what happened, you can be certain I won't be buying *anything* from those crooks and cheats again," he said, scowling.

"The gauntlet was used in a murder," she reminded him. "A man is dead."

Bergeron nodded gravely. "Of course, of course. You're right. Consider my lesson learned."

As soon as he said it, I went cold. *Consider my lesson learned.* It was possibly the most disingenuous thing I'd ever heard someone say. In that moment I understood exactly what kind of man Clarence Bergeron was. He wasn't going to stop. Not ever. Collecting and hoarding artifacts wasn't just a hobby for him. No one devoted an entire wing of their home to a hobby. No, this was his kink, just like keeping all those thousands of books his family had accrued over the generations. He couldn't care less that someone had been killed, only that someone had the audacity to steal from him. If helping us catch the killer meant giving up his kink, he wasn't going to lift a finger. We would be lucky if we ever saw that list of names from him.

The rich weren't just different from everyone else. They were untouchable, and they knew it.

"What happens when you recover the gauntlet?" Bergeron asked.

"We'll destroy it, if we can," she said. "Barring that, we'll send it back to the Avalonian Collection."

Bergeron's face clouded. "We seem to have a miscommunication, young woman. The only reason I let you in here and answered your questions is because I was under the impression you would help find what was stolen from *me*. That you would bring it back to *me*. I spent a small fortune on that gauntlet. If you destroy it or send it back to England, will the money I spent on it be returned to me? Where is *my* restitution, I ask you? I'm the victim here, too."

Bethany glared at him.

"Fine, I'll pay you," he continued. "If you find the gauntlet, I'll pay you to bring it back here instead. I assure you, money is no object. Just name your price."

"Goodbye, Mr. Bergeron," Bethany said. She walked out of the room. Philip and I followed her.

Bergeron hurried after us as we made our way to the front door. "I'll increase the security, if that's what you're worried about," he said. "No one will ever steal it or any of my other artifacts again. I'll make sure of that myself. You needn't worry."

At the door, Bethany turned to face him. "Thank you for your time. We'll be in touch."

Bergeron bid us goodbye, struggling to remain chipper in the face of his disappointment that we couldn't be bribed. He shook our hands as we left. I found myself reluctant to shake his, as if everything I despised about him—his arrogance, his callousness, his sense of entitlement—would stain me. But he grabbed my hand, shook it vigorously, and didn't let go.

"Tell me your name again, young man," he said.

"Trent."

He nodded. "Huh. Funny."

"What is?"

"Nothing. It's just . . . that name doesn't suit you at all." He let go of my hand. "Until we meet again."

Then he closed the door between us, leaving me to puzzle over what he meant by that.

I didn't have much time to dwell on it before my cell phone buzzed in my trench coat pocket. I took it out and saw Isaac's name on the screen. I answered the call.

"You'd better come to the warehouse right away," Isaac said. "I'm texting you the address. I found something. Or rather, some*one*."

# Fourteen

If there was one part of Brooklyn I still loved, one part I could still stand after the whole borough had taken on Underwood's stink, it was the Promenade. I'd only been there once, ages ago, in the timeless dark between midnight and dawn when no one else was around. I'd just finished a messy collection job for Underwood. Confused, delirious, covered in my own blood, half a dozen bullet holes perforating my shirt, I had stumbled through the dark cobblestone streets of Brooklyn Heights, past the quiet town house mansions of the rich. Eventually, I found myself on a half-mile-long flagstone terrace that wound along the edge of the East River. Across the water, the lights of the Manhattan skyline twinkled with signs of life. I was the man who never slept looking upon the city that never sleeps. I thought that somewhere in all that city, somewhere in all that light, someone was still awake. Someone confused and alone, just like me. Somehow, it was a balm for my wounds. I stood on the Promenade for what felt like hours as the sun rose over the river, slowly pulling back the curtain of night to reveal the Statue of Liberty, the South Street Seaport, the Brooklyn Bridge. I didn't want to leave. Looking at Manhattan sprawled out before me, I felt connected to something. I felt small, the way you feel small when you look up at the stars at night. The way you feel small when you're not alone.

But so much of New York City was an illusion, and the Promenade was no exception. Just below it, the exhaust-choked Brooklyn-Queens Expressway wound conveniently out of view, willfully ignored in favor of the Promenade's carefully cultivated metropolitan fantasy. And below the

BQE was Brooklyn's industrial waterfront. For decades it had sat as empty and decrepit as a ghost town, until they started bulldozing the area flat to make room for an expansion of Brooklyn Bridge Park. It was the inevitable next step of Brooklyn's gentrification—remove all signs of industry from the wealthiest neighborhoods so the rich never again had to be reminded of the working-class people they'd displaced when property values shot through the roof. But the entire waterfront hadn't been razed yet. One warehouse was left untouched by the bulldozers, as if it were protected by a ward. That wouldn't have surprised me, considering it was the warehouse where the Ghost Market held its auctions.

Crossing the machine-flattened dirt of the waterfront, I felt the Promenade at my back. I glanced over my shoulder at it, the memory of that night coming back to me. I had promised myself I would return to the Promenade one day. That I would stand on its flagstones and look out upon the city once again, only this time I would do it without fear, without blood, without bullet holes. And I would know who I was. When I went back, it would be with my real name and my memories intact. That was a promise I intended to keep. But I wasn't there yet.

The warehouse was a four-story, brick structure roughly the size of a city block. From the outside, it looked desolate, its arched windows and doorways shuttered with rusting metal slabs. Graffiti and gang tags had been painted all over the façade. A single shuttered doorway on the ground floor stood slightly open. Philip motioned for us to get behind him, then carefully pulled it open the rest of the way. The door's hinges didn't make a sound. They were the color and texture of rusted metal, but they were as quiet as any well-oiled hinge.

Walking inside, we found a short hallway cluttered with garbage—old coffee cups and beer cans, empty potato chip bags and cigarette butts, a moldy mattress up against the wall. It looked like the spot where the local high school kids held their parties. If Isaac hadn't already told me it was all a carefully crafted deception, and if the silent hinges hadn't tipped me off, I would have bought the lie without hesitation. Clarence Bergeron was right. The Ghost Market did a hell of a job covering its tracks.

At the end of the hallway, we passed through an open doorway into a ten-thousand-square-foot space. More piles of carefully arranged garbage stood stacked in the corners and along the walls. Dust coated everything.

The windows on the far wall were unshuttered, allowing a wan, yellow light to stream into the warehouse through the dust. It reminded me of the abandoned warehouse on the West Side Highway where I'd first met Bethany and Thornton, just before everything took a sharp turn into Crazytown. A sharp turn for me, anyway. The others, of course, were no strangers to it. They'd been at this a lot longer.

Though, for all I knew, I could have been at it a lot longer, too. As Lucas West. It would make sense. *Something* had happened to me, and magic was the likeliest answer.

I filed the thought away for later. Now wasn't the time to let myself get distracted again. On the other hand, it was getting harder and harder to keep Jordana Pike out of my head, and not just because she'd put a name to my face. That kiss . . .

Damn. So much for not letting myself get distracted. I shook my head and told myself to focus.

Isaac was standing in the middle of the warehouse, his hunter green duster billowing around him. His arms were raised as if he were holding something over his head, which in a way he was. A good five feet above him was another man, trapped inside a floating, translucent, reddish bubble. To my surprise, the man was laughing. He wore a yellow rain slicker, despite the clear weather outside. The slicker's hood was up over his head, but as I drew closer, I saw his face. His skin was deathly pale. He opened his mouth wide, laughing like a maniac, and revealed sharp fangs.

Shit. Another vampire. As far as I was concerned, one was more than enough. I turned to Philip to see what he thought. His expression was as stony and unreadable as ever, his eyes hidden behind his ever-present mirrored shades.

"I found him skulking about in the shadows," Isaac explained. "He's with the Ghost Market."

"Yes, but as I said, I'm just a lowly bookkeeper," the floating vampire said, breathless from laughter. "Now let me down, mage. Let me down so I can tear you open and bathe in your blood."

He threw his head back and resumed his crazy laughter. A string of glistening drool lengthened from his chin down to his chest. He didn't care. He just laughed and twitched and repeated the words *bathe in your blood* like it was the punch line to his favorite joke.

"He's insane," I said.

"He's infected," Isaac clarified. "Magic has twisted his mind."

The vampire looked down at Isaac. "Go away, mage! This place is mine! This is where *I* feed—go find someplace else!"

"What does he mean?" Bethany asked. "He feeds on the people who come to the Ghost Market?"

"I doubt it," I said. "Even thieves need people to buy their stolen goods. No crime syndicate in the world would let someone pick off their customer base like that. They'd kill him in a heartbeat. I don't think that's what he meant by feeding."

Philip crossed his arms and said, "It's not."

The floating vampire's gaze swept over us, finally registering our presence. His pale blue eyes were like a cold draft blowing through us. He stopped when he saw Philip. Recognition flickered in his eyes.

"Well, well, well. Renshu Chen," he said.

"Hello, Crixton," Philip said. "I go by Philip now."

Crixton grinned. "And here I was thinking I would never see you again."

"Thinking? Or hoping?" Philip's tone was as cold as a February blizzard.

"You know this guy?" I asked him.

"Unfortunately," Philip said. The two vampires kept their gazes locked onto each other like high-intensity laser sights. "Our families are bound by clan. I've known Crixton a long time. Too long. He was always a junkie. Though the last I saw him he was addicted to more . . . mundane substances."

"Junkie?" Crixton shook his head. "That's such a mean word. I prefer to think of myself as a connoisseur of heightened experiences, that's all."

Philip grunted in disgust. "How much magic have you taken into yourself, Crixton?"

"So much, Renshu. So much," Crixton said. "Why should I let it go to waste?"

"What do you mean *waste*?" Philip asked.

Crixton rolled his eyes as though the answer should be obvious. "Not every artifact sells at auction. Some are useless. Some are ugly. The curators give me all the unwanted artifacts to dispose of. But I don't dispose of them, not the way they think." He giggled and wiped the string of drool off his chin. "I break them open and drink their magic. I feed on them. Have you ever seen magic in its rawest form, Renshu? It sparks like a bonfire. Dazzles like fireworks. And it sings, Renshu. It sings in so many voices." Crixton drew his hands down his face, letting them linger by his mouth. "It tastes like smoke and shadows and earth; it tastes like everything, because it *is* everything. And when you let it inside you, it's glorious. Like no other drug in the world. It's a night-blooming flower that opens in your belly, only it's so much more than that. It *gives* you so much more. You can't imagine what it feels like. Don't even try. You have to experience it for yourself. You have to feel it." Crixton's icy gaze shifted to Isaac. "The mage knows. He carries magic inside him, just like I do. He can feel it flowering inside him. Can't you, mage? You know the more magic you carry, the more you want. The more you *have* to have."

Isaac narrowed his eyes at Crixton but didn't respond.

The vampire looked at Bethany next. "And this one. She's handled magic. I can smell it on her. And yet, she doesn't have any inside her. Not a drop. You must have the Sigil of the Phoenix upon you somewhere, woman. So foolish to think you need its protection when you could just let the magic in instead. When you could just let it grow inside you." He giggled a moment, and then his face grew grim. His eyes focused on Bethany more sharply. "Your vest. There's magic in it. I can hear it calling to me from every pocket. What do you have in there? Charms? Artifacts?"

He swallowed hungrily and began clawing at the bubble around him, trying to scratch his way out, trying to reach Bethany. The bubble didn't yield. He remained floating, scrabbling against it like a rat trying to dig through a metal wall.

"You're wasting all that magic, leaving it inside those baubles! Give them to me! Let me drink from them!"

Bethany stared at the vampire in disgust. "You're out of your mind."

"Once a junkie, always a junkie," Philip said. "That's what brought you back here, isn't it, Crixton? It's why you risked coming out in daylight. You needed a fix."

"It's been so long since my last one," Crixton said. "I thought there had to be more here somewhere, an artifact I overlooked, something they left behind by accident. But they know better than to leave anything behind.

There was nothing here." He eyed Bethany's cargo vest again. "Until now. Give them to me, woman. Let me drink them and I will spare your life."

"Hey!" Philip shouted, pulling Crixton's attention back to him. "Look at me, Crixton, not her. Focus. We want answers."

Crixton grinned. "About the Thracian Gauntlet? Yes, the mage mentioned it. I propose a trade. The woman's magic trinkets for the information you seek."

Bethany shook her head. "That's not going to happen."

Crixton shrugged. "Suit yourself. You all heard. I tried to be reasonable. *She's* the one who said no."

"You know me, Crixton," Philip interrupted. "You know what I'm capable of. Don't push me."

Crixton laughed. "Oh, I know what you're capable of. We all do, prodigal son. There might have been a time when your name instilled respect in a member of our clan. Maybe even fear. But not anymore."

"I can fix that right now," Philip growled, taking a step forward.

"Enough. We don't have time for this," Isaac interrupted. "We need answers, Crixton, and I'm running out of patience. So I'll ask you again, did the Ghost Market steal the Thracian Gauntlet back from Clarence Bergeron?"

"Let me down and I'll tell you." Crixton laughed but tried to keep it under control this time, as if attempting to show Isaac he was sane and trustworthy. It wasn't very convincing.

"Not on your life," Isaac replied.

Crixton giggled. "How about on *yours*?"

"I think we've been patient enough." Isaac moved his fingers in a tiny pattern. The bubble lifted higher, carrying Crixton toward the ceiling.

"You think I'm afraid of heights?" Crixton said. "I've jumped off of buildings three times as high, and landed with the grace of a cat to tear open the throats of humans like you."

Isaac ignored the taunt. "I don't think you're afraid of heights, Crixton. I think you're afraid of the sun. Look up."

Crixton looked up. The bubble was floating toward a sealed cargo hatch in the ceiling. He glared smugly down at Isaac. "It's closed."

"For now," Isaac said. "But it would be very easy for me to rectify that and send you outside, right into the sun. It's the simplest spell in the world to open a door from a distance. The kind of spell a magician learns on his first day."

The smugness drained from Crixton's face. He let slip a strained giggle. "You wouldn't dare. It would make you a murderer. Do you have the stomach for that, mage?"

"To rid the world of one more Infected? Oh yes, I have the stomach for that," Isaac said. "But I doubt it would kill you, at least not right away. First it'll hurt like hell. I've seen what sunlight does to vampires. It's excruciating, isn't it? The pain would drive you mad long before it kills you. Or madder, I should say."

"You're bluffing!" Crixton yelled, but he sounded terrified. His legs started kicking uselessly beneath him. The bubble carried him higher.

Isaac murmured something in the strange, eerie language of magic. I shuddered at the sound of it, but this incantation was short, at least. When Isaac was done, the cargo hatch in the ceiling burst open on its own to reveal the bright afternoon sky outside. A shaft of sunlight speared into the warehouse. The bubble floated higher, heading right for it.

"I told you, I'm running out of patience," Isaac said.

"All right, all right!" Crixton cried, scratching at his own face in terror. "I'll tell you whatever you want to know! Just stop it! Please! I'll tell you everything!"

Isaac murmured another incantation. The hatch slammed closed, cutting off the sunlight. With another gesture, Crixton's bubble started floating back down toward the floor.

"Big mistake, old man," Philip said. "You should have sent him out to fry when you had the chance."

Isaac ignored him. "Start talking, Crixton. The auction is supposed to be anonymous, but we already know the Ghost Market keeps information on everyone. How?"

"A telepath," Crixton said. "He sits in the audience with the others. They don't know he works for us. They think he's here for the same reason they are. He scans the crowd to see who's lying about how much money they have, who's carrying a weapon, that kind of thing."

"I presume he gathers names and addresses, too," Bethany pressed.

"Yes, yes, all of that. It's the kind of information that might prove valuable down the road, if things go bad or a buyer reneges on his commitment," Crixton said. "Our telepath scans them all and gives us everything he finds."

"What about the ones who bid over the phone or by proxy?" Isaac asked.

"There aren't a lot of remote bidders," Crixton said. "Most prefer to be here in person. They like to be near the artifacts. Near the magic." He giggled, then bit his lip to silence himself.

"Clarence Bergeron came in person," Bethany said. "That's how the telepath got his name and address. It's how Langstrom got it, too. Am I right?"

Crixton nodded.

"And then someone from the Ghost Market went to Bergeron's home and stole the Thracian Gauntlet. Why? To double your money by selling it to someone else?"

Crixton shook his head. "You're wrong. The curators would never allow that."

"Why not?" she demanded. "Honor among thieves? You don't really expect us to believe that, do you?"

"Nothing so dramatic," Crixton said. "The Ghost Market has a reputation to uphold. If we compromise that reputation, we stop making money. It's as simple as that. If the gauntlet was stolen, it wasn't us. If you want to know who took it, you should ask the man who almost won it before Bergeron swooped in at the last minute and outbid him."

"Another bidder?" Isaac asked.

"Bergeron took it right out from under him," Crixton said. "That kind of bid-sniping would be enough to tick off any serious collector. Maybe even make him think about stealing the gauntlet for himself."

"Who was he?" I asked. "Do you have a name?"

Crixton shrugged. "Maybe I do, maybe I don't. If I did, it would be in the ledger. And if you want that, you're going to have to let me out of this bubble. We keep the ledger in a very safe, very special place, you see. A pocket to our dimension. If you want the ledger, I'll have to summon it to me. But I can't do that from in here." He spread his arms to indicate the bubble around him.

"Don't do it," Philip said. "It's a trick."

Crixton gave a shark's smile. "Do you want the ledger or not?"

Isaac sighed. "We don't have a choice. We need that name. Keep him covered, Philip. Don't let him out of your sight."

Philip grunted. "This has mistake written all over it."

Isaac lowered his arms, and the bubble came to a rest on the floor. Crixton kept grinning, his eyes locked on Philip the whole time. Isaac gestured, and the bubble vanished.

So did Crixton. The vampire was a dark blur speeding toward the warehouse exit.

Philip raced after him, a faster blur. He reached the door first and blocked Crixton's path. Crixton bounced off Philip's chest, body-checked, and fell backward onto the floor. The yellow hood dropped back, revealing Crixton's bald head. A patch of what looked like mottled ivory grew out of the nape of his neck and up his skull. The infection hadn't just altered Crixton's mind, it was altering his body, too.

Philip glared down at him. "You forget who I am, Crixton. My standing in the clan."

"What standing?" Crixton spat. "Do you honestly think you're still the son of an elder? How delusional are you, Renshu?"

"What are you talking about?" Philip demanded.

Crixton laughed and wiped spittle from his chin. "Everyone knows a human saved your life. How pitiful. How humiliating. But even worse, you've taken up with humans now. You've gone soft. You're weak."

Philip frowned. "You know what our law says about the debt owed to one who saves your life."

"The debt is not owed to *humans*!" Crixton yelled, baring his fangs. "What good is the hundred-year debt of service to these cattle? They barely live that long to begin with!"

Philip gritted his teeth. His hands clenched into fists. I'd seen him angry before, but never like this. He was a ticking time bomb. "I don't need to explain myself to a junkie like you."

"What about your father? How will you explain it to him?" Crixton pressed. "He thinks the way I do about humans. The way we *all* do. Your father didn't become a clan elder by being weak like you. He would have thanked the human who saved his life by draining him dry. Instead, you swore fealty to him. When your father heard the news, he was ashamed. He disowned you as soon as he understood what you've become. You're *nothing* now, Renshu. Our clansmen spit when they mention your name." Crixton rose to his feet. "So does your father. That is, if he speaks your name at all."

The time bomb went off. Philip rushed Crixton and knocked him off his feet. He carried him in a blur across the warehouse floor and slammed him into the far wall. The wall cratered under the impact. A long crack tore its way up to the ceiling. Plaster dust rained down over them. Philip pinned Crixton to the wall and roared like a beast. I'd never seen him this angry before, or heard a noise like that come out of him. His lips pulled back to reveal his fangs. He looked like he was about to bite Crixton's face off.

Isaac, Bethany, and I ran over to them. Isaac yelled, "Philip, don't! We need him!"

Crixton turned his eyes toward Isaac. "Stay out of this, meat!"

Philip pulled Crixton off the wall and slammed him into it again. Cracks spiderwebbed through the plaster behind him. More dust rained down.

As painful as it looked, Crixton only laughed. "Ah, now I see. This mage is the human you serve. Trust me, were I in your shoes, I wouldn't make the same mistake. I would do what you didn't have the spine to do."

"I've got the spine now," Philip said. He shifted his grip, putting one hand at the base of Crixton's neck and the other on Crixton's chin. He pushed the two apart, baring Crixton's throat. Philip opened his jaws hungrily.

"Philip, don't!" Isaac yelled.

For a moment, it looked like Philip was going to disobey him. He brought his teeth closer to Crixton's throat. Then, with a frustrated growl, he pulled back and let go of Crixton's neck.

"You're his dog, Renshu Chen. He tells you to heel, and you heel," Crixton said, rubbing his neck. "I see you still wear those ridiculous sunglasses. Have you shown your human friends your eyes? Have you shown them what the clan elders did to you after your first transgression?"

The corner of Philip's lip curled. "Fuck you, Crixton."

Crixton turned his head to address us. "Didn't he tell you? Back in the day, your dear friend *Philip* was too reckless and violent even for us. He killed an entire family in one night. Four generations slaughtered at a wedding. How young was the smallest of your victims that night, Renshu? Eighteen months?"

Philip looked like he was just barely managing to keep it together. There was more emotion on his face now than I'd seen in the whole time I'd known him. I wished I could believe Crixton was lying, but there would be no point to it. It was easy enough to picture Philip taking out a roomful of humans. Surprisingly easy.

"That was a long time ago, Crixton," Philip said. "I'm not like that anymore."

Crixton ignored him. "He left no survivors. He erased an entire bloodline from the earth, and that's a no-no, even for us. He had to be punished. And so they punished you, didn't they, Renshu? I've seen your eyes. I saw what they did to them. It's enough to make shit crawl uphill. Tell me, Renshu, what punishment do you think they would give you if they could see you now?"

Isaac stared at Philip in shock. It was clear he hadn't heard this story before. None of us had. An entire bloodline . . . ?

Philip noticed the look on Isaac's face. He gave Crixton one last shove against the wall, then released him. "You're lucky I don't send you into the sunlight myself. Just give us what we need and be gone."

Crixton straightened up and brushed the dust and chunks of plaster off his shoulders. "You want the name of the other bidder for the Thracian Gauntlet? Fine. It'll be in the ledger."

"And we can trust what this ledger says?" Isaac asked, composing himself.

Crixton nodded. "We keep a record of every bid as they're made, handwritten in kraken ink. It's hearty stuff, and permanent, even against magic. We use it so the records can't be tampered with afterward." The vampire held up one pale hand and began his incantation. I shivered at the sound of it and tried not to listen. There was a sudden flash of light from his palm, accompanied by a puff of sulfurous smoke, and an oversized book appeared in his hand. The ledger, summoned from where it was being kept in "a pocket to our dimension," whatever that meant. A hole, like a gap in space? Or was it more like a sack where you could store things? Trying to figure it out made my head hurt.

The ledger looked old and worn, its spine and the corners of its covers reinforced with brass. The metal creaked as Crixton opened the book. I moved to look over his shoulder as he flipped through pages of tiny, cursive handwriting. I kept my guard up. I wasn't sure it was safe to stand this close to crazy.

Each page in the ledger had three columns. In the first were the dates of the auctions. In the second were the names of the bidders. In the third were the amounts of the bids. Some of the numbers sported a lot more zeroes than I would have imagined. Though maybe I shouldn't have been surprised. Artifacts were rare, unique, and valuable. Probably, there were a hell of a lot of wealthy collectors like Clarence Bergeron out there.

My next thought hit me so hard and fast I didn't see it coming. All those items I'd stolen for Underwood, the ones he'd ostensibly sold on the black market—had they wound up here? What if the things I'd stolen weren't just pieces of art or precious stones or briefcases full of cash? Given who and what Underwood turned out to be, what if I'd been stealing artifacts? Artifacts that were then sold at the Ghost Market for quick cash?

How many of the items in Clarence Bergeron's gallery had my fingerprints on them?

"Aha!" Crixton shouted. He held the book open for us to see as he drew a finger down one page. "The auction of the Thracian Gauntlet. As you can see here, a single name reappears over and over again, upping the dollar amount as each new bidder gets involved. This man was determined to have the gauntlet. Eventually the other bidders dropped out when the price got too high. For all intents and purposes, he was the winner. It was going once, going twice . . . and then *boom,* Clarence Bergeron topped his bid. Can you imagine how that must have felt? It's a wonder he only stole the gauntlet and didn't murder Bergeron when he had the chance."

I looked at the names on the page. It was true, one name appeared more than any other. The only problem was, it wasn't a name I'd heard before.

"Who the hell is Cargwirth Kroneski?" I asked.

Bethany shook her head. "That name hasn't come up in our investigation at all."

Crixton shrugged. "You asked, I answered. It's not my fault if the name doesn't mean anything to you."

"Did your telepath have anything to say about Kroneski?" Isaac asked.

"Nothing," Crixton said. "There are no notes here on the page, only the name. Kroneski must have bid over the phone."

"Damn," Isaac said. "Who is he? What does he have to do with any of this?"

"Cargwirth Kroneski doesn't even sound like a real name," I said.

Bethany bit her lower lip and narrowed her eyes, an expression I knew well. "You might be right about that. Hold on a moment."

She went over to a window. With her fingertip, she wrote the name in the dust on the glass. The light from outside streamed through the letters, making them glow.

CARGWIRTH KRONESKI.

She crossed off the A and wrote it again under the name. She did the same with the R.

"An anagram?" I asked.

"Maybe," she said, still concentrating. "Hold on."

The process continued, letter after letter, until she'd rearranged them all. Three new words glowed on the glass.

ARCHING TOWERS KIRK.

I'd seen those words before. "That's from Calliope's notebook."

"Hold on," Bethany said. She bit her lower lip and squinted at the window. Then she started crossing off letters again, rearranging them once more along a third line. It went a lot faster this time. When she was done, a new name glowed back at us from the dusty window. And this time it was one I recognized.

ERICKSON ARKWRIGHT.

"He's alive," Bethany said. "Calliope knew it, she just didn't know how to find him. That's why she needed Yrouel's help. This is the proof we were looking for. Erickson Arkwright is alive, and he's got the Thracian Gauntlet."

"So that *was* Arkwright in Chinatown," Philip said. "Damn. The son of a bitch is in good shape for someone who's supposed to be dead. He runs like a goddamn Olympic sprinter."

"There, you've figured out your little puzzle," Crixton said. "Can I go now?"

Isaac held out his hand. "Not until you give me the ledger."

Crixton pulled the book close to his chest. "You already have the name you were after. The ledger wasn't part of our agreement."

"We don't *have* an agreement," Isaac said. "Hand it over."

Crixton smirked. "Sorry, this is nonnegotiable."

With another flash of light and smoke, the ledger disappeared. Isaac's face reddened. He thrust out one hand. Crixton flew up and backward, slamming into the wall halfway toward the ceiling. He hung there, laughing, writhing, and screaming all at the same time.

"Bring it back," Isaac said.

Crixton laughed so hard, screamed so hard, that he spat all over his own face. "Or what, mage? How badly do you want it? How far are you willing to go?"

"I want that ledger, Crixton."

Isaac closed his hand into a fist. Crixton screamed even louder. Whatever he was doing to the vampire, it sounded agonizing. Philip watched, looking smugly satisfied. He was enjoying this.

"What do you care about the ledger?" Crixton cried. "You have the name you wanted!"

"Because the ledger can point me to all the artifacts the Ghost Market sold. Every one of them. All the artifacts they've *ever* sold," Isaac said. "I can get them back before anyone else gets hurt or killed. I can make this right. I can put right everything the Ghost Market did. *So give it to me!*"

Crixton screamed as if the pain had intensified.

"Do it, mage! Kill me! Feed the darkness inside you!" Crixton yelled. "Oh yes, I can see it. I can see the dark seed all that magic has planted inside you. Give in to it. Kill me and let it bloom!"

Isaac stared in horror at Crixton, the steely resolve leaving his eyes. He lowered his hand. Released from the spell, Crixton dropped to the floor. He landed in a crumpled ball and gripped his stomach in pain.

"Are you okay?" I asked Isaac.

He nodded, but he was breathing hard. "Too many artifacts have passed through here and ended up in the wrong hands. I'm a fool to think there's any way to make that right. We'd need a hundred of us, a thousand to find them all."

A strange noise came out of Crixton then. It sounded like a moan of pain at first, but then I realized he was chuckling. The chuckles grew into laughter as the vampire got to his feet.

"Oh, mage, you were so close to letting that dark seed inside you grow. But it's not too late. Not yet. Demonwar is coming. Can't you feel it in the air? Can't you hear it, like the burning hot scream of a furnace? Give in to the darkness inside you, mage, let it fortify you, and maybe you will survive what's coming the way *we* will. You call us infected. We call ourselves sanctified. And there are so many of us. So very many of us."

Isaac shook his head in disgust. "Get out of here, Crixton, before I change my mind."

With a grin, Crixton started toward the warehouse exit. Philip followed him to the door, glaring at him. Before Crixton left, he turned to Philip one last time.

"When your human friends are dead, your debt of service will die with them," he said. "But don't bother coming back to the clan. You won't be welcome there. Not even by your father. You're dead to him, Renshu. You're dead to all of us."

Then Crixton pulled the hood of his yellow rain slicker up over his head and walked out into the sun.

I wanted to tell Philip not to listen to him, but my tongue wasn't working. No one's seemed to be, because no one said a word. All I could see in my mind was Philip standing over the mangled, drained corpses of a family. An entire bloodline, wiped out in a single night. Grandparents, parents, children. A baby. Maybe that was all any of us could see.

Philip let out a frustrated roar and put his fist through the wall. The plaster and concrete cracked and split like dry earth.

# Fifteen

As soon as we were back at Citadel, I found myself thinking about Jordana again. I wanted to hear more of what she had to say, to be with her, to kiss her again—it was an undeniable urge, stronger than anything I'd felt before. But the doubts came back, too. Did she really know me? Was I really Lucas West? It was driving me crazy. I needed advice. I needed to talk to Isaac. As I approached the door of his study, Philip came stalking out.

I thought of the dead family at the wedding again. The dead baby. I couldn't help it. I knew Philip had a violent past. All vampires did, I supposed. But this was more than I could have imagined. I felt sick thinking about it. And yet, how many times had Philip saved my ass? Saved all our asses? Didn't he deserve better than my disgust? As he approached, I pushed it down and forced myself to find my voice.

"Hey, you okay?"

He walked past me down the hall without a word. I watched him go down the stairs to the first floor. Philip wasn't big on opening up. That was something he and I had in common. But I'd never seen him like he was at the warehouse before. I'd never seen anything get under his skin that badly. I supposed there was a reason I'd never heard Philip mention his clan before. Or his father.

Maybe we had more in common than I thought. It seemed to me we were both haunted by our victims in our own way. I had my list of names. He had the memory of wiping out an entire bloodline. We both had things we wanted to make up for. We were both striving to be something better than what we were, but the ghosts of our pasts just kept coming back to rub our faces in it.

I went into the study. Isaac was sitting at his desk with his head in his hands.

"Everything all right?" I asked.

He looked up at me. "What can I do for you, Trent? I assume you didn't come here just to check up on me."

I pulled up a chair and sat across the desk from him. "There's something I wanted to talk to you about. Something happened when we met with Jordana Pike today. Something important." I told him that Jordana had recognized me, that she said my name was Lucas West, that she'd filled in some of the blanks of my past. Not all of them, just a few, the tip of the iceberg. There was so much more to learn.

Isaac was surprised. "I thought for sure the Janus Endeavor would be how you found your identity, not someone you met by chance. What do you think? Do you trust her?"

I sighed. "That's why I wanted to talk to you. I *want* to trust her. It felt so real when I was there, but the more I think about it . . . I don't know. I looked up Lucas West online, but I didn't find anyone who looked like me. I thought that was strange. But then, the Janus Endeavor couldn't find anyone who looked like me, either. I felt a connection with Jordana, one that makes me think she's not lying. On the other hand, who the hell is Lucas West?"

"When you say a connection, are you talking about a romantic history?" he asked.

I thought of the kiss again, how it had thrilled through me like lightning, down to my core. "Maybe. What do you think? Should I trust her?"

Isaac leaned back in his chair. "I can't answer that for you. But I can tell you this: If she says she has information about your past, you need to hear her out. You can't afford not to. Right now, she's the only lead you have. You owe it to yourself to find out." He tented his fingers under his chin. "What does Bethany think about this connection between you and Jordana?"

The question took me by surprise. "Does it matter what Bethany thinks?"

"Doesn't it?" He studied my face for a moment. It made me uncomfortable. I didn't like being in the spotlight. I preferred the shadows. "You and Bethany are close. I get the feeling that normally this is something you would talk to *her* about. So why come to me instead?"

It was a good question. I didn't know the answer. Why *not* talk to Bethany? Was it because she didn't trust Jordana? Was I just looking for someone to tell me to go for it? Or was it something else?

"Not that it's my business, but you and Bethany are up in your room for hours every night," Isaac said.

"We play cards," I said.

He arched an eyebrow, clearly having trouble believing that. "You play cards. And that's all you do?"

The question made me fidget. I wasn't just in the spotlight anymore. Now I felt like I was being dissected. "That's all. Why?"

"Never mind. I guess I was wrong about you two," he said. "Today is one of those days where I'm wrong about everything, it seems. Even myself. I very nearly crossed the line with Crixton."

"How so?" I asked. "We've killed Infecteds before."

"This was different," he said. "This felt sadistic. Cruel. But the worst part is that I didn't care. I wanted Crixton to suffer for not giving me the ledger. I think I was going to kill him. It's one thing to kill in self-defense, or the defense of others. But to kill him out of frustration? To kill him because he said no to me? I wanted him dead so badly it shocked me. That's what brought me back to my senses. It's why I let him go."

He looked tired, his face drawn. For the first time since I'd known this nearly sixty-year-old man, he actually looked his age.

"Are you sure you're okay, Isaac?" I asked.

He sighed and waved off the question. "It's just stress. We haven't had much of a break since we started chasing down Infecteds. I suppose it's catching up with me."

"The past is catching up to all of us," I said. "I saw Philip in the hall just now. He didn't look very happy."

"Philip and happy seldom go together," Isaac said. "We may not see him again for a while. I sent him on a mission. He volunteered, actually. I think he needed to clear his head, and I can't argue that. He never wanted that story to come out. He even kept it from me, and I thought I knew everything about his past." He sighed and ran his hands over his face. "It's a lot to process. I think some time apart may do us good."

"Did you send him to find the fragments?" I asked.

"Something else, actually," Isaac said. "If we're lucky, we'll find the fragments ourselves before Arkwright does, and prevent a catastrophe. But if something goes wrong, if Arkwright gets his hands on the Codex Goetia before we do, we're going to need a way to tip the scales back in our favor. A Plan B. I sent Philip to get the one thing that will do that for us."

"A weapon?" I asked.

"Yes," he said, standing up. "Let's leave it at that for now. It's getting late, and I wanted to hit the books tonight to see if I can find out where the fragments are hidden. There have to be some clues out there. If there are, I'll find them."

I stood up, too. "Need some help?"

"Your head wouldn't be in it," he said with a patient smile. "Things are going to heat up soon, Trent. Once I figure out where the fragments are, I'm going to need all hands on deck with no distractions. If you want to talk to Jordana, you should do it now, while there's still time." He clapped me on the back. "And good luck. I hope she has the answers you're looking for."

So did I.

I went back to my room. Outside the window, the dusk cast a grayish-blue hue over Central Park. Kali stared at me from where she lay curled on my pillow. She'd claimed that part of the bed for herself and refused to relinquish it. It was just as well. I never slept. Someone might as well use it.

I dug my phone and Jordana's business card out of my pocket. I stared at the number she'd written at the bottom of the card, my thumb poised over the screen of my phone. I felt like I was bursting at the seams. There was so much I wanted to ask her, I hardly knew where to begin. But before I could dial, the doubts started nagging me again. If I was Lucas West, all-American high school football star from Norristown, Pennsylvania, why hadn't the Janus Endeavor found my likeness anywhere? Why hadn't there been anything about me online? Maybe I hadn't searched deep enough. What if there had been something about me on the very next page of search results when I stopped reading? But damn it, I'd gone ten pages deep already, and the results had started to repeat. I had to face it. There was nothing about me online. Nothing about me *anywhere*.

And yet . . . Lucas West. The name stuck in my head, impossible to ignore.

Clarence Bergeron's parting words were still fresh in my mind. He was a spoiled, privileged old asshole who thought his wealth entitled him to stand above the law. But even assholes could be right about some things, and Bergeron was right about this. The name Trent *didn't* fit me. It had been given to me by someone I despised, someone who had used and manipulated me. I should have dumped the name ages ago, but it was the only one I had.

Until now.

*If* Jordana was right. *If* I really was Lucas West.

I hated all these ifs. Somehow, being this close to the answer without knowing for sure made it worse. I felt like I was going to explode. Isaac was right. The questions were too big to ignore. I owed it to myself to find the answers.

How did Lucas West get this thing inside him that wouldn't let him die? How did he lose his memory? Why did magic go haywire around him? How did he know how to fight like he'd been doing it all his life?

Who the hell was Lucas West that he could do these things?

My aura wasn't human. Neither was my scent. These things I already knew. So what had happened to Lucas West to make him . . . me? Had he taken magic into himself? Been changed by it, like Biddy and Crixton and so many others? But the thing inside me was more than magic, wasn't it? Stealing other people's lives to cheat death was something no magic could do. Bethany had told me that. Something else must have happened. But what?

I felt like I was going round and round in circles. A knock on the door pulled me out of it. I put the business card and phone down on the dresser and opened the door. Bethany stood in the doorway, shuffling a deck of cards like a smooth Vegas dealer.

"I was thinking this time I'd let you win for a change, just to see what it feels like," she said.

"Do you mind if we skip tonight?" I asked.

She raised her eyebrows. This was the second time I'd turned her down. "What's going on?"

I sat down on my bed and sighed. Kali decided I was too close now and jumped down, vanishing into the dark space under the bed.

Bethany stopped shuffling the cards. She came a few more steps into the room and tucked the deck into the back pocket of her jeans. "Are you okay?"

I chuckled. I couldn't help it. "Am I ever?"

"You know what I mean," she said. "Comparatively."

I took a deep breath and said, "Lucas West." The name still sounded new to me. My tongue wasn't used to saying it. And yet how many times had I said it before my amnesia?

"Lucas West," Bethany repeated. "Does the name ring any bells?"

"No, but it wouldn't. I can't remember anything from before."

"You were sure some part of you would recognize your name if you heard it again," she said.

"I know. I thought hearing it would spark a memory, a feeling, *something*."

"Don't you think it's strange that it didn't?"

"I don't know. Something took my memories away, Bethany. All of them. Even my name. I know you're skeptical about Jordana, but it feels like . . ." I paused, not sure what I was trying to say. Sometimes it felt like whatever had taken my memories also took my words when I needed them. "It feels like she's all I've got."

Bethany came over to the bed and sat down next to me. Her hair smelled like lavender shampoo. "I know what it's like not to know where you come from, or why you're different from everyone else. But I also know how desperate it can make you for answers. It makes you willing to listen to anyone who claims to know something. I went down that road once, too. I wish I hadn't. I wish someone had warned me. I wish I'd been smart enough at the time . . ." She trailed off. Apparently, this was a story she wasn't ready to share yet.

She shook her head at the memory, her dark brown locks sweeping and bouncing along the shoulders of her blouse. It was only then that I realized she wasn't wearing her cargo vest. Funny, I was so used to seeing her in it that she looked even smaller to me without it. Delicate, even though I knew that was the furthest thing from the truth about her. But it made me feel protective. It made me want to keep her safe from that memory. From everything. I looked at her, marveling again at just how bright and blue her eyes were.

Then I got up off the bed, uncomfortable being so close to her. I kept thinking about the kiss she and I had shared on the tournament field at the Medieval Festival—that brief, amazing moment before she'd pulled away and told me she couldn't be with me. Then, as if my mind were flipping a page, I thought about Jordana and the kiss we shared in her office. Jordana hadn't pulled away. Jordana hadn't told me we couldn't be together. I was confused, a drowning man floundering for purchase and finding none. I walked to the opposite side of the room and leaned back against the wall between the door and the dresser, crossing my arms.

"You're preaching to the choir, Bethany," I said. "I believed Underhill for a long time when he was pretending to help me. But this is different. I felt something with her. A connection, like we . . . knew each other."

Bethany stood up off the bed and came toward me. I watched her. The air felt electrified, as if suddenly anything was possible, anything could happen, if we only wanted it to.

She stopped when she saw Jordana's business card resting on top of the dresser beside me.

"I was about to call her when you showed up," I said.

"You know I'm still not a hundred percent on this," she said. "I know Jordana's very pretty and all—"

"Is that what you think this is about?" I asked.

She looked up at me sharply. "Isn't it?"

"Bethany, I have to do this. It's the only lead I've got. I have to follow it. You know that. You would do the same thing in my shoes."

"What makes you so sure you can trust her? You still don't know anything about her."

"Then I'll get to know her," I said. "That's one of the reasons I wanted to call her. So I could spend time with her, get a sense of who she is, what she's like."

"You mean, like a date," she said.

"What if it *were* a date? Would that be so bad?" I asked.

She blinked at me, not answering. For the first time in a long time, I couldn't read what was going on behind her eyes. I decided to deflect the growing tension the way I always did, with humor.

"I know you think a guy like me doesn't stand a chance with someone like her, but—"

"I never said that," she interrupted.

"I know. I was kidding."

Suddenly everything felt awkward. I'd never felt this awkward with

Bethany before. We used to be able to joke around without missing a beat, completely in sync. Now it was like we were strangers speaking different languages.

"I should call Jordana before it gets too late," I said. I didn't want to have this conversation anymore.

I reached past Bethany for Jordana's business card and my phone on top of the dresser. Bethany didn't move out of my way. Suddenly, we were right up against each other. I could feel her unusually warm body heat passing through the thin layers of clothing between us. She looked up at me with eyes that flashed so blue they looked like pools of water.

"Take me with you when you see her," she said.

"What? No." I grabbed the card and phone off the dresser and backed away from her.

"I don't trust her, Trent," she said. "Something doesn't smell right about this. I'd feel a lot better about this if I were there, too."

"No," I said again. "This is *my* life, Bethany. *My* past. It's got nothing to do with you."

She stared at me, her mouth a hard, tight line. "And I would be a third wheel. On your date."

"I didn't say that."

"But you were thinking it," she said. She put up her hands in mock surrender. "Fine. I was just trying to look out for a friend. Don't let me stand in your way."

She started toward the door.

"Bethany, come on," I said.

She stormed out the door and slammed it behind her. I sighed, annoyed and confused. How had this conversation gone so bad so quickly? Was it something I said? It usually was.

A single playing card lay facedown on the floor. It must have fallen out of the deck when she put it in her pocket. I picked up the card and turned it over. The three of hearts. I glanced at the door, thinking about going after Bethany to give it back, but considering the way she'd left, I thought better of it. Besides, it was getting late and I had a phone call to make.

I sat down on the bed. From somewhere below me, Kali mewled a warning not to get too close.

"Shut up, cat," I groused. It seemed like everyone was trying to tell me what to do today. I was tired of it.

I dialed Jordana's number and listened to it ring, wondering if she would pick up. Wondering what I would say. Wondering what *she* would say. About me. About who I was. About us.

The ringing stopped, and suddenly I heard her voice in my ear. "Hello?"

My heart lurched into my throat. I fiddled nervously with the playing card in my other hand. "Hi, it's Trent," I said. "Um, I mean Lucas. I think. We met today at your office?" I winced. God, I sounded like an idiot. I'd fought gargoyles, revenants, shadowborn, infected magicians, even a mad, thirty-foot-tall Ancient, but talking to a beautiful woman on the phone? Apparently that was where my courage drew the line.

"I'm so glad you called," Jordana said. Her voice melted all the stress and confusion right off my shoulders. "Did you find the fragments?"

"Not yet," I said. "I was calling because I—I wanted to talk some more."

"Maybe we should talk after you find the Codex Goetia," she said. "You need to find it as soon as you can."

"We're working on it," I said. "But I don't think I can wait that long. I spent a year not knowing who I am. I don't want to spend another minute not knowing, not if you can tell me."

Her voice softened. "Well, you're in luck, Lucas. It turns out my plans for tonight fell through anyway. I could meet you for a drink if you're up for it."

Lucas. Hearing her say the name made me smile. Suddenly it felt really good to have a name that hadn't been given to me by a psychotic crime boss. A psychotic crime boss who turned out to be a reanimated dead body under the control of a deranged necromancer. Christ, was this really my life?

Lucas West's life couldn't be this fucked up. Lucas West's life had to be simpler. He was from Norristown. He played high school football. He sucked at algebra. Lucas West was normal. Blessedly, blissfully normal.

"Do you feel like getting away?" she asked.

"You have no idea," I said, and let go of the three of hearts. It fluttered to the floor and landed facedown.

# Sixteen

Jordana suggested a bar she liked in Brooklyn, the Bearded Lady on the corner of Washington and St. Marks Avenue. I took the 3 train to Prospect Heights, exiting onto a quiet, residential patch of Eastern Parkway in the shadow of the palatial Brooklyn Museum. The sky was already dark. I walked a few blocks down Washington, a street where new and old Brooklyn were still duking it out for space, trendy restaurants and lounges standing shoulder to shoulder with ancient Laundromats and dusty bodegas. The Bearded Lady belonged in the former category, a corner bar with big windows and brightly colored, retro-style furniture. There was a small weeknight crowd inside seated at the bar on plush yellow barstools. Jordana sat on a banquette at one of the candlelit tables that lined the perimeter of the room. The flame from the candle cast a warm glow on her cheeks, her hair, her eyes. She saw me, smiled, and waved.

I walked over. She stood up and kissed me again, a longer kiss than the one in her office. When we broke apart, I was still reeling from the heat of it. I sat down across from her. She sat down, too, straightening her knee-length black skirt and crossing her amazing legs in a display so hypnotic I would have done anything she told me to at that moment. Then she asked the question all Brooklynites felt obligated to ask their visitors from Manhattan.

"Did you have any trouble getting here?"

"No, I've been out this way before," I said. I didn't elaborate. I didn't want to scare her away by telling her it had been on a collection job for Underwood. I didn't think I could stand it if she looked at me the way Bethany did whenever that part of my past came up. Suddenly self-conscious, I changed the subject quickly. "Do you live around here?"

"Why?" she asked. "Did you think I was going to take you home with me tonight? What kind of a girl do you think I am?"

The blood drained out of my face. Breathless, I backpedaled as quickly as I could, feeling like I'd pulled the pin out of a grenade. "No, I just . . . I thought . . . I didn't . . ."

She broke into a smile. "Oh my God, don't have a heart attack. I was just kidding."

I nodded. "Oh. Okay." I felt clumsy, like I'd just bumped into a priceless Ming vase and watched it shatter all over the floor. Were all first dates this excruciating?

"Everything here is good," she said, handing me a small specialty drinks menu. I skimmed it quickly. The cocktails had names I didn't recognize: Bedford Nostrum, Town Destroyer, the Kinky Krown. It was like trying to read another language. Was every bar in this part of Brooklyn like this? How did anyone who wasn't a hipster survive in this neighborhood without going crazy? I felt like a fish out of water. Far, far out of water. A fish on the goddamn moon.

"I have no idea what to get," I said.

"Leave it to me," Jordana said. She got up and went to the bar to order. The bartender, a pretty, petite woman with wavy hair and a collared shirt, mixed two drinks in highball glasses and handed them to her. "Thanks, Mary," Jordana said, and slipped her a few bills. She brought the drinks back to the table, put one down in front of me, and sat down with the other.

I reached into my pocket for my wallet, but she waved a hand. "No, don't worry about it. I invited *you* out, remember? Isn't that how it works?"

"At least let me pay for my own," I said.

"You can get the next round," she said. Her eyes twinkled.

"Fair enough." I looked at the iced, yellow-green drink on the table. The end of a plastic straw pointed expectantly at me. "What's this one called?"

"It's a Ginger Prince," she said. "Go on. Try it."

I risked a sip. It was refreshing, crisp, with just a subtle bite of ginger. I was surprised how much I liked it. I downed half the glass thirstily before I remembered it was alcoholic and probably a lot stronger than it tasted.

"So," I said to fill the silence, "you and Gabrielle met in grief counseling?" I froze. Did I really just say that, just come right out and say it like some kind of insensitive oaf? When was I going to learn I was terrible at small talk? "I'm sorry, I didn't mean to pry . . ."

"No, it's okay," she said. "I don't mind talking about it. My mother passed away recently. She was very sick. The doctors didn't even know what the problem was. She died before they could diagnose it. You remember my mother, don't you?"

"I'm sorry," I said. "I don't remember anything."

She nodded. "Right. The amnesia. Of course you wouldn't remember her. Or me."

An awkward, uncomfortable silence fell over us. It felt like it stretched on for hours before she spoke again.

"Okay, that was depressing. Let's pretend it didn't happen with a flawless change of subject." Her eyes twinkled again. "I've been studying up on you. I know what you've been up to."

I nearly choked on my Ginger Prince. "You do?"

She looked around us to make sure no one was listening, then leaned forward with a mischievous grin. "The Immortal Storm? That's not a pretentious nickname at all, by the way. Do you have it as a vanity license plate, too?"

"Oh, God," I said, embarrassed. "Just for the record, I don't call myself that. Other people do. *Some* people. Not a lot. Anyway, just Trent is fine. Trent, or . . ." I stopped myself. I was about to say Lucas, but I wasn't ready to call myself that. Not yet. Not officially.

She looked at me strangely then, studying my features more closely.

"What?" I asked. Suddenly I was worried that she'd made a mistake. That she didn't see Lucas West in me after all. That it was all a horrible misunderstanding.

"You don't look like a gargoyle," she said, trying to suppress a laugh. "Aren't you the king of the gargoyles now, or something?"

I groaned and rubbed my face with my hands. "No, I'm not the king of the gargoyles. They were living as slaves and I set them free. They don't have a king anymore."

She cracked up, finally, unable to keep her laughter contained anymore. I liked the sound of it. It made everything feel okay. I couldn't help smiling.

"What's so funny?" I asked her.

"Who would have thought a small-town girl like me would be out on the town with gargoyle royalty?" She laughed so hard tears squeezed out of her eyes.

"All right," I said, "how about another flawless change of subject?" I took a sip of my drink while she pulled herself together. "Tell me about the rest of your family. I don't remember them."

"I don't have much family left. Just my stepfather," she said. "He and I never really got along, but he's all I've got now. With Mom and Pete gone, I'm doing what I can to get along better with him. Family is important to me. It's everything, really." She caught my gaze with hers. "It's very nice of you to ask, but I know that's not why you're here. You want to know what you were like when I knew you. When you were Lucas West. All this small talk must be killing you."

"Tell me," I said. "I want to know everything."

"I don't know everything. I just know the parts about you and me," she said. "You came back to Norristown once, a few years after you graduated college. I'd graduated by then, too. You don't remember this, either, I take it?" I shook my head. She looked down at her glass and cleared her throat. "We went out on a date. My parents were up in arms about it. You should have seen them. They were fine with you and my brother being friends, but they didn't like the idea of you and me dating. But I didn't care. I'd had a crush on you since high school and I wasn't about to let them stop me. I snuck out of the house and met you at this awful dive bar downtown. At the end of the night, your credit card was declined. You were so embarrassed and so adorable about it that I ended up paying for us both. You said you would pay me back by buying the drinks next time." She chuckled. "I have to admit, it was a pretty smooth line. Except, after that night you never called. I tried to call you a few times. I left messages, but you never got back to me. I—I just assumed you didn't like me."

She looked up at me. When her eyes met mine I felt as though I were levitating a few inches off my chair.

"I can't imagine not liking you," I said.

I bought the next round of drinks myself, just like I'd promised all those years ago.

When I returned to the table, I said, "You mentioned your brother Pete was gone, too. What happened?"

"I was surprised when I didn't see you at his funeral," she said. "You and he were so close. I thought maybe it was because you were still avoiding me, even after all these years."

Avoiding her? If I'd felt as bowled over by her then as I did now, there was no way I would have avoided her. Whatever had happened to me, whatever took my memories and put this life-stealing thing inside me, must have occurred sometime between my date with Jordana and her brother's death. It was the only thing I could think of that would explain why I'd disappeared on her, and why I hadn't shown up at the funeral.

"If you don't mind my asking, when did Pete die?"

"Two years ago," she said. "They robbed him in an alley in Tribeca. Took his wallet and cut his throat. I don't know why they had to do that. If he gave them his wallet, why did they have to . . . ?" She stopped and blinked back tears. "Sorry, I—I don't like talking about it."

"You don't have to apologize," I said, putting my hand over hers on the table. "I wish I could remember him. I wish I knew why I didn't go to his funeral. Or why I didn't call you."

Pete had died in 2011. That didn't line up with whatever had happened to me. My memories only covered the last year, give or take, starting around mid-2012. There must have been some other reason I disappeared on Jordana.

She squeezed my hand tight. "I'm glad I found you again, Lucas."

Lucas. It sounded right when she called me that. I liked it. I liked it a lot.

"I'm glad, too." I leaned across the table and kissed her. She pulled me closer. I got up from my chair and joined her on the banquette. We kissed again, hungrily, fiercely, her body pressed up against mine, warm and soft. My heart pounded like a drumbeat in my ears, in my head.

*Lucas West . . . Lucas West . . .*

She pulled away from me, breathing hard. I took the opportunity to catch my breath, too.

"Do you have any leads on the whereabouts of the fragments?" she asked.

I looked at her. "The what? Oh, the Codex. No, not yet." My brain felt fuzzy. After kissing her, the fragments weren't exactly on my mind.

"There isn't much time," she said. "You have to find them, Lucas. You have to find them before Arkwright does."

"I know," I said. "I will."

"It's not going to be easy. Nobody knows where they are."

"I know one thing," I said. "They're here in New York City."

She knit her brow. "How can you be sure?"

"Two reasons," I said. "First, New York is where the doomsday cult operated. It's where they summoned Nahash-Dred and tried to bring about the end of the world. That was the last time anyone saw the Codex Goetia. Second, Erickson Arkwright is here. He stole the Thracian Gauntlet and used it to kill someone in Chinatown. I think he might have killed someone in the Village, too. I'm starting to think Arkwright never left New York, not even after faking his death. It would have been much easier to create a new identity and start over somewhere else, but he didn't. He stayed. The only reason he would do that is if there were something here he still wanted."

"The Codex?"

I nodded.

"Okay, assuming you're right, New York City is still a lot of ground to cover," she said. "There are no clues. There's nothing to go on."

I thought of the strange phrases from Calliope's notebook. One of them, *Arching towers kirk,* turned out to be an anagram, an arrow pointing directly to Erickson Arkwright. What if they were all arrows? What if every phrase the spirits had given Calliope was pointing to something?

"There *are* clues," I said. "They were right in front of us all along. We just didn't realize what they were."

Her eyes lit up. "Then you can find the fragments?"

"Yes. I think I can." I felt bold and clever, so I kissed her again. This time, she pushed me back.

"You have to find them," she said.

I knew she was right, but all I wanted to do was kiss her some more. I leaned toward her.

"Promise me you'll keep me informed," she said. "Tell me everything you find."

I sighed and stood up. "I will. I promise. But it's just a hunch right now."

"A hunch is better than nothing," she said, also standing.

I wasn't ready to say goodbye just yet. I liked being with her, and not just because she could tell me about my past. I felt good around her. I felt like myself.

I reached for her hand. Our fingers twined around each other. Her lips had felt so good on mine I pulled her close for another taste. Mary the bartender yelled at us to get a room. Jordana gently pushed me away, grinning.

"You have to go," she reminded me, hitting me playfully on the chest. "You have a world to save, remember?"


I was back at Citadel forty minutes later, surprised to see Isaac still awake. He was sitting alone at the big table in the main room with his reading glasses perched at the end of his nose. On the table in front of him was Calliope's notebook, as well as nearly a dozen other books from his library and his laptop. He glanced studiously back and forth between the mess on the table and the words on the whiteboard.

"We were wrong, it's not a code," I said as I shrugged out of my trench coat.

Isaac looked up at me with a satisfied grin. "I know," he said, taking off his glasses. "It's a *map*."

# Seventeen

The hour was late, but this was too big to sit on until morning. With Philip away, we called Bethany and Gabrielle back at Citadel. Only, Gabrielle wasn't answering her phone. I tried calling her multiple times. It left me with a bad feeling. Where was she? I hoped she was okay. Bethany came in, but as we sat at the big table in the main room she barely looked my way. I could tell she was still upset from earlier.

Isaac stood in front of the whiteboard. "As soon as we learned the Codex Goetia was missing, things began to fall into place. I've been wondering all this time what Calliope was looking for, how she thought she could stop Arkwright before he summoned the demon. Now I understand. Calliope was looking for the Codex fragments. She knew if she could get to them before Arkwright did, she could stop it. The spirits she communed with gave her the information in her notebook, but I believe she was only just starting to decipher it when she was killed."

"The Codex was broken into three fragments, and each fragment was hidden separately," I said. I stood up and walked over to the whiteboard, studying the phrases written there:

*Eternal voice and inward word*
*Arching towers kirk*
*Hidden mariner lost at sea*
*Beneath the three monuments*
*Look to the Trefoil pieces*

*The Angel of the Waters*
*Codex Goetia*

"They're clues. All of them," I said. "Bethany figured out one of them earlier today." I erased *Arching towers kirk* and wrote in *Erickson Arkwright.* "Arkwright could have left New York City anytime to start a new life under his assumed identity, but he didn't. He stayed here. Why? Because he knew the three pieces of the Codex were here, too, and he wanted them. He just didn't know where they were. Somehow he must have discovered Calliope was asking questions about him, about his cult, and about the demon, Nahash-Dred. My guess is, he thought if Calliope knew this much, she might also know where the fragments are. He began watching her, following her, waiting to make his move." I thought of Calliope's gutted body nailed to the ceiling of her bedroom. "He must have tortured her for information. I'm guessing she died before he found out about her notebook."

"Hold on, Trent," Bethany said. She was looking at me finally, but her gaze felt as hard and sharp as drill points. "What makes you so sure these are clues to the fragments' locations?"

"That's not my name," I told her. "Call me Lucas."

Bethany's eyebrows lifted so high they nearly left her head. *"What?"*

"Trent isn't my name," I explained. "It never was. I know it's a lot to get used to. It's a lot for me to get used to, too. But Lucas is my name. And to answer your question, the reason I'm sure these are clues to where the fragments are hidden is because we wrote them down wrong. That's why we didn't know from the start that Calliope was creating a kind of map."

I erased one word from the third line, another word from the fourth line, and yet another from the fifth. Then I wrote them all together on their own line above the others, spelling out:

*Three hidden pieces*

"There's more," Isaac said. He picked up the dry-erase marker and circled the word *monuments* on the whiteboard. "There are thousands of monuments across New York City. Not just in our cemeteries. Our parks are filled with statuary, our plazas, squares, pedestrian malls. The façades of buildings like Grand Central Terminal. New York is a city of monuments, second in the country only to Washington, D.C. I think this is telling us the three fragments are hidden under three different monuments."

"I'm convinced the fragments are still out there," I said. "Calliope died before she could collect them herself. Now it's up to us. If we find them before Erickson Arkwright does, we can stop him from summoning Nahash-Dred. We can stop him from ending the world."

"So, *Lucas*," Bethany said, treating my name like a verbal eye roll. "Why don't you tell us what our next step is?"

I sighed. I was never going to hear the end of it from her. "Our next step is to figure out what all this means." I turned back to the whiteboard.

*Three hidden pieces*
*Eternal voice and inward word*
*Erickson Arkwright*
*Mariner lost at sea*
*Beneath the monuments*
*Look to the Trefoil*
*The Angel of the Waters*
*Codex Goetia*

This wasn't going to be easy. Even knowing that each phrase meant something important, it still looked like a bunch of gibberish to me.

We started at the top. Isaac ran the phrase *Eternal voice and inward word* through an Internet search engine. He spun the laptop around on the table so Bethany and I could see the results on the monitor.

"It's from a poem," he said. " 'The Shadow and the Light' by John Greenleaf Whittier."

"The Shadow and the Light" ran several pages long. Isaac scrolled through it until he reached the pertinent stanza:

> *O Beauty, old yet ever new!*
> *Eternal Voice, and Inward Word,*
> *The Logos of the Greek and Jew,*
> *The old sphere-music which the Samian heard!*

I had no fucking idea what it meant. I read it again and again until my eyes hurt, and all I learned from it was that I didn't like poetry. At least I'd discovered something new about myself. Did my dislike of poetry belong to Lucas West, too, I wondered? Was it something I'd carried with me through the amnesia, or was it new, something more Trent than Lucas?

The implications of that thought floored me. *Were* there things about me that were more Trent than Lucas? How far had I strayed from who I used to be? What would it mean to Jordana when she started to see I was no longer the same man she knew? Wasn't I the same man she'd had feelings for? I put the thought out of my head. I didn't want to think about it.

We scoured the Internet for more information about the poem. The poet Whittier was an American Quaker and abolitionist from Massachusetts who died in 1892. As far as we could tell, Whittier never lived in New York City. Never even visited it. So maybe the clue wasn't about the poet, but something in the poem itself. More research revealed the poem was about Pythagoras, known as the Samian because he was born on the island of Samos, and about religion, with Logos meaning the Word of God. That didn't make much sense in this context, either. None of it did. The poem was starting to feel like a dead end. But the spirits had given Calliope this phrase for a reason. I refused to give up until I knew why.

I took the notebook off the table and started leafing through it. The answer had to be in it somewhere. Maybe I'd overlooked something important. I found a page filled with the words *Eternal voice and inward word* scrawled all up and down the paper in varying sizes, some in all capitals. But something else was on the page, too. It was another of Calliope's sketches: a woman, naked and looking up to the sky. Her right hand was raised and holding one end of her removed gown. The rest of the gown wound behind her to wrap its other end around her left leg. She was leaning back against an unusually small, kneeling horse.

"Take a look at this," I said, showing the sketch to Isaac and Bethany. "Is there anything in the poem about a woman and a horse?"

Isaac scrolled quickly through it on his laptop. "Nothing."

Bethany studied the sketch, biting her lip in concentration. "I've seen this before. I know I have."

"Could it be a painting?" I asked.

She shook her head and looked at the whiteboard again. "No. The notebook references monuments, not paintings. Isaac, can I try something on your computer?"

"Of course." He slid the laptop over to her.

Bethany bent over the keyboard, the glow from the monitor lighting her face. Isaac and I leaned in to see what she was doing. Into the search field of an Internet search engine she typed the phrase *eternal voice and inward word*. Then she added *+monument* and hit the enter button. A screen of links appeared. She clicked on the first link. Our jaws dropped.

The Web page showed a photograph of a tall fountain in front of a marble wall. At the top of the fountain was the statue of a naked woman leaning back against a small, kneeling horse—exactly the same as the sketch in Calliope's notebook. Above the statue, a stone plaque on the wall was etched with the words:

BEAUTY

OLD YET EVER NEW

ETERNAL VOICE

AND INWARD WORD

"My God, that's it," Isaac said.

"Where is this?" I asked.

Bethany looked up at me, her blue eyes reflecting the light from the monitor. "I knew I'd seen it somewhere before. It's the New York Public Library, the main branch on Forty-Second and Fifth."

"Then that's where you'll go," Isaac said. "One of the fragments must be under that statue."

# Eighteen

It was still dark out when I parked the Escalade on a side street near the New York Public Library's main branch. The long, columned, museum-like building covered two city blocks along Fifth Avenue in Midtown. The nighttime floodlights were still on, illuminating the famous twin lion statues in front of the library and casting shadows across its tall, vaulted windows. Yet even at this predawn hour, Fifth Avenue was active. Off-duty cabs and delivery trucks barreled down the street, and the sidewalks were peppered with the occasional jogger and early morning commuter. There was no way Bethany and I could do this without being seen. Luckily, we had just the thing. I left my trench coat in the car and slipped on an orange, reflective construction vest instead—the closest thing to an invisibility cloak in New York City. Bethany wore her usual cargo vest. Together we looked enough like two Con Ed or Verizon workers on the job that nobody would give us a second look. We hoped.

We climbed the grand stairs toward the library's majestic, columned entrance. Directly on our left was the statue of the naked woman leaning back against her kneeling horse. It stood within an arched alcove in the library wall, at the top of an elaborately designed, multi-tiered fountain. Above the alcove was the plaque bearing the now familiar words from Whittier's poem. The fountain itself was dry, allowing us to climb right up to the statue. A fine mesh net hung in the alcove to protect the statue's delicate details from the crowds of people who passed it every day. We ducked under the net and into the narrow space between the statue and the alcove's back wall.

Bethany and I hadn't spoken a word to each other since leaving Citadel. She was still angry with me. I wasn't all that pleased with her, either. Why couldn't she just be happy for me? Didn't she understand how much it meant to me that someone *remembered* me? That someone *cared* about me?

I shook it off and focused on the statue in front of us. If a fragment of the Codex Goetia really was beneath it, how were we supposed to get to it? The quickest and easiest way would be to move the statue. I put my hands against the cool marble, braced my legs, and pushed. I was hoping it would slide along a hidden track to reveal a secret hatch, but that didn't happen. The statue didn't move an inch. I pushed harder, strained against it, but the damn thing didn't budge. It was solid stone, way too heavy for one man to move. Too heavy for a dozen men, probably. I let go, breathing hard from the exertion. Bethany stared at me.

I shrugged. "It was worth a shot."

She arched a skeptical eyebrow. "Was it? Really?"

"If you've got a better idea, let's hear it."

I looked up at the statue and rubbed my chin in thought. The skin on my jaw felt surprisingly smooth. I was used to stubble—there wasn't much time to shave when you were busy chasing monsters and Infecteds all over town—but I had wanted to look presentable for my date with Jordana. The thought of her put a smile on my face. I felt her kiss on my lips again. It was a warm, welcome memory on a cold October morning. But the memory wasn't enough. I wanted more, and soon.

"Are you going to help me look, or are you just going to stand there grinning like an idiot at a statue of a naked woman?" Bethany said.

I came back to myself and realized I'd been staring into space while lost in my thoughts about Jordana. Except the space I'd been staring into was occupied by the marble woman's nude body. Damn. I needed to pull it together.

"Help you look for what?" I asked.

Bethany sighed. She ran her hands along a portion of the statue's marble pedestal. "You didn't hear a word I said, did you? Fine, for the second time, there has to be a door here, or a panel. Some way of getting under the monument. Or there might be a lever or a button that opens it. If someone hid the fragment under the statue, they had to get down there somehow."

That made sense. It also made sense that if there were a door, or a mechanism to open one, it would be within easy reach. Whoever hid the fragment here wouldn't have put the entrance anywhere too high up or too hard to get to. They would have wanted quick access, a way to get under the statue before anyone saw them or figured out how they did it. They also certainly would have camouflaged it to look like part of the statue. While Bethany continued checking the pedestal, I ran my hands over the small marble horse, the highest point of the statue within easy reach. I felt for a switch or button on its hooves, in the bends in its raised front leg and the etched strands of its mane and tail, but there wasn't one. I didn't find any seams or hidden panels, either. There was nothing to indicate a secret entrance.

Damn. Why couldn't it be easy, just this once? I wanted to get back to Jordana and tell her we'd found the first fragment. No, what I really wanted was to kiss her again. The thought made me glow inside. What a fool Lucas West had been—what a fool *I'd* been—to let her slip away the first time. It made me wonder again just how different I'd been as Lucas West. Who was he? What was he like? The answer lay locked away in my memories. Memories Jordana held the key to.

But when I got those memories back, would I still be me? Or would I be him?

"You're doing it again," Bethany said, interrupting my thoughts. She was on her knees, feeling around the base of the pedestal. "Why did you bother coming if you're going to make me do this by myself? You need to get your head in the game."

She was right, but how the hell was I supposed to concentrate when I was closer than ever to knowing who I was? Closer than ever to the past I'd forgotten? Family. Friends. Loved ones. Lucas West's life might have been different from mine, but that was what I liked about it. He was normal. Lucas West wouldn't find himself poking around an old statue before the sun was even up, looking for a secret door. He had his own ambitions, his own routines, his own worries. All of which had come to an end when—

When something happened to him. When something turned him into me. But what?

At the foot of the pedestal, Bethany bent forward. Her hair shifted to reveal a pointed ear. Bethany's past was as much a mystery as mine. No wonder she was upset. I was getting answers while she was still in the dark.

"Do you remember anything about your family?" I asked. I figured if we had something this enormous in common, we should be talking about it, not giving each other the silent treatment.

Bethany looked up at me sharply. "Let's just focus on the task at hand," she said. The edge in her voice could cut the marble walls around us.

Fine. I squatted down and started examining the opposite corner of the pedestal from her, forcing myself to concentrate. The edge of the pedestal had been carved in the form of a horn of plenty, its mouth spilling forth a selection of marble fruit. I ran my fingers down the widening shape of the horn, feeling for anything out of the ordinary like a seam or a loose part. I stopped when I came across a single ram's head carved amid the apples and grapes. That was odd. What was it doing there? It was hidden in the design, but didn't fit with the rest of it. I poked at the ram's head, thinking it might be some kind of button or switch, but nothing happened.

Bethany looked over at me. "Did you find something?"

"Maybe."

I changed tactics. Instead of pressing it like a button, I tried spinning it like a dial. The ram's head turned easily, shifting clockwise. A soft groan came from the back wall of the alcove. I turned around to see a section of the wall slide aside. Beyond it was a narrow, empty space. There was no floor, only steps leading down into a thick darkness.

I gawked at it, astonished. A hidden staircase inside the wall of the New York Public Library. The secret parts of this city never ceased to amaze me.

I moved toward the steps, but Bethany stopped me. "Hold on, Trent, let me go first."

She fished the small, mirrored charm from her vest and muttered a spell. The charm blazed into light and she started down the steps. I followed her. When we were a few steps down, the door in the wall slid back into place, cutting off all light from outside.

"You keep calling me Trent," I said as we descended. "I told you, my name is Lucas."

She sighed in exasperation. Even though I couldn't see her face, I was pretty sure she was rolling her eyes. God, she was infuriating.

At the bottom of the steps, the stairwell opened into an enormous, pitch-black chamber. The air was as musty, cold, and stale as a tomb. Bethany held her glowing charm as high as she could, but the space was so immense the light barely penetrated its depths.

"This must run under the entire library," she said.

"What the hell is this place?" I asked.

We walked deeper into the darkness, our boots echoing on the smooth, stone floor. Up ahead, strange rectangular shapes seemed to float in the darkness. As we got closer and the light reached them, I saw they were actually huge cages. They hung from the darkness above us on thick chains. Inside them were the bones of creatures I couldn't identify. In one cage, a bearlike skull tapered into the long, coiled spine of a serpent. In another was a six-foot insect carapace with an elongated, toothy, gatorlike skull and multiple limbs that ended in humanlike hands. In other cages were a winged giant with three heads, each of a different animal, and a goat as big as a horse, its tailbones ending with another, smaller goat skull. The skeletons were grotesque and utterly alien. I'd never seen anything like them.

"What are they?" I asked.

Bethany shook her head. "I don't know."

"What's with the cages?"

She shone the light into another cage as we passed. Inside were the remains of something that looked like the love child of a giant spider and a komodo dragon. "I have a bad feeling about this place. Let's just get what we came for and get the hell out of here. The fragment has to be down here somewhere."

She led the way deeper into the chamber. More cages full of enormous, misshapen skeletons loomed out of the darkness. A bird with thick, crablike claws instead of wings. A gigantic, rusted warrior's helmet with hoofed legs and a spiny tail coming out of it. Eventually we came to an open, circular area about fifty feet in diameter. In the center of it lay a stone sarcophagus. Its surface was polished smooth and ornately patterned in gold leaf.

"A coffin?" I said. "What the hell is a coffin doing here?"

"And whose is it?" Bethany added.

Situated roughly in the center of its lid was the shallow imprint of a hand. The gold leaf pattern seemed to focus there, with separate, gilded strands coming together in the palm. Curious, I put my own hand inside the imprint.

"Trent, don't!" Bethany yelled.

Her warning came too late. Something sharp darted out of the stone under the tip of my index finger and pricked the skin. "Ah! Son of a bitch!" I yanked my hand back. In the light of the charm, I saw something small and needle-sharp retract into the stone. I shook my hand until the stinging subsided. "What the hell was that?"

"Let me see it," Bethany insisted. I held out my hand. She inspected my finger in the light. A small bubble of blood sat perched on my fingertip. "It doesn't look infected. Do you feel dizzy? Light-headed? Does your hand feel hot?"

I shook my head and pulled my hand back. "I'm fine. It barely hurt. It took me by surprise, that's all."

She breathed a sigh of relief even as she glared at me sternly. "How many times have I told you not to touch things you don't know anything about? You could have been poisoned, or put under a blood spell. Either one could have killed you in an instant."

"I told you I'm fine."

"It's not just about *you*," she pointed out. "You know what happens when you die, and I'm the one standing closest to you."

Shit. She was right. I hadn't been thinking. I'd been distracted and reckless.

I started to apologize but was cut off by a sudden, loud *ka-thunk* from inside the sarcophagus. The lid began to open on its own. Bethany shone her light into it. I expected to see a dead body inside, but there wasn't one. I didn't know whether to feel relieved or disappointed about that. And yet, the sarcophagus wasn't empty. A short, obsidian pedestal stood inside it, and on the pedestal was a piece of metal. Brass or some other copper alloy, it was roughly triangular in shape, with one side perfectly rounded and the other two jagged and broken. I moved closer for a better view.

"Be careful," she said. "This thing already got you once."

Strange patterns had been etched on the surface of the metal, crisscrossing each other at haphazard angles. There were words on it, too, written in a language I couldn't read. Then it hit me. They weren't words, they were names. Demon names.

"It's the fragment," I said. "Putting your hand on the lid must be the key to opening the sarcophagus. But why prick me first?" I looked down at the drying blood on my fingertip.

Bethany shrugged. "The equivalent of a blood sacrifice, maybe? Some kind of trade where you have to give up something important first before it lets you inside? I'm not sure."

"Usually you know everything," I said. "When you don't, I get nervous."

"That makes two of us." She leaned in to study the fragment. "Calliope was right. The fragment was right where she said it would be, under the monument. *Eternal voice and inward word.*"

I cleared my throat loudly.

"Okay, fine," she said, unimpressed. "You were right, too. The fragment was still in New York City. There's no need to be smug about it."

"I do sometimes get things right, you know."

"Says the man who doesn't know better than to go sticking his hand where it doesn't belong," she said. "Anyway, all we really know is that *this* fragment is here. The other two could still be anywhere."

"No, they're all in New York. I'm sure of it," I said. "Look at this place. It's not a garbage dump, it's a stash house."

"You think whoever hid this fragment meant to come back for it?"

"Definitely," I said. "Maybe someone was after him, the cops, or another cult, or maybe Nahash-Dred himself. He would need a safe place to stash the Codex Goetia for a while, until everything blew over. Maybe he thought it would be safer in pieces. But why go through all that trouble unless he was going to come back for them? If you wanted to get rid of the Codex for good, why not just bury it in cement at the bottom of the ocean or the Grand Canyon? No, my gut says this guy was planning to pick up the fragments again. Maybe even put the Codex back together. That means he was keeping them close by."

"But if Erickson Arkwright didn't hide them, who did?" she asked. "He was the only survivor of the cult. There *was* no one else."

As much as I wished I had an answer for that, I didn't.

I tried to lift the fragment off its pedestal, but it wouldn't budge. I examined its edges for brackets or nails that might be fastening to the pedestal, but I didn't see any. It was just . . . stuck. I dug my fingernails under the fragment's edges and strained to pull it free. Finally, it came loose with a snap. I stumbled backward, fumbling it like a clumsy drunk about to drop his bottle.

Bethany sucked in a nervous breath. "Don't drop it! We need it in one piece!"

"What the hell do you think I'm trying to do?" Still stumbling backward from the momentum, I finally managed to get a good, stable grip on the fragment. "There. See? I'm not as clumsy as you think, Bethany."

And with that, I backed into one of the hanging cages behind me. It jangled on its chains. Something inside it rustled and stirred slowly, as if waking from a long slumber. Hot breath touched the back of my neck, reeking of sulfur.

A voice behind me said, "You have come at last, my lord. I knew you would."

I leapt away, tossing the fragment to Bethany. She caught it with her free hand and clutched it protectively to her chest. I spun around to face the cage, pulling the Bersa semiautomatic from the back of my pants. Within the cage sat a gaunt shape whose shriveled skin was pulled tight over his bones. Wings drooped from his shoulder blades. His face looked almost human, though his eyes were too big and his nose was nearly a foot long, hanging off his face like a deli window sausage. Sharply pointed ears poked out of his messy gray mop of hair. Two long horns swept back from his temples like dull, twisted swords. As his enormous eyes focused on me, his face fell in disappointment. He stroked the small, bristly gray beard on his chin.

"You are not the one I expected," he said.

I kept my gun trained on the creature. He blinked at me, clearly not threatened.

"Who are you?" I demanded.

He took a deep breath through his tumescent nose. He straightened up, squaring his bony shoulders. "Do you not know me, wretch? There was a time when you would have. I am the Mad Affliction. Once, I commanded legions and drove whole villages from the clutches of sanity. My name alone was enough to loosen the bowels of the fiercest warrior. But now . . ." He paused, and seemed to deflate. "Now I am caged like an animal. Caged and starving. I have not tasted flesh in so long. Even the rats have eluded me. There are so many of them, plump and juicy, some as big as cats—but they're smart. They know to stay away from me." He moved closer to the bars, his big eyes gleaming with hunger. "Let me taste you. Just one finger. One finger is all I ask."

He reeled back and threw himself against the bars, rocking the cage on its chains. I took a step back, keeping my gun on him.

"Surely you won't miss one finger!" he implored.

"What is this place?" Bethany asked him.

The Mad Affliction looked at her, his lip curling in revulsion. He turned away. "Ugh. A female. Awful thing. Get it away!"

"Sounds like he's met you before," I said.

Bethany glared at me. "Don't encourage him."

The Mad Affliction harrumphed and spat in disgust. "The females of your species taste so bland, like flavorless pudding. Disgusting things! But the males . . . the males taste like the richest sweets." He threw himself against the bars again, grasping for me. "One finger for my stomach! Just one! To the first knuckle only!"

"Hey!" Bethany shone the light in his face to attract his attention. He lifted a bony, emaciated hand to shield his eyes. "I asked you what this place is."

"Surely the answer is obvious. This is a place of punishment. What other explanation can there be?" the Mad Affliction said. "I was summoned here, through the door between realms. We all were, all those you see caged here. The Walker in Nightmares. The Cruxshadow. The Dread Torment. The Queen of Tombs. He Who Strides Beneath the Waves. So many of us. One by one we were pulled through the doorway, only to be locked away forever."

"By who?" I asked.

"Men like you," the Mad Affliction replied bitterly. "Men who possessed the key that unlocks the door. They summoned me, but they could not bind me. They could not bind any of us. They did not understand the binding spell. But they had other spells at hand. Painful spells. That is how they forced me into this accursed cage. I have been here ever since."

"Is this part of the key you mentioned? The one that unlocks the door between realms?" Bethany asked, holding up the fragment. The Mad Affliction nodded. "Trent, the men who summoned him must have been the

Aeternis Tenebris, Erickson Arkwright's doomsday cult." With her free hand, she shone the light around us again, taking in the enormous chamber of bones and cages. "It all must have happened right here, under the library. This was their sanctum."

The Mad Affliction nodded, his long nose bouncing. "Aye, the Aeternis Tenebris, they called themselves that. They're the ones who summoned us."

"You're a demon," I said. Sometimes I was a little slow on the uptake. "All the things in the other cages, they were demons, too."

The Mad Affliction's bony, nearly concave chest swelled with pride. "Of course I am a demon! Was there any doubt? Did I not strike such terror in your heart that there was no mistaking what I am?" He sighed, his shoulders slumping, his wings rustling against his back. "No, of course not. Not now. Not when I am reduced to *this*. Those men, they had the key, they opened the door, but they did not know what they were doing. They were amateurs. Tinkerers. They summoned the wrong one of us time and time again. Tell me, how long have I been here? A century? Ten centuries?"

"Fourteen years, give or take," I said.

The Mad Affliction looked shocked. A shocked demon wasn't something you saw every day. "Fourteen years? Is that all? Time passes so strangely in your realm. I would have thought it much longer, given that all the others have perished. Starved to death. The men caged us, but they left us nothing to eat. Nothing to do. I slept the years away, and now I am the last one. Perhaps that is fitting, as I was the last of their mistakes before they finally managed to summon the one they truly wanted."

"Nahash-Dred," Bethany said.

The Mad Affliction cackled. "Indeed! The fools sought the Burning Hand, He Who Puts Out the Stars, the Wearer of Many Faces. Spawn of Leviathan, brother of Behemoth. They sought Nahash-Dred, Destroyer of Worlds!" He glared at us. "Are you so foolish that you do not tremble at his name? Beware, imprudent humans. Nahash-Dred could be anyone, anywhere. He could be listening to you even now, and you would not know until you felt his bare hand tear the dripping spine out of your back!"

"What do you mean *anyone*?" I asked.

It was Bethany who answered me. "The Wearer of Many Faces. Don't you see? Nahash-Dred isn't just a demon. He's a shape-shifter."

"There are demons that can change their shape?" I asked.

"Of course," she said, as if everyone knew that.

"Right. Of course," I said.

The Mad Affliction laughed at my ignorance, his long nose quivering. I was still holding the Bersa. I thought about shutting him up with a bullet between those big saucer eyes of his, but something told me a gun wouldn't be much use against a demon. I put it back in the holster at the small of my back.

"What happened when they summoned Nahash-Dred?" Bethany asked.

The demon grinned at the memory. "The fools could no more bind my lord than they could me. Nor were their other spells strong enough to overcome one so mighty. And so he slaughtered them. Oh, it was glorious! Nahash-Dred took them apart with but a thought. Some tore like paper. Others burst like overripe fruit. A hand here, a foot there, a loop of gut. Blood streamed across the floor like a beautiful red river."

Bethany pointed the glowing charm at the floor. The smooth stone was mottled with big, dark red patches of long-dried blood. There were no bones, though; no clothing. The rats must have gotten to them long ago. Rats as big as cats, the Mad Affliction had said. I thought of them dragging the pieces of the dead back to their nests, and shuddered.

"Oh, the hunger! My mouth waters just thinking of all that blood." The Mad Affliction glared at me again. "Let me have your toe. Even just your smallest toe!"

"Forget it," I said. "What happened next?"

The Mad Affliction sighed, annoyed. "When the slaughter was done, Nahash-Dred ignored our pleas to be released from our cages. Surely my lord had good reason why, though he did not share it with us. Instead, he left this place. But he will come back for us. I know he will. I thought you were him when you woke me."

"So Nahash-Dred killed the cult members and went back to his dimension?" I said.

"Back? No, Nahash-Dred did not go back. When he left this place, he did so in the shape of a man. Not through the doorway between worlds, but out into your realm. There he remains to this day."

"What?" Bethany demanded. "He can't be."

"What reason have I to lie?" the Mad Affliction asked. "I wish my lord had returned to our realm rather than stay in this forsaken one, and I wish he had taken me with him. But neither happened."

"Are you *sure* Nahash-Dred is still here?" I pressed.

"I am as sure of it as I am of the hunger that racks my body day and night," the Mad Affliction said. "I can sense him in this realm. I would not be able to were he on the other side of the doorway."

Shit. If Nahash-Dred never went back to his own dimension, then the demon was out there right now, hiding somewhere among the people of New York City. But how was that possible? In the footage Isaac showed us, Nahash-Dred looked a hundred feet tall. How exactly did the principles of shape-shifting work? Did the rule of conservation of mass not apply to demons? Could he be any size as well as any shape? Human? Mouse? Insect? And did it work the other way, too? Could he make himself *two* hundred feet tall? Five hundred? A thousand?

Bethany shook her head. "This changes everything."

A strong contender for understatement of the year.

"If Nahash-Dred can change what he looks like, then the Mad Affliction is right, he could be anyone, anywhere," I said. "There are ten million people in this city."

Bethany shut her eyes, trying to stay focused. "He changed his shape. That explains why no one saw a demon escaping out into the streets." She opened her eyes again and looked at the Mad Affliction. "Do you remember what Nahash-Dred looked like as a man?"

"Like him," the Mad Affliction said, pointing at me. "As a man, my lord looked as all men do. I cannot tell them apart."

"What color was his hair? How tall was he?" she pressed.

The Mad Affliction shrugged. "Man is man is man. Can you honestly say you see any difference from one to the other?"

Bethany groaned in frustration.

"You're telling me a shape-shifting demon just walked out onto Fifth Avenue and blended in with the crowd?" I asked. "Hailed a fucking cab after tearing everyone to pieces down here?"

"Not everyone," the Mad Affliction said. "Now that I think on it, he did not slaughter all of them. In the aftermath, one of the men was missing. He was not among the dead."

"That must have been Erickson Arkwright," Bethany said. "I don't suppose you remember what *he* looked like?"

The demon shrugged again. "As all men do."

"Great," I said. "How the hell are we supposed to find either of them?"

The Mad Affliction laughed at that. "You cannot find Nahash-Dred. Even I could not recognize my lord in another form. He cannot be found if he does not wish to be."

"Okay, but maybe you know where he would have gone," Bethany suggested.

"I have no inkling why he would stay in this awful realm when our home awaits," the Mad Affliction replied. "But I am sure he plans to return one day. I pray it is soon, and that he takes me with him."

"How would he go back?" I asked. "I thought you needed the Codex, the—the key to open the door between worlds."

"Ah, but he had the key," the Mad Affliction said. "Nahash-Dred took it with him."

I wasn't expecting that. I looked at Bethany, who appeared just as shocked.

"Nahash-Dred took the Codex Goetia?" Bethany asked.

"Aye, though how that piece of it got back here I do not know," the Mad Affliction said. "Perhaps it happened while I slept. I slept many of the years away."

"I don't understand," I said. "Nahash-Dred took the Codex. He could have used it to go home, but he didn't?"

The Mad Affliction nodded. "You share my confusion. All I know is he must have had good reason. Nahash-Dred is a prince in my realm. He would not abandon that role for nothing."

"Can you help us find him?" I asked.

The Mad Affliction laughed so hard I thought he was going to choke. "Why would I? Did you not hear me when I said Nahash-Dred is a prince? He is of royal blood—my lord and master! Clearly he does not wish to be found. I would not betray him for the likes of you. Nor for anyone."

"But he left you behind," I pointed out. "He betrayed *you*."

The Mad Affliction shook his head vehemently. "Never. I would sooner eat the disgusting flesh of this female than go against my lord."

"Fine," Bethany said. "Leave him. We've gotten everything out of him we're going to. If he doesn't know where Nahash-Dred is, there's nothing else we can learn from him."

She started to walk away. I turned to follow her.

"No, wait!" the Mad Affliction cried, his voice rising with panic. "You cannot just leave me here! I beg of you! I have no one left to talk to! You are the only ones who have talked with me in years! Please, come back! Do not leave me in this cage!"

Bethany didn't turn around, but I did. Something about the creature's desperate loneliness made me feel sorry for him. The Mad Affliction was caged and alone, the last of his kind in this dark and airless chamber. I'd been locked in a cage once myself, not knowing if I would ever get out. It was a fate I didn't wish on anyone. I didn't like feeling this kind of connection with a demon, but there it was. I couldn't ignore it. I went to the side of the cage where the door was secured by a heavy padlock.

"What are you doing?" Bethany asked, walking back toward me.

"He's right," I said. "We can't just leave him here."

"The lock is weak," the Mad Affliction said, watching me eagerly. "One good tug could break it. I cannot do it myself. When I touch it, it burns."

I bent down to inspect the padlock. A pentagram had been etched into the metal. Was that why it burned him? Did pentagrams hurt demons? It was another thing I needed to ask Jordana when I had the chance. I reached for the lock.

Bethany put her hand over mine, stopping me.

"You can't let him out, Trent," she said. "He's a demon, not a stray dog. You can't just set him free into the world."

"We could send him back to his dimension instead," I said. "What do you call it? Banishing?"

"We can't banish anyone without the other pieces of the Codex," she pointed out. "And even if we could, it's too risky. When you open a door between worlds like that, you don't know what's going to take the opportunity to sneak through into ours."

"So what are you saying? We're just going to leave him here to starve like the others?"

She didn't answer me. She didn't have to. I could see her mind was made up. Sometimes I forgot just how coldhearted Bethany could be when she was on the job.

The Mad Affliction's arm shot out of the cage, grasping for me. I jumped back. His long, ragged talons swiped the air in front of me.

"Free me!" the Mad Affliction cried. He grasped for Bethany, but she backed away, too. "Free me and know the living nightmare that is unending madness!"

"You're not doing yourself any favors," I told him.

Bethany grabbed my arm and started leading me away from the cage. "Come on, we can't stay."

I went with her, reluctantly. I didn't want to leave the Mad Affliction in that cage, but she was right. He was a demon. A hungry demon with a taste for human flesh. I couldn't just let that out into the world.

"Please, do not leave me here!" the Mad Affliction called after us as we walked back the way we came. I tried not to listen. I tried not to think of myself in the cage. We began to climb the stairs back toward the surface. As the secret door in the wall of the library slid open for us at the top of the stairs, I heard the Mad Affliction call out, "You will never find Nahash-Dred if he does not want to be found!"

Then we were back outside. The wall slid closed behind us, abruptly cutting off the demon's voice.

"I'm sorry," Bethany said. "There was nothing else we could do."

"It's not right, Bethany. I understand the reasons, but there should have been another way."

She started down the front steps of the library. "Come on. We have to get the fragment back to Citadel. If Nahash-Dred is still somewhere in New York City, we have to tell Isaac. We need a new plan."

The sun was up as we descended to the sidewalk. There were more people out now, heading to work. In the bleary morning rush, and with our vests camouflaging us as city workers, none of them gave a second glance our way, or at the Codex fragment tucked under Bethany's arm.

One down, two to go.

I watched people hurry past us on the sidewalk. Any of them could be Nahash-Dred. The gray-haired man in the long coat with the newspaper folded under his arm. The woman in the smart pantsuit drinking from a takeout coffee cup. The young man in the puffy winter coat. I studied everyone's face as they walked by, but if there was a way to tell if someone was a demon in hiding I didn't know it. Everyone looked normal to me.

Well, *New York* normal, I thought as a man walked by with facial tattoos and stretched-out earlobes.

On the walk back to the Escalade, I pulled out my cell phone and dialed Jordana's number. It rang until her voice mail picked up. I checked my watch and saw it was only seven thirty in the morning. Probably, she was in the shower or getting ready for work.

At the beep, I said, "Hey, it's me. My hunch was right. We found one of the fragments. But there's something else I need to tell you, something important about Nahash-Dred. Call me as soon as you get this, okay?" I was about to hang up when I realized there was more I wanted to say. Personal things. But as always, I found that to be a lot harder. "I, um, I'm really glad we got a chance to talk last night. I wish we could have talked longer. Maybe we can get together again soon. Besides, I'm pretty sure I owe you another drink." I ended the call and put the phone away. Bethany was watching me. "Jordana," I explained.

"I figured," she said. She kept looking at me.

"What?" I asked.

"I didn't say anything," she said.

"But you want to."

We reached the Escalade. I opened the driver's door. She opened the passenger door and took a seat.

"You already made it clear it's none of my business," she said.

I tossed my orange construction vest in the back of the Escalade, put my trench coat back on, and sat down behind the wheel. I started the car.

"But if you must know," Bethany continued, "this whole Lucas West thing . . ."

I glared at her.

She raised her hands in surrender. "Staying out of it."

I pulled into traffic and drove toward Central Park and Citadel. We took Sixth Avenue, riding in silence. That was fine with me. Whatever else Bethany had to say on the subject, I didn't want to hear it.

The traffic light turned red at Forty-Fourth Street. I braked at the edge of the crosswalk, directly beneath the arching metal post where the traffic light hung. A sudden movement in the periphery of my field of vision made me glance up. A shape was perched on the metal post, crouching on his hands and feet. Without warning, he sprang up, somersaulted through the air, and landed expertly on all fours on the hood of the Escalade. The car rocked with the impact.

I recognized the black sweats and ski mask right away, even before I saw the metal gauntlet on his hand.

Arkwright.

# Nineteen

Even though the traffic light was still red, I slammed my foot down on the accelerator. The Escalade squealed out into the crosstown traffic on Forty-Fourth Street. Horns blared at us, drivers shouted, and people stared from the sidewalks. I swerved around a yellow cab and sped into the empty lanes of Sixth Avenue in front of me. All the while, Arkwright hung on, gripping the top seam of the hood.

I twisted the steering wheel from side to side, trying to throw him off the car. He pulled back the Thracian Gauntlet. I braced myself for the blast, but instead he made a fist and smashed the gauntlet through the tinted windshield right in front of Bethany. She cried out as cubes of safety glass showered over her.

I continued swerving the car from side to side, blowing through another intersection, but Arkwright held tight. He reached through the hole in the windshield with his gauntlet and grabbed the fragment in Bethany's hands. She fought to keep it like a drowning woman holding onto a life preserver as the two of them tug-of-warred for the fragment. Keeping one hand on the steering wheel, I used the other to hit Arkwright's arm, trying to force him back. More cars honked and swerved to avoid us as we blew past Forty-Fifth Street. Finally, Arkwright managed to yank the fragment out of Bethany's hands. He pulled it out through the hole in the windshield.

Fuck it. I'd had enough of this asshole. I pulled my gun from the holster in the back of my pants and aimed it at him through the windshield. Before I could pull the trigger, Arkwright leapt backward off the hood of the Escalade, clutching the fragment. He somersaulted through the air and landed on top of the station wagon in front of us. The son of a bitch didn't even stumble.

I rolled down my window. I transferred my gun to my left hand and pointed it out the window at Arkwright. I adjusted the speed of the Escalade to match that of the station wagon. I had a clear shot.

"Don't shoot!" Bethany yelled. "The kids!"

I took my eyes off Arkwright. That was when I saw them, two little boys in the back cargo area of the station wagon, their faces and hands pressed against the rear window. One was looking up, trying to catch a glimpse of the man who had landed on top of their car. The other was staring at me. At my gun. His mouth was a round O of terror, his face as white as a sheet. Damn. There was no way I could guarantee my shot wouldn't go wrong and hit one of those kids. Cursing, I put my gun away.

Arkwright leapt off the roof of the station wagon and jumped from car to car, getting farther from us. If I didn't catch him now, he would get away. I hit the gas, but the morning rush-hour traffic kept me slow. Up ahead, Arkwright jumped off a car and onto the rear of a charter bus. He used the big vent grille for handholds and the bumper for his feet. Then he started to climb up the bus, the fragment tucked under one arm. When he reached the roof, he ran the length of it, then jumped again. He landed on the back of a fifty-foot-long tractor-trailer.

Damn, this guy was like a fucking gymnast. But if I wanted to stop him, I had to catch up. I spotted an opening in the traffic in front of me and floored it. I weaved the Escalade through traffic, cutting off vehicles as more angry drivers honked at me. A few seconds later, I pulled up alongside the truck. Through the window, I noticed a ladder running up the back of the trailer.

"Take the wheel," I told Bethany.

Her eyes went wider than I'd ever seen them. "Tell me you're not planning to do what I think you're planning to do."

"Just take the damn wheel!"

I let go of the steering wheel, giving her no choice but to lean over from the passenger seat and grab it. After everything we went through to get the fragment, there was no way I was letting that bastard take it from us. I opened the car door. Asphalt whipped by beneath me at flesh-ripping speed. Ahead, the early morning traffic thickened and slowed as we drew closer to Rockefeller Center. I crawled out the door, holding tight to the side of the Escalade to make sure I didn't fall.

"Trent!" Bethany shouted. "You're crazy! Get back in here!"

I squared my feet, readying myself.

"Don't you dare!" Bethany yelled.

If we were going to catch Arkwright, it was now or never. I jumped. I grabbed hold of the ladder on the back of the truck and clung to it. The Escalade kept pace beside me. I saw Bethany crawl into the driver's seat and close the door. She shook her head and mouthed something I was pretty sure wasn't a compliment.

People shouted in alarm on the sidewalks. I saw cell phones and tablets lifting into the air as everyone snapped pictures of the lunatic holding onto the back of a moving truck. So much for keeping a low public profile. Isaac wasn't going to like this.

I climbed up the ladder toward the roof of the trailer. My arms already hurt from grabbing the ladder in mid-jump, and my boots barely fit on the rungs. I slipped, cursing, but held on and righted myself. Wasn't this kind of thing usually Philip's job? I started climbing again. I made it to the top of the ladder and pulled myself up onto the roof.

Arkwright was standing at the front end of the trailer, his back to me. I moved forward, keeping my center of gravity low so I wouldn't lose my balance. I pulled my gun and tried to line up a shot. I would shoot that son of a bitch right in the back if I had to.

Arkwright spun around and pointed the Thracian Gauntlet in my direction. I heard the high-pitched whine and hit the deck. The blast from the gauntlet sizzled through the air over me, smelling of ozone. Across the street, an office building's second-story window exploded as the blast struck it. Glass rained onto the sidewalk below. I heard screams.

Shit. I got back on my feet. Arkwright was already running toward me. I couldn't shoot without risking hitting a bystander. I holstered the gun and ran at him. Before he could get the gauntlet up for another blast, I tackled him. Our bodies hit the metal roof with a loud clang. We grappled on top of the trailer. I pinned the gauntlet down with one hand. With the other I tried to yank the fragment away from him. He kneed me in the gut, knocking the wind out of me. He broke away and got back on his feet. I did the same, struggling to catch my breath.

From the corner of my eye I saw something rocket toward us. I turned my head and saw an advancing traffic light dangling from its long metal post, the rapidly approaching green circle shining like a comet. There was no clearance—it was heading right for us. Arkwright and I both dropped onto our stomachs as the truck passed under the traffic light.

An instant later, we were both back on our feet. I reached for my gun, but the tractor-trailer beneath us changed lanes suddenly and I lost my balance. I fell, sliding toward the edge of the boxy trailer. My legs went off the side, then my torso, but I caught hold of the metal rim along the edge and hung on for dear life. As soon as one of my boots found purchase, I clambered back up.

Arkwright was waiting for me. Before I could get back on my feet, he kicked me in the face. I fell onto my side, tasting blood.

Arkwright turned away and started moving down the length of the trailer. I could tell he was getting ready to jump again, to make his escape with the fragment. There was no way in hell I was going to let him.

I was on my feet and chasing after him before I'd even finished the thought. I tackled Arkwright from behind. This time I got a good hold on him. The fragment fell out of his hands and landed a few feet away. Arkwright struggled, but I had both my arms around him tight.

Something felt strange through his clothes. It was like he had bandages wrapped around his body. I thought of Lon Chaney, Jr. in the old Universal mummy sequels, covered head to toe in his wrappings. Was that what Arkwright looked like under the black sweats? I thought about what the demon might have done to him. It'd been a massacre in the cult's sanctum under the library. Just because Arkwright survived didn't mean he'd survived unharmed. But if that was the case, if he was that seriously injured, how the hell was he running, jumping, and flipping around like that? A spell?

First things first. I had more pressing questions.

"How did you know where to find us?" I demanded. "How did you know we had the fragment?"

By way of an answer, he elbowed me in the face. My grip on him loosened, and he managed to wriggle away.

Arkwright pointed the gauntlet at me again. I heard another high-pitched whine as it powered up. I kicked his hand up. The gauntlet discharged into the air, its blast disappearing into the sky above us. I didn't know what its range was, but I hoped like hell there were no airplanes flying overhead just then.

Arkwright ran for the fallen fragment and scooped it up. I threw myself at him, but he jumped out of my reach. My breath was coming hard and fast, but the bastard wasn't even winded. His eyes, the only part of his face I could see thanks to the black ski mask, looked past me. I turned, saw another fast-approaching traffic light, and hit the deck.

Arkwright didn't. He jumped and landed on top of the metal post of the traffic light. He stayed perched there, falling farther and farther back as the truck carried me away from him.

Shit. We were approaching Radio City Music Hall on Fiftieth Street. I got to my feet and jumped off the truck. My boots hit Radio City's red-and-blue, neon-lit marquee with a loud bang, while the tractor-trailer continued up Sixth Avenue without me. As soon as I looked up at the traffic light again, Arkwright was gone.

And the fragment was gone with him.

Damn.

I clambered down from the marquee to the sidewalk below. I got a few curious looks and a couple of sneers from passing tourists, but no one stopped me or asked what I was doing there. Good old New York. You could always count on no one wanting to get involved.

I waited on the corner in front of Radio City until Bethany rolled up in the Escalade. I opened the passenger door and climbed into the seat, wincing. Every muscle in my body felt sore. She pulled back into traffic and glanced over at me.

"Are you okay?"

"I'm fine," I said.

"Well, you're still in one piece, anyway. That's more than can be said for people who've done things a lot less foolish."

"I thought I could catch Arkwright," I said. "I couldn't. He's too fast. How the hell is he so fast?"

The more I thought about Arkwright, the angrier I got. He'd killed Calliope and Yrouel. He'd stolen the fragment from us. He'd gotten away because I wasn't fast enough or strong enough to stop him.

Somehow, he'd figured out one fragment was at the library. He must have seen us get there first and decided to ambush us when we came back out. We should have been expecting it. We should have been smarter.

But if Arkwright knew the location of one fragment, there was a good chance he knew where the others were hidden, too.

Now it was a race. If we didn't find the other two fragments before he did, the whole world was toast. Arkwright would bind Nahash-Dred and use the demon as his own personal weapon of mass destruction. It would be the end of everything.

# Twenty

I fidgeted on the edge of my bed. Bethany sat on a chair in front of me and brought a cotton ball soaked in rubbing alcohol toward my face. I pushed her hand away. "I told you, I'm fine. Stop fussing over me."

"Arkwright beat you up pretty good," she said. "I just want to make sure these cuts don't get infected."

"I got in a few good punches, too, you know," I grumbled. I touched the cut on my lip and winced.

"Are you going to let me take care of it, or are you going to keep up this stupid macho act?"

I sighed. "Fine. Do whatever you want, if it'll make you feel better."

"Riiiight, this is about making *me* feel better," she said.

She dabbed the cotton ball on a cut over my left eyebrow. The alcohol stung against the open wound. I winced a little. Kali sat in the corner and watched with intent fascination, clearly enjoying seeing me in pain.

"What are you staring at, stupid cat?" I grumbled at her. Kali only blinked in reply.

"Sounds like you two are really hitting it off," Bethany said. She dropped the cotton ball onto a pile of used ones next to her chair. "Now take off your shirt."

I unbuttoned my shirt and pulled it off. "Sometimes I think you only do this because you like getting me to take my shirt off."

"Keep flattering yourself," she said. "No one else will."

I chuckled. For a moment it felt like old times again, before things had gotten tense between us.

Bethany gently inspected the dark, softball-sized bruise on my chest near my left arm. I fidgeted again, trying not to think about what the feel of her warm hands on my skin was doing to me. Then she poked the bruise a little too hard, and a sharp pain spiked through me. Problem solved.

"Don't be such a baby," she said. "The bruise isn't that bad. It'll be gone in no time, and then you can go back to jumping onto moving trucks like a maniac."

I pulled my shirt back on. "Your bedside manner could use some work."

Bethany stood, picked up the bottle of rubbing alcohol, and started collecting the cotton balls off the floor. "Are you ready to come downstairs?"

"Give me a second," I said. "I'll catch up."

"Don't take too long," she said, heading for the door. "Isaac wanted to see us ASAP."

When she was gone, I called Jordana. Once again, it rang and rang until the voice mail picked up. I was starting to worry.

"It's me again," I said after the beep. "Arkwright ambushed us. The son of a bitch stole the fragment right out of our hands. I don't know where you are, but call me soon, okay? Let me know you're all right." I ended the call. It was just after nine in the morning. Where was she? At work, presumably. Maybe her cell was in her purse and she couldn't hear it. I dug out her business card and called her direct work number. Again there was no answer, just her voice mail. I ended the call without leaving a message.

I tried not to worry, but I kept imagining Arkwright going after her. Blasting her with the Thracian Gauntlet, or worse, gutting her like Calliope. But Arkwright didn't know about Jordana, did he? She wasn't like Calliope or Yrouel. She wasn't on his radar.

Was she?

Kali blinked at me from the corner of the room.

"Where the hell is she?" I asked, but the cat didn't have any more answers than I did.


Downstairs in the main room, I found Isaac and Bethany already seated at the big table, waiting for me.

"Arkwright attacked you in broad daylight, in full view of the public?" Isaac was asking.

"He wants to end the world," Bethany said. "I don't think he cares if anyone sees him running through traffic or taking shots at us with the gauntlet."

"I don't know about that," I said, pulling up a chair. "Arkwright was wearing a mask. He's hiding *something*."

"I suppose you were seen, too?" Isaac asked.

"By pretty much everyone, yeah," I said. "Probably a few security cameras, too. Especially when I ran that red light on Sixth Avenue. Sorry."

Isaac sighed. "You did what you had to. If we're lucky, people will just assume it was another movie shoot."

I looked at the empty chairs on the other side of the table. After losing the fragment to Arkwright and learning the demon was still in New York, I would have felt better if we were back up to full strength, all five of us working together. It felt wrong, just the three of us. Like everything was off-balance.

"Still no word from Gabrielle?" I asked.

"Nothing," Isaac said. "She hasn't answered a single phone call, text, or e-mail I've sent."

Damn. Now I was getting really worried about her. "Where is she?"

"I wish I knew, but we can't wait for her," Isaac said. "Especially now that we know Nahash-Dred never left New York City."

"Does Arkwright know the demon is here?" Bethany asked.

"We have to assume he does," Isaac said. "But even so, he still needs the Codex Goetia to bind Nahash-Dred to his will."

"Okay, but if the demon's still in New York," she asked, "what's he been doing all this time?"

Good question. If the Destroyer of Worlds was here, why hadn't he begun destroying it yet? From the trail of carnage he'd left over the ages, I got the sense Nahash-Dred wasn't exactly shy about wiping out entire civilizations. So why hadn't there been reports of entire cities, countries, *continents* left in ruin? Fourteen years had passed since Arkwright's cult summoned him here. If Nahash-Dred never left, what had he been doing since then? Preparing? I could see how destroying the world would take a lot of effort and energy. Maybe he needed to rest up first, let his power build. But fourteen years? Did it take *that* long?

It occurred to me there might be a much simpler answer. Maybe

Nahash-Dred had no interest in destroying the world because he liked it here. He'd been summoned into New York City, after all. We had more murders every year than just about any other place in the world. On paper, we were practically a city of homicidal maniacs. Where else would a death-dealing demon want to live but someplace where he could kill with impunity, as often as he wanted? As a shape-shifter, he wouldn't have to worry about getting caught, even if there were witnesses. All he had to do was change what he looked like. White to black. Tall to short. Male to female.

For Nahash-Dred, New York City was the perfect killing field. It was fucking Disneyland.

A chill came over me. It occurred to me I might have already seen Nahash-Dred's handiwork. Given the bizarreness and brutality of Calliope's murder, and how different it was from Yrouel's, could the demon have killed her? Maybe it wasn't just Arkwright she'd gotten too close to. Maybe it was the demon, too.

"The fact that Nahash-Dred is a shape-shifter isn't going to make this any easier," Isaac said. "Though now I understand why no two artists could agree on what he looks like."

"How do you track down a shape-shifter?" Bethany asked. "No description would matter. Even his fingerprints could change. He's been hiding in New York City for over a decade without drawing attention to himself, so he clearly knows how to cover his tracks."

"And what do we do if we *do* find him?" I asked.

Nahash-Dred was much more powerful than we were. We would be like ants taking on an elephant. Slingshots against a hydrogen bomb. *Nahash-Dred took them apart with but a thought.* None of us had signed up for the Five-Pointed Star because we thought the job would be easy or safe, but I didn't exactly relish the idea of being taken apart by a greater demon. Was that something I could come back from, or would it be as much the end for me as for anyone else? Nahash-Dred wasn't from our dimension. He was a demon with powers I knew nothing about. If he killed me, would I stay dead? Or would I come back like all the other times? I took it a step further, following the train of thought down the rabbit hole: What happened if we failed and Nahash-Dred eradicated all life on earth? Would I still be here? Just me, Nahash-Dred, and Erickson Arkwright on a smoldering rock in space?

That raised another question, one I hadn't thought of before. What was Arkwright's endgame in all this? Did his insane desire to see all life extinguished include his own? Arkwright was clearly nuts, but was he also suicidal?

"For now, our mission hasn't changed," Isaac said. "We keep looking for the fragments. Once we have them all in our possession, we can use the Codex Goetia to banish Nahash-Dred back to his dimension before Arkwright has the chance to bind him."

"Even if we manage to get the stolen fragment back from him, and even if we successfully banish the demon, Arkwright's not going to give up," I said. "He's that tenacious."

"Then we'll be waiting for him," Isaac said.

"How do you propose to use the Codex at all?" Bethany asked. "None of us know how it works."

"Jordana does," I said.

"Will she help?" Isaac asked.

I nodded. "Definitely. She wants to help."

Bethany leaned forward in her seat. "Wait, so Jordana is part of the team now? When did that happen?"

"If she's the only one who knows how to use the Codex, then we can't do this without her," Isaac said.

Bethany shook her head in disbelief. "You can't be serious. You're really going to hand over a powerful and dangerous artifact like the Codex Goetia to someone we barely know?"

"I can vouch for her," I said.

"You only just met her," Bethany insisted.

"You vouched for me once," I pointed out. "I'm doing the same for her."

Bethany sighed and rubbed her forehead. "How do you even know she can work the Codex properly? Arkwright's cult thought they could, too. The minute they slipped up, Nahash-Dred butchered them. You're putting a lot of faith in someone you don't really know."

"It's not like we have time to take out a Craigslist ad looking for an experienced demonologist with references. We're working with what we've got," I said. "Besides, I trust her."

"With your life?" she asked. "Wow. That must have been one hell of a date."

"What's that supposed to mean?" I demanded.

Isaac interrupted quickly. "Enough, you two. Whatever's going on here, give it a rest for now. The clock is ticking."

Bethany put up her hands. "Fine. Let's just get on with it."

"Trent—" Isaac began.

"Lucas," I corrected him. Bethany rolled her eyes.

"Sorry. Lucas," Isaac said. "I need you to get in touch with Jordana. Ask her if she'll help us with the Codex once we have it."

"I will if I can get ahold of her," I said. "I've tried twice already. All I've gotten is her voice mail."

Isaac knit his brow. "Do you have any reason to be worried about her?"

"No," I said, which was true enough, but it didn't mean I *wasn't* worried. I kept thinking how Arkwright had already killed at least one person connected to this, maybe two. He wouldn't balk at another. "I'll keep trying her. I'm sure I'll get through eventually."

"You mean our new and completely untested demon expert is proving unreliable?" Bethany muttered. "I'm shocked."

I gave her a look telling her to back off. Yet some part of me wondered if Bethany was right. How much did I really know about Jordana? Maybe I *was* taking too much on faith. But I'd always trusted my instincts, and whenever I was with Jordana I didn't have any doubts about her. So how come when she wasn't around I felt less certain?

We'd found one fragment of the Codex Goetia, only to lose it to Arkwright. But the race wasn't over yet. There were still two more fragments out there, and like Isaac said, the clock was ticking.

The next clue from Calliope's notebook was *Mariner lost at sea.* The phrase wasn't part of a poem or inscription this time, but knowing the fragments were all hidden beneath monuments helped us narrow our Internet search. New York City was one of the country's oldest port cities. We figured there had to be a monument somewhere dedicated to those lost at sea. We were right, it didn't take long before we hit pay dirt. There was an American Merchant Mariners' Memorial in Battery Park, at the southern tip of Manhattan.

"Is that the place?" Bethany asked, leaning over Isaac's shoulder to get a better view of the laptop.

"Can you pull up a picture?" I asked.

Isaac brought up a photograph on the screen. On top of a small pier off the shore in the Hudson River was the bronze sculpture of a tipped, sinking lifeboat. There were four bronze figures as well, three men on the boat and one, in a macabre touch, below them in the river itself. The grimacing figure in the water was reaching up with one arm, about to either be saved by his comrades or lost to the waves, depending on the whims of the sea. The bronze had turned green from exposure to the elements. It made all four of them look like drowned spirits who'd risen from the sea.

I was certain I'd seen this image sketched in Calliope's notebook. I flipped through the pages until I found it. Her drawing of a sinking boat mirrored the monument exactly, except for one startling difference. Calliope had drawn herself as the figure in the water, desperately reaching up to be saved as the waves closed around her. The hopelessness of it put a knot in my gut, a reminder that I couldn't protect her. She had reached out to me for help, just like the figure in the sketch, and I'd failed her. I'd let the sea take her.

Isaac read the monument's inscription off the computer screen. "'This memorial serves as a marker for America's Merchant Mariners resting in the unmarked ocean depths.'"

"That's the one," I said. "Calliope drew it in the book. That must be where the second fragment is."

"If we figured it out, Arkwright will have, too," Isaac said, standing up. "We should get it now, before he does."

"You're coming with us?" Bethany asked.

"If Arkwright shows up again, I want to be there," Isaac said. "He's already got one fragment. There's no way I'm letting him get the other two."

My cell phone rang, startling me. I fished it out and looked at the name on the screen.

"It's Jordana," I said. "Give me a minute. I'll meet you at the car."

"Don't take too long," Isaac said. "Arkwright might have a head start already."

Isaac and Bethany went out the front door. I answered Jordana's call.

"Are you okay?" I blurted into the phone. I didn't even say hello.

"Yes, of course," she said. "I was in meetings all morning, but I got your messages. Are *you* okay?"

I sighed with relief. "I'm fine. I was worried something had happened to you."

"You don't have to worry about me. No one's getting past the Bay Ridge Harpy at the front desk," she said. "But are you sure you're okay? You said Arkwright ambushed you. You'd tell me if you weren't okay, wouldn't you?"

"I fought him off, but he got away with the fragment," I said. "Jordana, I want you to be careful. If Arkwright knows you're helping us, then you're in danger. He's already got blood on his hands. Don't take your usual route home tonight. Don't let any strangers approach you."

"You're being silly," she said. "I know how to take care of myself."

"Then just humor me, please," I said. "I know what Arkwright is capable of."

"Okay, okay," she said. "Message received. I'll be careful. I suppose I should be flattered that you're so concerned about me."

"There's more," I said. "Nahash-Dred is already in New York City. Apparently, he never went back to his dimension after the cult summoned him here."

She didn't answer me. The line was silent for what felt like a very long time. When she finally spoke, it was with a fearful urgency.

"Lucas, if Nahash-Dred is here, you can't waste any more time," she said. "He's a prince of demonkind. He's bred for destruction. It's what he does. He destroys, he kills, he annihilates. You have to bring the fragments to me. I know how to send the demon back, but I need the Codex Goetia. All of it."

"That's what I wanted to know," I said. "We're heading out to Battery Park now. We're pretty sure another fragment is hidden there."

"Lucas, listen to me," she said. "I—I saw a demon once. It was a couple of years ago, shortly after Pete died. My family went on a ski trip to Aspen. I guess we were trying to find a sense of normalcy again. We rented a private cabin near the woods. One night, my mother and stepfather were arguing. They did that a lot after Pete died, but this one was really bad. I couldn't take it. I had to get out of there and clear my head, so I went out into the woods alone. I saw this—this light in the trees and went toward it. That was when I saw it. I thought it was a bear at first, but it had a head like a wolf and these big, staglike antlers. The antlers were on fire, they were *burning*. It was crouched over the carcass of a dead dog. It was . . . eating. Then it turned around and saw me. Lucas, its eyes were like fire, they burned just like its antlers. Then it—it just went back to eating the dead dog, like I didn't matter. I know now that it must have been a lesser demon, because only the Codex Goetia can summon greater demons. I don't know who summoned this one or why it was there, but it scared the hell out of me. It's why I started studying demonology. I never wanted to be that scared or feel that helpless again."

"I had no idea," I said. I couldn't begin to image how terrifying that must have been for her.

"Please be careful, Lucas. What I saw in the woods that day is *nothing* compared to Nahash-Dred. Check in with me as soon as you've got the next fragment. Promise me you'll call."

"Will you pick up this time?"

"Even the Bay Ridge Harpy couldn't stop me," she said.

From outside, the car horn blared impatiently.

"I have to go," I said.

"Then go," she told me. "Bring me the fragments before it's too late."

I ended the call. I was about to leave when my eyes fell on Calliope's notebook, still lying open to her sketch of the American Merchant Mariners' Memorial. Something about it jumped out at me then—another difference between the sketch and the actual monument, one so subtle I hadn't noticed it before. But now that I saw it, I wished I hadn't. It took a moment for me to remember to breathe.

Calliope had drawn the three figures aboard the lifeboat in their exact poses. One was reaching down for his comrade in the water. The second had his cupped hands around his mouth, shouting for help. The third was kneeling, his hands on his knees as he faced forward. But Calliope had given this last figure a different face. One I recognized instantly.

I couldn't believe it. I blinked and rubbed my eyes, but it didn't change. It was there. It was real. It was unmistakable.

She had given him Underwood's face.

# Twenty-One

By the time we got to Battery Park all the way at the bottom of Manhattan, it had started raining. Fat droplets drummed furiously around us. I pulled up the collar of my trench coat against the cold rain. I wished I had a hat, too, something to keep my head dry. Of course, with both a trench coat *and* a hat, I would look like I'd stepped out of a 1940s film noir.

The path into the park led us past well-manicured green lawns and rows of park benches. The rain hadn't kept the tourists away. They huddled under umbrellas and in their dollar-store plastic ponchos, exploring the park and admiring the south Manhattan skyline or New Jersey across the water. Isaac and I wore the orange construction vests. Bethany wore her usual cargo vest. I had mine on under my trench coat this time. I was sure I looked ridiculous and wasn't fooling anyone, but no one gave us a second look. Part of me wished I'd known about the construction-vest trick back in my thieving days. It would have come in handy anytime I had to go . . . well, anywhere.

A battered, twenty-five-foot, spherical bronze sculpture towered beside the path. Once, the sphere had adorned the plaza between the Twin Towers of the World Trade Center. Now it was a memorial, still bearing the scars of that terrible day in its torn bronze. As the raindrops *pinged* against it, Isaac regarded the sphere with haunted eyes. He'd been at the Towers that day, I recalled, helping rescue survivors from the rubble. One of those survivors had been a vampire named Philip, who'd pledged him one hundred years of service in gratitude. That moment had marked the birth of Isaac's little team of artifact thieves and, ultimately, the renewed Five-

Pointed Star. Yet even now, twelve years on, I could still see the pain and loss in Isaac's eyes when he thought of that day. I saw it in the eyes of all New Yorkers.

My thoughts went back to Gabrielle. I couldn't help it. Her absence felt like a lost limb. Why couldn't we reach her? Where was she? Was she avoiding us, purposely not answering our calls? I couldn't help thinking about what she'd said after the Fetch attacked us, how she didn't think she was cut out for this kind of life anymore. But damn it, didn't she know how much was at stake?

We reached the far end of the park, where Castle Clinton stood near the water. A castle in name only, it was actually a circular, brownstone fortress that dated back to the War of 1812. We walked into Castle Clinton to find an open-air courtyard. At its center was a ticket booth for boat tours to the Statue of Liberty and Ellis Island. We left the fortress through the opposite side, exiting onto a cement walkway along the river's edge. Off to our right, in the shadow of the clock tower of the abandoned City Pier A, was the American Merchant Mariners' Memorial.

The monument stood several yards out from the shore. Rain pelted the surface of the Hudson River like bullets. Waves churned against the monument's base, slapping at the bronze figure half-submerged in the water. Up close, the desperate grimace on its face was even more harrowing than the online pictures conveyed. Only a few small inches separated his outstretched fingers from those of his comrade on the boat above him. I glanced at the kneeling figure at the far end of the monument, worried he would have Underwood's face like in Calliope's sketch. To my relief, he did not.

Why had she drawn Underwood? What did it mean? It felt like a message, one meant specifically for me, but how was that possible? Calliope hadn't met me yet when she drew it. If she'd used automatic writing, then technically the spirits had drawn it, not her. But why?

A short, concrete bridge led across the water to the monument, but it was blocked by a chain-link fence. A heavy padlock secured its gate. The fence was only eight feet high and there was no barbed wire across the top.

"We can climb it," I said.

Isaac took the padlock in one hand. "No need. Just make sure no one is watching."

I looked to see if the coast was clear. The rain had picked up in the last few minutes, turning into one of those lashing monsoons New York got in the summer and fall. Throughout the park, people were dashing madly toward the street or under trees to get out of the rain. No one was paying attention to us.

A flash of black caught my eye. In the distance, a figure in a black, hooded cloak stood watching us. A crow was perched on his shoulder. A shiver went through me as I remembered our encounter in the Village. What was he doing here? Why was he watching us?

A small flame flared in Isaac's palm, drawing my attention. The padlock went up like flash paper. He brushed the ashes off his hand, glancing quickly over his shoulder to make sure we were still in the clear, then pulled the gate open. I glanced back at the cloaked figure. He was gone. Had he really been there? Or was it just a trick of the rain? Isaac and Bethany strode quickly across the bridge to the monument. I hurried after them.

Standing on the monument's pier, the artist's tricks became evident, like the forced perspective of the sinking lifeboat, which was actually just a diagonally positioned slab of metal. There was more detail to be found in the figures' faces and clothing, but there was something eerie about them, too. Something almost inhuman about the weathered green of their faces and the black, empty holes of their eyes. They looked like corpses.

What I didn't see, even up close, was any way of getting inside the monument. There was no door. No visible seams that could mark a hidden entrance. The rainwater rolled straight off the long, metal slab of the lifeboat, not disappearing into any secret crevices or hatches.

"How did you find your way into the last one?" Isaac asked.

"We searched every inch of that statue," Bethany said, squinting against the rain. "Trent found a secret button hidden in its base."

"Lucas," I corrected her. She didn't reply, which I supposed was better than another one of her wisecracks. It was progress, anyway.

I wiped the rainwater from my face and bent to inspect the bronze figure closest to me. He lay prone across the width of the lifeboat, reaching down to help his fallen comrade in the water. I swept my hands over his back and legs, the wet metal cold against my palms, but I didn't find anything out of the ordinary. I reached into the figure's empty eye sockets and mouth, hoping to find a switch or lever, but there wasn't one. Isaac and

Bethany searched the other two figures and came up just as empty-handed as I did. Damn. How the hell were we supposed to get inside? If only we had some clue . . .

But there was a clue, I realized. Calliope had already provided it, and as usual we hadn't seen it for what it was. In her notebook, she'd written, *Mariner lost at sea.* Not *mariners,* plural. Just *mariner.* Just one.

A mariner lost at sea.

Only one of the figures fit that description.

I got down on my stomach on the cold, wet monument and looked over the edge at the figure in the water. He was reaching up to the boat. The back of his hand lay flat against the wall, leaving his palm exposed. From this angle, it almost looked as though he were reaching up for me. Maybe he was.

I reached down toward his hand, but it was farther than I thought. My fingers barely grazed his. I stretched my arm as far as I could until I touched his palm. With a metallic creak, his cold, bronze fingers began to move on hidden hinges. They closed around mine, as if the drowning mariner were holding on for dear life. The grip tightened, crushing my hand. I gritted my teeth against the pain. Had I made a mistake and tripped a booby trap? Was this thing going to crush my hand into ground chuck? But the grip loosened then, and the sound of a metal door springing came from the other side of the monument. I pulled my hand free and got to my feet.

At the farthest end of the bronze lifeboat, where it was tipped the highest, a trapdoor had opened. I wiped the rain out of my eyes. First a secret chamber under the New York Public Library; now another one under a monument in the Hudson River. I would never get tired of this city.

We looked down into the opening. Metal stairs descended into darkness.

"Stay behind me," Isaac said, starting down the stairs. "We don't know what's down there."

We descended in silence. I took up the rear, stepping carefully. The stairs were metal and already slippery from the rain. The stairwell went down so deep I was sure we were descending far below the surface of the river. Behind us, the doorway slid closed again, cutting off the rain, but also cutting off the daylight and enveloping us in absolute darkness. Isaac pronounced a quick incantation, and a ball of fire appeared in the air above his fingers. It didn't give off any heat—though, shivering from the cold rain, I wished it did—but it radiated enough light to see by.

The stairs terminated at a wall, but on our left was an open archway. We stepped through into a chamber considerably smaller than the enormous sanctum under the library. This one was probably five or six hundred square feet in total, with walls decorated in arcane patterns and designs. There were no hanging cages; no bones or trapped demons. There was only one object here, right in the center of the room. Another gilded sarcophagus. It was identical to the first, right down to the shallow imprint of a hand on its lid.

Isaac snapped his wrist. The fireball leapt from his fingertips into the air, where it hovered above us, a tiny sun keeping the room lit.

"The sarcophagus is just as you described," he said, walking a circle around it. He stopped at the hand-shaped imprint. "This is how you opened the other one?"

I nodded. "Be careful. It likes to bite."

He placed his hand in the shallow imprint. A second later he yelped in surprise and yanked his hand away. I caught a glimpse of the needle as it retracted into the stone.

"You weren't kidding," he said.

"You'll be all right," I said. "It's some kind of blood offering to get the lid to open, that's all."

He shook his hand and stuck his finger in his mouth. We waited, but the lid stayed closed.

"Did I do it wrong?" Isaac asked.

"Let me try," Bethany said.

Isaac stepped back. Bethany put her hand where his had been. Hers was much smaller, but she positioned her fingers so that they filled as much of the imprint's fingers as they could. She winced as the needle pricked her, but unlike Isaac—or me, for that matter—she didn't cry out or pull her hand away. Even so, nothing happened.

"I don't understand," she said. "Is this one different somehow?"

I walked over to it. "I don't know. What else would it want us to do?"

I put my hand in the imprint. Instantly, I felt a sharp prick to the tip of my index finger.

"God damn it!" I cried out, yanking my hand away. Even expecting it, the damn thing still hurt like hell. A dollop of blood clung to my fingertip.

A loud *ka-thunk* came from inside the sarcophagus as it unlocked. The lid began to open.

"Apparently, it likes your blood better than ours," Isaac said. "Why is that?"

"Guess I'm just lucky," I said, sucking on my fingertip. One more thing to add to the list of my abnormalities. Special blood, the kind preferred by vampiric sarcophagi. Was there *anything* about me that was normal?

Inside the sarcophagus, resting on a short, obsidian pedestal, was another fragment of the Codex Goetia. It was identical in shape to the first one, a thick triangle with one side rounded and smooth and the other two jagged and broken. Its surface was covered with etched patterns at odd angles, plus three hundred and thirty-three more demon names, all in a language only Jordana could read. I wished she were here. Not just to translate, but so she could see this. I wanted to share the thrill of discovery with her.

Isaac struggled to pull the fragment out of the sarcophagus. Finally, it released with a *snap,* and he stumbled back a few steps.

I turned to Bethany as if to say, *See, it's not just me.* She rolled her eyes.

"Two down," I said, "one to go."

"It makes you wonder," Isaac said, looking around the chamber. "Who's responsible for all this? Who broke the Codex Goetia and hid the pieces? And what about this chamber? Was it here already? Where did the sarcophagus come from? What does it mean?"

"Whoever did this would have to be very powerful," Bethany said. "The Mad Affliction said Nahash-Dred took the Codex with him after he massacred the cult. Whoever's responsible for hiding the fragments would have had to get it back from Nahash-Dred first. But I can't imagine the demon handing it over without a fight."

Neither could I. How could anyone get the Codex from Nahash-Dred without being turned into body-part stew like the cultists?

The answers, if there were any, would have to wait. We walked back to the stairs. I started up the steps first. Far above us, the door in the monument slid open again. A shape appeared silhouetted in the doorway, too far away to see clearly. He pointed down the stairs at us. As soon as I heard the high-pitched whine, I knew exactly who it was.

"Get back!" I shouted to the others.

We raced down the stairs and back into the chamber just as the blast from the Thracian Gauntlet came crackling down. It struck the wall at the bottom of the stairs. A section of the wall exploded in a cloud of dust and rubble, leaving a big, scorched divot in the concrete. A long crack tore through the floor to the center of the chamber, beneath the sarcophagus.

I drew my gun and aimed up the stairs at Arkwright, but before I could squeeze off a shot Isaac pushed past me. He motioned like a pitcher throwing a fastball, only what came out of his hand was a sizzling red torpedo that arrowed up toward Arkwright. Arkwright jumped aside. Isaac's spell struck the doorway, obliterating a chunk of it and the top stairs. Arkwright reappeared in the opening, his gauntlet powering up again. I grabbed Isaac and threw both of us out of the way.

The second blast struck the wall in the same spot as the first, tearing through the concrete. A big hole opened into the depths of the Hudson. Torrents of freezing cold, silty river water rushed into the chamber. The crack in the floor widened and deepened. We backed up to the far end of the chamber as the water splashed violently across the floor. It was a small space, and it filled fast. The icy water was up to my thighs before I knew it. It smelled terrible, the stench of centuries of garbage and industrial waste dumped into the Hudson.

Bethany pulled a charm out of her vest, the same emerald she'd used to shield me from the Thracian Gauntlet in Chinatown. She affixed it to her hand with the leather strap, then pointed it toward the archway that separated us from the stairwell. The charm projected its translucent green barrier over it. The river water smashed against it but couldn't pass. With nowhere else to go, the water began to fill up the stairwell instead. We'd kept the flood out, but in the process we'd cut off our only exit.

Blast after blast from the Thracian Gauntlet hit the chamber wall from the other side. Arkwright was trying to break his way through to us. He knew we had the Codex. The wall shuddered and cracked. It wouldn't hold him, or the water, out for long.

"We have to hurry!" Bethany cried. The translucent green barrier over the archway was already starting to flicker. The emerald strapped to her palm glowed so brightly it looked hot. "The spell won't last much longer! If we don't find another way out soon, we'll all drown!"

I waded forward, sloshing quickly around the chamber. I inspected the walls, but there was no other way out. I looked back at the others and shook my head. "There's nothing. We're trapped."

Arkwright blasted at the wall again from the other side. The chamber floor quaked and shifted under my feet. Through the muddy river water I saw the crack in the floor grow bigger, spiderwebbing across the chamber. I expected to see more water bubble up from the crack, but instead the water began to drain through it, forming small whirlpools in the surface. Was there empty space under the chamber? Another room, maybe? If there was, and the water kept rushing through the already structurally weakened floor like that . . .

"Ah, shit," I said.

A section of the floor crumbled and gave way with a monstrous noise, opening a hole into darkness beneath us. The sarcophagus fell through. Rushing water poured into the hole and pulled us with it. The emerald charm was torn from Bethany's hand as the flood swept her up. The barrier disappeared instantly. A roaring tide of water came crashing into the chamber. Bethany and Isaac went under.

I sucked in a deep breath and held it. The current dragged me down through the hole in the floor. The freezing water closed over me. I was pulled in free fall for several long, panic-filled seconds. Then I dropped into another room far beneath the chamber we'd left. I landed on my back—but not on the floor. I hung suspended above it, floating on a web of netting over the smashed remains of the stone sarcophagus. If I hadn't stopped, I would have broken my back on them.

Isaac stood on the floor below me. He'd saved me with a spell. Bethany stood beside him. They were both drenched, their hair plastered to their heads, their clothes sopping wet and muddy with Hudson River silt. A new fireball floated near the ceiling, lighting the chamber.

But water was still coming down on me with the force of a fire hose. I coughed, nearly swallowing a mouthful of the Hudson River. I tried to scramble away, but the force of the water was too much. I couldn't get enough air in my lungs—

The web shifted as Isaac swung me away from the waterfall. He set me down gently on my feet on the water-covered floor. The web vanished. Then he cast another spell, up at the hole this time, and sealed it over with a big, glowing, blue disc. The water stopped.

"It won't hold for long," Isaac said. "We're going to want to be gone by the time it gives way."

I coughed more water out of my lungs. I took out my gun and inspected it. It didn't look damaged. I tipped it forward, pouring a stream of water out of the muzzle. I didn't know if it would fire now. The ammo was high quality, which meant it was waterproof, or damn close to it. The crimp was airtight and the primer sealed. But as my lungs could attest, that had been a hell of a lot of river water. It could have washed away the oil and injected silt into the action. When we got back to Citadel, I would have to clean it, oil it, and just to be safe, replace the ammo.

I holstered the gun again and took in the room around me. It was long and narrow with walls fashioned from marble blocks. Much larger than the chamber above, the water spread out over the floor and only came up to my shins. A row of tall, standing candelabras lined both sides of the room, unlit. At the far end, on a slightly raised marble platform, were three chairs of heavy, polished wood. The one in the middle was bigger than the other two, more ornately designed and with a taller back.

"Where are we?" I asked.

Bethany pushed her wet hair out of her eyes. "Is that a *throne*?"

"Never mind that, I found the door," Isaac said behind us. He was standing in front of two tall, metal doors in the wall. "It's a tight seal," he groaned as he pushed them. They swung outward, and the water flooded out of the room. Isaac glanced up at the glowing disc on the ceiling one last time. "Come on. We should get out of here while we can."

"Arkwright's not going to give up that easily," I said. "Is there any way he can follow us through that seal?"

"The Thracian Gauntlet could blast through it easily," he said. "But in doing so, he would flood this whole place and risk losing the fragment. Let's hope he's more concerned about putting the Codex back together than killing us."

Bethany and I followed him through the doors into a marble-walled corridor, sloshing through the water at our feet. My wet clothes weighed me down. The waterlogged trench coat on my back felt like a hundred extra pounds, but I wasn't about to leave it behind. The coat had belonged to Morbius once, founder of the original Five-Pointed Star. I was probably the last person anyone would call sentimental, but I didn't want to give it up.

The fireball floated along with us, lighting the way through the pitch-black surroundings. Other passages branched off from the corridor, their metal doors closed to our prying eyes. What was this place? And where had everyone gone? It looked deserted.

Passing through an arch at the end of the corridor, we found ourselves in a huge chamber with redbrick walls. The earthen floor was muddy from the water that had preceded us down the hall. In the center of the chamber was a wide, deep, stone pit. Dark stains painted the pit's walls and floor.

"What is that?" I asked.

Isaac stared at the stains. "It's blood."

"Whatever this place is, it reeks of death," Bethany said. "The sooner we get out of here, the better."

She and Isaac kept walking. I lingered a moment, looking into the pit. If the stains were blood, there'd been a lot of it. Someone had died in there. Probably more than one person. Why? What *was* this place, a slaughterhouse? A torture chamber? The room grew darker as the fireball followed Isaac away from me.

"Trent, come on!" Bethany called back.

"Lucas," I corrected her, so softly I barely heard it myself.

I tore my gaze from the pit and followed them. How many had died here? I had a bad feeling about this place, a terrible sense deep in my gut. I wanted to get out as quickly as I could and never think about this place again.

I caught up to Isaac and Bethany in a tunnel off the pit chamber. There was graffiti all over the walls, some carved crudely into the brick, others written in chalk. Much of it was in languages I couldn't read, let alone identify. They didn't look like any alphabet I'd ever seen. Only one was in English, a poem written over a large section of the wall:

> *Rich or poor*
> *With most or least*
> *You'll never go wrong*
> *Betting on the Beast*

I didn't know what it meant, and frankly I wasn't interested in sticking around to find out.

Bethany pointed down the tunnel. "Look!"

In the distance, the thin shape of a ladder stood upright in the tunnel. We hurried toward it. As I passed another tunnel that branched off to the left, I glanced quickly down it. It was a habit I'd picked up while on Underwood's crew, when I'd had to make sure no one was waiting in an alley to slip a knife between my ribs. I barely registered a tunnel extending deep into the darkness before I continued on.

Then I froze.

My heart jammed itself into my throat.

I backed up a few steps and looked into the tunnel again.

Something had been etched into the brick wall, near the tunnel's mouth.

An eye inside a circle.

The Ehrlendarr rune for magic.

I swallowed, my throat as dry as sandpaper. I walked up to the rune. I touched it, traced it with my finger. I'd seen this before. I knew it very well. An eye inside a circle etched on a brick wall. The image had haunted me for the past year.

It was my first memory, the very first thing I'd seen after losing my identity—the Ehrlendarr rune for magic carved into a brick wall, along with sparks in the air and a wisp of smoke, as if something had just happened, something I couldn't remember.

But this wasn't a coincidence. This wasn't déjà vu. This was the wall. This was the symbol. I was certain of it. I felt it in every fiber of my being.

I'd been here before.

# Twenty-Two

Isaac and Bethany doubled back, rounding the corner to find me standing in the mouth of the tunnel. The floating fireball followed them, casting a brighter light on the rune etched in the brick wall before me.

"What are you doing?" Bethany asked.

"We have to go, we don't have much time," Isaac said. He gripped the Codex fragment tightly in one hand.

I didn't turn from the wall to look at them. I couldn't. All I could do was stare at that damn rune. I tried to tap into what I'd felt the first time I saw it, the confusion and fear, the sense of something having *just* happened before I woke. I tried to force the lost memories to come back, but they wouldn't. They were gone.

"There are a thousand things I don't remember. My family. My home. But *this* I remember," I told them. "I've been here before."

Bethany looked at me, astonished. "What?"

"This is where I woke up without knowing my name. This is where I lost my memories. I was right *here*, in *this* spot, in *this* place."

"How do you know?" Isaac asked.

"Because of this." I pointed at the rune etched in the brick.

Isaac came closer to examine it. "It's Ehrlendarr. What's it doing here?"

"It's the symbol for magic," I said. Though not just magic. Calliope had told me it also meant change and transcendence. "It's my earliest memory. This rune, on this wall. I was here."

"You're sure?" Bethany asked.

"I've never been more sure of anything," I said. But *why* had I been here, in the same underground complex as that awful, bloodstained pit? And why did I have such a strong urge to get the hell out? I studied the rune, desperate for answers.

A loud crash came from somewhere deeper in the complex. Isaac and Bethany jumped, but the noise barely registered with me. I was lost in my thoughts.

What had taken me from Norristown, Pennsylvania, to this hellhole beneath Battery Park? Why had I lost my memories here? I wanted to stay. To explore, to learn everything this place had to tell me. I needed to know why I'd been here.

"Trent," Isaac said from a thousand miles away. He repeated it, loud enough to pull me out of my thoughts. "Trent! We have to get out of here. That noise was the seal giving way in the throne room. The water is breaking through!"

"I'm not leaving, not yet," I said, only half listening.

Another crash came from somewhere behind us. I heard a rushing roar in the distance, the sound of things being knocked over.

"We have to go! Now!" Bethany cried. She grabbed my arm and tried to yank me away.

I resisted, pulling myself out of her grasp. "I was *here*, Bethany! Don't you get it? I have to know why! What if there's something else here I recognize, something that sparks another memory?"

Isaac glanced down the tunnel in the direction we'd come from, then back at me. His eyes were big and wild. "Move!"

He grabbed me by the trench coat, dragged me back into the main tunnel, and pulled me along with him toward the ladder up ahead. I tried to break free, tried to brake with my boots against the floor, but Isaac wouldn't stop. He pulled me farther and farther from the rune on the wall, and I hated him for it every step of the way.

A loud rumble behind us made me glance over my shoulder. A wild, rushing wave filled the long tunnel, barreling after us.

That brought me back to my senses. I stopped resisting and sprinted down the tunnel toward the ladder. Was this the way I'd run before? A year ago, when I awoke without my memories in front of that Ehrlendarr rune, I'd been so confused, so scared, that all I could do was run. I didn't have any memory of my escape, only that suddenly I was outside. I risked a glance back at the rapidly approaching floodwaters. Had something been chasing me then, too? Was that why I'd run?

Ahead of us was the ladder, bolted to the floor in the middle of the tunnel. It extended up into a wide, round shaftway in the ceiling. I didn't know where it led, but we didn't have much choice. The ladder was our only escape from the flood. Bethany reached it first and quickly ascended. Isaac tucked the Codex fragment inside his duster and followed her. The fireball went with him. In the dimming light, I looked back one last time. A hundred feet back, the rushing wall of water slammed into the corner where the two tunnels diverged, and then the place where I'd had my first memory was gone. There was only the water, pushing forward, coming at me. My chest went tight with anguish. The Ehrlendarr rune, the first physical clue I had to my past—I had no idea if it had been destroyed, lost forever.

The water rushed toward me. I jumped, grabbing high rungs of the ladder, and pulled myself up after the others as quickly as I could. As soon as I had climbed into the shaftway, the floodwater swept by beneath me. The force of it shook the ladder. If I'd been a second slower, I would be dead. Again.

I started climbing up after the others. My heavy, waterlogged clothes slowed my progress. Water dripped out of my hair and into my eyes. I tried to wipe it away with the back of my coat sleeve, but the sleeve was wet, too, and only made it worse. Water, water, everywhere. If I never saw water again, I would be happy.

My heart felt like a dense cannonball sitting in my chest. I hated leaving the underground complex behind without knowing why I'd been there before. But what choice did I have? We had to get the fragment back to Citadel before Arkwright made another attempt to steal it. All the answers to my questions were underwater now anyway, inaccessible, even if we had the time to go back and look. I knew all these things, and I hated leaving anyway.

The ladder went up three or four stories into an enclosed, dimly lit space. By the time I reached the top, my arms and legs ached from the effort of climbing. I rolled onto my back on the blessedly dry floor to catch my breath. We were in a room big enough to hold maybe ten men. In the center of the room was the brick-lined hole in the floor I'd crawled out of. There were no windows, but there were horizontal slits in the wall high above us that let in a little air and a small amount of light. There was a door in one wall. Isaac's fireball was gone, no longer needed.

I coughed, feeling completely waterlogged. I sucked air into my lungs, grateful for it even if it was the stale air of this room.

"Where are we now?" Bethany asked.

Isaac looked down into the shaftway. "The entrance to wherever we just were, I'd say. This must be how you get in."

I got on my knees and stared down into the shaftway. I couldn't see anything down there. Whatever lay below, I'd lost it.

"I was so close," I said. "So fucking close."

"I'm sorry, Trent, I truly am, but we can't stay," Isaac said. "Arkwright's still out there somewhere, probably looking for us. We need to go. But I promise you, we'll come back when we can."

"Provided there's anything down there anymore that the flood didn't wash away," I said, shaking my head. "No. You two can bring the fragment back to Citadel. I'm staying. I have to know."

Bethany knelt down in front of me and looked me in the eye. "If there's anything to find, you'll find it. That's what you're good at—figuring things out, putting things together that no one else sees. Which, come to think of it, is pretty remarkable for someone who tends to punch first and ask questions later. But you can't go back down there now. It's not safe. And neither are we, not until we get back to Citadel."

I took a deep breath and let it out slowly. I knew she was right, but what I was feeling was too big to let go of just yet. "I was there, Bethany. Back when I was Lucas West. Whatever happened to me, whatever made me like this, it happened *down there*."

"We'll come back," she said. "If we survive this, if we stop the world from ending, we'll come back."

"Those are some pretty big ifs," I said, but I nodded. She squeezed my hand.

Bethany stood and walked to the door. She tried the handle and found it unlocked. She pulled the door open a crack and peeked outside.

"I don't see Arkwright," she said.

She pulled the door open wider, revealing trees and grass in a corner of Battery Park. We hadn't traveled all that far underground. The three of us left the little room and walked out into the cold, hammering rain. I looked back and saw we'd been inside a tall, angular, concrete structure in the middle of a lawn. It was white and featureless, aside from a patterned black trim around the top. A ventilation building for the nearby Brooklyn-Battery Tunnel, most likely. When Bethany closed the door again, it blended seamlessly with the rest of the concrete slabs in the building's façade, utterly camouflaged. The secrecy only made me more curious. Whatever the underground complex was, it had been deserted, its entrance left unguarded. Whatever it had been used for, it no longer was.

I thought about the bloodstained pit again. Something violent and terrible had taken place down there. Why the hell had I been in a place like that?

As we walked away from the structure, I kept an eye out for Arkwright. The autumn treetops made excellent hiding places, and I already knew Arkwright had no fear of heights. But there was no sign of him. That surprised me. He didn't seem the type to have just gone home. He was desperate for the fragment. He wouldn't give up that easily. No, if Arkwright was gone, there was a reason for it. Something had driven him away.

When we turned the corner of the ventilation building, a group of people were waiting for us, blocking our way. The stench of wet, rotting flesh hit me before I realized what they were.

Revenants. On quick count, there were seven of them. Now I had an idea what must have spooked Arkwright.

Standing front and center amid the revenants, with his arms crossed smugly across his chest, was Thornton. Or rather, his reanimated corpse. His pupils glowed red from Reve Azrael's magic. His pale, bloodless lips parted in a grin.

"Hello, little fly," Reve Azrael said through Thornton's mouth.

I had my gun out in a flash, pointed right at her head. After being submerged in all that river water, I didn't know if the gun would fire, jam, or blow up in my hand, but one shot to the head was all I needed—

A revenant I hadn't seen came up behind me and yanked the gun out of my hand. I glared at the revenant, a male corpse whose mouth was frozen in a twisted, rictus grin. Smiley tossed my gun to Reve Azrael, who tucked it into her belt. Then Smiley yanked my arms behind my back and held them there. Looking over at Isaac and Bethany, I saw two additional revenants had restrained them the same way.

Okay, so there weren't seven revenants. There were ten.

They were fresh bodies, the kind that could pass for living if you didn't look too closely, and there were so many people in New York City that no one ever looked all that closely. It made me wonder where Reve Azrael got her stock. Did she just hang around graveyards waiting for fresh bodies to arrive?

Actually, I could see her doing that.

"Looks like you still have a knack for finding me, Reve Azrael," I said. "Yesterday you sent the Fetch, but today you're actually gracing us with your presence. Or as close to your presence as you ever get, anyway. I'm touched."

"Do not be. You are not the only one I have come for," Reve Azrael said. She approached Isaac. "You have something I want, mage."

"I'm not surprised," Isaac said. "Why don't you start doing your own legwork for a change?"

"Why, when you can always be counted on to do it for me?" She pulled his duster open, reached inside, and pulled out the Codex fragment.

Isaac glared at her. "You wearing Thornton's face like that is an abomination."

She laughed. "I rather like it. His corpse is still strong from the spell his woman employed when she tried to save his life. It is a nice change from the host bodies that are usually available to me." As if to illustrate the point, the other revenants pressed closer, the stench of their rot overpowering.

"And you, little fly," Reve Azrael said, coming over to me. "You have something I want, too."

I looked hard into those glowing red eyes. "I'm flattered, but I've got a girlfriend now."

"I am here to offer you another chance," she said. "Join me in what is to come."

"What makes you think I'll say yes this time?"

"I can be very persuasive," she said.

I narrowed my eyes at her. "Give it your best shot."

She stepped aside. The crowd of revenants parted. I'd miscounted again. One revenant had been hiding behind the others, waiting to be brought forward. An eleventh.

He looked just as I remembered him. The same clothes, the same bullish stance, the same dark sunglasses. But his skin was mottled and discolored now, decaying in patches. The ocean of cologne he used to wear to mask his rot was gone. He smelled sickly sweet and foul.

"Good dog," Underwood said.

# Twenty-Three

The revenant I had once known as Underwood shuffled toward me with stiff, jerking movements. "Good dog," he said.

It all came crashing back then. The loneliness of the fallout shelter where I'd been kept like a pet. The torture room behind the black door. The threats, the violence and death he'd manipulated me into. All the damn lies about helping me while only stringing me along. Promises made to keep me under his thumb.

"Good dog," Underwood rasped again. Part of his cheek had turned green with rot. One spot had worn through, leaving a hole in which I caught a glimpse of his teeth. He limped closer.

The horror-movie zombie act was just that, I knew—an act. Reve Azrael was making Underwood behave this way to play with my head. It was working. I couldn't think straight.

"Stop it," I told her.

"Does it bring back fond memories, little fly?" she asked.

Underwood stopped in front of me and slapped my cheek lightly. His hand was cold and clammy like uncooked meat. "You're my go-to guy."

"Call it off!" I shouted, struggling against Smiley's iron grip on my arms.

Now, at last, I understood why Calliope had drawn Underwood's face in her sketch. It was more than a message. It was a warning. The spirits had known what would be waiting for me when I came here.

"You're not real," I told Underwood. "You never were. You're a trick, a lie, just like before."

"Careful," Reve Azrael said. "You're hurting his feelings."

Underwood straightened, the horror-movie charade over. He wrapped one cold, waxy hand around my neck and squeezed, choking me as his grip tightened.

"Let him go!" Bethany yelled.

Reve Azrael ignored her. She walked over to me. "You still have something I want, little fly."

Underwood squeezed harder, strangling me. I couldn't get any air. A dark gray haze began to crowd the edges of my vision. I didn't have much time before I passed out.

"You can join me," Reve Azrael said, "or I can take it from you."

"You won't get it by squeezing it out of him!" Isaac yelled.

"I gave him the chance to come with me willingly, and he threw it back in my face," Reve Azrael said. "Clearly, he needs convincing."

I gasped, trying to breathe, but it was no good. Underwood was crushing my windpipe. I struggled against Smiley behind me, but the revenant was too strong and I was growing weaker. I tried to kick Underwood away, but there was no strength left in my legs. He continued to throttle the life out of me.

"Tell me, little fly, after he kills you, whose life force will you steal to cheat death this time?" Reve Azrael asked. "There are only two living beings close enough to choose from. Will it be the mage? That would leave your little team of misfits weak and vulnerable, without a leader. Or will it be the small, annoying woman? Oh, how that would destroy you. Perhaps it is a good thing, then, that you do not get to choose. The luck of the draw, isn't that what they call it? Perhaps after you come back from death and see which card has been dealt you will reconsider your refusal."

I would have spat in her face, but my mouth was too dry and my tongue too swollen.

The gray haze started to turn black. I only had seconds left. I panicked. I would rather die and stay dead this time than let Isaac or Bethany take my place. I couldn't let them die like this. Not because of me.

"Let him go!" someone called out. Whoever it was, they sounded a thousand miles away.

A sudden shock wave knocked me back, knocked all of us off our feet. It was like a bomb had gone off right in the middle of us, but there was no explosion, no fire or smoke. And yet, something forceful had sent us reeling. I landed in a heap on top of Smiley. Freed from Underwood's choking grasp, I breathed in huge mouthfuls of air, my lungs aching and burning. My neck felt sore and bruised.

Beneath me, Smiley didn't move. The revenant's skull had broken open against a rock, damaging the brain enough that Reve Azrael couldn't control it anymore. Now it was just a harmless dead body.

Still dizzy from the shock wave's impact, I had trouble standing. I noticed Bethany and Isaac were having the same trouble, struggling to their feet and trying to shake it off. Unfortunately, the revenants were unaffected. Reve Azrael, Underwood, and the rest of them got back on their feet easily.

"The hell was that?" Isaac demanded.

Bethany pointed into the sky behind me. "Look!"

I turned. My jaw fell open.

Gabrielle flew through the air over Castle Clinton, moving toward us. Her leather coat flapped in the wind behind her. Her braided dreadlocks whipped in the air around her head like serpents. The air felt charged, electrified, and it was coming from her.

Hovering above us, she shouted, "Get out of my fiancé's body, you bitch!"

She brought her arms together in front of her. The ground exploded under Reve Azrael's feet, throwing her back several yards. She landed on her back, stunned. The other revenants froze as her connection to them was temporarily severed. I watched, astonished, as Gabrielle sent down another shock wave. The ground exploded again, hurling Reve Azrael through the air like a rag doll. When she crashed back to the ground, she didn't move. The other revenants crumpled in limp piles. Gabrielle swooped down and landed.

"Gabrielle, what . . . ?" I fumbled for the words. "How . . . ?"

She turned to me, her eyes hard and angry. "Philip was right. I was weak and Reve Azrael knew it. She exploited it time and again. But no more. Now I'm strong. Now I'm ready for her."

Isaac regarded her cautiously. "You're carrying magic inside you."

"You're damn right I am," she said. She opened and closed her hands into fists. "God, I've never felt so powerful. I feel like I could beat Philip in a fight now, if I wanted to. Where is he, anyway? I want to thank him for the good advice."

Isaac didn't answer. He just looked at her, half angry, half alarmed.

"Philip's on a mission," I said.

Gabrielle didn't ask for details. She didn't seem all that interested. She shrugged and said, "It's just as well. We don't need him. Not while I'm here. Not when I can do this." She looked down at the revenant at her feet, a heavyset, middle-aged, male corpse still in the dark blue suit he'd been buried in. All she did was point at him, and his skull shattered, crumbling inward as if a sledgehammer had pulverized it.

Isaac watched her with horror. "Do you know what you've done to yourself, Gabrielle? How dangerous this is? You *know* what magic does when it gets inside people. It infects them. You've *seen* it. It's what we've been fighting against this whole time."

"You're carrying magic and you're not infected," she said.

"I'm a mage."

"And I'm a woman with nothing left to lose," Gabrielle said. "If I get the infection, then that's the price I'll pay. If it means I get to put that bitch in the ground once and for all, it'll be worth it."

"Gabrielle—" Isaac started.

"Save it," she said. "You can either help me, or you can get out of the way."

She stalked over to Thornton's corpse on the wet grass. She bent over him to take the Codex fragment out of his hand. She didn't see his red-glowing eyes open. Reve Azrael had control of his body again. Before I could yell out a warning, Reve Azrael brought up the triangular fragment and drove its sharp, jagged point into Gabrielle's side. It slipped under her rib cage like a dagger blade. The side of her shirt blossomed red. Blood splashed from the wound onto her dead fiancé's chest, neck, and face, while Reve Azrael laughed and laughed.

I ran toward Gabrielle, but a revenant stepped in front of me and landed a cold, meaty right hook to my jaw. I fell on the wet grass and looked up. It was Underwood. He loomed over me, his knuckles raw where the brittle skin of his fist had connected with my face. I tried to get back up. He kicked me in the stomach, and I went down again. Behind Underwood, the other revenants swarmed Bethany and Isaac before they could help Gabrielle.

Reve Azrael grinned cruelly as she drove the sharp point of the Codex fragment deeper into Gabrielle's side. Gabrielle cried out and throttled Reve Azrael, but of course it did no good. You couldn't strangle a dead body. Her grip on Reve Azrael's neck slipped as she grew weaker.

"It is time you joined your beloved in death," Reve Azrael hissed. Gabrielle let out a soft moan and started to fall over. Reve Azrael yanked her back up and pulled her limp body close. "Know this, witch. After you die, I will wear your body like I wear his. I will make you do terrible things. To yourself. To those you loved. Perhaps I will start with your family."

Gabrielle spat blood in Reve Azrael's face. "You're sick."

"No," Reve Azrael replied. "I *win.*"

With that, she tore the fragment out of Gabrielle. Its bloody point trailed an arc of red through the air. Gabrielle fell onto her side, bleeding into the wet grass. She shivered and curled up in the rain, hugging her midsection, her knees at her chest.

"No!" Bethany yelled. She struggled furiously against the revenants holding her back.

Reve Azrael stood, clutching the Codex fragment at her side. The heavy rain washed Gabrielle's blood off the metal and into the dirt below. I got to my feet. This time, Underwood didn't stop me. Watching Gabrielle lie in the grass, bleeding, dying, a white-hot rage built inside me.

"You had your chance, little fly," Reve Azrael said. "The witch's death is on your head, not mine. All their deaths will be."

The revenants swarmed Bethany and Isaac until I couldn't see them through all the dead flesh. I ran toward them, but Underwood grabbed me. He lifted me off my feet with unnatural strength and threw me to the ground. I hit the hard-packed earth. Pain shot through my back. I rolled over and stumbled to my feet. Underwood landed a hard punch across my face. I fell again.

"Where you going, Trent?" Underwood asked. The rotten hole in his cheek gave his voice an airy sibilance. "I thought this might be a good chance for you and me to catch up. It'll be just like old times."

I knew it was Reve Azrael speaking through the corpse, trying to trip me up, trying to keep me off guard. It was working. Underwood kicked me again, his boot striking me in the face. I flipped over and fell in the rain-soaked grass.

"I'll start," he said. "Did you know that when I burned Tomo and Big Joe alive, Tomo screamed like a woman? But not Big Joe. He was a tough soldier to the end. I needed them both to die, but of course neither of them wanted to. Tomo screamed and screamed as the flames surrounded them, but Big Joe just stared at me. I could see the hatred in his eyes as I watched him die. So much for loyalty, huh?"

I tasted copper on my tongue and spat on the ground. My saliva was tinged with blood. I rose to my feet.

"It's so hard to find good help these days," I said.

Underwood's fist struck my face before I even saw it coming. For a dead man, he was quick. But then, that was the thing about revenants. They might be corpses, but they were fast and strong. The punch sent me reeling. I fell again.

I got back up, wobbly and off-balance. "You're lucky they took my gun."

"You should have remembered the Golden Rule," Underwood said. "Never, ever lose your gun. You never know when—"

I silenced him with a sucker punch to the face. His nose broke under the impact, the cartilage snapping like a twig. There was no blood, of course. Underwood's heart had stopped pumping a long time ago. But the force of the punch sent him staggering backward.

Damn, but that felt *good*. So good that I did it again, hitting him this time with a powerful haymaker that sent him reeling until he flopped back against a tree trunk. I punched him again. The rain had made his waxy skin slippery and loose. A patch of it sheared off under my knuckles. My fury numbed me to the pain as my fist scraped bone. Underwood's face was ruined. His nose was a flattened turnip. Several teeth were missing. More of his skull had been revealed beneath his skin. My knuckles were raw and bleeding. I didn't care.

Underwood laughed. His jaw hung crooked.

"What's so funny?" I demanded.

"That you think this changes anything," Underwood said. "That you think this matters."

"It does to me," I said. I hit him again. His cheek crumbled.

He laughed more. "I taught you well. You can take the criminal off the street, but you can't take the street out of the—"

I hit him again, silencing him. His face was starting to look like hamburger mixed with jam.

He grinned at me through the wreckage of his features. "Don't stop now. Embrace your true nature, little fly. Let it out!"

I punched him so hard his loose jaw came off. It hung on a strand of rotten flesh for a moment, and then the strand broke. The jawbone fell at his feet. Underwood's black, withered tongue waggled beneath his upper teeth.

I continued pounding my fists into him. Even as his body began to sag against the tree trunk, I kept whaling on him. Every punch was a weight removed from the load on my shoulders, a load Underwood himself had put there. Every punch brought back the face of the dead little boy in the crack house. Every punch was the punch I should have thrown when Underwood told me the boy's death didn't matter. I wondered why I had ever been afraid of this man.

Underwood's skull crumbled under my bleeding knuckles. After a while, I didn't even feel the resistance of bone anymore. It was like putting my fists into pudding.

Hands gripped my shoulder and pulled me away. Trembling with rage, my blood pounding hot in my ears, I spun around, ready to keep fighting. Then I saw it was Bethany and Isaac standing behind me. I lowered my fists.

"It's okay, Trent," Bethany said gently. "It's over."

The grass was littered with destroyed revenants, their heads broken and cracked like eggs. Apparently, Bethany and Isaac had been busy while I was fighting Underwood. Catching my breath, I scanned the bodies. One was missing. The most important one.

"Where's Reve Azrael?" I asked.

"She got away," Isaac said. "Are you all right?"

I looked down at Underwood's body slumped at the base of the tree. His face wasn't recognizable anymore. The blood from my knuckles ran in red streams down my fingers.

"Yeah," I said. "I'm good."

One of the revenants on the ground stirred, an elderly female corpse in a dirty, gingham dress. As she rose to her feet I saw the wound on her head was only superficial, not deep enough to sever Reve Azrael's connection. The revenant lurched forward, groping for Isaac.

"Look out!" I shouted.

Isaac spun around, his palms crackling. He didn't get a chance to cast his spell. Instead, the revenant burst apart in an explosion of dried meat, bone dust, and gingham. Behind it stood Gabrielle. She was hunched over, one hand clutching her wound. The entire right side of her shirt was slick with blood.

"Reve Azrael thinks she *wins*?" Gabrielle snarled. "No. Wrong again, bitch."

We ran over to her, but she motioned for us to stay back. She pulled her hand away from her side. Her palm was wet with blood. She spoke an incantation, and a bright, green light spilled out of the wound. She winced in pain as the light filled the wound, then disappeared. Gabrielle lifted the side of her shirt to let the rain wash the blood away. Beneath it, she was completely healed, as if she hadn't been stabbed at all. I blinked, amazed. I had never seen a healing spell like that before.

"That's twice Reve Azrael tried to kill me," Gabrielle said. "And twice she's failed."

Bethany put her hand on Gabrielle's arm. "Are you okay now? How did you . . . ?"

Gabrielle shrugged off Bethany's hand. Bethany backed away, confused.

"I'm fine," Gabrielle snapped. "But I'll be even better once Reve Azrael is dead."

"That makes two of us," I agreed.

Bethany and Isaac both shot me a look, but I didn't care. Maybe Gabrielle had gone off the rails, but she was right about this. It was time to put the rabid necromancer down. It was time to end this once and for all.

"Reve Azrael has the fragment," I said. "But she couldn't have gotten far, not yet. We can still find her."

Isaac nodded. "Agreed. Fan out, search the park."

We split up. I started down one of the long paths that ran parallel to the water. A hundred yards ahead of me, the path took a sharp turn onto an access road that ran north out of the park. A crowd rounded the corner of the access road and lumbered down the path toward me. They moved stiffly, and as they came closer I saw pale, discolored skin, dirty clothes, and bright red blood.

Shit. More revenants. I turned and ran back toward Castle Clinton. But it was too late. Revenants were flooding into the park everywhere. A small army of them proceeded down the central path past the battered bronze sphere. More came shambling down the winding side paths. There had to be a hundred of them, and they were all coming our way.

# Twenty-Four

The revenants poured into the park, blocking the paths as they converged on us. The few remaining park visitors who'd braved the rainstorm stopped what they were doing and watched the revenants go by with puzzled expressions. What was wrong with them? Why weren't they running? I looked around for Bethany, Isaac, and Gabrielle, but there was no time to regroup. I turned and bolted back the way I came, down the path toward the access road that led out of the park.

Unfortunately, that meant running right toward the revenants. They surged forward in a tide of dead, groping flesh. These revenants moved slowly—perhaps they weren't as fresh as the last batch—but there were a hell of a lot of them. I didn't see any way around them. I stopped and looked back quickly. The paths were filling up. The revenants ignored the gawkers in the park, lumbering past them, staying on target. And that target was us—or, more accurately, me. I was the one Reve Azrael wanted.

I ran toward the oncoming horde. Reve Azrael had taken my gun, but that didn't mean I was helpless. I still had my fists. I would bash in as many rotting skulls as I needed to. But as I ran into the crowd, the revenants didn't seem to take any notice of me. They marched right by me, moaning and growling like animals. I stopped, letting them file past. I'd never seen Reve Azrael's revenants act this way. None of them tried to subdue me. None of them spoke. I turned in circles, watching as they flowed around me and continued on. Where the hell were they going?

A short, male revenant walked past me, his hair a shaggy mop of unruly gray. I put a hand on the shoulder of his torn blazer and spun him toward me. His face was green and craggy, the lower half of it glistening red with blood. His eyes widened in surprise. I dropped my hand from his shoulder.

There was no red glow inside his pupils. This wasn't a revenant.

The dead man squinted against the rain, brought the straw of a Gray's Papaya cup to his lips, and took a sip. "Dude, where's your makeup?" he asked.

I frowned at him. "What?"

"Your makeup," he repeated. "Aren't you here for the zombie walk?"

"Zombie . . . walk?" I asked, confused. I looked around. Rotting, bloody-mouthed "zombies" talked on their cell phones. Some pushed baby strollers, with the babies inside made up to look like zombies as well. A zombie Santa Claus lumbered by with a bag full of rubber limbs and heads. Behind him staggered a zombie in a "sexy nurse" costume, her ample cleavage spattered with stage blood.

It was fake. It was all fake. How could I have been stupid enough to think these were revenants?

The man in front of me took another sip from his Gray's Papaya cup. I clearly saw now that it was just makeup on his face. It was starting to run a little in the rain.

"Um, it's a flash mob in honor of Halloween?" he said. I still didn't know what the hell he was talking about. He sighed in annoyance. "You should check out this new thing they call the Internet sometime."

He walked off, dragging one leg behind him in the way he assumed the living dead moved. If only he knew how wrong he was.

I started pushing my way through the zombie walk, but it was going to be next to impossible to find Reve Azrael in this crowd. Battery Park was twenty-five acres, the largest public open space in downtown Manhattan. That left a lot of places to hide and a lot of fake zombies to blend in with. And that was if she was even still here. For all I knew, she'd already left the park. If she had, we'd never find her. She could disappear down the side streets, vanish into the subway tunnels or sewer system and be untraceable.

I kept moving, trying to see past the zombie walkers or over their heads. Some of them were getting a little too into it, snarling at me, pawing at me, gnashing their teeth. From the corner of my eye I thought I saw a truly rotting face, its eyes burning with red light, but when I turned there were only more zombie walkers in makeup and costumes.

"They're out to get you," a voice rasped, close to my ear. "There's demons closing in on every side."

I spun around, ready to defend myself, but the voice only belonged to another zombie walker. This one was wearing a red-and-black leather jacket and matching red leather pants. He wasn't talking to me. He was singing, in what he thought was a suitably zombielike voice, Michael Jackson's "Thriller."

I had to get a grip. I would never find Reve Azrael if I kept letting myself get distracted by these idiots. I continued to wade against the tide of zombie walkers until I managed to break free of the crowd. I found myself in the open space of Battery Park's World War II memorial. Standing between the two rows of massive, granite pylons that stood like gravestones leading down the waterfront, I tried to gather my thoughts.

None of us knew where Reve Azrael had gone. None of us knew how many revenants she'd left behind. The zombie walk was a perfect distraction, slowing us down and breaking our focus. I was tempted to think she'd planned it this way, but Reve Azrael didn't give a damn about flash mobs or the Internet or any of that. She only wanted one thing. To turn every last New Yorker into a revenant and rule over a city of the dead.

So what did she want with the fragment? Summoning demons wasn't her style. Then again, Nahash-Dred, the Destroyer of Worlds, would certainly leave her a lot of dead bodies to play with.

Movement at the entrance to the World War II memorial caught my eye, where a huge bronze eagle stood atop a polished, black granite pedestal. I thought I saw someone duck behind it—a muscular, bald man, the right half of his face mushy like oatmeal. Had I seen glowing red eyes? Was he a revenant, or just another zombie walker? I didn't know, but my nerves had me on high alert. I moved toward the eagle, wishing I still had my gun. I turned the corner of the pedestal. No one was there.

More zombie walkers limped past, growling and pretending to grab at me. These damn fools were driving me crazy. If they didn't stop soon I was going to deck someone.

I kept moving through them like a salmon swimming upstream. Finally, I reached the access road. I continued up it until I exited the park. I was on State Street, a busy road that wrapped around Battery Park and became Water Street where it ran parallel to the East River. The last of the zombie walkers were filing into the park now, leaving amused pedestrians on the sidewalks laughing and murmuring to each other. Shielding my eyes from the rain, I looked up and down State Street but didn't see Reve Azrael. Damn. She could be anywhere by now.

My cell phone buzzed in my pocket. It was Isaac.

"Do you have her?" he asked.

"No," I said. "What about the others?"

"Nothing. This flash mob isn't making it any easier," he said. "I've got Gabrielle in the sky, searching from above, but so far she hasn't spotted Reve Azrael anywhere."

"She's probably long gone," I said.

My neck prickled. Someone was watching me. I turned around. The muscular, balding man stood behind me, his eyes glowing red in his half-oatmeal face. His fist connected with my chin in a powerful punch. I reeled backward, losing my grip on the phone. I heard Isaac call my name as it fell to the sidewalk. A van raced up on the street behind me. Its brakes squealed. The side door slid open before it came to a full stop, and the revenant pushed me inside. I landed flat on my back. There were others waiting in the van—bony, tattered shapes looming over me with glowing red eyes. The side and rear windows had been blocked off with cardboard. Oatmeal Face jumped into the van and slid the door closed, sealing me into the dark interior. The inside of the van reeked with the stench of rotting flesh. The engine revved, and we squealed away from the curb.

Cold, bony hands affixed a zip tie around my wrists. Another pair of hands grabbed my shoulders and hauled me into a sitting position against the wall. I counted five revenants with me in the van: one in the driver's seat, and four with me in the back, including Oatmeal Face. Their red eyes glowed eerily in the dim light.

"Where are you taking me?" I asked.

None of them answered. They just stared. She was watching me through them.

"Not feeling talkative anymore, Reve Azrael? That's a first."

The van took a corner fast and hard, the tires shrieking against the asphalt. I tipped over as we turned. A revenant missing his lower jaw reached over and pushed me upright again. The stretched, torn skin of his cheeks hung low over his neck, wobbling as the van jostled and bounced over the road.

"You might want to slow down," I called to the driver. She was the corpse of a young woman who had obviously been in some kind of accident. Most of the skin had been scraped from the front of her skull, leaving bits of shorn flesh stuck in her long, auburn hair. In the rearview, her wide, lidless eyes looked like marbles. "If the cops pull you over, you're going to have a hell of a time explaining why it looks like you fell face-first into a meat grinder."

Like the others, she ignored me. Fine. Reve Azrael was obviously toying with me. She wanted me to wonder where I was being taken, and what she had in store for me.

Isaac and the others would be wondering the same thing. By now, they would have figured out I'd been kidnapped. They would have found my phone on the sidewalk outside the park. It wouldn't be a lot to go on, but it would be enough to tell them I hadn't left voluntarily. They would try to find me, but they would almost certainly fail. They didn't know about the van, and judging by our high speed we were already far, far away. A bystander might have seen me get taken, might even have caught the license plate, but with the zombie walk distracting everyone it was doubtful. Once they realized they were running out of time, they would stop looking for me and focus on finding the last fragment of the Codex Goetia instead. It would be the right thing to do.

But it meant I was on my own.

The first thing I needed to do was figure out where I was. I got up on my knees and craned my neck to look out the windshield. Through the sheets of rain on the glass, I caught a glimpse of the East River on our right and the Brooklyn skyline beyond it. Then Oatmeal Face shoved me back down again. I'd seen enough to guess we were heading north on the FDR Drive, the highway that ran along the eastern edge of Manhattan. After a few minutes, the van took an exit and turned onto a side street. We drove a small distance farther, then turned into a structure of some kind. The natural light coming through the windshield was cut off instantly, as was the sound of the rain drumming on the roof. I was in complete darkness, with only the red glow of the revenants' eyes in the dark with me.

Then the van's headlights snapped on. Where were we? I tried to look out the windshield once again, being sure to stay seated this time so Oatmeal Face wouldn't get grabby with me again, but I couldn't see anything, just the twin headlights spearing out into the dark. It had to be a tunnel. I felt us descending as we drove, until we were several stories below the street. Then Eyeballs behind the wheel brought us to a stop and parked the van. The headlights went out. I was in pitch-blackness again.

I heard Eyeballs get out of the front and come around to open the side door from the outside. Oatmeal Face, Jawless, and the other revenants dragged me out of the van by the zip tie between my hands. The sharp plastic bit painfully into my wrists.

"All right, all right, I'm coming," I said. "Keep your faces on."

No reaction from any of them. Humor was wasted on the dead.

In the dark, all I could see were five pairs of glowing red eyes. There was no noise to tell me where I was. I smelled mud and rust and old, stagnant water. The revenants dragged me forward. I slid my feet along the ground instead of lifting them so I wouldn't trip over anything. The ground shifted under my feet like dirt. It wasn't wood or cement, then. That told me something about my surroundings, anyway, even if it wasn't enough to draw any conclusions from.

We had to be close to the FDR Drive. Maybe just a few blocks inland from it. But how far north had we come from Battery Park? Were we near the South Street Seaport, or had we gone farther? Stuyvesant Town? The United Nations Plaza? I tried to think of other landmarks, important buildings, anything that could be a clue to where I was, but I couldn't concentrate with the revenants yanking me along. Hell, for all I knew I was completely wrong and we were under a field in the Bronx somewhere.

I heard the sound of a door opening. A rectangle of light poured into the darkness around me. They led me through the door into a stone corridor. Eyeballs closed the door behind us again and drew a bolt across it. We were in a catacomb that looked old enough to have been built centuries ago. Thick cobwebs clung to the corners and hung from the ceiling in ghostly tendrils. Torches burned in sconces at intervals along the walls. It reminded me of the ancient, subterranean corridors leading to the Nethercity, and of the strange, sunken tower where the oracles had dwelt. Once again I got the sense that New York City had been built on top of some ancient civilization that had been abandoned and forgotten.

We descended a spiral staircase of cracked stone. At the bottom, the revenants led me through a doorway into another torchlit catacomb. I paused, startled to see dead bodies hanging all along the walls—male, female, old, young, clothed, naked, all of them suspended a couple of feet off the floor by ropes tied around their wrists. They looked like marionettes waiting to be picked up by their puppeteer. I didn't want to go anywhere near them, but the revenants pulled me forward. None of the suspended bodies moved or opened their eyes. I was grateful for that, at least.

We passed through corridor after corridor, each one lined with bodies in various states of decay. This place was a maze. I tried to remember the way we'd come, but I quickly lost track. Finally, we stopped before a rusted, iron door. Eyeballs opened it, and the others dragged me through.

Inside was a small room with an earthen floor and rough-hewn stone walls. There, waiting for me, was the same woman I remembered skulking about the fallout shelter. The woman I'd thought was Underwood's girlfriend. Now, of course, I knew better. This was Reve Azrael in her true body. She turned her thin face toward me, her eyes as dark as midnight, her long, unruly black hair falling across her face. The five revenants pulled me in front of her and held me there.

I didn't take my eyes off her. This was her lair, her turf. She had the advantage here. That made her more dangerous than ever.

She stared back at me silently.

"It's just like old times," I said. "You used to stare at me a lot back then, too. Never said much, though. At least, not with your *own* mouth."

Beside me, Oatmeal Face said, "I did what was necessary."

I looked at the revenant, momentarily confused. Then I turned back to Reve Azrael. "Oh, I get it. You can't talk, can you? You can only talk through the dead. No wonder you went crazy."

"It is true, I communicate only through my revenants," Oatmeal Face said. "It was the price I paid for my power, and I gave it willingly. What need have I of my own voice, when I can speak with the voice of hundreds? Thousands?"

"Like Underwood," I said. "Or whoever he was before you turned him into a revenant. Do you even remember his real name? Do you even remember who he was before he became part of your little charade?"

"His name is irrelevant. It is the name Underwood that has meaning. At one time, it was my own. But the other syndicates and the black market were all run by men. And like so many men, they preferred to deal only with other men. Underwood provided me with the face I needed to do business with them. He had other uses, too. When I needed a decoy, he played the role of Melanthius. And when I needed to keep you in line, little fly, his was the perfect face for that, too."

"I'm sorry to break it to you," I said, "but Underwood doesn't have a face anymore. In fact, he doesn't have much in the way of a head anymore."

"No matter. That body has served its purpose. I have no use for an Underwood now, or a Melanthius. The time for such games is over. The witch, Gabrielle, knows that. She knows it better than the rest of you. I almost respect her for it." Reve Azrael studied my face. "It surprises you that I am aware she is still alive. I would know if she had crossed through the dark, but she has not. There is so much anger burning inside her. Even through the cold, dead flesh of my revenants, I could feel it. It reached through them all the way here, to me. Her anger gives her strength, and her strength makes her a threat."

"What did you expect after you started playing dress-up in her dead fiancé's body, a bouquet of flowers and a thank-you card?"

Reve Azrael walked deeper into the room. My gaze fell on a small table by the wall. Resting on it, tantalizingly close, was my gun. If I weren't surrounded by revenants, and if my hands weren't tied, I could have snatched it up in a heartbeat. As it was, the damn thing might as well be a hundred miles away.

On the table next to the gun was the fragment she'd stolen from us.

"I would have thought all this squabbling over the Codex Goetia was beneath you," I said. "What do you want with it?"

"To tame the demon, of course. Should it prove necessary."

"You know about Nahash-Dred, then?"

"Of course. The dead are abuzz with portents of catastrophe. Erickson Arkwright's plan is a good one. To end all life on earth. I approve."

"You've been keeping tabs on him," I said.

"I have eyes and ears all over this city. No one is ever far from something dead. But there is a flaw in Arkwright's plan. He has not made room in it for *me*. My existence means nothing to him. He would just as soon have me among the dead, instead of commanding them. I find that unacceptable. And here, I believe, we find common ground in our disdain for Erickson Arkwright. Join me and we can stop him together. I with my army of revenants. You with your . . . abilities."

"And what happens after we stop him?" I asked.

"We will rule this world together. Arkwright has inspired me, little fly. Why stop with just a city of the dead? Why not a kingdom? Why not a planet?"

"I had a feeling that's what you were going to say," I replied. "You're insane. The answer is no. It will always be no."

Her thin face registered no emotion, not even disappointment. "It is a shame you refuse to use the power locked inside you for its true purpose. To use it the way I would. But I will not be denied my greatest weapon. And that is what you are. I do not need your consent. I merely thought it expedient to ask."

She stopped on the other side of the room, before a freestanding, stone arch. It measured five feet across and about nine feet from the dirt floor to its rounded top. Its stones were a dusty gray, all except for the keystone at the top, which sat red and polished as a ruby.

"Do you know what this is, little fly?"

"Mail-order Stonehenge?" I said.

"It is the Prometheus Arch, an artifact that dates back to the earliest days after the Shift. It was created by the elves in an attempt to cure the so-called *Infected*."

Elves. This wasn't the first time I'd heard of them. Bethany had mentioned them before, though she'd said no one had seen them in decades.

"They used the Prometheus Arch to remove the magic from inside one entity and transfer it to another, usually some unfortunate animal they would then be forced to put out of its misery. You see, they thought if the Prometheus Arch took your magic, it would take the infection from you as well. But they were wrong. They misunderstood. It is not a disease to be cured. It is a gift, the legacy of the Shift. Once it takes hold, it is irreversible."

"That's not true," I said. "The Black Knight beat it before he died. The infection *can* be reversed."

She shook her head, but it was Oatmeal Face who spoke, a disorienting double act. "You are wrong. The Shift has lasted a thousand years already, and no one has ever reversed its legacy. It may last a thousand more. Tell me, who will come out on top then? Those who embrace its gift, or those who fight against it?"

I held my tongue. There was no point in answering. She was insane, and I already knew you couldn't argue with crazy. I also knew what I had seen. The Black Knight *had* broken the infection's hold on his mind. At the end, he was sane again. He'd died a hero.

Reve Azrael ran one hand along the smooth, ancient stone of the Prometheus Arch. "The arch did not cure anyone. But it was soon discovered to work well in other, unforeseen ways. It could do more than transfer magic from one vessel to another. It could transfer *power*, too. The strength and speed of a vampire. The metamorphosis of a shape-shifter. The second sight of a seer. And so, as men have done throughout history, they turned the Prometheus Arch into a weapon. An instrument of torture and theft. After the second Great War swept through Europe and Asia, the elves finally had their fill of the atrocities of man. They took leave of our world. It was said they took the Prometheus Arch with them so it could no longer be misused. But that was a lie; the Prometheus Arch was merely lost. Until recently, it was in the Black Knight's possession. Did you know that? It was how he planned to steal Stryge's power for himself. And yours."

I hadn't seen the arch while the Black Knight kept me as his prisoner-slash–experimental guinea pig, but it answered a few of my lingering questions. After the Black Knight died and the gargoyles took off for greener pastures, their cavern in the Palisades cliffs had been left open and unguarded. It would have been easy enough for Reve Azrael to steal the arch.

"Fun history lesson, but you'd better cut to the chase," I said. "The others are looking for me. It's only a matter of time before they find this place. So either make your move or let me go."

Reve Azrael smiled. She knew I was bluffing. There was no way the others could track me here.

"You owe me for what you did, little fly. You robbed me of my chance to remake this city in my own image. The Prometheus Arch will rectify that. It will take the power locked deep within you and give it to me. I had planned to take your power from the Fetch, had it succeeded in its mission, but even then it would have merely been a facsimile, a copy of a copy. How much better to take it right from the source."

She was as obsessive and single-minded as ever, still hung up on wielding Stryge's power herself. Worse, she finally had the means to take it. I kept my poker face, trying not to look worried, but I doubted it was working. Stryge's power was dangerous. It had completely overwhelmed me. It had nearly driven me to kill Bethany, Isaac, Gabrielle, and Philip, and tear the world in half. Even now I could still feel it inside me, a low flame that burned just out of reach. If the Prometheus Arch really could siphon it out of me, that kind of power in Reve Azrael's hands would be unthinkable.

"Good luck getting Stryge's power out of me," I said, trying to sound confident. "It shouldn't even be inside me anymore, but it's holding on like it's got claws. It doesn't want to go anywhere."

She laughed. That wasn't the response I expected.

"You still do not understand. The power that sleeps inside you, the force that can unmake everything—it is not Stryge's. The Ancient's power merely awakened it, but it does not belong to him. The power is still inside you, little fly, because it is yours. It was *always* yours."

My poker face fell. I thought back to that day in Fort Tryon Park when the raw power had erupted inside me. It had shown me the inner workings of everything around me, and the threads that bound it all together. I had plucked one of those threads, just one, and the earth had quaked and broken open. That limitless, destructive power . . . was mine? It came from *me*?

The voices of the oracles echoed in my head again, too insistent to ignore: *It is a threat. It is a danger to all who live.* But they were wrong. That wasn't who I was. The power wasn't mine, it couldn't be. *A menace. An abomination. As long as it walks upon this world, it puts us all in peril.* I refused to believe that. It was a lie. Reve Azrael and the oracles were in on it together. I was human. I was Lucas West, damn it.

I shook my head vehemently. "No, you're lying."

I struggled to break free of the revenants holding me. I didn't care if my hands were tied. I would beat her head to a pulp, make it a matching pair with Underwood's.

From behind me, Eyeballs dug her hard, bony fingers into the tender flesh between my neck and shoulders. I cried out in pain as she forced me to my knees.

"You still do not know who you are. *What* you are."

I looked up at Reve Azrael, gritting my teeth as Eyeballs continued digging her claws painfully into me. "My name is Lucas West. I'm human. Something happened to me beneath Battery Park. Something changed me, but I'm human!"

"Oh, it changed you, little fly. Just not the way you think."

The revenants pulled me to my feet and dragged me toward the arch. I resisted, digging my boots into the earthen floor. But it was five against one. While the others held me tight, Oatmeal Face cut the zip tie from my wrists. I struggled to get away, but I was surrounded and outnumbered. There was no place to go. Eyeballs took one wrist, and Jawless took the other. Together, they pulled me toward a pillar of the arch, where two empty holes waited. I tried to pull away.

"You're making a big mistake," I said. "You don't know what happens when I come in contact with magic. It goes crazy!"

Ignoring me, the revenants plunged my hands into the holes. Inside, the stone seemed to tighten around my wrists like the coils of a python. I shook and shouted and yanked my arms, trying to break free. A cold, dead hand on the back of my neck warned me to stop.

"Try not to resist. The Prometheus Arch is known for many things, but gentleness is not one of them."

Reve Azrael put her own hands into two holes in the opposite pillar. She spoke through Oatmeal Face again, intoning a spell. The red keystone at the top began to throb slowly with a soft glow.

I gasped in pain. It felt like someone had stuck me in a food processor and hit puree. I closed my eyes and gritted my teeth, trying to endure it, but the pain kept building in intensity. So did the light from the keystone. I could see it through the thin skin of my eyelids, throbbing brighter, faster.

"Can you feel it pulling the power out of you? Pulling the wings off my little fly?"

"Go to hell!" I shouted back. Tears squeezed out from between my clenched eyelids.

"Once your power is mine, I will be the queen of this wretched city. I will command the dust and bone left behind."

"You're insane," I said.

"No. Merely determined."

The pain increased, a thousand serrated knives hollowing me out. I felt feverish, burning from the inside. Sweat dripped down my face. Moisture coated my body, sticking my clothes to my skin. I didn't know how much longer I could hang on. If the Prometheus Arch killed me, would the thing inside me steal Reve Azrael's life force before the transfer was complete? Or would Reve Azrael take *that* power from me, too? Was it all connected somehow?

The thing inside me—the thing that wouldn't let me die, the thing that had made my life a living hell—oh God, had that been my own from the start, too?

The pain held my entire body in its searing grip. Through my eyelids, I could see the keystone throbbing so quickly now it gave off a consistent, unbroken light.

I opened my eyes. Everything looked different.

Reve Azrael was a dark silhouette filled with tiny black suns, diseased and corrupted by the infection. The revenants were dark silhouettes, too, but what filled them was hard and cold, like dead moons hanging in space. Inside the Prometheus Arch, atoms flashed and sparked and pinwheeled as it drained the power from me. I was too weak to do anything but watch.

"I can see it," Reve Azrael said, awed. "The structure of the universe. The building blocks of life and death. I can bring it all crashing down!"

Thousands of silken threads filled the room, tying everything together. I tried to reach them with my mind, pluck them or cut them, but I was too weak.

And then I saw him, sitting in the corner of the room. A wolf. He didn't appear as atoms and threads. He was something else, something bright and translucent. The wolf stared at me, panting with his long tongue hanging out of his mouth.

*You're being followed, too. . . . It's not a person. It's a wolf.*

"Thornton?" I said.

I could have sworn the wolf smiled.

# Twenty-Five

I knew what dying felt like. Over the past year, I had done it twelve times already. That was how I knew the Prometheus Arch was killing me. I recognized the sensation. My knees buckled under me, too weak to support my weight anymore. I slid down the pillar, my hands still stuck inside the holes, until I was on my knees with my arms over my head. My breath came in shallow bursts. My chest hurt, as if my heart were being squeezed by a massive fist. I'd been shot more times than I could count, had my throat slashed, been stabbed, but this was the worst death of all. I was being hollowed out, the power ripped out of me. My body shuddered and convulsed like I was holding a live wire. My thirteenth death. Unlucky thirteen. Maybe, like a video game character, I'd used up all my extra lives. Maybe this time it would stick.

Was that why Thornton was here? To be my guide to the afterlife and take me across the dark to the plains of mist and seas of ash? It wasn't fair. I knew where my parents were now, but I hadn't had the chance to see them. I knew my name, finally, but hadn't had the chance to learn about myself. I hadn't had the chance to say goodbye to . . . to . . .

It was Bethany who came into my mind then, not Jordana. As I wondered why, the pain ripped even that thought away.

But there was something strange about me and magic. It went haywire around me. I didn't know why. When I touched a broken artifact or charm, it suddenly worked. When I touched a working one, it overloaded. The Prometheus Arch was clearly working. I wasn't surprised when it began to shake and groan. Cracks tore through the stone, erupting in showers of sparks. The pain stopped. My vision shifted back to normal. I struggled to my feet, my strength slowly returning.

"I warned you this would happen," I said.

The overload built and built inside the arch like a head of steam. The keystone at the top of the arch exploded, sending a huge fireball into the room. The fire caught on the revenants' clothes. The old, dry cloth went up in flames. So did the revenants. The desiccated corpses flared like kindling.

The stone around my wrists loosened, releasing me. I fell back from the arch. I was still weak, but I got back on my feet quickly. I looked to the corner of the room, but I didn't see Thornton. Had he really been here, or had I hallucinated from the pain?

I had to find a way out of the room, but it was filled with stumbling, lurching, human-sized bonfires. The revenants were just dead bodies, they couldn't actually feel the fire, and yet they were all screaming. When I turned back to the Prometheus Arch, I saw why. Reve Azrael's hands were still stuck inside the holes. She hadn't been released. The fire surrounded her, catching on her clothes, her hair. I watched in horror as she struggled inside a blanket of flames.

I forced myself to move. I had to get out before the fire found me, too. I ran for the door, weaving around the screaming, flailing revenants that burned all around me. Eyeballs, the van driver, appeared before me. The fire had already taken her hair. Her skull-face screamed with Reve Azrael's agony. I kicked her out of the way. She crumpled like burning leaves. I ran to the small table and scooped up the Codex fragment. The metal was already warm from the fire. I took my gun back, too, stuffing it in the holster at the small of my back.

Four shrieking, burning revenants stumbled toward me. I couldn't tell one from another anymore, couldn't tell which one was Oatmeal Face or Jawless. Their features were completely burned away. I darted past them, grabbed the hot handle of the iron door, and pulled it open. Reve Azrael's agonized screams followed me as I ran out of the room and into the stone corridor outside. I looked up and down the torchlit hallway, trying to get my bearings. I knew there was an empty van parked nearby, but I couldn't remember which direction led back to it. Every part of these damn catacombs looked the same to me. If I took a wrong turn, I might never find my way out.

The ghost wolf came loping toward me. My vision was back to normal, but I could still see him somehow. His body glowed as bright as a ray of sunlight. He stopped halfway down the corridor and looked at me, his tongue lolling from his open mouth.

"Calliope was right," I said. "You *are* following me."

Thornton turned and sprang back the way he'd come. He stopped, looked back at me, then ran again. He wanted me to follow.

I ran after him. He disappeared around a corner. I turned the corner a few seconds later and caught a glimpse of his shining haunches already turning the next corner up ahead. He was way ahead of me. All along the walls, the suspended corpses thrashed and screamed with Reve Azrael's pain. I moved past them carefully, avoiding their kicking legs. Their eyes were open now, the red light spearing out of their pupils. Could Reve Azrael see me through them, or was she too lost in the pain? I hurried past, following Thornton around the next corner. I saw him in the distance again, turning yet another corner up ahead.

"Damn it, slow down," I called, but Thornton was already out of sight.

This corridor, too, was lined with dead bodies that thrashed and screamed. One of the ropes snapped as I passed, dropping a revenant on top of me. She was a woman with nut-brown skin, black hair, and a blue sundress. She couldn't have been older than her mid-twenties when she died. The three bullet holes in her chest explained what had happened to her, while the sundress and the stiffness of her limbs told me she'd been dead since the summer. She continued thrashing on top of me, clubbing me with her arms as bits of brittle, rotting skin sloughed off her bones. Her glowing red eyes looked right at me, but I couldn't tell if there was any consciousness behind them. She just screamed and screamed.

I managed to push the shrieking revenant away and scramble out from under her. I ran. I heard her moving behind me, but I didn't waste time turning to see if she was following me or just continuing her spastic dance of agony. Thornton came bounding back down the corridor toward me. I tried to slow down and duck out of his path, but he was too fast. Thornton leapt—

And passed through me.

I felt a chill, like a sudden, cutting wind, and then I was someplace else. A room with walls shrouded in black velvet curtains. A circular table stood in the center of the room, also draped in black velvet. A crystal ball on a wooden stand sat in the middle of the table. I knew this place. It was the downstairs parlor of Calliope's row house. Calliope herself was sitting at the table, her face slack and her eyes vacant, as if she were in a trance. She was holding a pen, her hand scribbling of its own accord in a notebook open on the table in front of her. Thornton, translucent and brightly glowing, sat beside her in his human form and whispered frantically in her ear.

And then I was back in the corridor, still running. What the hell . . . ? I shook my head clear, trying to focus on my surroundings. Behind me, I heard noises from Thornton and the revenant that I didn't want to think about. I didn't know what a ghost wolf could do to a magically reanimated dead body. I didn't *want* to know.

A moment later, Thornton came bounding past me and around the corner up ahead. Following him, I found myself in another corridor, only this time there were no revenants suspended along the walls. The walls had changed from stone to metal. Pipes traced the length of the corridor along the ceiling. The floor was wet with shallow water that splashed under the soles of my boots. This was most certainly not the way back to the van.

"Where are we going?" I called after Thornton. Of course he couldn't answer. That would have been too easy, and apparently nothing in my life was ever allowed to be easy. I could only assume he was leading me toward an exit. What choice did I have? I kept following him.

We raced down more metal hallways, each grading slightly upward toward ground level. At least we were headed in the right direction. Finally, I saw Thornton pass, immaterial, through a windowless steel door. When I reached it, I pulled it open and stepped out into a well-lit, generically institutional corridor of fluorescent lights, white walls, and a neutral, gray, tiled floor. I looked up and down the hallway and saw several other windowless steel doors like the one I'd come through. I caught a glimpse of Thornton rounding another corner and hurried after him.

The wolf jumped straight through an emergency exit door like it wasn't even there. I hit the crash bar and shoved the door open, exiting into a parking lot by the side of a building. The rain battered my head. A sudden, high-pitched shriek made me cover my ears. Damn. Opening the emergency exit had set off an alarm. As the door closed on its hydraulic hinge, I saw an official seal affixed to it that read OFFICE OF THE CHIEF MEDICAL EXAMINER—THE CITY OF NEW YORK.

The city morgue. Of course. The perfect hiding place for Reve Azrael. With her lair right below, she would have access to unlimited bodies to turn into revenants—the bodies of crime and accident victims, prison inmates, and most importantly, the John Does, those unclaimed bodies that wouldn't necessarily be missed if they disappeared. All those bodies suspended in the catacombs below—how long had she been harvesting from this place? How many had she taken?

I glanced around the parking lot but didn't see Thornton. Was he gone again? I couldn't hang around to find out. This was an official government building; the alarm would bring someone soon. I tucked the fragment into the interior pocket of my trench coat and ran for the parking lot exit. When I was out, I kept running until I reached the corner. Then I stopped and got my bearings. I was on Thirtieth Street and First Avenue, right next to the NYU Medical Center.

Part of me knew I should find a pay phone, call Isaac, and let him know I was okay. But there was something I needed to do first, something that felt a hell of a lot more pressing. I started walking toward the subway. If Thornton was still following me, he didn't show himself.


In the reception area of Gamma Solutions, LLC, the Bay Ridge Harpy stood up indignantly from behind the reception desk. "Hey, you can't just go in there! There's protocol!" she shouted, pronouncing it *prota-cawl*.

I didn't stop. I didn't say anything. I hadn't since I stepped off the elevator. I just walked through the reception area and into the hallway. I knew the way. Three doors down on the left. I reached the door beside the plaque that read *Jordana Pike, Systems Analyst,* and opened it.

Jordana was sitting at her desk, one finger on the speaker button of her phone. She looked up at me as I stormed into her office. The receptionist's voice was coming through the speakerphone: ". . . barged right through like an asshole!" *Ayass-howall.*

"Sorry about that. Everything's okay. There's no need to call security," Jordana replied, then released the button. She looked at my wet, blood-stained clothes and the bruises and dried blood on my face. "Oh my God, what happened to you, Lucas? Are you all right?"

I closed the door behind me. She got up out of her chair and tried to put her arms around me. I backed away from her.

"Is my name really Lucas West?" I said.

She froze. She looked confused and hurt, and for a moment my heart broke that I was the one who'd put such a pained expression on her face. I forced the feeling away. I couldn't trust my feelings right now. I couldn't trust anything.

"I don't understand. What's going on?" Jordana asked.

"I want the truth," I said. "How can I be a normal guy from Pennsylvania when there's this—this *thing* inside me—"

"Lucas, stop." She stepped closer and put her hands on my chest. Her touch instantly calmed me. "Tell me what happened. Did you find another fragment?"

"Jordana, please, I have to know," I insisted. "What am I? Where does this power come from? Is it—is it mine?"

"I told you, you're Lucas West," she said.

She gripped the lapels of my trench coat, pulled herself up onto her toes, and kissed me. The moment our lips touched all my questions evaporated, as ephemeral as steam. Jordana pulled away and touched a cool, comforting hand to my face.

"I've been looking for you for years, Lucas, and now that I've finally found you, I'm not letting you slip away from me again."

I pulled her to me, crushing her so tightly I thought she might break. We kissed again, fiercely, and the next thing I knew we were in the small, cramped supply room around the corner from her office. My fingers worked the buttons of her blouse. I kissed her neck while she gasped and tangled her fingers in my hair. I didn't want to think about the destructive power locked inside me. I didn't want to think about Reve Azrael or Nahash-Dred or Erickson Arkwright or the end of the world. Let the world take care of itself for once—or let it burn if it had to, I didn't care. I just wanted to be normal, even if only for a moment. I wanted to not care about anything. I wanted to be human.

# Twenty-Six

When the fire inside us had burned itself out, we lay on my trench coat spread open on the bare supply room floor. I held Jordana for a while. She rested her head on my chest. My fingers traced lazy lines up and down her back through the thin material of her blouse.

"Tell me more about your brother," I said.

She looked up at me. "Pete?"

"It sounds like he was my closest friend," I said. My closest friend until I disappeared on him, anyway. Until I disappeared on them both. I wished I knew why.

Something passed through her eyes. I could feel her pulling away, as if a wall had come down between us. "I don't want to talk about Pete right now," she said, her voice hitching with emotion. She put her head on my chest again. "I—I can't."

"It's okay," I said apologetically. Clearly, I needed to work on my pillow talk. I didn't mean to touch a nerve. She was still mourning Pete's loss, and her mother's, too. The world had taken a lot from Jordana. She'd told me how much family meant to her. To suddenly be without her brother and mother, to lose everyone but the stepfather she barely got along with, I couldn't even imagine that.

She put a hand on my chest, still not looking at me. "I have nightmares every night, but in the morning I don't remember them. I'm just left with this strange feeling that it had something to do with Pete and my mother. Like they want to tell me something important, but when I try to remember, it's gone."

I stroked her hair. The gesture felt feeble, but I didn't know how else to comfort her.

"Do you ever—do you ever feel like you're not in control sometimes?" she asked. "Like you're falling toward something and can't stop?" She stiffened almost imperceptibly, but I felt it through her body. She looked up at me, her eyes guarded. "I—I shouldn't have said that. I don't know why I did."

"It's okay," I said. "I want to know things about you. I want to know everything about you."

She smiled, but there was something missing. I felt like I was looking at a completely different person now. She rolled away from me, putting her back against me. She looked at the pointed edge of the Codex fragment peeking out from my coat's interior pocket.

"Is that the fragment?" she asked.

"Yeah. It was in Battery Park, just like we thought. Arkwright didn't get it from us this time, but he sure as hell tried."

I didn't mention what else we'd found there, the underground complex and the brick wall with the Ehrlendarr rune from my first memory. I didn't want to scare her. I also didn't know what to make of it yet. What was that place? What had happened to me there? What had brought Lucas West, just a normal guy from Pennsylvania, to a place like that?

The doubts crept back into my mind on the tail of a headache. How could I be Lucas West if what Reve Azrael said about me was true? If that terrible power was mine all along? She had to be lying, that was all. Lying was what Reve Azrael did. Time and again, she had tricked me, manipulated me for her own reasons. What she'd said was impossible. Lucas West made sense. The rest of it didn't.

And yet, hadn't the oracles said Reve Azrael knew the truth about me?

*Seek out the Mistress of the Dead. She knows. She knows all who have passed through the dark that separates the cities of the living from the cities of the dead.*

"Jordana," I said slowly. "There's something I need to know—"

"Can I see it?" she interrupted, still looking at the fragment. "I've read all about the Codex Goetia, but I've never seen the real thing."

"Wait," I said. "First, tell me something. Tell me how Lucas—"

Jordana rolled to face me again. She kissed me, and whatever I was going to ask her melted away faster than ice in a New York City August. My headache disappeared, too.

"Please can I see the fragment?" she asked.

I nodded. She took the triangular slab of metal out of my coat and stood up. She smoothed her skirt over her stockinged legs, then crossed the room to sit on a stack of copy paper cartons. She studied the fragment, turning it in her hands, admiring its details. Her blouse was still unbuttoned, revealing the dark red bra against her olive skin. I had trouble keeping my eyes on the fragment.

"It's amazing," she said. "It's everything I thought it would be. The craftsmanship is remarkable. Some demonologists say the Codex Goetia dates back to 900 B.C., but others say it's even older. Some claim it's not actually from Tulemkust, that it's not even from our world. Whoever broke an artifact this old and this beautiful should be in jail, or worse." She placed her hand flat against the fragment. "The metal looks like copper or brass, but it's not, it's something else. There's almost a subtle vibration to it."

While she inspected the fragment, I managed to take my eyes off her and sit up. I glanced at the supply room door. We'd locked it from the inside so no one would find us, but now that the fragment was out in the open I was getting nervous. It was only a matter of time before someone came looking for a legal pad or a fresh pen or whatever it was office workers came to supply rooms for. It would be awkward enough to explain what we were doing in here half-naked without also having to explain why we had a priceless, antique artifact with us.

Jordana studied the lettering on the fragment's face. "None of these are Nahash-Dred's name. It must be on one of the other fragments. How close are you to putting the Codex back together?"

"Not as close as I'd like," I said. "Arkwright still has the fragment he stole from us, and there's one more fragment still hidden somewhere out there. Isaac and the others are probably already trying to find it."

"Lucas, you *have* to bring me all three pieces," she said. "I told you, the Codex Goetia won't work unless it's whole. There's no other way to banish Nahash-Dred back to his dimension."

"I'm sure Isaac's got a handle on it. I just . . ." I paused, sighing. When I spoke again, it all came spilling out of me. "I just want to be normal. I want to forget about it all, the demons, the supernatural conspiracies, the infection. I don't want this life anymore. I want to be Lucas West again. I want to go see my parents. I want to be with you and live a regular life."

"You can do that," she said. "You can have that life again—*we* can have that life—but you need to bring me the fragments first."

The headache slipped back behind my eyes. I rubbed my forehead. Something wasn't right. It felt like my thoughts were trying to force themselves through a solid wall.

"Isaac can do it without me," I managed to say.

"No, he can't. None of them can. They're not like you. You're stronger than they are. You're the Immortal Storm."

I groaned, the pain in my head growing sharper. The Immortal Storm. I hated that name. Hated everything that came with it.

"Without the Codex Goetia, there won't be anything left for you to go back to, Lucas," Jordana said. "Nahash-Dred is no joke. They call him the Destroyer of Worlds for a reason. He will annihilate all life on earth if we don't use the Codex to banish him."

She was right, there would be no life to go back to if Arkwright unleashed Nahash-Dred on the world. If I wanted to reclaim my life, all I had to do was save the world first. No pressure.

"You're going to have to find the other fragments, and fast," Jordana said. "In the meantime, I'll hold onto this one. I can study it while you look for the others. Maybe I'll find something that can help."

I stood and took the fragment out of her hands. "No, it's safer if I hold onto it."

"Let me keep it for now," she insisted. "Please. I can study it. I've *been* studying it, but only in books. This may be my only chance with the real thing."

I picked up my trench coat and slid the fragment back inside the interior pocket. "I can't. It's too dangerous. Arkwright is out there right now looking for it. I don't want to put you in his crosshairs. Remember what I said before about not taking your usual route home tonight."

"Stop worrying, I'll be fine," she said.

"He's dangerous, Jordana. He wants to destroy the world. You can't reason with someone like that. He's got nothing to lose. Arkwright has already killed people to get this far. He won't hesitate to kill more if he has to. Please, just for now, just until this is over, start taking different routes home. Do it for me."

"Okay, okay, I'll be careful, I promise. Just please let me keep the fragment."

She walked into my arms and kissed me. Her body pressed against mine, so soft and warm. For a moment, I lost myself in the sensation. I wondered if I was overreacting. Jordana was a demonologist, after all. She was the only one who knew how to use the Codex. Letting her study it couldn't hurt, could it? There might be some hidden clue, some other way to banish or defeat Nahash-Dred we didn't know about. Maybe I *should* let her keep it. Why had I thought it wasn't a good idea? I couldn't even remember. I started to reach into my trench coat again to pull out the fragment.

A man's voice came from the hallway outside, calling Jordana's name. Damn. Someone was looking for her. I'd forgotten her office was right around the corner.

Jordana broke away. I came to my senses and left the fragment in my pocket.

"Damn it, not *now*," she hissed under her breath. She started buttoning her blouse quickly. She looked angry enough to kill her coworker for interrupting us. I almost felt sorry for the poor guy, except I kind of wanted to kill him, too.

"I'd better go before they find us in here," I said, straightening my disheveled clothes. I pulled on the trench coat. "I'll get a new phone from Isaac. Call me when you're home. I want to know you're safe."

"Just go," she said. She sounded angry, but I didn't know if she was angry at her coworker or at me for not letting her keep the fragment.

I opened the door quietly and peeked out. The hallway was empty, but I heard footsteps coming my way from the direction of Jordana's office. I ducked down the hall in the opposite direction. I took the long way around the office, eventually finding my way back to the reception area. The Bay Ridge Harpy glared at me from behind the desk, snapping her gum like she was cocking a revolver.

I rang for the elevator, stepped inside, and pressed the lobby button. It didn't sink in until I was halfway down how close I'd come to giving Jordana the fragment, despite my better judgment. I'd lost myself somehow. It wasn't the first time, either. I'd felt it in her office, too, when all the questions I'd meant to ask her died on my tongue. I'd felt it since the first time we met.

Why did I never feel in control around her?

When I got back to Citadel, I found Isaac, Bethany, and Gabrielle seated around the big table. Calliope's notebook and Isaac's laptop sat on the table between them. When they saw me, they got up and came over.

"My God, man, are you all right?" Isaac asked, sounding relieved. "What happened?"

"I had a run-in with Reve Azrael and her revenants, but I'm fine," I said. "I got the fragment back." I took it out of my pocket and put it on the table. "She knows about the demon. She knows about Arkwright. She knows about all of it."

"Does she know the name Arkwright is using now, or where the demon is?" Isaac asked.

"I don't know. She was definitely holding something back. She knows more than she's saying. But one thing's for certain, she doesn't like Arkwright any more than we do. She offered an alliance, but it came with the usual caveat: rule over a city of the dead by her side. I told her no."

"I'm guessing she didn't take that well," Bethany said.

"About as well as I expected," I said. I filled them in on the rest of it— Reve Azrael's lair under the city morgue, the Prometheus Arch, and the fire. I didn't tell them what Reve Azrael had said about the power being mine, not Stryge's. I still didn't know if that was true or just a ruse.

"We tried to find you," Bethany said apologetically, "but the trail went cold at the FDR Drive. All we found was this. It still works." She took my cell phone out of her pocket and handed it to me.

I felt like I was seeing a long-lost friend again. "Thanks."

"You're sure you're okay?" Bethany asked.

"Yeah, I'm fine."

Gabrielle snickered. "I bet you are, Casanova."

Surprised, I raised my eyebrows. "What?"

Bethany glared at Gabrielle. Then she turned back to me and said, "You've got lipstick on your neck." She pulled a white cloth handkerchief from her pocket and passed it to me.

Embarrassed, I rubbed my neck with it. The handkerchief came away with a smear of red. Damn. I must have looked like a fool sauntering in here like that. I stuffed the handkerchief in my pocket. I was pretty sure Bethany wouldn't want it back.

"After I got away from Reve Azrael, I went to see Jordana," I admitted.

"No kidding," Gabrielle said, still grinning.

"Why?" Isaac asked. "Why didn't you come back right away?"

"I had questions that needed answers," I said.

"Did you get them?" Bethany asked.

"Not exactly," I said. I thought again about how I seemed to lose my will around Jordana.

"All I want to know," Gabrielle said, "is whether that bitch Reve Azrael is finally dead."

"I wish I knew," I said. "She could be. It was a hell of a fire. Revenants make damn good kindling."

Gabrielle steeled herself before asking her next question. "What about Thornton's body? Did it—did it burn, too?"

"I don't know. I didn't see his body anywhere," I said. "But there's something I need to tell you. Something important." She looked at me, curious, waiting. They all did. I took a deep breath, hoping they wouldn't think I'd lost my mind. "I didn't see Thornton's body, but . . . I saw Thornton."

Gabrielle knit her brow in confusion. "What do you mean?"

"He was there," I said. "His ghost, or spirit, or whatever you want to call it. It was him, in wolf form. He led me out of the catacombs to safety. There's no way I would have gotten out of there without his help. Trust me, I know how this sounds, but—"

Gabrielle cut me off with a chuckle. She wiped a hand under one eye, smearing a tear against her cheek.

"He's okay," she said, relieved. "Even dead and gone, he's okay. I knew that, or I hoped it was true, but to have proof . . ." She broke down, covering her face with her hands.

"Calliope tried to tell me Thornton's spirit was following me, but I didn't believe her," I said. "I'm sorry I didn't mention it to you. But after this, I thought you'd want to know."

"Hell yes, I want to know," Gabrielle said, laughing and crying at the same time. "I'm such a fool. Things have been turning up around my apartment for weeks now, things that were important to both of us. I thought I was losing my mind." She pushed up her sleeve and looked at the brown leather bracelet around her wrist. "He's been with me all this time, and I didn't even know it. But what is he doing here? Why isn't he on the other side?"

"I don't know," I said. "But there's something else. I don't know how to explain it. At one point, Thornton passed through me and I—I saw something. It was like I was somewhere else for a moment. I saw Calliope and Thornton. She was in a trance. He was whispering things to her, and she was writing them down in the notebook." I turned to Isaac. "We know Calliope could talk to the dead. We know it was the spirits who warned her about Arkwright's plan. But we never stopped to ask who those spirits were. I . . . I think it was Thornton. I think Thornton is the one who warned her. I think he's the one who set all this in motion."

The others didn't speak. They stood around the table in stunned silence for a moment.

Finally, Gabrielle said, "I don't see why you're all so surprised. It sounds just like him. Still trying to save the world, even after he's dead."

"Thornton," Bethany said, shaking her head. "Even now, he keeps surprising me."

"Join the club, hon," Gabrielle said. "Now you know why I wanted to marry the man."

Erickson Arkwright had a fragment of the Codex Goetia. So did we. That left one last fragment to be found. It turned out Isaac, Bethany, and Gabrielle had been hard at work trying to find it while I was gone. On the whiteboard, they had crossed off all the clues we already deciphered. Only two were left.

~~Three hidden pieces~~
~~Eternal voice and inward word~~
~~Erickson Arkwright~~
~~Mariner lost at sea~~

~~Beneath the monuments~~
Look to the Trefoil
The Angel of the Waters
~~Codex Goetia~~

"Who is the Angel of the Waters?" I asked. "Is it a person, or another monument?"

"We figured that one out while you were with Jordana getting your, um, questions answered," Gabrielle said, suppressing a chuckle.

"The Angel of the Waters is a reference to the Gospel of John, in which an angel blesses the Pool of Bethesda and gives it healing powers," Isaac said.

He opened his laptop and turned it to face me. On the screen was a photograph of a tall, two-tiered, bronze fountain that stood at the center of a wide, circular pool of water. At the top of the fountain was the statue of a winged woman. An angel. The fountain looked familiar to me, though I couldn't place it.

"The Angel of the Waters is also another name for the statue on top of Bethesda Fountain in Central Park," he said.

Of course. Now I recognized it. You could see Bethesda Fountain from the highest windows in Citadel, especially now that it was autumn and the trees had shed their leaves.

"So the fountain is the third monument," I said. I looked at the whiteboard again. "What about the last clue? *Look to the Trefoil.* What does that mean?"

"We don't know yet," Isaac said. "We haven't had any luck figuring it out."

"What's a trefoil, anyway?" I asked.

"A plant with three leaves, like a clover," Bethany said with a shrug. "But for some reason Calliope capitalized the word every time she wrote it, as if it were a name. We don't know why, or what it has to do with the Codex."

"Maybe it doesn't," I said. "Now that we know where the third fragment is, maybe this trefoil thing doesn't matter."

"I doubt that," she said. "Everything Calliope wrote down has mattered so far."

Isaac closed his laptop. "We were about to head out to the fountain when you showed up."

"Before we go, we need a plan in case Arkwright shows up again," I said. "He has a nasty habit of being one step ahead of us."

"If he shows up, we'll deal with him," Gabrielle said.

"He's got the Thracian Gauntlet," I reminded her. "That thing can kill from a hundred feet away. Even with a mage on our side, Arkwright still has the advantage."

"Two mages," Gabrielle corrected me. "I'm every bit as powerful as Isaac now. Let Arkwright try to come at us. I'll make him wish he'd died with the rest of his doomsday cult buddies."

Isaac's face clouded. "You may be powerful, Gabrielle, but you're no mage. You're still at risk of being infected."

"So are you," Gabrielle pointed out. "I know you mages pride yourself on supposedly being immune, but there have been plenty of mages who have turned."

"That's different," he said. "It takes decades of study and experience to be able to carry magic inside you safely. There are no shortcuts, Gabrielle."

Gabrielle sighed, exasperated. "I've got a handle on it. Now, are we going to keep talking about this, or are we going to find the last fragment before Arkwright does?"

Isaac crossed his arms and glared at her. Even if the conversation was over for now, it was clear he wasn't finished talking about this.

"Arkwright is faster than any of us," I said. "He's got a long-range weapon he doesn't have to come out of the shadows to use. We'll be sitting ducks. I'd feel better if we had Philip with us."

Those were words I never thought I'd say. Especially after learning what he'd done in his past. I still didn't know how I felt about him. Philip was dangerous and unstable at the best of times, but his strength and speed were a huge advantage. He could see body heat in the dark, and we already knew he could survive a direct blast from the Thracian Gauntlet.

But Isaac shook his head. "Arkwright's going to set his plan in motion at midnight tomorrow. We don't have time to wait for Philip. We're going to have to make do without him."

"You still haven't told us where he is," Bethany pointed out.

Isaac sighed. "I sent him to get something for me. Something we may need if things don't go according to plan."

"What?" she asked.

"Nightclaw," Isaac said.

Bethany and Gabrielle both sat up straight in their chairs.

"You can't be serious," Bethany said.

"I thought nobody knew where Nightclaw is," Gabrielle said. "Do you?"

"No," he said. "But I know someone who does. Aiyana, the Goblin Queen. She was appointed Nightclaw's guardian and protector. She's sworn to secrecy about its resting place. But she and I have a history. She owes me. She won't turn Philip away. I just wish it wasn't taking so damn long."

"What *is* Nightclaw?" I asked.

Isaac shook his head. "Nothing you need to worry about right now. I'd prefer to focus on finding the last fragment before Arkwright does."

"Fine," I said. I didn't like being brushed off, but when Isaac didn't want to talk about something, you couldn't get it out of him. I pulled my waterlogged Bersa from its holster. I ejected the magazine from the handgrip, emptied the chamber, and began field-stripping the pistol. If we ran into trouble, I wanted to be ready. "I'll need ten minutes," I said. "And some gun oil."

# Twenty-Seven

Bethesda Fountain wasn't far from Citadel. We walked to it down the long, concrete path through Central Park's Literary Walk. On either side of the path stood statues and busts of famous poets and authors, their names carved on the statues' bases—Robert Burns, Sir Walter Scott, Fitz-Greene Halleck. The only name I recognized was William Shakespeare. Even amnesiacs have heard of Shakespeare. My gun, freshly cleaned, oiled, and reloaded, sat in the holster at the small of my back. If Erickson Arkwright made another appearance, I planned on putting a bullet in his head before he had the chance to unleash Nahash-Dred on the world. Provided I could catch him. The son of a bitch was fast.

Leafless elm trees flanked the path and formed a skeletal canopy above us. Sheets of rain poured down as the sky grew dark. I looked at my watch. It was almost six p.m. Was Jordana on her way home now? Was she already there? My cell phone sat in my trench coat pocket, worrying me with its silence.

The weather had kept people out of the park, save for a few brave tourists in plastic ponchos determined to get their money's worth from a trip to the big city. They didn't pay us any attention. The orange construction vests worked their magic.

Bethesda Terrace, a two-level structure of sandstone and Roman brick, overlooked the fountain plaza below. We proceeded down the terrace's wide, granite stairs into the enclosed arcade underneath. Here, under the thousands of colorful, hand-patterned tiles that lined the ceiling, more park visitors huddled to wait out the rain in their sopping wet coats. They chatted among themselves or on their cell phones, ignoring us as we marched through the arcade and out through the archways into the open-air plaza.

The rain shimmered on the brick pavement. Puddles splashed under my boots. At the far end of the plaza was Bethesda Fountain. The water had already been turned off for the winter, leaving the pool basin empty, except for the rainwater that had collected there and was seeping into the drains at the base. The fountain itself rose twenty-six feet into the air in multiple levels. At the bottom, two rows of short, stone pillars rose from a pedestal to support a second, smaller basin. Above that, four bronze cherubs posed around a central column. At the top stood the eight-foot-tall statue of the Angel of the Waters. She wore flowing robes, her wings outstretched as though she were just touching down atop the fountain. One hand clutched a lily. The other pointed down at the pool basin below.

Past the fountain, a fence and some metal barricades separated the plaza from the rain-battered waters of a lake. Off to the left were the distant skyscrapers of Central Park West, their windows glowing beneath the darkening sky. To the right, the lights of the nearby Boathouse restaurant shimmered softly through the rain.

I felt a sudden sense of déjà vu. I'd been here recently. But when? It hit me a moment later. Just a few days ago, I'd been looking at the Boathouse from the opposite side. Only a few hundred yards northeast from here was the *Alice in Wonderland* statue, and Biddy's lair beneath it.

I snapped my fingers. "I know why Calliope was in the park when Biddy kidnapped her. She was doing the same thing we are. She must have figured out there was a fragment under the fountain and came to get it. But Biddy nabbed her before she could. That's why she had the knife with her, too. She brought it for protection because she knew she was being followed."

It was ironic. If Biddy hadn't kidnapped Calliope, there was a good chance her stalker would have killed her that night. If he had, we never would have known about her or Erickson Arkwright or Nahash-Dred or any of it. I still didn't believe in fate—I refused to, it felt too much like a cage—but it was hard to shake the feeling that *something* had gone through a lot of trouble to get our attention.

"Her knife wouldn't have been any match for the Thracian Gauntlet," Gabrielle pointed out.

True, but then, the gauntlet wasn't what killed Calliope. She'd been

Die and Stay Dead

cut open, her body spiked to the ceiling of her bedroom. I wasn't ruling out Nahash-Dred as her murderer, but Arkwright still seemed the likelier suspect. But why would he kill Calliope that way when he had the gauntlet? Did he hate women, and reserve a different fate for them? It wouldn't be the first time I'd seen violent insanity and misogyny go hand in hand. Biddy had only targeted women. Was Arkwright cut from the same cloth?

We searched the fountain slowly, methodically, keeping an eye out for hidden doors or switches. The fountain was much larger than either of the previous monuments, so we split it into quadrants: Isaac searched the pool basin, Bethany checked the cluster of stone pillars, and I climbed to the smaller basin and inspected the four cherubs. Gabrielle examined the angel itself, magically levitating to the top of the fountain.

"Be careful," Isaac hissed at her. "If anyone sees you . . ."

"Relax, red. Don't get your panties in a bunch." She stepped onto the fountain in front of the angel. "There. Happy now?"

Isaac glowered at her. I could tell he was worried about Gabrielle now that she was carrying magic inside her. I was worried, too. She'd become reckless. She'd shown us that much when she turned into a loose cannon in Battery Park and nearly got herself killed in the process. But it wasn't just that. There were more subtle changes, too. She'd become smug, arrogant, the complete opposite of the woman she used to be. Was the magic altering her mind? If she was infected, did that mean that she would become a threat?

No. This was Gabrielle. She was a member of the team. She'd risked her life for us more times than I could count. Infected or not, she would never turn on us. Would she?

I hated asking myself questions I couldn't answer. I shifted my focus to examining the cherubs instead. As the cold rain soaked me to the bone, I scoured the bronze curls of their hair, the folds of their robes, the hidden spots behind their knees and under their feet. I inspected the column behind them, too, where the bronze was molded into thick leaves and palm fronds. I got my wet fingers into every empty space I could, but I didn't find anything. Isaac, Bethany, and Gabrielle didn't have any better luck.

"There's got to be *something*," Bethany said, frustrated. She brushed wet hair out of her eyes. "There was a way to get under the other two monuments, there has to be a way to get under this one."

"Maybe we should just blow the damn thing up. That would get us under fast enough," Gabrielle said. She floated brazenly down to the pool basin to land beside Isaac. "I can do it. Just say the word."

"That's enough," Isaac growled at her. "We're not blowing anything up. The last thing we want to do is draw anyone's attention, especially Arkwright's."

"Or the cops," I added.

I jumped down into the empty pool basin. Bethany was right, there had to be a way to get under the fountain. We just weren't seeing it. I looked up at the winged statue. *The Angel of the Waters*. That was what Calliope had written in the notebook. It stood to reason the statue had something to do with getting inside. But what? Gabrielle had already examined it. I looked at the angel's extended hand pointing down at the pool basin. Wait, no, that wasn't exactly right. She was pointing downward, but not at the basin. She was pointing at one of the cherubs right below her.

I climbed back up and began searching every inch of that cherub. He was standing with his left foot up on a small stone. I checked the foot and the stone but found nothing. The cherub's right hand crossed his body to hold part of his robe. I checked the arm, hand, robe, and again there was nothing. Damn. I could have sworn I was on to something, but it was starting to feel like another dead end. I looked into the cherub's face, wishing he could tell me what I wanted to know. His round, pupilless eyes stared back at me blankly. Thanks for nothing.

I watched drops of rainwater stream down from the top of the cherub's head. They disappeared before reaching his face. Odd. I looked closer. A slight seam ran around the perimeter of the cherub's face, along the hairline and under the jaw. Was it a result of the casting process, or something more? Holding my breath, I gripped the bronze face and pulled. It slid off the statue like a mask.

"I found something," I called to the others.

But what exactly had I found? There was no switch or button beneath the cherub's face, only a flat bronze surface. At its center was a round hole, roughly the size of a baseball. I poked a finger inside. It was shallow and rounded at the back, as if it were made to hold something spherical.

Gabrielle floated into the air behind me and peered over my shoulder.

"People are going to see you," I said.

"You sound like Isaac," she said, hovering. "If anyone sees me, let them gawk. What do I care?" Her arrogance made me nervous, but I wasn't in the mood to argue. I nodded at the hole in the cherub's head. "Any idea what that is?"

"If the door's locked," she said, "that must be the keyhole."

"The other monuments didn't need a key."

She shrugged. "This one does."

I jumped down to the pool basin. Gabrielle floated down next to me, ignoring Isaac's angry glare.

"If we're looking for a key," I said, "it's got to be something that fits into that space, something round like a ball. But from the size of the hole, I'm thinking it's something too big to carry on a key chain."

"Could it be hidden somewhere else on the fountain?" Isaac asked.

I shook my head. "Only a fool would keep a key right next to the lock. But it'll be stashed somewhere nearby, I'm sure of it. Hidden but easy to get to in a pinch."

We split into two groups to search the surrounding area. Bethany and I went east toward the Boathouse. Isaac and Gabrielle went west toward a long, cast-iron bridge that spanned the lake. I suspected he didn't want to let her out of his sight.

Bethany and I followed a path that traced a bend in the lake. Wet, dead leaves squished under my boots. I'd grown used to the rain after being drenched all day, but with the sun down it was getting colder out. I shivered and lifted the collar of my trench coat around my neck. Bethany took out the glowing charm and used it as a flashlight in the dark. She shone it on the path and the leafless trees around us, but we hardly knew what we were looking for. I was certain the key would be as hidden as the keyhole. Inside a hollow tree or under a random brick in the path, maybe. Someplace only the person who'd hidden it would think to look.

"Kind of like old times, huh?" I said.

She looked at me. "What do you mean?"

"You, me, stumbling around in the dark looking for mysterious objects. It's weird the things you feel nostalgic about."

She smiled briefly. "We've only known each other a month. That's hardly long enough to start feeling nostalgic."

She was probably right about that, but she'd been my first partner on the team, before I even knew there *was* a team. She was still the one I felt the most comfortable with. The one I felt the closest to, even when she was infuriating. Which was always.

"This is pointless," she said. "We don't know what we're looking for. For all I know, we could have passed it already. Did Jordana mention anything about a key or what it might look like?"

"No, nothing," I said. "I don't think she knew."

"Huh," Bethany said. "So there's something Jordana *doesn't* know. Imagine that."

She continued up the path, but I stopped for a moment, watching her. Why couldn't she just give it a rest? Why did she have to keep picking on Jordana? Except, I knew it wasn't really about Jordana. It was about me. On some level, I'd known that all along.

"Did you expect me to wait for you?" I called after her.

Bethany stopped walking. For a long moment, she stood with her back to me.

"You turned me down, remember?" I said. "You told me the timing wasn't right. Did you expect me to wait?"

She turned around. "Yes," she said. Then she sighed, her shoulders slumping. "No. Maybe. I don't know. This is all new to me."

I walked up to her. "It's new to me, too."

"Look, I'm not heartless," Bethany said. "I'm happy for you that you're learning about your past. Really, I am. I wish I knew half as much about where *I* came from. And I know I've been acting like an ass about Jordana. It's just that it's all happening so fast. I didn't think I would lose you so quickly. Or that she would be so . . ."

"Beautiful?"

"Tall," she said.

I shook my head. "You're not losing me. I'm not going anywhere—"

She raised a hand to stop me from saying more. "Everyone leaves eventually. So let's call a truce, okay? I'm just going to wish you good luck and stay out of it. Just don't ask me to call you Lucas. Because even if that's your real name, it's not who you are to me."

I looked at her, the rain running down her face. There was nothing for me to say, but a thousand things I wanted to.

Bethany looked past me then, her eyes widening in surprise. She lifted the charm to point its light behind me. "Look."

I turned around. Behind me, a flight of concrete steps led downhill to the underpass of a pedestrian bridge. Its round, brownstone archway was nearly obscured by the dead, brown shrubbery that hung over it like cobwebs. A lamppost next to the stairs was affixed with a sign that read TREFOIL ARCH.

"*Look to the Trefoil,*" I said.

We descended into the dark underpass. The glowing charm showed us brick walls and a low, wooden ceiling that slanted down at forty-five-degree angles at the sides. There was another arch at the far end of the underpass, different in shape from the one we'd come in through. This one had three lobes, almost like a clover's leaves. A trefoil. Hence the name.

A raspy voice came from behind me. "Spare some change?"

I turned around. A homeless man with a long, tangled beard and filthy clothes sat on the floor, his back against the wall. I hadn't noticed him when we came in.

I shook my head. "Sorry, pal."

"Rainy night," he said. "You want to stay under my bridge, you gotta gimme some change." He made a strange braying noise, then laughed. "Three billy goats gruff."

Bethany pulled some change out of her pocket and handed it to him. His thick, dirty fingers closed quickly around the coins.

"God bless you," he said. "This'll help me get a hot meal." At that moment, an empty forty-ounce bottle of Olde English 800 rolled out from behind him on the floor. He looked at it and sighed. "Busted."

"It's all right," she said. "Just do us a favor: Keep an eye out and make sure no one else comes in here?"

"Okay," he said. "But if you two are looking for a place to get your freak on, the public bathroom's gonna be a lot more private."

"Just keep a lookout," she said.

He stood up, balancing himself tipsily against the wall. He went to stand in the archway with his back to us. "All right, I ain't lookin'. Just make it quick. And keep it down. Don't wanna hear none of your nasty business."

Bethany walked to the center of the underpass. She stood on her toes and knocked on the angled part of the wooden ceiling. It sounded hollow.

"It's a drop ceiling," she said. "There's empty space inside."

"Enough space for the key?" I asked.

"I don't know," she said. "But the notebook mentioned this place for a reason."

I noticed a plain wooden panel set into the ceiling, lighter in color than the rest of the wood. I knocked on it. It, too, sounded hollow, and the panel jostled slightly in its frame, as if it weren't fixed in place. I pushed it, and the panel lifted. I gave it a shove, and it fell inside the dark space above it.

"I think I found something," I said. "Bring that light over here."

"The fuck you two doing?" our drunk watchman demanded, turning around.

"Just let us know if anyone is coming," I told him. He turned back again with an annoyed grunt.

Bethany shone the light up into the hole. I stretched to reach in as far as I could. I felt around and touched something cold, hard, and rounded. I pulled it out. It was a crystalline sphere, although it wasn't quite as round as I thought. Instead of smooth curves, the surface was comprised of many identical, equilateral triangular faces. Bethany shone the light into it. The sphere absorbed it somehow. No light came out the other side.

"It's an icosahedron," she said.

"A what?"

"A fancy word for an object with twenty sides," she explained. "It looks like it's made of glass or crystal, but I've never seen anything with this kind of light absorption capability."

"Magic?" I asked, keeping my voice down so our drunk friend wouldn't hear.

"Undoubtedly. It's also the right shape to be the key."

So the same person who hid the fragments had also hidden the key here inside the Trefoil Arch. But there was one thing I couldn't figure out. If they'd gone through the trouble of breaking the Codex into pieces and hiding them around the city, why hadn't they tried to stop us from collecting them? None of the fragments had been guarded or moved. What happened to the person who hid them?

As we walked out of the underpass, the homeless man gaped at the crystalline sphere in my hand.

"Thanks for keeping watch for us," Bethany said.

The homeless man went back to his spot on the floor, shaking his head. "Can't believe that motherfucker was up in the ceiling this whole time. Screw spare change. I coulda bought me some high-end shit with that. *Sophisticated* shit."

Outside, I called Isaac's cell and told him we'd found the key. He and Gabrielle met us back at the fountain. I climbed up to the faceless cherub and inserted the crystal sphere into the hole. It fit perfectly. As soon as it was in place, the sphere erupted with a sudden, bright light that shot out across the rainy sky like a search beam. Startled and momentarily blinded, I fell backward off the fountain. Gabrielle caught me in midair.

"I've got you," she said. She floated back down and deposited me safely on my feet. "Any idea what that light is?"

"An alarm system," I said, blinking until my vision came back. "It's warning whoever hid the fragments that someone's getting in."

A low rumbling came from under our feet. The fountain began to slide across the pool basin, revealing a wide, round hole beneath it.

"Why does this one have an alarm system when the others didn't?" Isaac asked.

"The others didn't need a key, either," Bethany pointed out.

"I don't know," I said. "But let's get in there, grab the fragment, and get the hell out before someone answers the alarm."

Gabrielle offered to stay behind and keep watch in case anyone came. I could tell Isaac didn't like the idea of leaving her alone, but he didn't argue. Considering how powerful she was now, even he had to admit she was a good choice to guard our backs.

I looked down into the hole. Granite steps led down into the shadows. I was starting to feel like nothing good ever came from following stairs down into the dark, but it was an occupational hazard.

Isaac led the way down, a fireball appearing above his hand like a torch flame. At the bottom of the steps was a small chamber with another sarcophagus. Like the others, this one was ornately patterned with gold leaf and sported the imprint of a hand on its lid.

"Would you like to do the honors?" Isaac asked me.

Here we go again. I took a deep breath and put my hand in the imprint. The needle stung my finger.

"Ow! God damn it!" I yanked my hand back and sucked the blood off my fingertip. That was three times now, on the same finger. It was never going to heal.

There was a loud, familiar *ka-thunk* as the sarcophagus unlocked from the inside. The lid began to open.

"I wish I understood why it only likes Trent's blood," Isaac said.

"I've been wondering about that, too," Bethany said.

"It doesn't matter," I said. "All that matters is that it opens."

Inside the sarcophagus was the third and final fragment of the Codex Goetia. It was identical to the others, triangular in shape with two sides broken and one side rounded and smooth. Isaac pulled it out of the sarcophagus. Then he retrieved the other fragment from the pocket of his duster. He held the two of them close together, trying to line up their broken sides like puzzle pieces. The fragments didn't let him finish. A bright, crackling light filled the space between them, and the two fragments jumped toward each other like long-lost lovers reuniting. They snapped together seamlessly. I couldn't even see a crack.

With only the one fragment still missing, the Codex Goetia was much closer to its original disc shape. I could also see more clearly the strange, geometrical patterns that decorated its face, and the demon names written in a language I couldn't read. Six hundred and sixty-six of them now. I wondered if Nahash-Dred's name was among them.

"It's astonishing," Isaac said, staring at the object in his hand. "It's like the Codex *wants* to be whole again."

"We should get it back to Citadel," Bethany said. "It'll be safer there."

We went back up the stairs to the plaza. When we reached the top, the fountain started to slide back into place behind us, hiding the stairwell once more. The beam of light from the crystalline sphere shut off.

I didn't see Gabrielle at first. Then I turned. She stood with her back to us, her hands in the air. Facing her was Clarence Bergeron. The old man wore a long, brown coat and a fedora. He leaned his weight on the cane in one hand. In his other hand was a pistol. His two security guards, LaValle and Francisco, had their pistols out, too.

"Well, isn't this nice?" Bergeron said. "I had a feeling we'd meet again."

# Twenty-Eight

Bergeron waggled his pistol at us, the rain pouring off the brim of his fedora. "Hand over the Codex Goetia."

Isaac clutched the Codex tightly. "That's not going to happen."

"Why do you want it anyway?" Bethany demanded. "So you can add it to your artifact collection?"

"Because I'm the one with the gun, that's why," Bergeron said. "Three guns, actually, counting my associates here."

LaValle and Francisco scowled as the rain dripped down their faces.

"We've only got two of the three fragments," Bethany pointed out. "The Codex isn't even complete. It's worthless like this."

"On the contrary," Bergeron said. "It is very valuable to me. If you don't hand it over, I'm afraid my trigger-happy associates and I will be forced to make a very nasty mess out of the four of you. And I do so hate the sight of blood these days."

"Boss, you said the vampire would be here. Where is he?" Francisco demanded, an angry sneer on his baby face. "You promised. You said he would be mine when the time came."

"Not now, Francisco," Bergeron hissed at him, taking his eyes off us for a moment.

But a moment was all Gabrielle needed to make a move. She lifted her hands from her side, green flames flickering hungrily around her fingers.

Bergeron pointed his gun at her. "I wouldn't if I were you."

"If you think a gun can protect you," Gabrielle said, "you don't know who you're messing with."

"Now, now," Bergeron said. "I didn't survive this long by being stupid."

He whistled. In response, dozens of figures came out of the dark. They positioned themselves along the top of Bethesda Terrace and the grand stairways on either side of it. The people huddled inside the arcade caught sight of the creatures on the steps and screamed, stampeding away from us. These things weren't human. Their bodies were thin, almost skeletal, with leathery, rust-brown skin stretched tight over their bones. Their heads were bald and insectlike, with two big, black, irisless eyes and two nubby horns on their brows. They wore no clothing, only swords in scabbards that hung at their bony hips. They hadn't drawn their weapons yet. They stayed in formation and awaited orders like a well-trained army.

Gabrielle reluctantly lowered her hands. The green flames faded away.

Isaac regarded the creatures with narrowed eyes. "Demons," he said.

"*Lesser* demons, of course," Bergeron replied. "The kind you don't need the Codex Goetia to summon. Just some blood, powdered bone, and the right incantations. I've gotten a lot better at summoning and binding demons over the years. I learned the hard way how important that is."

I looked down at the withered leg he'd shown us in Westchester.

*An old injury that never quite healed right.*

Damn. What a fool I'd been. He'd been right under our noses all along.

"You're Erickson Arkwright," I said.

The old man smiled. "It's been a long time since anyone called me that. The last time I used that name I was hiding half-dead beneath a pile of my friends' body parts. Waiting until it was safe to come out again. Dragging myself through their blood and entrails to the door."

He was getting worked up as he spoke, his anger growing. He started coughing, but brought it under control quickly. Specks of blood dotted his lower lip. When he spoke again, his tone was calm and even.

"Forgive me. As you can see, not all the damage was external. I have a collapsed lung, and kidneys that no longer function properly. What was done to me, what I lived through, was grueling. An unimaginable hell. After enduring that, a new name was a blessing, a chance to put the horror behind me. Even a name as bland as Clarence Bergeron. But then, the real Clarence Bergeron was quite bland himself. Killing him and assuming his identity felt like doing the world a favor."

I had no doubt he was telling the truth. And yet, how *could* he be Erickson Arkwright? I couldn't see the connection between this sick, old man with a bum leg and the nimble, black-clad killer who'd attacked us with the Thracian Gauntlet. Had Arkwright used a spell to give himself such acrobatic use of his legs again? I couldn't think of any other explanation. But if that was the case, why wasn't he using the spell now? Why bother with the cane?

LaValle and Francisco stood stoically beside their boss, jaws tight, ready to start throwing bullets on his orders. It seemed more likely that one of them had donned the black sweats and Thracian Gauntlet, not Arkwright himself.

Arkwright had purchased the gauntlet at the Ghost Market auction, then faked its theft from his mansion so he could use it to murder Yrouel without suspicion falling back on him. That much was clear. What wasn't clear was where the gauntlet was now. Why threaten us with pistols and a small army of lesser demons when he had such a powerful, deadly weapon in his arsenal?

"Why all the games at the Ghost Market, Arkwright?" Bethany asked. "Bidding on the Thracian Gauntlet under two different names? Why create a fake bidding war?"

Arkwright raised his eyebrows, surprised. Evidently, he hadn't expected us to know anything about that. "I see you've been poking your nose where it doesn't belong. The two identities were a necessary obfuscation in case anyone started to ask questions. Who would even look at Clarence Bergeron when Cargwirth Kroneski was a far more likely suspect, what with his name being such a simple anagram."

"But you were *seen* at the auction," I said. "How did you bid over the phone, too? You couldn't be in two places at once."

Arkwright arched a smug eyebrow. "Enough talk. I want the Codex Goetia. I won't ask again."

"I told you," Isaac said. "That's not going to happen."

In unison, the demons took a single, threatening step toward us. Their hands went to the hilts of their swords.

"I assure you 'lesser demon' is just an academic classification," Arkwright said. "They are quite formidable, and quite deadly. I will not hesitate to use them to take the Codex from you if I have to."

"You want it?" Isaac asked, slipping it back inside his duster. "Come and get it."

Arkwright glared at him. Then he called to the demons, "Kill them. Leave their bodies in the lake."

The demons ran down the stairs toward us, drawing curved, scimitar-like swords from their scabbards. They outnumbered us by at least ten to one. I didn't like those odds. Throw in a madman and his two thugs, each armed with a gun, and I liked them even less. But we'd been through too much to let this lunatic walk away with the Codex Goetia now.

I pulled my Bersa from its holster and started shooting. My bullets chewed into demon flesh. None of them even slowed down. I shot again, this time aiming for the spot between the nearest demon's black, buglike eyes. The bullet lodged in its head, but it kept coming. Damn, these things were hard to put down. The demon got close enough to swing its sword at my head. I shot a third time. My bullet went into the fleshy meat of its left eye, exploding it in a burst of gelatinous goo. The demon dropped like a sack of bricks.

"Aim for their eyes!" I shouted.

The others attacked the demons with magic. Isaac sent out crackling, electrical blasts. Gabrielle flew into the air and unleashed her shock waves, knocking handfuls of demons off their feet. Bethany pulled a small, blade-less sword hilt from her cargo vest. When she gripped it in her fist, a blade of fire burst out of it.

The demons came at us in a relentless wave, so many of them that I couldn't see Arkwright and his thugs anymore. I dropped more of them, but for each demon I shot it seemed like there were three more ready to take its place. How many of these damn things were there? I couldn't tell. All I knew was that there were more of them than bullets in my gun. As if on cue, the gun started clicking, its magazine empty. Shit. I'd only killed five of them. Barely a drop in the bucket.

Demons swarmed over Isaac, pulling him to the ground and tearing his duster open. One of them pulled the Codex from the inside pocket and scrabbled away. I ran after it and tackled it. The Codex slipped out of its grasp. The demon struggled, but I kicked it aside and threw myself on top of the Codex.

I heard the sound of guns being cocked. I looked up. Arkwright, La-Valle, and Francisco stood over me, their guns trained on me.

"Give me the Codex Goetia," Arkwright said.

I stayed on top of it, preventing them from taking it.

"Don't be an idiot," Arkwright said. "If you don't hand it over, we'll just shoot you dead and take it from you anyway."

"Try it," I said. "Stay real close and see what happens."

LaValle's boot struck me in the face, knocking me off the Codex. Arkwright put his pistol away, freeing his hand to pick it up. I scrambled to my knees and grabbed the other end of it. Arkwright held on. He locked eyes with me and smiled.

"I recognized you the moment I saw you, you know," he said. "How could I not, after everything we've been through together?"

I narrowed my eyes at him. "You know me?"

"Haven't you figured it out yet? Why the sarcophagi only open for you? Not for me or anyone else, just for you?"

"Tell me," I insisted. "Tell me why."

He sighed. He looked almost sad as he yanked the Codex out of my hand. "Such a pity. You had so much potential."

"What's that supposed to mean?"

I got to my feet, but LaValle and Francisco aimed their guns at me, warning me to stay back. Arkwright tucked his cane under one arm. He reached into his right coat pocket and pulled out the fragment that had been stolen from us outside the library. He brought the big and small pieces of the Codex together. As before, a bright light crackled in the space between them. They jumped toward each other, snapping seamlessly into a single object, a perfect circle. The Codex Goetia was whole again. Gleaming in the rain, the overlapping geometric designs on its face appeared as concentric shapes now, each smaller than the last as they approached the center—a circle, then a heptagon, then a seven-pointed star, then a smaller heptagon, and finally, at the very center of the Codex, a miniature five-pointed star. Etched all around and inside these shapes were the names of the greater demons.

All nine hundred and ninety-nine of them, in Erickson Arkwright's hands.

He put the Codex in his coat's interior pocket. "Look around you," he said, gesturing at his army of lesser demons. "Look at what I did *without* the Codex. Imagine what I could do *with* it."

I glared at him. "You can't do this, Arkwright. We won't let you."

He leaned his weight on his cane again and smiled. "I told you the name Trent doesn't suit you, didn't I? Of course, I'm not the only one who recognized you. There was another. Not to worry." He leaned close and dropped his voice to a poisonous whisper. "I'll make sure your secret stays just between us."

My chest squeezed tight. Jordana—the son of a bitch was threatening Jordana! My hands clenched into fists.

"If you hurt her, I'll kill you," I said.

"I doubt that," he said.

Arkwright turned and walked away, his cane tapping the brick pavement of the plaza with each step. LaValle and Francisco followed him, walking backward with their guns still trained on me.

The bastard was getting away. If I let him, Jordana was as good as dead. I couldn't let that happen. I grabbed a fallen demon's sword off the ground and ran after him.

But there were more demons between us. Lots more. I swung the sword as I pressed forward, knocking aside their flashing blades and cutting into their flesh when I could. But it was like swimming against the current. I barely moved more than a few feet forward. In the distance, Arkwright, LaValle, and Francisco walked into the arcade beneath Bethesda Terrace. I pushed and chopped my way through the demons. I wasn't going to stop until Arkwright was dead. I would kill him with my bare hands if I had to. I would kill him even if it meant never knowing how he knew me, or what he knew about me. It was the only way to keep Jordana safe.

A demon's sword struck my arm, slicing through my coat and sleeve and into my skin. I kicked the demon away and kept running. I blocked another sword coming at me and shouldered a demon out of my way. I felt a sword bite into my leg. I fell to one knee on the hard, wet bricks. I pushed myself back up and kept limping forward. I couldn't let Arkwright get away.

I was almost at the arcade. Through the archways, I saw Arkwright and his men stop. He reached into his pocket for something.

My back erupted with sudden, burning pain. A demon had slashed me from behind. I could feel the hot blood drooling down my back from the wound. I forced myself to keep moving forward. I limped into the arcade.

"Arkwright!" I yelled.

He turned, surprised to see me. LaValle and Francisco pointed their guns at me. I braced myself for the bullets. I didn't care how many times they shot me, I wasn't going down until Arkwright was dead.

But they didn't shoot. Instead, a demon stepped in front of me. I'd been so focused on Arkwright I hadn't even heard it come up on me. It swung its sword in a quick arc, slashing open my stomach. I dropped my sword and fell to my knees. I clutched my reddening shirt, trying to keep my insides from spilling out.

"If you hurt her . . ." I snarled at Arkwright.

He pulled an object out of his pocket and threw it onto the floor. It burst on impact, and a hole appeared in the air above it, flickering and blue. A portal spell. Damn it, I couldn't let him get away. I couldn't.

With a smug grin, Arkwright stepped into the portal, followed by his men. They disappeared into the light, and the portal closed.

I looked up at the demon standing over me.

It drove its sword right through my heart.

# Twenty-Nine

I came gasping back to life on top of the dead demon's withered corpse. My fingers were sore from having grabbed hold of the demon as I died and refusing to let go. It had done the trick. The thing inside me stole the demon's life force to bring me back. Good riddance. That guy was an asshole.

I stood up. My shirt, pants, and trench coat were torn and spattered with blood, but as usual my wounds were completely healed. Not even so much as a scar. It was strange how fine I felt. I was used to more of a shock when I came back. I was used to feeling groggy, confused, and not knowing where I was. But this time was different. I felt charged. Energized the way I imagined people felt after a good night's sleep. Maybe after thirteen deaths I was finally getting the hang of this resurrection thing. Or maybe it was because I'd stolen the life force of a creature from another dimension. But it wasn't a good idea to look a gift horse in the mouth. Whatever the reason, the demon's life force agreed with me. I left it at that.

Out on the plaza, Bethany, Gabrielle, and Isaac congregated by Bethesda Fountain. They were stacking dead demon bodies, so many that they were forced to make several different piles. With a wave of his hand, Isaac set them on fire. The pyres worked quickly, reducing the dead demons to ash in seconds. The wind took care of the rest, dispersing the ashes across the lake and into the forest beyond. The Parks Department owed us a big thank-you for the cleanup. Not that they would ever know.

I walked over to them. Bethany saw me first, her eyes going wide at the sight of my torn, bloodstained clothes.

"Are you all right?" she asked.

"I've had worse deaths." I turned to Isaac. "Arkwright threatened Jordana. She needs protection. That's where I'll be."

I turned around and started walking. The three of them hurried after me.

"Wait," Isaac said. "We need a plan."

"How's this for a plan?" I suggested. "I keep Jordana alive while the rest of you find Arkwright and put him in the fucking ground."

Gabrielle grabbed my arm. "Trent, don't. If they're going to go after Arkwright, they'll need you. Let me get Jordana. I can bring her back to Citadel. She'll be safe there. I'll call as soon as I have her."

"Forget it," I said. "It's my fault she's in danger. She was just a consultant until I brought her deeper into this mess. I put her right in Arkwright's crosshairs by getting involved with her."

"Damn it, Trent, she's my friend, too," Gabrielle insisted. "I can help. I have the power to protect her, and I can reach her a hell of a lot faster than you can."

I turned to her. "How?"

"Watch me." She launched herself straight up into the air and flew off into the night, out of sight before I could protest.

I looked at Isaac. "Fine. We'll get Arkwright. You drive."


The Escalade sped north on the Henry Hudson Parkway to Bronxville. I leaned forward in the passenger seat and opened the glove compartment. I ejected the spent magazine from my gun and tossed it in.

"How the hell did Arkwright find us?" I asked. "That's three times now he's been waiting to ambush us."

Isaac said, "He must have been following us."

"Or the light from the sphere," Bethany said from the backseat. "You said yourself it was an alarm system."

"But Arkwright can't be the one who hid the fragments," I said. "He told me he couldn't open the sarcophagi."

Bethany shook her head. "I don't get it. In his condition, how can he be the same person who came after us with the Thracian Gauntlet?"

"It had to be one of his henchmen," I said. I rooted around the glove compartment until I found a fresh magazine of bullets. "One of them must have bid remotely for him at the auction, too, so there would appear to be two different bidders for the gauntlet."

"He's been one step ahead of us the whole time," Bethany said.

"Well, the son of a bitch forgot something," I said, slamming the new magazine into the butt of my gun. "We know where he lives."

When we pulled into the driveway of Arkwright's mansion in Bronxville, I expected to be greeted with a hail of gunfire or a blast from the Thracian Gauntlet. Instead, we didn't meet any resistance at all. The grounds were empty. The only sign of life was the light in the windows. Someone was home. We pulled up to the columned portico entrance and got out. I stalked up to the front door, gun in hand. Yesterday, I'd stood right here talking with a murderer and hadn't even realized it. I'd shaken his goddamn hand.

My phone sat silent in my pocket. Gabrielle hadn't called yet to tell me she and Jordana were safe. What the hell was taking so long?

I waved Isaac and Bethany behind me, then tried the door. It was locked. No surprise there. I kicked it open and stepped inside, my gun raised in front of me. I didn't hear an alarm, but that didn't mean I hadn't tripped a silent one. I led Bethany and Isaac through the entrance hallway, past the hanging portraits and cabinets filled with finery.

I kept my gun in front of me as we moved deeper into the house. I was ready for Arkwright's goons to come blasting out of every door we passed, but it never happened. I didn't see *anyone*. The whole house was eerily quiet. I led us toward the three-story library at the center of the mansion. No one was there, either. In the ceiling, the stained-glass angel stared down at us indifferently.

I made a beeline for the door to Arkwright's private artifact gallery. If he were holed up anywhere, it would be in there. With its extensive collection of deadly artifacts, it was the safest place in the house. I tried the handle. It was locked. I gave the door a few hard kicks. Unlike the front door, this one refused to budge. Bethany took a door-buster charm from her vest and fixed it to the doorknob. She motioned for us to get back. The charm exploded with light, followed by the sound of rending metal and the stench of burning. When it was done, Bethany put her hand in the hole where the doorknob used to be and opened the door.

The gallery was empty. Completely empty. Not only was Arkwright not there, all the artifacts had been cleared out. Damn. Arkwright's collection was the most important thing in the world to him. It was the only thing he would never leave behind. If it was gone, then he was gone, too. He'd probably started packing the moment we left yesterday. But where had he gone? Another residence? A safe house?

The only object left in the room was the painting on the wall, still covered with a heavy curtain. I grabbed the curtain and yanked. It fell, pulling the curtain rod down with it to thump and clatter to the floor. Behind the curtain, painted right onto the marble wall, was a landscape of two seaside cities. They were built on the side of a mountain range, and separated by a long, winding wall. In the foreground, two small figures flew over the water toward the cities. They were wearing suits of armor.

The Gemini Sentinels. It was a painting of Tulemkust and Sevastumi, the cities where the Thracian Gauntlets originated. Supposedly the home of the Codex Goetia, too. The true cause of the war between them.

Something in the bottom right corner of the painting stood out amid the aqua blue brushstrokes of the water. It was just a flourish, barely noticeable if you weren't looking for it, but it was there. The letter Y. I'd seen it before. The signature of an artist too egotistical not to leave his mark, even on forgeries.

Yrouel.

The pieces were starting to fall into place. Clarence Bergeron had hired Yrouel to come paint this for him. Yrouel must have seen something that made him realize Bergeron was really Erickson Arkwright, the sole surviving member of the Aeternis Tenebris doomsday cult. Yrouel had then tried to sell that information to Calliope, but Arkwright got to her first. Then he'd killed Yrouel, too. No loose ends, or so he thought.

What I didn't understand was, why *this* painting? Why Tulemkust and Sevastumi? What did the legend mean to Arkwright?

I looked up from the painting, up to the ceiling and the little black cameras embedded in it. I could have kicked myself for being so stupid. I ran out of the gallery and back through the house. I stopped in front of the security office where we'd reviewed the doctored footage of the gauntlet's "theft" yesterday.

"Stay back," I told Bethany and Isaac as they came running up behind me.

I kicked the door open and went inside, gun first.

LaValle leapt up from where he was sitting in front of the surveillance equipment. He reached for the pistol at his hip, but I pointed my Bersa semiautomatic at his face. His hand froze on the grip of his gun.

"Don't," I said. "Where's Arkwright, LaValle?"

LaValle grinned smugly. "Someplace you'll never find him. You can't stop him. Nothing can stop him now."

He drew his gun. I put three bullets in him, center mass, before he could fire. He fell back against the far wall, then slid down to the floor. He looked pretty damn dead to me, but I kicked his gun away from his hand anyway. I wasn't taking any chances.

"You shouldn't have killed him," Isaac said. "He might have had information."

"He said everything he was going to say." I holstered my gun. I went to the bank of surveillance equipment, but I couldn't make heads or tails of all the buttons and dials in front of me. "Can you operate this thing? There might be footage that tells us where Arkwright went."

Bethany and Isaac went to work on the equipment, but after a minute they stopped.

"It's been erased, all of it," Isaac said. "There's nothing saved on the hard drives. LaValle was keeping an eye on us. These are live feeds from all over the house, but nothing's being recorded. Arkwright wasn't taking any chances."

"Now what?" Bethany asked. "Arkwright could be anywhere. We're no closer to finding him than we were before."

I looked at the monitors, the various rooms under surveillance around the house—the living room, a den, the master bedroom, the gallery, guest rooms, hallways. There had to be something here, something that could tell us where Arkwright was.

"We should split up and search the house," I said. "Nobody takes off this quickly without leaving something behind. Papers, a receipt, a Post-it note with a phone number, *something*."

Bethany looked down at LaValle's dead body. "Be careful. LaValle was part of Arkwright's security detail. If he's still here, he was guarding something. Or someone."

We split up, searching different parts of the house. I took a carpeted stairway to the top floor, three stories up, keeping the gun in front of me. I checked behind door after door—a bathroom, a linen closet, a laundry room—but there was nothing to tell me where Arkwright had gone. Finally, I found a study. It was a big room with an antique wooden desk, a plush, leather couch, and a marble-topped, wrought iron coffee table. I searched the desk but didn't find anything except for a few stray pens and pencils rolling around its drawers.

A fireplace stood on the wall opposite the door. Several framed photographs had been arranged on the stone mantel. I studied them closely, hoping to find a clue. The photos were all of Arkwright at various landmarks around the world, the Eiffel Tower, the pyramids of Giza, the Great Wall. The man certainly got around. Maybe it was his farewell tour, one last hurrah before he commanded Nahash-Dred to destroy it all.

The picture at the far end of the mantel caught my eye. It showed Arkwright standing beside a woman about his age. She was wearing a red parka, matching knit cap, and yellow, buglike goggles. They were standing at the bottom of a ski slope. Above them, part of a banner had been captured in the photograph. It read ASPEN SN.

I picked it up. I'd seen the woman before. I'd seen this *picture* before, but . . . different. I turned the frame over and started to undo the back.

My phone went off. Gabrielle's name flashed on the screen. I put the photograph down and answered the call.

"Gabrielle, where are you? Do you have Jordana?"

"Trent," she said, her voice shaking. "Jordana never told me where she lives, so I—I came to her office first. I thought she might still be here, or that I'd find her home address."

"Do you *have* her?" I asked again.

"When I got here, they were—they were all dead," she said. "Everyone in the office. They were murdered. Their bodies are burnt. There are burn marks all over the walls. It—it had to be the Thracian Gauntlet. It had to be Arkwright."

My fingers tightened on the phone so hard I thought it might break.

"God damn it," I said. "Why were they still at the office at this hour? What were they doing there?"

"That's the thing," Gabrielle said. "I don't think they stayed late. They're already cold. They've been dead for hours."

It felt like the floor dropped out from under me. "Did you see Jordana? Is she there, too?"

"I don't know. Her—her office is empty. I didn't see any burn marks in there, but that doesn't mean . . . God, Trent, I don't know how she could have gotten out if she was here when Arkwright came. He was thorough. It's—it's like he was enjoying himself. He didn't spare anyone. There are bodies huddled together in the break room like they were hiding from him, but—but they . . ."

She trailed off, unable to continue. I picked up the photograph again in my other hand. I smashed it against the corner of the mantel, shattering the glass. I pulled the picture out of the frame. It had been folded to show only part of the photograph. I unfolded it, making the image complete. The banner at the top now read, in full, ASPEN SNOWMASS 2011. Standing next to the older woman was Jordana. It was the same picture I'd seen on Jordana's desk at work.

*My family went on a ski trip to Aspen . . .*

"I'm sorry you had to find out this way," Jordana said behind me.

I dropped the photograph, dropped the phone, and spun around, pulling my gun. She was standing partially in the doorway. I could only see her head and one shoulder.

"Jordana," I said. "There are easier ways to quit your job."

"But none quite so satisfying," she said. "Luckily, I wasn't looking for a reference."

She stepped fully into the doorway. She was holding Bethany by the arm, pulling her along. On Jordana's other hand was the Thracian Gauntlet, its palm pressed to the side of Bethany's head.

"Put your gun on the floor," Jordana said. "Now."

# Thirty

"Put the gun down," Jordana repeated, keeping Bethany between herself and me as a human shield. "You know what this gauntlet is capable of."

"Okay, okay," I said. Keeping my hands where she could see them, I bent down to put the gun on the floor.

"Don't do it, Trent," Bethany said. "Don't you dare put that gun down!"

Jordana shook her. "Shut up, unless you want those to be your last words."

I put the gun on the floor. I didn't have a choice. Even if I had a clear shot at Jordana, there was no guarantee she wouldn't blast Bethany's head off her shoulders first.

"Now kick the gun away," Jordana said.

I did. It slid across the polished hardwood and didn't stop until it hit the leg of the desk.

"You're why LaValle was here. You're what he was guarding," I said. "You were in this with Arkwright all along."

"Gold star," Jordana said. "And now you're going to give me safe passage out of this house. Unless, of course, you want to see what the gauntlet can do to someone at point-blank range."

Bethany's eyes stayed hard and focused. If she was afraid, she wasn't showing it. Where the hell was Isaac? Did he know what was happening? Or had Jordana already killed him?

Jordana narrowed her eyes at me. "Isaac? Someone *else* is here, too?"

"You're a mind reader?" I asked, surprised.

"I'm a lot of things," she said. "Anyway, it doesn't matter that you're not alone. It's a big house, and I'll be long gone before Isaac finds me. Right?"

She backed toward the door, staying behind Bethany. I glanced at the gun on the floor.

"I said, *right*?" Jordana snapped.

"Right," I said. "Safe passage."

"Then you're coming with me, too," she said. "Try anything and I'll kill both of you."

She backed out the door and into the hallway. I followed, leaving the gun on the floor behind me. I hated abandoning it, but I didn't have a choice. I already knew what Jordana was capable of. I followed her and Bethany into the hallway.

"Stay back," Jordana warned.

I kept my hands up. "You were the second bidder at the Ghost Market," I said. "You killed Yrouel in Chinatown."

"That fat piece of garbage brought it on himself," she spat. "Yrouel wasn't even supposed to be here that day, but he came in to put some finishing touches on that stupid painting in the gallery. He overheard Erickson and me talking in the library. He was right on the other side of the door. He heard *everything*. The cult. The demon. I told Erickson that damn painting would be nothing but trouble, but he wouldn't listen. He said it was 'important family history.' He said it was his heritage, proof that the Codex Goetia rightfully belonged to him. He should have listened to me. That painting compromised us. Yrouel had to be taken out."

"And I suppose I brought it on myself, too, when you tried to kill me," I said. "Three times."

"Oh, don't look so wounded," she said. "As I recall, you took a few shots at me yourself on top of that truck. Didn't anyone ever tell you you're not supposed to hit a woman?"

I remembered our fight on the truck, the feel of bandages under her black sweats. Now I understood. It had been part of her disguise, a way to make sure nothing could be traced back to her. She'd bound herself so she wouldn't look female.

"Why are you doing this, Jordana?" I demanded.

"He's my stepfather. It's like I told you, he's all the family I have left. I would do anything for him. He needed the Codex Goetia. I knew you would lead us to it, so I did what I had to."

"You got in my head. You read my mind so you'd know where the fragments were as soon as I did," I said. "Neat trick."

"My birth father was human. My mother was a succubus. That left me with a few tricks up my sleeve. All it took was one kiss and I had a bridge directly into your mind. I could read your thoughts. I could influence you. Make you think things. Feel things."

"That's sick," Bethany said.

"Jealous much?" Jordana hissed in her ear.

"That's how you kept finding us," I said. "The library. Battery Park. I'm guessing you would have been at the fountain, too, but Arkwright wanted to be there himself to take the last fragment. Some men can't resist the urge to grandstand."

"You don't know anything about him," she snapped. "Don't pretend you know him!"

She pushed the gauntlet against Bethany's head. There was something unhinged in Jordana's eyes. I didn't have any doubt that she would kill Bethany if I pushed her too far.

"Okay, okay," I said, showing her my hands, trying to keep her calm. "I'm sorry. I spoke out of turn. Let's not let things get out of hand."

She laughed bitterly. She sounded nothing like the Jordana I knew. But which one was the real one? The one who'd laughed and cried with me over drinks in Brooklyn, or the murderer currently threatening Bethany's life? How much of what she'd told me was true, and how much were lies meant to keep me wriggling on the line? Was Lucas West real?

"I can still read your thoughts, Trent," Jordana said. "And the answer is no. You're not Lucas West. The Lucas West I told you about was a boy I knew in high school. He died in a car crash before graduation. Drunk driving. I just told you what you wanted to hear—that you had a normal family, a normal life. You're so pathetic. I didn't even have a bridge into your mind yet when I fed you that story. I didn't need it. You were so easy to read."

A lie. Lucas West was a lie. It tore a hole in me. I'd wanted to believe it so badly I was blind to all the red flags. Bethany had seen them. She'd tried to warn me, but I didn't listen. If I had, then maybe Bethany's life wouldn't be in danger right now. Maybe we wouldn't be in this mess at all.

"You should have just given me that fragment when I asked you to," Jordana said, dragging Bethany backward down the hallway. "It would have saved you a lot of trouble."

"Jordana, please," I said, hoping I could still reason with her. "It doesn't have to be like this."

"Doesn't it?" she said. "In the end, which side did you think I'd be on, yours or my stepfather's? I told you, he's all the family I have left."

"So not everything was a lie," I said. "The things you told me about your mother, your brother, they were real. The trip to Aspen, the demon you saw there, that was real, too."

Her mouth made a hard, tight line, and for a moment she didn't say anything. I thought I'd gotten through to her, thought maybe I saw a hint of the Jordana I knew in her face, but it was gone in a flash.

She smirked. "Lies work best when there's some truth to them."

"Jordana, your stepfather isn't who you think he is. He's using you—"

"He's not using me, he loves me!" she yelled. "He's all I have left, and I'm all he has left. I would do anything for him. I even carried magic when he asked me to, spells that gave me unbelievable speed and agility. I took that magic inside me willingly, because it was what he wanted and I knew it would help him. That's what you do for family. Not that you would know."

A chill came over me. "My God, Jordana, he infected you. Arkwright purposely infected you."

She laughed. "Do I look infected to you? Am I growing an extra arm, or a tail? Do you see any mutations anywhere on my body? As I recall, the last time we were together you got a pretty good look."

"The infection doesn't always change you physically," I said. "But it affects your mind. Always. You know that."

"You're wrong," she said. "There's nothing wrong with me. In fact, I've never seen things so clearly before. I won't let anyone come between me and my stepfather. Especially not *you*."

If I thought my heart couldn't break any more, I was wrong. "Was it *all* a lie?"

She looked at me with mock pity. "You were so easy to manipulate. So lonely, so desperate for someone to know you. But look at you. Did you really think I could love you? That *anyone* could? Every time you kissed me, every time you touched me, I cringed inside."

Bethany squirmed in Jordana's grip. "Don't worry about me, Trent. Just take this bitch out already. She's earned it."

But I didn't. I couldn't. Not Jordana. There had to be another way. I was starting to think this was all a mistake. A misunderstanding. I cared about this woman. I loved her. I couldn't hurt her.

Jordana laughed. "See? Even now, your thoughts are so easy to mold."

I snapped out of it. Damn. I was like putty in her hands. How much had she influenced my thoughts over the past two days? How often had she steered me away from realizing the truth about her?

"What about Calliope?" I asked. "You killed her, too, because she was getting too close. Only you got your inner sadist on, big time. Why? What did she ever do to you?"

"I hate to break it to you, loverboy, but I never even met the woman," she said.

"You mean Arkwright killed her himself?" That could explain the different M.O., but Arkwright didn't strike me as someone who liked to get his hands dirty.

Jordana laughed derisively. "Please. That injury to his leg is real, courtesy of Nahash-Dred. It'll never heal right. He can barely walk without a cane. Doesn't exactly make him the perfect killer, now does it? Sure, Erickson was keeping tabs on Calliope after she started getting cozy with Yrouel, but he didn't kill her and neither did I. Much as I would have loved to off that nosy bitch for him, I didn't get the chance. Someone beat me to it."

Someone else killed Calliope? That sealed it. It had to have been Nahash-Dred himself. Somehow, the demon had found her. He'd broken in through the attic window and killed her. But that still didn't feel right. There'd been no sign of a struggle, just some blood on the stairs and the horror show in the bedroom. *Nahash-Dred killed them with but a thought.* Was that how he'd pulled it off? With magic?

Jordana dragged Bethany around a corner. Turning the corner after them, I saw Isaac standing farther down the hall. He was holding my gun in his hand. I'd never been so happy to see anyone.

"You're going to want to let her go now, Jordana," Isaac said.

Jordana spun around, startled. She backed against the wall, keeping Bethany in front of her. She pressed the gauntlet against the back of Bethany's head.

"Don't come any closer, either of you!" she yelled.

"Jordana, we can help you," I said. "The magic inside you is infecting your mind. This isn't you. I know it's not."

"Shut up!" she yelled. "Just shut up! I need to think!"

"The things you told me about yourself were true. The tears you cried for your brother and your mother were real," I said. "Look at what you're doing. You're hurting people. Killing people. Is this what they would have wanted?"

Something snapped in her. Her face reddened with fury. "You leave them out of this! Don't you talk about them!"

She took the gauntlet off of Bethany's head and pointed it at me. It started to whine, powering up. I dove to the floor as the blast tore a blackened chunk out of the wall behind me. Several burning, framed paintings flew over me. An antique wooden end table exploded just inches from where I lay with my hands over my head. Pieces rained down around me like hailstones.

I looked up to see Jordana swing the gauntlet toward Isaac, the blast moving in a wide arc across the hallway and destroying more of the walls. Isaac threw himself through a nearby door and into the room beyond it. The blast tore a chasm in the floor and blew apart a section of the wall.

The hallway was filled with smoke and dust. I coughed it out of my lungs and got to my feet. Through the haze, I saw Jordana drag Bethany away, farther into the house.

# Thirty-One

Isaac came back into the hallway, a black smear of ash on one cheek. He brushed plaster dust off his shoulders and arms. "We need to talk about your girlfriend," he said.

"Save it," I said. "Jordana's our only link to finding Arkwright, and she's got Bethany."

I jumped over the hole Jordana had blasted in the hallway floor, and started after them. Isaac walked quickly to keep up.

"Trent, I heard the awful things Jordana said—"

I cut him off. I didn't want to talk about it. "If we don't get through to her first, she'll kill Bethany the moment she doesn't need her anymore. We can't let her leave this house."

Isaac nodded. "Agreed. I take it you have a plan?"

"This is my fault," I said. "I'll finish it, one way or the other. You just make sure Bethany is safe."

He handed me my Bersa. "You'll need this."

I took the gun from him and holstered it. "Not like that. I can get through to her. I know I can. Some part of the real Jordana is still in there."

"And if you're wrong?" he asked.

I didn't reply. We both knew what the answer was.

Figuring out where Jordana had gone wasn't hard. She and Bethany had both left smeary, plaster-dust footprints on the carpet. We followed the trail to a door at the center of the house. On the other side we found ourselves on the top level of Erickson Arkwright's prized, three-story library.

We were on the south side of the balcony that wrapped around the perimeter of the room.

Jordana was directly across from us, on the north side. She was dragging Bethany toward a door in the wall.

"Jordana, wait!" I called. "Let her go. Take me instead, okay? Then we can talk. We can talk about everything. It's not too late."

"You just don't give up, do you?" Jordana pushed the Thracian Gauntlet into the side of Bethany's face. "Stay back, or I'll turn her skull into dust. You know I will."

Isaac whispered to me, "I can kill her from here, Trent. There's a spell that's quick and painless. She won't suffer, I promise you. She won't even know what hit her."

"Don't," I hissed back.

"We may not have a choice."

"Don't!"

"Safe passage out of the house," Jordana continued. "That's what you said. Safe passage so I can get back to Erickson."

"Why help him, Jordana? He wants to end the world," I said.

"I *want* it to end!" she cried. "This world took *everything* from me! My brother. My mother. It took my birth father before I was even born. So if the world has to burn, I say let it!"

Above us, the stained-glass window in the library's ceiling exploded inward as Gabrielle came crashing through it. Shards of glass rained down three stories to shatter on the floor below. Gabrielle flew down into the atrium. She cast a spell, and suddenly the door behind Jordana swelled and warped in its frame. Jordana tried to pull the door open, but it was stuck. She was trapped on the balcony with nowhere to run.

"Let Bethany go," Gabrielle said, hovering in midair.

"Stay back!" Jordana yelled. She was breathing hard. Her eyes darted nervously around the room, trying to find a way out. She was like a cornered animal. That made me nervous, especially with the gauntlet still pressed against the side of Bethany's face. Jordana was too unpredictable to be certain what she would do next.

"You've been planning this from the start, Jordana," Gabrielle said. "You gained my trust. Got me to make the necessary introductions. You used me."

Jordana looked at her again, but her expression was one of confusion. The anger and determination were gone, as if some part of her was trying to push through the infection.

"No, I . . . that's not why . . ." she said, her voice trembling.

"That's not why you went to those meetings, is it, Jordana?" I said. I started along the wraparound balcony toward her. I kept my voice calm and my hands up to show her I didn't mean any harm. "Your grief over your mother's death was real. And when you met Gabrielle at the meetings, maybe your friendship was real, too, at first. Maybe it still can be."

"I—I told Erickson I was spending time with Gabrielle, and that she worked with the—the Five-Pointed Star," Jordana stammered. We were getting a glimpse of the real Jordana now, I was sure of it. She was fighting to break the infection's hold on her. "Erickson told me there was someone else in the Five-Pointed Star, the Immortal Storm, a man who—who doesn't know who he is. He put—he put more magic inside me. He told me what to do, and I *had* to . . ."

"He took advantage of your friendship with Gabrielle," I said, edging closer. "He twisted it to serve his own ends. He did the same to you. He turned you into a tool he could use. Let Bethany go and put the gauntlet down, Jordana. You don't owe that man anything."

"No! He's all I have left!"

Just as I thought we were starting to get through to her, her face changed, hardening. Her eyes focused on me like lasers. Damn. The infection was too strong.

She smirked. "Erickson's plan was brilliant. Use your amnesia to keep you on the hook and get the Five-Pointed Star to find the fragments for us. I wish I'd thought of it myself." She pulled Bethany closer. "Better keep your distance, loverboy. This could get messy. You, too, Gabrielle. Stay back."

I stopped where I was, halfway to her. I kept my hands up. There was nothing in Jordana's eyes I recognized anymore. The infection and Arkwright's hold on her were too strong. Was any part of the real her left?

"It's over, Jordana," Isaac said. "You're outnumbered. There's no place left for you to run. Let's end this now."

"You're right, it's time to end this," she said. She pushed Bethany face-first into the wall of books. She put the gauntlet to the back of Bethany's head.

"Jordana, don't," I said.

She locked eyes with me. "You promised me safe passage. You should have let me go."

"Jordana . . ."

"When you think back on this moment, remember: *You* made me do this."

The gauntlet began its high-pitched whine. Bethany gritted her teeth and squeezed her eyes shut.

"No!" I shouted.

In my desperation, something snapped inside me. Time slowed to a crawl. My vision changed. Everything became atoms, sparking and blazing like suns. Around them wound the silken threads, binding it all together. I saw a dark cloud growing inside Jordana, swallowing the tiny stars within her and turning them dark. There was so little left untouched by the infection inside her. So little, but there was still *some*. I held onto that.

Instinct took over immediately, as if some part of me knew what to do. With my mind, I pulled and tore at the threads all around Jordana. The north balcony shook, destabilized. Then it buckled, knocking Jordana and Bethany off their feet. Jordana fell backward just as the blast erupted out of the gauntlet. Bethany was knocked forward. The blast clipped her across the back before it continued on to strike the north wall. Shelves of books were destroyed in a fiery explosion. An entire section of the north balcony floor was obliterated. Being grazed by the blast had extinguished some of the starry atoms inside Bethany, I saw, but not all of them. She was injured and unconscious, but not dead. Not yet. Though she would be if she didn't get help soon.

Threads began snapping all across the north side of the library. Between destabilizing the balcony and the blast from Jordana's gauntlet, the structure of the entire north wall was seriously weakened. It was all going to come down and take what was left of the balcony, plus Bethany and Jordana, with it. Books tumbled out of the shelves. Shelves fell out of the wall and crashed to the floor far below.

Gabrielle swooped down toward Bethany's unconscious body. I saw a dark cloud within her, too. It was small, much smaller than Jordana's, but it was there. Damn. The infection was already in her.

Gabrielle pulled Bethany off the balcony just as another section fell away, taking the metal railing with it. The rest of the north balcony warped and tipped. Jordana slid toward the edge. She grabbed hold of it before she fell and dangled some thirty feet above the floor below.

Gabrielle flew Bethany to the south balcony and laid her gently down beside Isaac. They bent over her, tending to her. Now that Bethany was safe, my vision began to return to normal—but not before I had another flash of those seven dazzling, titanic figures watching me. Watching while the whole world went to hell. They were so bright they seemed to sizzle. I only saw them for a moment. Then they were gone, and everything looked normal again.

I ran to what was left of the north balcony. As soon as I stepped foot on it, it bounced and shifted under my weight. I heard a bolt slide out of the wall somewhere beneath me and tumble to the floor. Jordana, dangling off the edge, gave a sharp cry. I didn't know how much longer the balcony would stay up, but I refused to leave her here. I threw myself prone onto the balcony and grabbed her wrist with both hands.

"Get away from me!" she shouted.

"I've got you," I said.

Her expression softened. She looked up at me. In her eyes, a sliver of her humanity rose to the surface through the infection.

"Let me go," she pleaded. "Just let me fall."

I looked past her at the floor below. Under normal circumstances, it would have been survivable if she landed right, maybe gaining her a broken leg or arm as a souvenir. But these weren't normal circumstances. The floor was cluttered with jagged, bulky debris—wood, concrete, twisted bits of rebar and steel joists. If she fell, she would break her back, or her neck, or both. It would kill her.

"I won't do it," I said.

Jordana released her grip on the edge of the balcony and dangled from my hands. "Just let go."

I got on my knees and started to pull her up. She struggled against me, bracing her feet against the underside of the balcony so I couldn't lift her.

"Damn it, Jordana, I'm not going to let you fall!"

"Why?" she demanded. "I never loved you, Trent, not even for a minute. None of it was real. Don't you get it? I *used* you."

"I get it," I said. "I just don't care. Call it a character flaw."

"I can make you let go," she said. She raised her other arm and wrapped the cold metal fingers of the Thracian Gauntlet around my forearm.

I shook my head. "Don't."

The gauntlet began its high-pitched whine as it powered up.

Tears streamed down Jordana's cheeks. "Let go. I don't want to hurt you. I've hurt enough people."

"Jordana, don't!"

I refused to let go. I braced myself, ready for the blast to take my arm off, or kill me, or whatever else it would do at this close range, but instead the gauntlet began to spark. Arcs of electricity crackled across its metal surface like twisting serpents. It didn't fire its blast, but it still hurt like hell, searing the flesh of my arm through my trench coat and my shirt-sleeve. I gritted my teeth through the pain and held onto Jordana as tightly as I could, refusing to drop her. She took the gauntlet away from my arm, and the pain subsided.

She looked up at me in confusion. "What—what happened?"

"Magic acts weird around me," I said. "I can't explain it. It goes haywire. Either it doesn't work right, or it gets stronger than it's supposed to be. It must have caused the gauntlet to short out."

I started pulling her up, but she stopped me with her feet again.

"Why are you doing this?" she demanded. "Why would you want to help me, after everything I did?"

"Because it's not too late," I said. "I saw the real you, Jordana, even if it was only for a moment. You showed it to me when we were in the supply room together. Remember? You asked me if I ever felt like I wasn't in control, if I ever felt like I was falling toward something and couldn't stop. You were reaching out. Not the infection. Not Arkwright. That was you, Jordana, the real you reaching out for help, only I didn't know it at the time. But I know you're still in there. I know the infection hasn't taken over fully yet."

"Then let me go," she said as more tears spilled down her face. "Let me die while I'm still me."

I struggled to pull her up. She grabbed my arm with the gauntlet.

"Don't make me do this again," she said.

"Stop!" I shouted. "The gauntlet is already malfunctioning. I don't know how much more it can take—"

But it was too late. The gauntlet sparked and fizzled again. The pain was excruciating, but for Jordana it was worse. This time, the electrical arcs that had crackled across the gauntlet spread over her whole body. We both cried out in pain.

When she took the gauntlet off my arm, she was weeping, and not just from the pain. There was horror in her eyes, revulsion and regret.

"I—I killed . . . so many people . . ." she sobbed.

"You can still come back from this, Jordana," I said. "I know. I've killed people, too. Some of them were innocent, just in the wrong place at the wrong time. It was because of something inside me, something I couldn't control, just like you. But I found a second chance. You can, too. The infection can be reversed. I know it can, I've seen it."

She shook her head violently. "Everyone at the office . . . they begged me for mercy, and I—I killed them without a second thought. I didn't care. I thought it was fun. But now I can't stop hearing them scream. I can't stop seeing their faces. I just want it to stop."

"I can help you, Jordana. Together we can figure out how to reverse the infection. Let me help you."

"You don't understand," she said. "How am I supposed to live with this?"

Sobbing, she put the gauntlet on my arm again.

"Please, don't do this," I said.

"I'm sorry," she said. "I can't."

The gauntlet sparked against my arm. I cried out and clamped my eyes shut against the pain. But it wasn't me she was trying to hurt. She knew the gauntlet would malfunction if it was touching me. She held it against my arm, taking the brunt of its backfire herself. I could feel her body jerking below me. I smelled burning hair and clothes. I held onto her as long as I could, but it wasn't long enough. Her arm slipped out of my grasp. I opened my eyes as the pain subsided and saw her falling toward the floor. She was completely enveloped in flames, a falling comet, a shooting star. She fell silently, without so much as a scream, and I realized she was already dead. It took only seconds for her to hit the debris below, but by then there was nothing left of her but a smoldering, blackened husk that burst apart into ashes and charred bone. The gauntlet, weakened by its own malfunction, broke in two. A stream of sparks erupted from each piece, then lessened and died.

I knelt on the edge of the broken, ruined balcony, feeling cold and empty inside. Everything had been a lie. Our relationship. Lucas West. It had all been a trap set by Arkwright. Yet even knowing that, there was a part of me that wished I really had known Jordana before, because I was sure *that* Jordana, the one I'd seen snippets of through the infection, was someone special. But she'd had the bad luck to have Erickson Arkwright as a stepfather. He'd taken advantage of her loyalty, her sense of family, her need to hold onto the one thing she valued above all else. He'd infected her. He'd turned her into a cold-blooded killer, something she couldn't stand to be. Something she would rather die than be.

The infection was supposed to be irreversible, but this was the second time I'd seen someone break through it. First the Black Knight, and now Jordana. What was the connection between them? Nothing. I couldn't think of a single thing they had in common.

Isaac came up behind me and put a hand on my shoulder.

"Are you okay?" he asked.

"Yeah," I said, but it was as much a lie as the rest of it. I wasn't okay. I didn't want to be okay. Not until Erickson Arkwright got what was coming to him. I stood up, my hands curling into fists.

"What happened to the balcony?" Isaac asked. "The blast from the gauntlet couldn't have done this much damage."

"I'm what happened," I said. "I couldn't control it. It just came through me again, like a reflex."

"You mean Stryge's power?" Isaac asked.

"Something like that," I said. Whether the power was Stryge's or mine, I didn't care just then. I only cared about one thing. Finding Arkwright.

I walked back to where Gabrielle was bent over Bethany. Bethany was still unconscious, lying on her stomach to keep the pressure off of the angry-looking burn that ran diagonally across her back.

"How is she?" I asked.

"Isaac and I were able to stabilize her with healing spells, but she's hurt bad," Gabrielle said. "We should get her back to Citadel. I can take better care of her there."

"Take her," Isaac said. "You can get there faster than we can."

Gabrielle didn't wait to be told twice. She scooped Bethany up in her arms and flew out the hole in the stained-glass window above us.

"I want Arkwright," I told Isaac. "When we find him, he's mine."

I turned and walked back into the third-floor hallway. Isaac followed me.

"Trent, I'm sorry about Jordana, but you need to keep a level head. If you go looking for revenge, you're going to get sloppy and slip up. You'll give Arkwright even more of an advantage than he's already got."

He was wrong. The only thing I would be giving Arkwright was a bullet in his brain. Erickson Arkwright should have died fourteen years ago with the rest of his doomsday cult. Now, the son of a bitch would die and stay dead. I would see to it myself.

I found the stairs and started down.

"Slow down," Isaac said. "Where are you going? We don't even know where Arkwright is."

"There's nothing left in this house that will tell us where he went," I said. "He covered his tracks too well. I'll turn over every damn stone in this city if I have to, but I'm going to end this."

"Wait," Isaac said, grabbing my arm. I stopped and turned to face him. "Trent, listen to me. Arkwright has the Codex Goetia. Tomorrow at midnight he's going to use it to order Nahash-Dred to destroy the world. That only leaves twenty-four hours. We have to use that time wisely."

"It's been one dead end after another," I said. "Even the oracles aren't around to ask. They saw what was coming and hightailed it out of here. You want to use these twenty-four hours wisely? Try finding them."

I turned and continued down the stairs.

"We don't have to," Isaac said. "There's another option. It's a long shot, but there's a higher authority we can appeal to for help."

I stopped and looked up at him. "Who?"

"The Guardians," he said.

I glared at him. "Don't fuck with me, Isaac. I'm not in the mood."

"I'm serious. Like I said, it's a long shot. But I don't see how we have any other choice. We've exhausted every other option and we're running out of time. We have to try."

"I thought the Guardians didn't get involved," I said.

"Let's hope this time they do," Isaac said. He started down the stairs. "This is their world to protect. If they're going to live up to their name, they can't just let it be destroyed. They won't."

It sounded like wishful thinking to me, but I was willing to try anything. I followed him down the stairs.

"So how do we reach them? Is there some hotline to the Guardians I don't know about?"

"No," Isaac said, continuing down the stairs to the ground floor. "We're going to pay them a visit."

I stopped in mid-step. "*What?*"

# Thirty-Two

Isaac drove the Escalade through the streets of Manhattan's East Village. We'd come straight from Bronxville, nearly an hour's drive that felt like an eternity. My blood was still boiling. Every minute I didn't have my hands around Arkwright's neck felt like a minute wasted. Isaac thought the Guardians could help us find him. I hoped he was right, because they were our last hope.

"We should have asked the Guardians for help from the start," I said. I watched the pedestrians on the sidewalk holding their identical small, black umbrellas, as if they'd all bought them cheap from the same corner bodega. It was pouring and almost midnight, but the bars and restaurants in the East Village were as active as ever. "It would have saved us a lot of time and trouble."

"It's not as easy as that," Isaac said. "There's a reason people don't just go to the Guardians any time they need something. There's a price, and it's not cheap."

"How much?" I asked.

"Don't worry about it," he said. "Just leave it to me."

I looked out the window again. I knew Isaac was rich, but something told me this particular price wasn't measured in dollars. These things rarely were.

He parked the car on Lafayette just south of Astor Place, in front of a big building with a brick-and-brownstone façade. The arched windows glowed from within. I stepped out onto the sidewalk. Banners hung off the front of the building. One read JOE'S PUB. The other, SHAKESPEARE IN THE PARK.

"This is it," Isaac said, getting out and closing the driver's-side door behind him.

I knew this place. I'd passed it plenty of times but never paid it much attention. "This is the Public Theater. What are we doing here?"

"We're not here for the theater, we're here for what's underneath," Isaac said. "Follow me. Stay close."

We walked into an alley next to the building, skirting around piles of overstuffed garbage bags and through a veritable minefield of cigarette butts. A plain metal door was set into the side of the Public Theater. Isaac knocked on it.

"So what's under this place?" I asked.

"The Library of Keys," he said.

The door opened, swinging out toward us. A tall, burly man stood in the doorway. He had a full beard, a black patch over his left eye, and a scar that ran down his cheek. A white ouroboros had been painted on the black patch, only it wasn't a snake eating its own tail, it was a dragon. The man glanced past us down the alleyway to make sure we were alone.

"Theater entrance is around the front, lads," he said. His thick Scottish accent did very little to hide the annoyance in his voice. He started to close the door.

"Serapeum," Isaac said.

The man froze. He looked at us again, his entire demeanor changing. With a nod, he opened the door wider to let us in. "Right this way."

We entered a narrow, dimly lit hallway with cement walls. The old, bare floorboards creaked under our feet. The man slammed the metal door closed behind us, then squeezed past Isaac and me into the hallway ahead, no easy feat for a man of his size. He led the way deeper into the building.

"Who's Serapeum?" I asked Isaac.

"Not who, what," Isaac said. "The Serapeum was a temple in Egypt that housed the books rescued from the destruction of the Library of Alexandria. The Library of Keys uses it as a password. It seems appropriate."

"I've never heard of a library needing a password before," I said.

"This isn't just any old library, lad," the man said, glancing over his shoulder at me. "It's the Library of Keys. Every key to every door, every gate, every lock in the world has a copy here. The doors people know about, and the doors they don't. Something like that has to be protected. No one gets in without the password."

"Wait, did you say every lock in the *world*?" I asked.

"Aye, and a few from other worlds," the man said. "It took the work of many powerful mages to create a library like this."

"And they put it here, in the East Village?" I shook my head. "I guess all those people who think New York City is the center of the universe are right."

The man laughed at that. He stopped at the end of the hallway, in front of an open ironwork elevator. He slid open the accordion gate. Isaac and I stepped inside. The man remained in the hallway.

I scanned the elevator walls. "There are no buttons."

"You don't control the elevator," the man said, sliding the gate closed again. "I do."

The elevator began to descend, though all the man did was watch us with his arms crossed over his barrel chest. We descended into a concrete shaft.

"The Library of Keys has been here since long before there was an East Village, or even a New York City," Isaac explained. "In the 1850s, John Jacob Astor built the Astor Library on this spot, but not before coming to an agreement with the Library of Keys first. If they let him build here, he would help keep their existence a secret. The Astor Library is long gone. Now it's the Public Theater, but they still honor Astor's agreement. In fact, this used to be Astor's private elevator to his own secret reading room on the top floor. His son, William, extended it down to the Library of Keys when he took over. Rumor has it he was having an affair with one of the librarians."

"So there's a key down here that will take us to the Radiant Lands to see the Guardians?" I asked.

"In a manner of speaking," he said.

"What does that mean?"

He smiled. "You'll see."

"You've done this before," I said. "Been to see the Guardians, I mean."

"Yes, once," he said.

"To be honest, I kind of didn't think they were real. It all sounds so . . . New Agey."

"I assure you the Guardians are quite real," he said. "When I was younger, I came here to ask them for help. They chose not to interfere. I suppose I shouldn't have been surprised."

The elevator stopped. Through the open ironwork, I saw an enormous room with high, vaulted ceilings and electric lights. The walls were polished cherrywood. The floor was marble tile.

"What did you ask the Guardians to do?" I asked.

Isaac slid open the gate and stepped out of the elevator. "Save Morbius's life."

Damn. I blew out my breath. I hadn't been expecting that.

I followed him into the Library of Keys. Before us, tall shelves stretched from floor to ceiling, only instead of books they held keys of all shapes and sizes, each on its own peg. A wide, central aisle ran down the middle of the room. On either side, row after row of shelves seemed to extend into an infinite distance. On any other day, under any other circumstances, I would have been excited to see the place Bethany was always talking about. Today, all I wanted was to get what I needed and get out again. Bethany was hurt because of me. Jordana was dead because of me. Erickson Arkwright had manipulated me—manipulated all of us—to this point. I didn't just want him stopped. I wanted him dead. For that, I needed the Guardians' help.

Heavy footsteps came from somewhere deep in the stacks, shaking the floor. A massive creature emerged and started toward us down the central aisle. It was big, and definitely not human. It wore a three-piece tweed suit over its fleshy, misshapen form, its pale skin loose and flabby. Its wide, flat feet were bare, and each had only four toes. Its jowly, triple-chinned face remained slack as it approached. Its lower lip drooped to reveal a row of teeth like square, yellow bricks. In its big, hairy-knuckled hands it carried a water-filled glass cylinder. Unsure what this creature was, I took an involuntary step back.

"Relax, Trent," Isaac said. "This is the librarian."

I looked at the creature again, surprised. This was the librarian? Its eyes were as blank and glazed as a frog's. There was no sign of intelligence or curiosity in them. Then another, far more disturbing thought struck me. If William Astor was rumored to have had an affair with a librarian, did that mean it was with a creature like this one? It wasn't my place to judge, but good God.

Something moved within the glass cylinder, catching my attention. I immediately wished it hadn't. Inside the cylinder was a head. It wasn't human, either. Its hairless flesh was the color of bronze. Eight tentacles sprouted from the head like limbs, waving sinuously in the water. It blinked its slate gray eyes at us.

"May I be of assistance?" the head asked. Somehow, its voice came through the water and glass loud and clear.

I realized my mistake then. I'd misunderstood what Isaac said. *This* was the librarian. The creature carrying it was merely its helper. Though that didn't make me feel any better about William Astor's alleged affair.

"We seek an audience with the Guardians," Isaac said.

The head tipped forward slightly in the cylinder, its version of a nod. "As you wish. You are aware of the price for access to the Guardians?"

"I am," Isaac said. "I've been here before."

The librarian looked surprised. "The Guardians do not often get repeat visitors. For most, once is enough. You know why, surely."

"This is an emergency," Isaac explained.

"Then I will not detain you any longer," the librarian replied. "Please, follow me."

The hulking, expressionless creature turned around and started walking down the central aisle, still holding the cylinder. Its footfalls rattled the keys on their pegs. Following it, I looked down every row of shelves we passed. They all stretched into the distance farther than I could see. On the pegs hung every kind of key imaginable, fashioned from metal, plastic, wood, ceramic, and glass. There were long and short keys, thick and thin, toothy and smooth, even plain electronic fobs. Every key to every lock in the world. This library was a thief's wet dream. But it couldn't truly hold *every* key in the world . . . could it? Was there a replica here of the key to Citadel? To Underwood's fallout shelter? What about the twenty-sided, crystalline sphere that had opened the secret chamber below Bethesda Fountain?

The creature turned a corner into an aisle that was much shorter than the others. This one terminated in a blank, wood-paneled wall. The rectangular outline of a door stood in the wall, but there was no handle to open it. The hulking creature stopped beside two wooden ledges on the wall near the door. One ledge was empty. The other held a plain, metal box. The creature put the cylinder on the empty ledge, turning it so the head inside faced us. Then it picked up the box and turned back to us. A round hole had been cut into one side of the box.

"Only one of you need pay for access to the Guardians," the librarian said. "Which will it be?"

Isaac stepped forward. "Me."

The librarian regarded him quizzically. "You offer to pay even though you have paid once before?"

"Yes," Isaac said.

The librarian nodded. "Very well. Place your hand inside the box."

The creature held out the box. Isaac reached into the hole, his hand disappearing up to the wrist. I watched nervously. Were they going to take his hand as payment? One of his fingers?

A light flared inside the box, quick as a camera flash. Isaac pulled his hand out of the box and flexed his fingers. There were still five. The creature put the box back on the ledge.

"Payment to the Guardians has been made," the librarian announced.

"What was that?" I asked Isaac. "What did they take?"

"Don't worry about it," he said.

"One year," the librarian said. Isaac shot it an angry look.

"A year?" I asked. "Of what, service?"

"No," the librarian said. "Of life."

"You took a year of his *life*?" I demanded, shocked. "What kind of sick bastard—"

"Not I. The Guardians," the librarian interrupted. "It is not our place to ask why they set this price. Their reasons are their own."

I turned to Isaac, still reeling from this. "You should have let me do it. One year off my life won't matter. I'm not like you. I don't have an end date."

He shook his head. "You don't know that. Besides, coming here was my decision. I couldn't ask you to pay the price. I wouldn't."

"You should have told me."

"Would you have let me do it if I had?"

"Of course not," I said.

"Now you know why I didn't tell you."

The door in the wood-paneled wall slid open. I couldn't see anything beyond it but a bright, white light. I shielded my eyes.

"Step through," the librarian said. The tweed-suited creature picked up the cylinder again.

Isaac walked into the doorway and was swallowed by the light. I lingered a moment in front of the door, glaring at the librarian.

"You should have told me what the price was," I said. "He already paid once before. That's *two* years they've taken off his life. It's not right."

"The price was not yours to pay, Immortal Storm," the librarian replied. I was surprised it knew who I was. "Step through. The Guardians do not like to be kept waiting."

The creature carried the librarian away, its loud, heavy footfalls receding into the stacks. Frankly, I didn't give a damn what the Guardians liked or didn't like, but Isaac was waiting. I looked at the bright light blazing through the doorway, shielding my eyes again. I couldn't see Isaac inside. I sighed and stepped through.

Despite the bright light, my eyes adjusted quickly. I found myself in a square room with glowing white walls. A low, steady hum came from all around me. Floating in the middle of the room was a huge key roughly the length of my forearm.

Isaac was standing before it, studying it. I watched him a moment. How much time did he have left in him? He'd shaved a year off his life to get us into this room. What did that mean for him? If he was destined to die next year, did that mean he would drop dead tomorrow instead?

I pushed the thought away. I didn't believe in destiny, especially when it came to death. I refused to.

I walked up to join Isaac and examine the key. The blade was long and forged from iron. There were two square teeth with hollow centers at the end. The bow was fashioned into an ouroboros of a dragon, just like on the man's eye patch upstairs. The key didn't appear to be resting on anything. It wasn't hanging on wire, either. It simply floated.

Isaac wrapped one hand around the key. Instantly, the lights and the loud hum dimmed and died. We were left in complete darkness, complete silence. Then a doorway opened in the blackness before us. Through it I saw a pure, blinding white ground below a blue, cloudless sky. Wind howled.

"Is that how we get to the Radiant Lands?" I asked.

"No," Isaac said. "We're already there."

He let go of the floating key and walked through the door. I took a deep breath, hoping he knew what he was doing, and followed him.

# Thirty-Three

As I stepped through the doorway, the white ground crunched beneath my boots. Snow. I shivered in the sudden cold and pulled my trench coat closed around me. My breath steamed in the air. Luminous and untouched, the snow blanketed everything as far as I could see, from horizon to horizon. Frosty mountains rose in the distance. Was this the Radiant Lands?

In the distance, eight plain, wooden chairs were arranged in a semicircle in the snow. Only seven of them were occupied. In three chairs, old men sat with their white beards in their laps. In the other four were old women whose long white hair blew in the wind behind them. All of them wore jet-black robes that stood out in stark contrast against the white snow. They wore sandals on their feet, as if the bitter cold didn't bother them.

The eighth chair remained empty.

"You have requested an audience, Isaac Keene," one of the women said as we approached. "We are here."

Isaac stopped, keeping a respectful distance from them. He bowed. "Thank you for seeing us, Guardians. We need your help. We seek a man named Erickson Arkwright."

*These* were the Guardians? Somehow, I'd expected something a little more impressive than seven elderly men and women sitting in the middle of the arctic tundra. Weren't they supposed to be omnipotent immortals with dominion over the elements? These seven didn't look like Guardians to me. They looked like residents of an old age home waiting for *Wheel of Fortune* to come on.

The Guardians turned in unison to look at me. Shit. They'd heard my thoughts. I should have been more careful. They were all-knowing, weren't they?

One of the male Guardians addressed me, his long beard blowing in the breeze. "You are wise not to believe your eyes."

"What you see are merely illusions," a female Guardian said. "Our forms, this landscape, they were chosen to put you at ease. But if we have misjudged and you are displeased, we can change it."

"That won't be necessary," Isaac said quickly, bowing again in deference. "Please don't mind my friend here—"

"No, hold on," I said. "He gave up a year of his life to see you. That may not mean anything to you, but it does to us. The least you can do is stop with the bullshit and show him your real faces."

"Trent, don't," Isaac warned.

The Guardians nodded in unison. One said, "Very well. If it is the truth you want, then you shall have it."

Instantly, the arctic landscape was gone. We were surrounded by a light so bright I had trouble keeping my eyes open against it. I raised a hand to shield my eyes, but it did no good. I had no sense of the space around me, or even which way was up. There was only the light and Isaac at my side, trying to shield his eyes just like I was. Was this the Radiant Lands in its true state? I sensed more than saw the Guardians nearby— seven titanic shapes encircling us, their features hidden by the light. The Guardians spoke then, but it wasn't in any language I understood. It was a horrible sound. Every syllable was like nails scratching at a tomb door. I put my hands over my ears. It barely muffled the sound, but at least I was able to think. I'd heard this language before. I recognized it. It was the same language Bethany, Gabrielle, and Isaac used when they spoke their incantations. If Ehrlendarr was the language of the Ancients, then the eerie language of magic belonged to the Guardians.

Suddenly we were back on the snow, beneath the clear blue sky. The seven Guardians sat in their chairs as before.

"You will agree that perhaps this is better after all?" one of them asked.

I blinked, letting my eyes adjust from the intense light. The terrible sounds still echoed in my ears. "Point taken."

Isaac scowled at me. "I told you to leave it alone."

"Do not scold him, Isaac Keene," another Guardian said. "He is a good friend to you. His desire to defend you is admirable. Only a good friend would feel the price you paid is unjust. But know, both of you, that the price is necessary. There are those who would abuse the privilege of an audience with the Guardians. Only this way can we separate those who truly need us from those who seek power and personal gain."

"But even so, we have our own code," another Guardian continued. "We observe but do not interfere. What makes you think we will help you find Erickson Arkwright?"

"You know what he's done," Isaac said. "You know what he's capable of."

"We know all," a third Guardian said. "All is playing out as it is supposed to."

"Supposed to?" Isaac asked. "But surely you know what Arkwright is planning to do."

"We know all," another repeated.

"We do not interfere."

"We cannot give you what you ask, Isaac Keene."

Isaac looked crestfallen. "Guardians, I beseech you. You're our last hope."

"You have our answer. All is playing out as it is supposed to."

That was all I could take. My fuse was already short. My anger had been simmering since we left Arkwright's mansion. Now it boiled over.

"The mighty Guardians," I sneered. "What a joke. You know what I think? I think you're a bunch of charlatans. You don't tell people anything because you don't *know* anything. You don't do anything because you *can't*. Well, congratulations, you've pulled the wool over everyone's eyes. And for what? So you can steal years off desperate people's lives to add to your own?"

"Is that what you think?" a female Guardian asked.

"Trent, stop it," Isaac hissed at me. "They've made their decision. We'll abide by it."

"It's bullshit." I stomped through the snow toward the Guardians. "If you're not going to help, then give him back the year you took from him."

"Trent!" Isaac shouted after me.

"You are wrong about us," another Guardian said. "We do not steal life from others for ourselves. We are not like you."

That was a low blow.

"Go on, then, prove me wrong and give it back to him," I said, furious. "Give back *both* years you took, because twice now he's come to you for help and twice now you've turned him away with nothing."

One of the female Guardians stood. She raised a hand. The snow under my feet broke apart. A thick, wooden vine sprouted from the ground and wrapped itself around my leg, stopping me. I tried to move my leg, but the vine held firm, refusing to snap no matter how hard I strained. I looked at the female Guardian again. If each Guardian ruled over an element, she had to be the Guardian of Wood.

"Isaac Keene knew the risk when he paid the price," she said. "Both times. He does not need you to fight his battles for him."

I looked back at Isaac. He glared at me and said, "I gave it willingly."

I turned back to the Guardians. "Fine, I get it, no refunds. Just tell me, what do you need a year from his life for? A year from *anyone's* life? You're immortal, aren't you?"

The vine unwound from my leg and retreated beneath the snow. The Guardian of Wood sat again.

"It is not for us. We have no need of it," she said. "The years are given to another. Someone who does."

"I thought it went against the laws of magic to take the life force from one person and give it to another," I said.

"Mortal magic, yes. Not ours." The Guardian of Wood turned to Isaac. "I am sorry, Isaac Keene, but we cannot give you what you ask. We must remain neutral. For the balance."

"What balance?" I demanded. "In case you haven't noticed, everything's gone to shit. On *your* watch. What have you done to fix it?"

"It is our existence that keeps the balance, not our actions." She looked at the empty chair beside her. "Our brother's absence is responsible for the current state of things, not us. But even if we could set things right in his place, we do not interfere. It is not our way."

"If you know everything like you say you do, then you know if Arkwright binds Nahash-Dred, it's all over," I said. "The world you're supposed to protect will be destroyed."

"All is playing out as it is supposed to."

I groaned. I was starting to hate those words.

"We do not interfere," the Guardian of Wood said.

"Well, maybe it's time you fucking started," I said.

Isaac grabbed my arm and began pulling me away. "That's it, Trent. We're going." He whispered angrily in my ear, "You do *not* lecture the Guardians."

"I think it's high time someone did," I said.

"We don't have time for this," Isaac said. He spun me around and marched me back the way we came. A black, rectangular doorway stood on the snowdrift ahead of us, a hole in space leading back to the Library of Keys. Isaac let go of my arm and went through first. I was about to follow him when the Guardians spoke again.

"Immortal Storm."

I stopped and turned around. The Guardians had moved. The chairs were gone, and now the seven of them stood in a semicircle right in front of me.

"We see you," one said.

"We keep seeing you," another said. "And you see us."

I nodded, remembering the times I'd glimpsed them. "I do, I see you whenever I . . ." I trailed off, not sure how to describe it. "When my vision changes."

"When you look through the skin of the world, you see us," the Guardian of Wood said. "What does that tell you of our role? Of our power?"

"Fine," I said. "I get it. You're at the center of everything, you're all-powerful. You just don't give a damn."

The Guardian of Wood said, "But we *keep* seeing each other, Immortal Storm. There is a connection between us." She cocked her head at me. "There is something . . . familiar about you."

The other Guardians chimed in.

"So like our lost brother."

"Hotheaded. Stubborn. Impatient."

"There is a sense of him about you. You are endless, like him."

"You walk in eternity, like him."

"And yet, you are not him."

"No, you are not."

"You cannot be. The Guardian of Magic is gone from this world."

Great, so I wasn't Lucas West and I wasn't the Guardian of Magic. If I were using the process of elimination, that only left seven billion other possibilities. But maybe there was a faster way to find out.

"You know who I am, don't you?" I asked.

They looked at me. None of them answered.

"Right. I should have known better. We're done here." I pointed over my shoulder at the doorway in the snow. "Isaac is waiting for me on the other side. We don't have a lot of time to stop the world from ending. No thanks to you."

One of the Guardians stepped forward, his long beard waving in the wind. "You speak prematurely. Are you so sure we will not give the information to you?"

I squinted at him. "But you said . . ."

"We told Isaac Keene we could not give it to him. We said nothing of you." The Guardian opened one hand, palm up like he was holding something, but his hand was empty. "After the sky is torn open and the demon comes, when all that is to be said is said, and all that is to be done is done, the information you seek will be lost. It will be burnt and scattered to the winds. But that is the interesting thing about time. For most, it is a long, unceasing forward march. But for others, it flows in many different directions."

Tiny, partially burned pieces of parchment appeared on the wind, blowing toward the Guardian and gathering in his palm. They cycloned there, the small bits fusing together into larger ones, the scorch marks fading. Finally, he held a scroll in his hand, rolled up and bound with a black ribbon.

"What is lost in the future still exists in the past," the Guardian said. The Guardian of Time, I presumed.

I reached for the scroll. He pulled it away from me.

"Heed me. It does not matter where Erickson Arkwright is now. What matters is where he will be. On midnight of All Hallows' Eve, when the wall between worlds is easiest to breach, he will open the doorway at the location written in this scroll, for this location is where the wall will be thinnest."

"I don't understand," I said. "Why would he open the doorway between dimensions if Nahash-Dred is already here?"

The Guardian held up a hand to silence me. It was clear he had no intention of answering my question. "Know this, too. At this location, at the appointed time, Nahash-Dred will be revealed. Are you prepared for that, Immortal Storm? You must be prepared."

"I am," I said.

"Are you truly? I wonder," the Guardian of Time said.

He handed the scroll to me. I quickly undid the ribbon and opened it. Written on the parchment was a blocky, ancient-looking alphabet I couldn't read. Maybe Isaac could. I closed it again and looked up at the Guardian of Time.

"Why are you helping us?" I asked. "I thought you didn't get involved."

He smiled. "All is playing out—"

"As it is supposed to," I finished. "Right. You guys sound like a broken record. But thank you for this. You might have just saved everyone's life."

"Not everyone's," the Guardian of Time said. "Lives will be lost, and the infection will claim another. Someone close to you."

"The infection?" I thought of the darkness I'd seen growing inside Gabrielle. Was that what the Guardian meant? Was there no way to stop it before it claimed her?

"Listen to me, Immortal Storm," the Guardian of Time said. "Be sure you are ready. You cannot control what dwells inside you. It will control you first. It has already begun."

The Guardian of Wood nodded, her long, white hair trailing in the breeze. "The Immortal Storm is the force that will destroy us all. So it is prophesied."

"Unless," said another Guardian.

"Unless," added another.

"Unless you die."

"Die a true death."

"I don't believe in prophecies," I told them.

"Belief has nothing to do with it. Not believing in snow will not stop a blizzard," the Guardian of Time said. "Find a way to die, Immortal Storm. Before the prophecy comes true."

# Thirty-Four

Isaac drove us back to Citadel. The rain had finally stopped. The wet blacktop glistened under the Escalade's wheels.

"I can't believe the Guardians gave you the information," he said, shaking his head in disbelief. "How did you convince them to help?"

"Must be my natural charm," I said.

I was still trying to process what the Guardians had told me. *The Immortal Storm is the force that will destroy us all.* It hit a nerve, reminding me too much of what the oracles had said. For a while, I'd thought I was free of the curse of the Immortal Storm when I was Lucas West. But that had been a lie. I wasn't free at all. I was starting to think I never would be.

"Charm? After the way you spoke to them, you're lucky the Guardians didn't turn you into a frog," Isaac said.

"Can they do that?"

"I think they can do pretty much anything," he said. "That's why it stings so much when they refuse to get involved."

But they'd gotten involved this time. Why? They refused to say, other than that everything was playing out the way it was supposed to, whatever that meant. I unrolled the scroll again, looking over the strange, blocky letters. At first I'd thought they'd been written in ink. Now I saw they'd been expertly burned into the parchment, without burning *through* it. It was amazing workmanship. Impossible workmanship.

"You're sure you can translate this?" I said.

"I think so," he said. "If I'm right, it's a very old language, one that hasn't been seen in a long time. But there are texts I can consult. I just need time."

"What language is it?" I asked.

"I think it's Elvish," he said.

"I thought there weren't any elves left. Didn't they all take off for greener pastures after World War Two?"

"They did," he said. "But look at the scroll again. It doesn't look particularly new to me. It could have been written centuries ago."

"Why would elves write a scroll centuries ago with the information we need now, in 2013?" I asked.

Isaac shrugged. "Where the Guardians are concerned, I've found it's best not to ask too many questions."

When we reached Citadel, Gabrielle met us at the door. I grilled her for an update on Bethany.

"She's resting comfortably," Gabrielle said. "I put her in your room. I hope that's okay. I didn't know where else to put her."

"It's fine," I said.

"I've been treating her burns with Sanare moss," Gabrielle continued. "She's stable now. She'll pull through, but she'll almost certainly have a scar."

I sighed with relief. Bethany was going to be okay. The three of us climbed the stairs to the second floor. Isaac took the scroll with him to his study. He paused at the door.

"I'm not to be interrupted," he said. "Not for any reason. I need to concentrate if I'm going to translate this."

"Is there anything we can do?" Gabrielle asked.

He shook his head. "I just need time." He shut himself in his study.

I looked down the hall at the door to my room. "Can I see her?"

Gabrielle nodded. "She asked me to send you in when you got back. Just be sure to let her rest, okay? She's going to need another treatment soon. Come get me when you're ready and I'll take care of it."

I nodded. "Thanks."

Gabrielle went back downstairs. I started at the door to my room for a moment. The last time I'd been here with Bethany, we'd gotten into an argument about Jordana. I felt like a fool for not listening to her. I knocked softly, opened the door, and went in. The room was dark. The shades had been drawn over the window. After I gently shut the door behind me, the only light was the dim gray of the approaching dawn seeping in around the shades. Bethany was sleeping on the bed, facing away from me. Kali was curled up on the covers by Bethany's legs, purring and dozing. It was obvious the cat liked Bethany more than she liked me. She'd made the right choice.

I sat down in the chair across the room and put my head in my hands. This was my fault. I was the reason Bethany was hurt. Gabrielle said she'd be all right, but what if the wound had been worse? What if the Thracian Gauntlet's blast had hit her full on? I'd almost gotten Bethany killed. My blindness—my stubbornness—had almost killed my closest friend.

In the darkness of the room, I heard Bethany speak. "You asked me once if I remembered my family. I don't."

"I didn't realize you were awake," I said, sitting up.

"My parents gave me up when I was very young, too young to remember them," she said. "But that doesn't mean I don't think about them. I do, all the time."

She turned to face me. She grimaced a little as she did, as though it hurt to move. More guilt surged within me. Upset at having lost her dozing spot, Kali jumped off the bed and scurried into the darkness beneath it.

"I'm going to tell you something I've never told anyone," Bethany said. "When I was young, I would think about my parents for hours on end, but I didn't know how to picture them. When I thought of my mother, I imagined the illustration of a queen I saw in a storybook once. She didn't look anything like me. She was tall and blond. But she was also beautiful and strong, just the way I hoped my mother was. When I thought of my father, I pictured . . . God, I can't believe I'm telling you this."

"It's okay," I said. "Go on."

She sighed. "The man I pictured was Patrick Stewart. I watched a lot of *Star Trek: The Next Generation* in the foster homes back then. I guess I wished my father was Captain Picard. Or someone like him, anyway. Decent. Honorable. A man who lived a life of dignity, a life in control. The opposite of the life I had. I made up this whole story about how my parents never wanted to give me up, but were forced to for some epic, tragic reason. It was childish. I know that now."

"It wasn't childish," I said. "You invented a story you could live with. I did the same thing. I invented a lot of stories trying to come up with a past for myself."

"I'm sure none of them involved Captain Picard," she said.

"No," I said. "Captain Sisko was more my style. He was a badass. He didn't take shit from anyone."

She laughed. It was remarkable how much I'd missed that sound.

"Remind me again how an amnesiac knows so much pop culture?" she asked.

"A television in the fallout shelter and a lot of sleepless nights."

She sat up in bed. She switched on the bedside lamp, bathing the room in a warm, golden light. She had changed out of her street clothes and into a loose-fitting nightgown that presumably wouldn't irritate her wounds. Her face scrunched in pain and she let out a small groan.

"Are you okay?" I asked.

"The burn on my back is flaring up again," she said. "I need more Sanare moss. Could you get Gabrielle? I'd apply it myself, but there are spots on my back I can't reach."

"How about I do it for you?"

She looked at me, surprised. "Are you sure?"

I stood up. "I haven't exactly been a good friend to you lately. I'm sorry for that. I want to make it up to you, but I don't know how. Taking care of you seems like a start."

She regarded me for a moment, looking deep into me with those bright blue eyes. Then she nodded and pointed at a clay bowl on a table at the foot of the bed.

I picked up the bowl. Inside it was a lumpy green goo. I'd seen Sanare moss in action before. It sped up the healing process at an astronomical rate. I hoped it would do the same for Bethany's burns.

Bethany turned her back to me and lifted her nightgown off over her head. Most of her back was covered with the tattoo of a fiery phoenix, a sigil that prevented magic from getting inside her and infecting her. But strong as it was, it couldn't protect her from physical harm. A long band of red, burned skin stretched diagonally from her left shoulder blade to the small of her back, just above the waistband of her panties. But it wasn't as bad as I thought it would be. The previous Sanare moss treatments were already helping. Bethany held her crumpled nightgown to her chest, covering herself as she sat cross-legged on the bed. With one hand, she gathered her dark hair together and draped it forward over one shoulder so it would be out of the way.

I sat down behind her, unsure what to do. I thought for sure if I touched her, it would hurt her. She'd already been hurt once today because of me. I couldn't stand the idea of hurting her again.

She sensed my hesitation and looked over her shoulder at me. "It's okay, just be gentle."

I could do a lot of things. I could fight creatures twice my size. I could die and come back. I could pluck the threads of the world and make it shudder. But gentle was something I didn't know if I could do. Gentle was something I'd never been.

I dipped my fingers into the Sanare moss. It felt cool and gelatinous, tingling against my fingertips. I scooped out a dollop and began to spread it on Bethany's back. The moss appeared green and lumpy in the bowl, but it went on clear and slick like an ointment. She shivered as I applied it.

"Does it hurt?" I asked.

"No," she said. "It feels good."

I spread the Sanare moss across her shoulders first, then worked my way down her back. In the few places where her skin wasn't burned or colored by the tattoo, it looked as pale as china compared to mine. The burnt skin felt rough to the touch at first, but the moss turned it smooth almost immediately. The tattoo had essentially been cut in two by the long stripe of the burn, but it began to knit itself back together under the moss, tendrils of color joining together and becoming whole again. Clearly, the shaman who'd tattooed her had not used regular ink.

Bethany was warm under my hands. Her body temperature had always been higher than normal, but now, touching her bare skin, she felt almost hot. It was like warming my hands before a fire.

"It's funny, usually *you're* the one fixing *me* up," I said, because suddenly I needed to say something. I needed to be doing something other than just touching her. The sensation was confusing me, making me feel things I thought I didn't feel anymore.

"It must really be the end of the world," Bethany joked.

"If it is, the Guardians don't seem all that worked up about it," I said. While I applied the moss, I told her about our visit with the Guardians and the scroll they'd given us. "It's supposed to tell us the location where Arkwright is going to open a doorway between dimensions, but it's in another language. I couldn't read it. Isaac is trying to translate it now. He thinks it's written in Elvish."

She looked at me over her shoulder again. "Elvish?"

I shrugged.

"Why would Arkwright need to open the doorway?" she asked. "Nahash-Dred is already here."

"I asked the Guardians the same question. They didn't elaborate."

"It figures," she said. "So you actually saw the Guardians? I never have."

I thought that was a good thing, considering the price of admission.

"What did they look like?" she asked.

"A bunch of old geezers with a serious ego problem," I said. "They made a big stink about staying neutral and not getting involved, but in the end they helped. Sort of. If the scroll can be translated, they helped. If it can't be, then they're just assholes."

"It's probably a little from column A, a little from column B," Bethany said. She glanced at me again. "I've been thinking about why you asked me that question before. About whether I remember my family."

"It was on my mind, that's all," I said.

"Because of Jordana. Trent, I'm so sorry. For all of it. I wanted to be wrong about her. I wanted you to be happy and know who you are."

"I'm the one who should be apologizing," I said. "If I'd listened to you, none of this would have happened. I was too blind to see I was being played, but you saw it. You had suspicions about Jordana from the start. I suppose you're dying to say 'I told you so.'"

"Not particularly," she said. "In a way, Jordana was a victim in this, too."

That was true enough. The anger flared inside me again, hot and ferocious. "Arkwright knew exactly what he was doing when he infected her. He knew it would affect her mind. It would silence any doubts she might have about killing to protect him and his secret. He turned her into a murderer.

He used her to get me to lower my guard and deliver the Codex right into his hands."

"Whoever Jordana was before Arkwright infected her, this wasn't her," Bethany said. "Not the *real* her."

I spread another handful of Sanare moss on Bethany's skin, down near the phoenix's tail feathers at the small of her back. "I guess I've always had bad timing with women, huh?"

She looked back at me, arching an eyebrow. "There's bad timing, and then there's bad timing."

I chuckled, but it was short-lived. There was just too much weighing me down. I opened my mouth to speak, but the words stuck in my throat. They seemed so tiny compared to everything I felt.

"I'm never going to know who I am, am I?" I said when I found my voice again. "Every time I think I'm getting close, it falls apart. Every time someone says they know, they're lying. The kicker is, out of everyone, the only one who seems to know the truth is Reve Azrael, and I don't even know if she's dead or alive."

"I wouldn't trust the answer from her, either," Bethany said. "I guess at the end of the day you have to ask yourself if you're okay with not knowing. If you can live without the answer."

Could I? I didn't know. Every time I thought I was close, the answer was pulled away from me. The frustration and disappointment were chipping away at me piece by piece. How much more could I take? How much more until there was nothing left of me to chip away?

"What about you?" I asked. "Can you live with not knowing why your parents gave you up?"

"I've lived with it this long. If I have to go on not knowing, then I guess that's what I'll do."

I finished applying the Sanare moss. I stood and put the bowl back on the table at the foot of the bed.

"You should get some rest," I said.

She slipped the nightgown back on over her head, then turned on the bed to face me. "Thank you."

I shrugged. "It was nothing. You're an easy patient to treat."

"Not just for the Sanare moss, that's not what I mean," she said. "For still being my friend after I acted like an ass. For listening to me go on about my parents. For talking to me. I don't think I've ever seen you open up like that before."

"A friend once told me I needed to open up more," I said. "I guess this is me trying to do that."

"Well, I like it," she said. "This friend of yours must be extremely smart."

"Yeah, she's annoying that way," I said. "Now get some rest."

"I'll be all right soon," she said. "The Sanare moss works fast. Promise me you'll come get me as soon as Isaac translates the scroll. Don't go after Arkwright without me."

"I wouldn't dream of it."

She lay down on her side and pulled the blanket up to her chin again. I walked to the door.

"Trent?"

I looked back at her.

"He was no Picard, but Sisko was okay, too," she said.

# Thirty-Five

I left Bethany to her rest and started down the stairs to the first floor. I ran into Gabrielle on the landing halfway down. She was staring at the portrait of Thornton mounted on the wall, lost in her thoughts.

"You okay?" I said.

"I miss him, Trent. I miss him so much," she said. "He still hasn't shown himself to me. Not like he did to you."

"I haven't seen him since."

"Do you think he . . . went back?"

"I don't know," I said. "But I have a hard time believing he would come all the way here without seeing you, even if just to say goodbye."

She looked up at the portrait again. "You never know how much time you're going to have with someone. It's not fair, but it's the way life is. Time isn't on anyone's side."

She winced suddenly and doubled over, clutching her stomach. Sweat beaded on her forehead.

"Are you okay?" I asked, reaching for her.

She backed away. "I'm fine."

"You're not fine," I said. "It's the magic inside you. It's infecting you. You shouldn't have done it, Gabrielle. You should have left it alone."

"I can make my own decisions," she snapped. "We're not all like you, Trent. We don't all have the luxury of coming back to life. When people like me die, we *stay* dead. So we either die, or we find some way to even the odds. We all make the choices we have to."

"I didn't choose to be like this," I said. "I didn't choose any of it. I'd give it up in a second to be normal. You know that."

She laughed bitterly. "What's normal, Trent? In this world, what exactly does *normal* mean?"

She winced again and doubled over, gritting her teeth. This attack seemed stronger than the last. She groaned in pain, but she still wouldn't let me touch her. When it passed, she straightened up again.

"I just need some air," she said. She started down the stairs to the first floor.

I followed her. "I'll go with you."

"I don't need a chaperone," she said.

"I could use some air, too," I said.

She shrugged. "Suit yourself."

I followed her out of Citadel and into Central Park. The sun was rising in the east, silhouetting the tall buildings of the Fifth Avenue skyline. With the sun behind them, they looked like featureless, monolithic stones in a prehistoric landscape. For a moment, the world felt new and unspoiled. The autumn morning was crisp and invigorating. After all the rain yesterday, it was good to see the sun again. We walked across the grass and into the nearby trees, our boots crunching the dead leaves that carpeted the forest floor. Not all the leaves had fallen yet. Some still clung stubbornly to their branches, red and gold and burnt umber, all of them ablaze with the morning sun. Everything felt right. Everything was in its place. There was no indication at all that the world could end tonight at midnight.

"You never really notice how beautiful something is until you realize it could go away," I said.

Gabrielle nodded, looking around her. She seemed calmer now. "The world is a beautiful place when the sun is up, and sometimes even when it's down. But it wasn't always like this. Before the Guardians came, the world was very different. Hot and barren, with nothing but rocks and fire and lakes of molten lava from one pole to the other. Back then, the world belonged to a race called the Voyavold. In Ehrlendarr, their name means Suneaters. They loved the dark so much they tried to eat the sun right out of the sky."

"I thought the Ancients were the first creatures on earth," I said.

"The first in recorded history," Gabrielle said. "Legend says the Voyavold were here before them, when the world was young. We only know about the Voyavold from stories and books that were locked away from the public long ago. They were supposed to be violent, monstrous creatures. The Guardians drove them out and tamed the earth."

It was hard to imagine the Guardians getting off their asses to drive a race of monsters from the world. It was hard to imagine them getting off their asses to do *anything*.

"Where did the Voyavold go?" I asked.

She shrugged. "Somewhere else."

"Ah," I said. "Another apartment in the cosmic condo."

"Something like that," she said. "But they say the Voyavold are always trying to come back. Always trying to take back what was theirs. You see, Trent? Even monsters miss things when they're gone. Even monsters know all too well that nothing lasts forever."

The sound of snapping twigs froze us in our tracks. Gabrielle grabbed my arm and pulled me down behind a thick bush. She peeked over the top.

"Look," she whispered.

I peered over the bush. A dense copse of trees stood in front of us. As I watched, humanoid forms peeled themselves off the bark along the thick, upper branches. They looked almost two-dimensional as they pulled free of the wood, but when they dropped to the ground they were as three-dimensional as the trees themselves. All of them were female, and all of them were unclothed, their skin the same color and texture as the bark, their hair matching every shade of the autumn leaves. They didn't see us. Their expressions were somber as they walked single file away from the trees.

"Dryads," Gabrielle said. "Where are they going?"

"It's the exodus," I said. "Yrouel told us about it before he died. He said he could sense something terrible was about to happen, and that others could, too. He said they were moving down to the Nethercity while there was still time, to be under Gregor's protection." I watched more dryads pull free of the trees and join the others in their slow, melancholy march. "Do you think they'll be safe from Nahash-Dred down there?"

"Maybe, maybe not," Gabrielle said. "But it's safer than being up here when the shit hits the fan."

The last of the dryads disappeared from view. The forest felt strangely empty, though nothing had visibly changed. The trees, the grass, the leaves, it all looked the same. But there was a sense of loneliness to it now, as if the dryads had taken something essential with them when they left. We stood up again.

"I'm sorry about what I said back there," Gabrielle said. "I was out of line. There's a lot of anger in me right now. I know that. It's getting harder and harder to keep it under control. It's just . . ." She paused and shook her head. "You can't imagine how alone I am now. How alone I *feel* without Thornton."

"But you're not alone," I said. "The rest of us are still here."

"That's different. You know that," she said. "You don't know how lucky you are. We don't all have someone who'll stay up all night with us playing cards just so we don't get lonely."

"That's different, too," I said.

"Is it? She loves you, Trent. She has from the start. She just doesn't know how to say it, or what to do with it. She hasn't had an easy life. She hasn't let herself feel anything in a very long time. I guess for a long time it was safer not to let herself get close to anyone. But things are different now. I know you have feelings for her, too. I would know it even if I hadn't crawled inside your head once upon a time. I saw the way you tore that library apart to get her back."

I took a deep breath. "I don't think she feels that way. She told me—"

"I know what she told you," Gabrielle interrupted. "What, you think she and I don't talk? Please. You two need to stop dancing around this and talk it out. Because what I said before is true. You don't know how much time you have left together. You know what's coming. It could all end tonight."


While Bethany slept, Gabrielle and I spent the rest of the day scouring Isaac's library for demonology books. The library was extensive, taking up most of Citadel's third story. The unfinished birch floor and row after row of maple bookshelves made the whole room smell like wood. But Isaac was right when he said his collection was woefully lacking in information on demons. We didn't find much. Sitting at a table amid the library's overstuffed bookshelves, Gabrielle and I pored over what little we found.

According to Bankoff's annotated *Libri Arcanum,* the king of the demons was named Leviathan. He and his queen, Lamia, had two sons together. The firstborn, and crown prince, was Behemoth. The second was Nahash-Dred. Apparently, the two brothers had a frosty relationship that spread to the rest of demonkind. Their kingdom had split into two camps: those loyal to Behemoth, and those loyal to Nahash-Dred. None of the rest of the royal family shared Nahash-Dred's ability to change his shape. Apparently, the demon would use his power to move undetected through worlds before destroying them. Why he did this or what, if anything, he was looking for was not mentioned.

I thought of the Mad Affliction again, the last of the greater demons Arkwright's cult had accidentally summoned. He belonged to a culture that was a lot more advanced, a lot more complex than I thought. I felt a pang of guilt. I hated that we'd left him in that cage under the library, all alone. Demon or not, it didn't sit right with me. There should have been another way.

If Isaac's library didn't have much on demons, it had even less on the Codex Goetia. In a yellowing old tome called *De Sacra Artificialia Caradras,* I found only one small chapter on it. The book hinted at mysterious, otherworldly origins for the artifact and warned it should never be used improperly, though it refused to offer any instructions on the proper way to use it. I flipped through the pages, hoping to find information on the Codex Goetia's banishing spell, but there was nothing, just more useless warnings to leave the Codex alone. I slammed the book closed in frustration, causing a cloud of dust to billow out from between its pages.

"Listen to this," Gabrielle said. She was reading a musty, leather-bound volume titled *The Book of Eibon.* "It says once a demon is bound to someone, if that person dies the demon returns to its own dimension."

"So Arkwright has to die," I said.

She looked up at me from the book. "You don't sound too upset about that."

I met her eye, but I didn't say anything.

"You have a terrible poker face," she said. "I saw it in your eyes when you couldn't save Jordana. You want Arkwright dead. I don't blame you. Jordana was my friend, too. He messed with her head and took my friend from me. I want him dead just as much as you do. But he also said he recognized you. He may know who you are, Trent. Don't you want to know?"

"Lots of people claimed to know who I am," I said. "They were all lying."

"What if Arkwright isn't?"

I didn't have an answer for that, so I let the question hang in the air.

I did want Arkwright dead. Not just because of what he did to Jordana, although that was a big part of it. But also because of what he'd done to me. He'd dangled a life in front of me, a good life I'd been made to believe was mine. And then he'd cruelly yanked it away. He hadn't just lied to me, he'd shown me that I would never, *could* never have that life. For that, too, I wanted to make him pay.

I let the shower's hot water run over me, unwinding my muscles and washing away the day's dirt. Bethany was still asleep in my room and I hadn't wanted to disturb her, so I'd helped myself to Isaac's shower instead. My jaw had dropped at the sight of a bathroom that was bigger than some of the apartments I'd seen. In one corner stood the marble-lined, glass-doored shower stall I was currently occupying.

The sun had crossed the sky and gone down again. There'd been no sign of Isaac all day. He never came out of his study, not even to join me and Gabrielle for meals. Deciphering the scroll was taking all his time. I wished I could help somehow. I felt useless just waiting around, but translating Elvish wasn't part of my limited skill set. Not unless you could translate scrolls by punching them.

I adjusted the gold-plated temperature-control knobs until the water was so hot I could barely see through the steam. I lathered soap over my torso, thinking about how I'd been stabbed to death with swords twice already this week. Once in the stomach and once in the chest. For anyone else, that would be some kind of record. For me, it was business as usual. There were no scars to show for it, of course. Looking at myself, I looked like a perfectly normal man. You'd never know I had died thirteen times already. You'd never know I could see through the skin of the world and pluck its threads.

How could I have ever believed I was Lucas West from Norristown, Pennsylvania? Who was I kidding? Myself, apparently.

When I finished showering, I stepped out of the stall into the steam-filled bathroom. A granite counter ran along one wall, embedded with a large, enamel sink. Above it was a wall-length mirror. I wiped the steam away and studied my reflection. Despite all my strange abilities, despite all the mysteries of my identity, I looked human enough.

That was an odd way to put it, I thought. Human enough for what?

My shirt lay crumpled on the bathroom floor, torn and bloodstained from the lesser demon's sword. My black jeans lay beside it, also spattered with blood. More casualties in the ongoing war on my clothing. Outside, in Isaac's sprawling bedroom, I found an enormous, walk-in closet. I took out a new shirt and pants, both black and pristine. Would he mind my taking them? Probably. But all my clothes were in my room and I didn't want to wake Bethany. I needed something to wear. Besides, his closet looked like it had enough clothes for months on end. He wouldn't even notice the shirt and pants were missing. It wasn't like I was taking his favorite hunter green duster, right?

When I was done dressing, I checked my reflection in the antique, oval-framed mirror on the bedroom wall. I cleaned up well, I thought, though part of me wondered why I was bothering. If the world didn't end tonight at midnight, odds were I'd just be covered in blood and dirt again, with yet another destroyed shirt. So why had I cleaned myself and dressed in nicer clothes? For Bethany? God, what was I doing? It wasn't that long ago that I'd been a lowlife stealing artifacts for a crime boss in Brooklyn. Did I really think I was good enough for her? There I went, kidding myself again.

Movement in the mirror's reflection caught my eye. A shape appeared behind me. He wore a familiar black, hooded cloak that covered most of his face, leaving only his mouth and chin visible. His paper-white flesh was veined with black. The crow on his shoulder cocked its head and stared at me with beady eyes. The cloaked man grinned, revealing yellow teeth and black gums.

"Pave the way," he said, his voice rumbling like thunder.

I pulled my gun from its holster and spun around. The room was empty. He was gone.

I barreled down the stairs, yelling for Gabrielle. I nearly collided with Bethany. She was finally awake and just leaving my bedroom, a white terry cloth robe over her nightgown. She and Gabrielle sat me down at the big table in the main room, asking questions and trying to calm me down.

"What you're saying is impossible," Bethany said. "No one can get into Citadel."

"The ward has been breached before," I pointed out.

"That was different," Gabrielle said. "That time, Reve Azrael followed you here."

"Who's to say this guy didn't follow me, too?"

"Tell us again who it was?" Bethany asked.

"I don't know his name. It was the same hooded man I saw before, in the Village near Calliope's house."

"The one who showed you the vision?"

Bodies everywhere. Ruined buildings. A tidal wave of blood crashing through the subway tunnel. A haggard, one-armed Isaac. Bethany covered in blood, screaming in my face, *What have you done? What have you done?* I shook the images out of my head.

"What the hell was he doing here?" I demanded. "How did he get in? Where did he go?"

"I didn't see him," Gabrielle said.

"Neither did I," Bethany said. "If he was here, he would have had to pass both of us."

"I'm not crazy," I said. "He was here."

"I don't think you're crazy, but I don't think he was necessarily here, either," Bethany said. "Whoever this man is, he obviously has magic."

"He showed me the future," I said.

"*A* future," she corrected me. "I told you before, nothing is set in stone. But if he has magic powerful enough to do that, who's to say he doesn't have other spells, too? He could appear in the mirror without having to be in Citadel at all."

"It's true," Gabrielle said. "The ward would have no effect on that kind of spell."

That didn't make me feel any better. "What does he want from me?"

It was a rhetorical question. I knew neither of them could answer it. Only the cloaked man could. If he *was* a man.

It occurred to me that all this time we'd been looking for Nahash-Dred, the demon might have already made himself known to us.

So where the hell was he? Where was this goddamn demon? Not knowing was driving me crazy.

A door slammed closed upstairs. I twisted around in my chair. I half expected the cloaked man to come creeping down the stairs. Or maybe floating down, which struck me as more appropriate. Instead, it was Isaac. He held up the scroll in triumph.

"I've got it," he said. He unrolled the scroll on the table, pinning it open with a heavy book on either end. "It took me a long time to translate. Elvish isn't as simple as most other languages. It's read horizontally *and* vertically. See this column here? Those aren't words, they're numbers. And this column here? They're constellations. Aquarius, Cepheus, Pegasus."

"They're coordinates," Bethany said.

"Precisely. Only, there's one small problem." Isaac opened his laptop. He typed the coordinates into a Web site, then turned the computer around so it faced us. On the monitor was a map of the western edge of Midtown Manhattan, between Forty-Second and Fifty-Seventh Streets. A small star sat on the map, marking the coordinates Isaac had typed in. I saw the problem right away.

"It's in the middle of the Hudson River," I said.

"Right," he said. "At first I thought it might be one of the piers in that area, but the coordinates are farther out in the water than the piers go. There's nothing there. According to the map, it's just water. Either Arkwright is planning to use the Codex at the bottom of the Hudson, which I doubt, or there *is* something there, just something that's not on the map."

"But what?" Gabrielle asked. "There are no islands or reefs in the Hudson. So what is it?"

"Let's find out," Isaac said. He turned the laptop toward himself again and started typing furiously on the keyboard. "There must be some traffic cameras or security cameras I can hack into. With any luck, one of them will have a clear view of . . . Ah!" He paused, his face freezing in surprise. "Oh. Oh, of course. Stupid of me."

Bethany, Gabrielle, and I got up and looked over his shoulder. Isaac had hacked into a traffic camera across the street from the waterfront. I saw a footbridge spanning Twelfth Avenue and traffic speeding past the piers. Men and women walked by in their Halloween costumes, ghouls and witches and zombies on their way to parties, bars, and the Halloween Parade downtown. I thought of the dryads again on their exodus to the Nethercity. What better night for supernatural creatures to be out in the open than Halloween, when they could blend in?

But on the water just past Twelfth Avenue was what had taken Isaac's breath away. A hulking, gray World War II–era aircraft carrier extended into the river from the pier. I recognized it right away. Any New Yorker would. The USS *Intrepid*. Decommissioned and turned into a floating museum, its nearly nine-hundred-foot-long flight deck was now home to a collection of various historical aircraft.

"It's perfect," Isaac said. "One giant altar for Arkwright's ritual."

"The Guardians said this spot is where the wall between dimensions would be thinnest at midnight tonight," I said. "But there's something we're missing. Nahash-Dred is already in New York City. Why bother opening the doorway at all? It's like taking the time to reload when you've still got a full magazine."

"Maybe he's not taking any chances," Bethany said. "If something goes wrong with Nahash-Dred, the Codex Goetia gives him nearly a thousand other greater demons to choose from."

That could be it, but something still didn't feel right. There was something important we still didn't know. I hated not knowing things. Everything we didn't know was another thing we weren't prepared for.

"Let's not give Arkwright the chance to call for backup," Isaac said. He rolled up the scroll again. "Get ready. We leave in ten minutes."

"Shouldn't we wait for Philip?" I asked.

Isaac looked at his watch and shook his head. "If he hasn't come back with Nightclaw yet, something must have gone wrong. It's almost ten now. That only gives us two hours to stop Arkwright. We can't wait for Philip. Not when we're looking down the barrel of a gun this big." He paused and looked at each of us. "The last time we faced something this catastrophic, I asked you to make a stand with me. Since then, I know I've had my doubts, I know I've had my moments of weakness, but I also know we've made a dent. We've beaten back the darkness, even if only by inches.

What I'm asking you to do now is help me stand our ground. Defend the advances we've made. No matter what happens, no matter the sacrifices we have to make, we do not cede an inch. Not to Arkwright. Not to Nahash-Dred. Not to anyone. We've fought too hard and lost too many to let it all be in vain."

"I've got your back," I said.

"We all do," Bethany said.

"Good." Isaac climbed the stairs, the scroll in his hand. "Ten minutes."

Bethany got out of her chair and started toward the stairs.

"Bethany, wait," I said, going over to her. I'd been thinking about what Gabrielle said, how you never know how much time you'll have with someone. There were things I wanted to tell Bethany, things I thought she should know, things we needed to talk about before time ran out.

"I'm fine, Trent," she said before I could continue. "Don't worry, I'm up for this. My back doesn't even hurt anymore."

"No, that's not what . . ." I started to say, but she was already hurrying up the stairs to get dressed. I sighed. "Damn it."

At the table, Gabrielle shook her head at me. "Smooth operator."


Ten minutes later, we were in the Escalade. Isaac and Bethany sat up front. I sat in back with Gabrielle.

I thought about Arkwright. I thought about my hands around his throat. But I knew that would never happen. Arkwright wouldn't be alone at the *Intrepid*. Given how important this moment was to him, how close he was to his goal, he wouldn't want anything to interrupt him. He would likely have summoned another horde of lesser demons to guard him, probably even more than he'd brought with him to Bethesda Fountain. There was no way I could get close enough to take him out. No way, that was, except one. I'd been giving it a lot of thought. Thinking about it all day, in fact. It wasn't the safest plan. It probably wasn't even the smartest plan. And it would take a hell of a lot to convince the others to go along with it. But the more I thought about it, the more I realized it was my only shot. Isaac always said it was important to have a Plan B. This was mine.

I leaned forward in the backseat. "There's someplace we need to go first. Something we need to pick up."

# Thirty-Six

A short time later, we parked the Escalade in the small pedestrian plaza in front of the Intrepid Sea, Air & Space Museum's Welcome Center on Twelfth Avenue. I opened the door and jumped out in front of the NO PARKING sign. Whatever. A parking ticket was the least of our worries.

The Welcome Center was a square, two-story building at the foot of the cement pier. Just past it, the USS *Intrepid* sat moored by thick, knotted anchor lines. The first thing I noticed was that the Welcome Center's glass front doors hung shattered and crooked from their hinges. I waved the others behind me, pulled my gun, and nudged one of the doors open. I stepped inside cautiously. On the floor, the bodies of five uniformed security guards had been piled on top of each other. From what I could tell, they'd been stabbed to death, their bodies marred by long slashes and deep puncture wounds. Their clothes were soaked in blood, with more pooling on the floor around them. Two had their guns out. If they'd managed to fire any shots, it hadn't made a difference.

My anger flared. These men had families. People who cared about them, who relied on them. But to Arkwright they were nothing but an obstacle. That was how Arkwright thought of everyone. They were either tools to be used or obstacles to be eliminated.

Isaac pulled me away from the bodies. "Come on. It's too late to do anything for them. We need to get to the ship, and there's no way to board it from in here."

We hurried back outside and continued along the pier toward a tower of stairs that led up to the *Intrepid*'s flight deck. A bright shaft of ice-blue light shot suddenly into the night sky from the ship's deck. It pooled against the low clouds like a search beam. But this was no ordinary light. An ordinary light wouldn't make every hair on my body stand on end.

"It's started," Bethany said. "Arkwright is opening the doorway. We're running out of time."

We raced up the stairs and across the short bridge onto the *Intrepid*'s flight deck. Immediately on our right was a bank of helicopters on display. We climbed over the safety rail and crouched down behind the bulky cabin of a red-and-white Sikorsky Sea Guardian Coast Guard chopper. The shaft of light was emanating from a spot somewhere in front of us, near the ship's stern.

I saw Arkwright. He stood in front of the wide pavilion where the decommissioned space shuttle *Enterprise* was housed. I could see its huge white tail and rounded engine modules inside. Arkwright's shadow flickered and danced behind him on the wall of the island, the hundred-and-fifty-foot superstructure that housed the aircraft carrier's bridges and control tower. At its top stood a tall array of radar dishes and communication antennas.

I could hear Arkwright chanting, but I couldn't make out what he was doing. My view was blocked by the army of lesser demons that surrounded him. Skeletal, bald, and big-eyed, they were identical to the ones at Bethesda Fountain. They encircled him, facing outward like sentinels, watching for intruders. Their swords were drawn, some of them already stained with the blood of the murdered security guards. I tried to count how many demons there were. I stopped when I reached two dozen and realized there were still at least that many left uncounted.

Arkwright's baby-faced thug, Francisco, stood inside the circle with him. Without his partner LaValle at his side, Francisco looked out of place, like a child playing dress-up. He didn't look comfortable being this close to the demons. He looked tense, one hand positioned on the butt of his holstered pistol.

From somewhere at the center of that circle of demons, the bright shaft of light poured into the sky.

"There are too many of them," Bethany whispered. "We'll never get past them all."

"We may not have to," Gabrielle said. "These demons are bound to

Arkwright. Remember what the book said. If we kill him, they'll return to their dimension. If Trent's plan works—"

She was interrupted by the sudden *clank* of metal against metal from somewhere nearby. I motioned for the others to stay down. I straightened, lifting my gun. A demon appeared, creeping along the edge of the deck toward us, its sword drawn. I leveled my gun at it, aiming for its eye.

I didn't have a chance to pull the trigger before a crowd of demons rushed us from the other side, swarming around the helicopter. Damn. I'd fallen for the oldest trick in the book. I turned to the oncoming demons and squeezed off shot after shot. I hit two of them in their eyes, killing them, but that was all I managed before the others were upon us. I pushed through them, trying to fight my way toward Arkwright. Behind me, Bethany already had the fire sword out. Gabrielle and Isaac attacked the demons with spells.

I shot my way through the horde, taking out demons on either side of me. When my gun ran out of bullets, I holstered it and used my fists, elbows, and knees instead. I grabbed the sword out of one demon's grasp, stabbed it in the eye, and kept moving, kept pressing forward.

I didn't get as far as I'd hoped. Not by a long shot. The demons were on me like sharks on chum, ripping the sword out of my hands and forcing me to my knees. I felt the cold steel of a demon's sword against the back of my neck.

Do it, I thought angrily. Kill me and see how well that goes for you.

Arkwright yelled, "Bring him to me! Bring all of them!"

I was hoisted back onto my feet and dragged in front of Arkwright. There, the demons forced me to my knees again. Two of them held my arms out to my sides. A third put its sword against the back of my neck, a warning not to try anything. Bethany, Gabrielle, and Isaac were dragged over and thrown on their knees next to me. Swords were put to their necks as well.

At last I was close enough to see what Arkwright was doing. The Codex Goetia hovered in the air at chest level before him, spinning with constant, unceasing momentum. Bursting out of the center of the Codex was the ice-blue shaft of light that shot up into the sky.

Arkwright glared at me. "You're too late. The ritual is complete."

"You're using the Codex to bring Nahash-Dred here?" I demanded.

He smiled. "I don't need to. He's already here. He came of his own free will, just like I knew he would."

I looked around for the cloaked man, but I didn't see him anywhere. "So where is he?"

"Waiting. Just like he's been waiting all these years."

"He hasn't just been waiting around, Arkwright. He's been a lot busier than you think," I said.

"Is that so?" Arkwright said with a condescending smirk. "Tell me more."

"All this time, I was wondering who broke the Codex Goetia into fragments and hid them around the city," I said. "But there was no good answer. Nahash-Dred had the Codex when he left the sanctum. No one could have taken it from him and lived, not from a demon that can wipe out whole civilizations. So that left only one person who could have done it all."

From where she knelt, Bethany looked up at me. "But that would mean—"

"No!" Arkwright yelled, interrupting her. "Not from you! From *him*! I want to hear it from *him*!" He turned to me. "Say it. Say the words."

"Nahash-Dred hid the fragments himself," I said.

Arkwright smiled. "Very good. You're starting to understand. But do you know why he did it? Why the demon broke it and hid the pieces?"

I was reluctant to admit I didn't. I wasn't sure how Arkwright would react. He was insane, but up until now at least he'd been methodical. This close to achieving his goal, though, he was coming undone. The lid was coming off the pressure cooker. But lying to him in this state would be an even bigger gamble, especially with our lives on the line.

"No," I told him. "I couldn't figure it out. Why would Nahash-Dred destroy his only way of getting home?"

"Isn't it obvious?" Arkwright said. "So he could stay. You see, there was something we didn't know about Nahash-Dred when we summoned him. A secret no one knew. The Destroyer of Worlds was tired of killing. He took no joy in it anymore. All he wanted was to be left alone."

Damn. I'd been wrong about Nahash-Dred. I assumed he'd stayed in our dimension because New York City was a fertile hunting ground for him. Instead, he stayed because he didn't want to go back to what was essentially a life of slavery, of being forced to kill again and again regardless of whether he wanted to. I had misjudged him. Hell, I could sympathize with him. I'd had a taste of that life myself. I didn't want to go back, either. But did that mean Nahash-Dred *wasn't* Calliope's killer? If not the demon, then who?

I understood one thing, though—why the fragment under Bethesda Fountain had been specially protected. Ten to one it was the piece with Nahash-Dred's name on it. Names had a lot of power, especially for controlling a greater demon. He'd locked that fragment away with a key and an alarm because he didn't want anyone to have that power over him anymore.

"Can you even imagine such a thing?" Arkwright went on, growing angrier. "Can you for one moment wrap your mind around what a cosmic *joke* that is? After so much effort, so much trial and error on the most important night of the millennium, the Aeternis Tenebris *finally* summoned the Destroyer of Worlds . . . and he said no. He. Said. *No.*"

"I take it that's a word you don't like hearing," I said.

He ignored me. "We tried to force Nahash-Dred to do it, of course, but our efforts at binding him failed. We paid a brutal, bloody price for that. When he was done with us, I was half dead and my brethren were in pieces on the floor. So much for Nahash-Dred not wanting to kill anymore, eh? But afterward, he hid the Codex and made sure no one could find it—or him."

"But he didn't stay hidden," I said, thinking of the cloaked man again. "He came to me. I've seen him twice now."

"Have you?" He laughed. For some reason, Arkwright was deeply amused by this. "Now *that* would be something!"

I shook my head in frustration. We were getting nowhere. "You said Nahash-Dred was here. So where is he?"

"I'm surprised you still haven't figured it out," he said. "But then, you're not the man you used to be. I suppose none of us are anymore."

"What does that mean?" I demanded. "Enough with the cryptic remarks. You said you recognized me, so why don't you tell me who you think I am?"

"You don't remember. Do you have any idea how frustrating that is for me?" Arkwright grew angry again. "You were *there*! You've *been* there from the start! You were in the sanctum that night, and you don't even remember!"

"That's not possible," I said. "I couldn't have been there. You're the only survivor."

"I'm the only survivor of the Aeternis Tenebris, yes, but who *else* was there that night?" Arkwright pressed. "Think, man! If you have the answer to that question, you have the answer to who you are. *Who else was there?*"

I racked my brain trying to figure it out, but I came up blank. The idea that someone else had been there at the same time just didn't make sense.

"Bah! You're useless. You still don't get it." He waved his hand dismissively. He looked up at where the beam of light speared the clouds. "It doesn't matter. It will all be over soon enough."

"You sound pretty convinced of that," I said. "So before we all die, how about you just tell me the answer?"

He laughed. "Where's the fun in that?"

"Fine, how about a different question, then," I said. "Why open the doorway between dimensions if Nahash-Dred is already here, like you said?"

Arkwright paused before he spoke, as if mentally debating how much to tell me. "I thought for a long time of punishing Nahash-Dred for what he did to me and my brethren. I thought of all kinds of ways to hurt him. Ways to really make him suffer. Then I realized *this* would be my revenge. To bind him. To force him to destroy the very world he has grown so pathetically fond of. But I discovered one small snag, a temporary setback. Nahash-Dred has left his true nature behind. Until he embraces it once more, I cannot bind him. That's why I needed the Codex Goetia. Not just to bind one demon, but to summon another. His brother, Behemoth, Lord of Ruination. Behemoth has the power to tear this world apart, too. It's different from his brother's, of course, but it's no less effective. After I bind Behemoth, he will begin his work. If Nahash-Dred wants to stop his brother, if he wants to prevent his adopted world from being destroyed, he will be forced out into the open. He will be forced to embrace his true nature again. And then he will be mine."

There it was, the missing piece of the puzzle. The reason none of this added up until now. It was a trap. This whole plot was a trap to get revenge on the demon who'd done him wrong. Arkwright would kill everyone on earth and leave our world a barren, broken husk if he had to, just to teach Nahash-Dred a lesson. The bastard was even crazier than I thought.

"What if Nahash-Dred won't fight?" I asked.

"He will. There's no love lost between brothers. Sibling rivalry exists even among demonkind. Once Nahash-Dred embraces his true nature, I will bind him. Then the two brothers will destroy this world together. It will be *glorious* to behold."

Damn. One world-destroying demon would be hard enough to stop, but two?

I looked up at Arkwright. I was close enough to kill him. Close enough to wrap my hands around his neck, crush the life out of him, and end this right now. He deserved no less. But I knew I would never make it that far. Even if somehow I got away from the demons holding me, even if by some miracle I got away from the demon poised to chop my head off, the other demons would be all over me before I reached Arkwright. They would cut me to ribbons, and when I came back there was no guarantee it would be a demon's life force I stole this time. It could just as easily be Isaac's, Gabrielle's, or Bethany's. We were all crowded so close together, I couldn't risk it.

Far above us, where the shaft of light struck the clouds, they parted and the sky tore open. A brightly glowing crack formed in the night sky. A rift in the fabric of reality. A doorway between dimensions.

"Behemoth is answering the call," Arkwright said.

"Damn it, Arkwright, stop this!" I yelled.

"It can't *be* stopped," Arkwright said, gloating. "Once summoned by name, a demon has no choice but to appear."

A sudden commotion arose behind us. The lesser demons made loud, agitated noises. Before I could see what was happening, a demon soared over us and landed on the nose cone of a tiger-striped MiG-21 fighter jet. The demon slid limply down to the deck. Its eyes were gooey messes, as if they'd been torn out.

I turned my head as far as I could, careful of the sword against the back of my neck. At first, all I could see was a swarm of the demons trying to wrestle someone to the floor. Instead, they were being tossed aside like rag dolls. Finally, a shape broke through the crowd for a moment before being swarmed again. It was Philip. His fingers were covered in demon eye goo. He swung the corpse of a dead demon in one hand like a club.

Arkwright panicked. He grabbed the floating, spinning Codex Goetia out of the air. As soon as he did, the shaft of light cut off, though the rift in the sky remained. Carrying the Codex, Arkwright ran up the stairs along the side of the towering steel island. The demons released us and followed him, covering his retreat. Philip hurried over to us, tossing his makeshift club aside.

Isaac grasped his hand. "I don't think I've ever been happier to see you, Philip. Welcome back. I was getting worried about you."

"It's going to take a lot to get rid of me, old man," Philip said.

I rubbed the back of my neck where the demon had pressed its sword into my skin. "I can't believe I'm about to say this, but I actually missed you."

"I'll try not to let it go to my head," Philip said.

"Guys, we can play catch-up later," Gabrielle said. "We're not out of the water yet. Look." She pointed.

Arkwright had reached vulture's row, the protruding, railed viewing platform at the very top of the island, roughly a hundred feet above the flight deck. The lesser demons surrounded him in a defensive phalanx. In the shadow of the communication antenna array and an enormous radar dish, Arkwright held up the Codex Goetia with both hands. He pointed it in the direction of the rift and began chanting again.

The rift bulged and warped as if something were trying to push through from the other side. There was a bright flash. A thick pillar of bloodred light erupted from the rift, blasting down to the aft end of the flight deck. It struck the space shuttle pavilion, instantly obliterating it in a violent explosion that knocked us to the deck. Smoldering debris and wreckage rained down, clanging off the flight deck around us and splashing into the Hudson.

Within the pillar of light, something moved.

# Thirty-Seven

I rose to my feet amid the flaming wreckage scattered across the deck. The pillar of red light stood in the destroyed pavilion's place, stretching between the flight deck and the rift in the sky above. The light looked almost solid, a containment field for whatever was moving inside it. I took cover with the others, squatting down behind a sleek, gray Marine fighter jet.

"So Clarence Bergeron and Erickson Arkwright are the same person, huh?" Philip asked. "I knew he was bad news the minute I saw him, but I never would have guessed the old cripple was the same one taking potshots at us in Chinatown."

"He wasn't," I told him. "That was Jordana. She was Arkwright's stepdaughter, and a part of this all along. Arkwright infected her with magic. He brainwashed her into doing his dirty work. She's dead."

"That chick you liked?" Philip said. "Damn, man, that's harsh. Did you at least get to tap that?"

I squinted at him. "I take back what I said about missing you."

I peeked around the fighter jet for a better look at the pillar of red light. Dark shapes moved and swirled inside it, slowly beginning to coalesce.

"Shit, what is that?" I asked.

"It's Behemoth. He's coming through," Isaac said. "Philip, did you get Nightclaw?"

"Yeah, sorry it took so long," Philip said. "We ran into some trouble. But Aiyana came through, just like you said she would. She also told me to tell you she's sorry. She said you would know what that meant."

Isaac nodded. "I do." Whatever history he had with the Goblin Queen gave him a faraway look in his eye.

Philip pulled a bundle of black velvet cloth from inside his coat and unwrapped it. Inside was a dagger, its hilt and blade as black as starless space.

I regarded it skeptically. "A magic dagger? Are you kidding me?" Just once why couldn't it be a magic bazooka, or a magic howitzer? Something that actually looked like it could do some damage?

Philip turned his mirrored shades my way. "You're fighting demons on Halloween, there's a doorway to another dimension in the sky, but the *dagger* is the part you're having trouble buying into?"

"Point taken," I said.

"It's no ordinary dagger," Isaac explained. "Nightclaw is also called the Voyavold Slayer. It was forged by the Guardians themselves during their war against the Voyavold. It's the oldest and deadliest blade there is. A single cut from Nightclaw can kill anything. It doesn't even have to be a mortal wound. Just one stab, one cut, anywhere on the body is lethal."

"If you want to kill a greater demon, you're going to need a weapon like this," Philip said. He wrapped it up again and put it back in his coat. "Unfortunately, it's a close-range weapon. We'll have to get up close and personal with whatever's coming through that doorway."

"Hopefully it won't come to that," Isaac said. "Behemoth hasn't fully materialized yet. I might be able to close the doorway before he does. Trent, once I close it, that's when I want you to put your plan into action. You'll have to take Arkwright out quickly. Otherwise, he could use the Codex Goetia to summon more demons. We can't let him. This has to end now."

"I'm ready when you are," I said.

Isaac stood, raising both his hands toward the rift in the sky. His whole body seemed to glow as he shouted an incantation. Bright beams shot out of his hands, soaring through the sky and into the rift. The rift began to dim. Isaac grimaced with effort, but it was working. The pillar of red light began to flicker. The shape coalescing inside it faded.

Up in vulture's row, Arkwright gesticulated wildly and yelled orders at his army of lesser demons. A small handful stayed behind as his personal guard. The rest raced down the stairs toward us.

"Shit, here they come!" I shouted.

Above us, the rift seemed to resist Isaac's spell, bulging and pushing back. The pillar of light brightened again.

"Hold them off!" Isaac said, forcing the words out from between clenched teeth. His face glistened with sweat. "I need more time!"

"I'm out of bullets," I said.

"Here, take this." Bethany threw me the hilt of the fire sword. As soon as I caught it, the blade of fire sprang out of it.

"Thanks. I owe you one."

"Buy me a beer," she said.

She pulled a charm from her vest. This one was a small, metal bracelet that she clamped around her wrist. A long, sharp blade sprang out of it, extending past her fist to the length of a sword.

Gabrielle flew into the air and started knocking lesser demons off their feet with shock waves.

Philip watched her in awe, his mouth hanging open. "Whoa. Gabrielle can fly now?"

"You missed some stuff," I said. "If we survive this, I'll fill you in."

Gabrielle was doing a good job keeping the demons busy, but there were too many for her to handle on her own. They began slipping past her, running directly for Isaac, determined to stop him from closing the rift. Bethany, Philip, and I intercepted them. The fire sword was lighter than I expected. I could swing it faster and with greater precision than a metal sword. When the first demon reached me, I cleaved its head in two, right down the center. Remarkably, the demon stayed upright and kept fighting, the two halves of its head bobbing on either side of its neck. I parried its blade with mine, relieved that the fire sword was solid enough to use defensively. Then I jabbed it into one of the demon's eyes. The eye ruptured and bubbled from the heat. The demon dropped dead.

One down, only an entire army to go.

I didn't waste time aiming for anything but the demons' eyes. In the chaos of the fight, I caught glimpses of Bethany stabbing demons through the eyes, too, her gore-soaked bracelet-sword lancing straight through the backs of their heads. Philip fought them with his bare hands, tearing the eyes out of their heads. Above us, Gabrielle continued her shock wave attacks, keeping the demons off-balance. And all the while, Isaac continued bombarding the doorway in the sky with his spell. The rift dimmed again. The pillar of red light flickered and grew fainter, then stronger again. I heard Isaac cry out.

"It's too much!" he shouted.

I ran to him. Gabrielle flew past me overhead and landed beside Isaac before I got there.

"Let me help," Gabrielle said. "I have magic. Tell me what to do."

"No," he said. His face was completely coated in sweat. It poured off his forehead and dripped from his chin. "Go. The others need your help."

"Isaac—"

"It's too dangerous," he interrupted, grimacing with pain. "Using this much magic could—could trigger the infection inside you. Go, damn it!"

Gabrielle looked at me, but there was nothing I could do to change Isaac's mind. Reluctantly, she flew into the air again.

"You, too," Isaac growled at me. "Go!"

I didn't want to leave him, but there was no point in arguing. I returned to the battle, but I was distracted by my concern for Isaac. A demon got around my defenses and struck me in the face with the hilt of its sword. I fell backward, tasting blood on my tongue. The fire sword fell out of my hand, its blade extinguishing instantly. The demon knelt over me, pinning my arms to the floor with its bony knees. It lifted its sword over its head, the point aimed straight down at my heart.

But the demon didn't get a chance to strike. Its left eye popped in an explosion of goo as the tip of Bethany's sword burst from its socket. More of the disgusting goo dribbled down on me as I tried to squirm out from under the demon. Bethany pulled her sword back out of the demon's head. It fell on top of me. I groaned in disgust and pushed the body away. There was demon eyeball goo all over my face, neck, and chest. I'd ruined Isaac's shirt, too. Maybe that was my true power: ruining shirts.

I stood up, wiping the goo off my face and trying to shake it off my hands. "Not enough showers in the *world*," I muttered.

"You're welcome," Bethany said.

"I had it under control," I said. "I was lulling the demon into a false sense of security."

She rolled her eyes. "Right. Now that's two beers you owe me."

"It's a date," I said.

She grinned and ran back into the fray. I watched her stab one demon through the eye while kicking another away from her. She pulled her sword free and dispatched the second demon before it could rush her again.

Sometimes Bethany took my breath away.

No, scratch that. Not sometimes. All the time.

Isaac cried out suddenly. I spun around. He was on his knees, his hands still raised over his head as the spell poured out of him. He was soaked with sweat. His entire body trembled with exhaustion. In the sky above, the rift bulged and fought to stay open.

"I can't!" Isaac said. "I can't close it!"

The spell ended. His arms dropped to his sides, and he collapsed onto the deck. The rift burst back to life above us. The pillar of red light brightened and thickened. The shape within it began to solidify once more.

I ran to Isaac. He sat up, grimacing in intense pain. He held one hand close to his body, trying to hide it from me.

"I'm fine, Trent," he said hoarsely. "I'm fine."

"Isaac, let me see your hand," I said.

He looked up at me angrily. "I told you, I'm fine."

"You're not." I knelt down beside him. "Show me."

Reluctantly, he held out his hand. I drew back in surprise. It wasn't a hand anymore—at least, not a *human* hand. It was a twisted, grotesque appendage, halfway between a cockroach's leg and a bird's talon. It twitched and writhed at the end of his arm.

"The doorway was too strong," he said, staring at his hand in horror. "I had to push myself further than I've ever gone. I've never tapped into that much magic before. It was too much." He looked up at me. "It's the infection, Trent. I'm infected."

# Thirty-Eight

"It's not possible," I said. "You can't be infected. You're a mage. Mages don't get infected. That's the rule."

Isaac shrugged off his duster. With his good hand, he started rolling up his shirtsleeve. "It's happened before. Other mages have gotten infected. Some were already predisposed to darkness. Others couldn't keep the magic inside them under control anymore . . ." He paused, looking off into the distance. "Crixton knew. He said the magic had planted a dark seed inside me. He could sense it. One infected soul sensing another."

"He was crazy," I pointed out.

"He was right," Isaac said.

He undid his belt and yanked it out of its loops. Using his good hand and his teeth, he wrapped it tightly around his forearm.

"What are you doing?" I asked.

He fastened the belt tight, just below his elbow. He held out his good hand to me. "Give me the fire sword."

I shook my head. "Jesus, Isaac—"

"Now, Trent!"

His tone told me there wasn't time to argue. I picked up the fallen hilt and handed it to him. As soon as he gripped it, the fire sword blazed to life. He held it over his infected hand. He gritted his teeth and paused a moment to steel himself.

"Isaac, wait!" I said.

"It's the only way to stop the infection from spreading," he said.

"But you've stopped infections before," I insisted. "You did it for Thornton—"

"There's no time," Isaac interrupted. "It's spreading too fast."

He was right. Already the flesh on his wrist and forearm was starting to change, turning squamous, mutating into an extension of the twisted thing where his hand used to be.

"But the infection can be reversed," I said. "We've seen it!"

He raised the fire sword. "We don't know how, and we don't have *time!*"

I flashed on the vision the cloaked man had given me—an older, haggard-looking Isaac with only one hand—and then he brought the fire sword down. He cried out as it sliced cleanly through his forearm just below the belt's makeshift tourniquet. The infected flesh fell to the deck with a sickening *slap*. The fire sword had cauterized the wound at the same time it cut through the flesh, filling the air with the odor of cooked meat. Isaac's face dripped with sweat. He dropped the fire sword to the floor next to his own amputated appendage. He tried to stand but nearly fell over. I caught him. He leaned against me, his face buried in my chest.

"No matter what happens," he murmured. "That's what I said. No matter the sacrifices we have to make, we don't—we don't cede an inch . . ."

Philip came sprinting across the flight deck, body-checking demons out of his way. When he reached us, he pulled Isaac out of my grasp and supported the mage himself.

"I've got you, old man. You're going to be fine," he said. "Trent, what the hell happened?"

"The infection," I said. "It came out of nowhere."

"I'm okay, I'm okay," Isaac repeated.

His eyes were glazed over, but he fought to stay upright. Any other man would have passed out from shock, but somehow Isaac was managing to stay conscious, forcing himself, drawing on enormous reserves of strength just to keep standing.

At the ship's stern, something massive was taking shape inside the pillar of red light. I could make out bits here and there: a thickly muscled arm the size of a tree, the ridged spine of a back, something that looked like a tail.

"We're running out of time," I said.

"Nightclaw," Isaac muttered. He slumped against Philip. The vampire held him upright.

"I'm not leaving your side, old man," Philip said.

Isaac shook his head. "Trent's . . . not fast enough . . . has to be you."

"I told you, I'm not—"

"Don't argue . . . no time," Isaac interrupted.

Reluctantly, Philip passed Isaac to me. While I supported the mage, Philip pulled the black velvet bundle out of his coat. He peeled off the cloth and gripped the dagger in his fist.

"Look after Isaac," he told me, poking a finger into my chest. "If anything happens to him, I will hold you personally responsible."

"I'll keep him safe," I said.

Then Philip was off and running through the battlefield. He slashed any demons who got too close. Wherever Nightclaw cut them, crooked black veins spread out over their bodies. A second later, they dropped to the floor, dead. I'd seen my share of strange and brutal weapons, but I'd never seen one so coldly efficient. All it took was one cut. No wonder the Guardians had kept its location a secret. Who could be trusted with a weapon like that?

Isaac leaned his weight against the fighter jet's fuselage. "You can let go now."

I released him. He didn't fall. How he was staying upright was beyond me. I picked up the fire sword, prepared to defend us both if any demons came. I felt restless, like a coiled viper that wasn't allowed to strike. I wanted to be out there fighting alongside the others. I knew someone needed to stay and protect Isaac, but hanging back and watching the others put their lives on the line made me feel useless.

But Gabrielle and Bethany were holding their own for now. They stood atop a pile of bodies, back to back, both of them covered in demon blood and eyeball goo as they continued to fight the horde. Philip battled his way through the crowd until he was through and running freely on the other side. He closed the distance to the churning pillar of light. A hundred feet, seventy-five, fifty—and then a missile of fire seemed to come out of nowhere. It struck him, exploding on impact. Philip was engulfed in flames and blown forcefully off his feet. He was hurled backward several yards, landing between two fighter jets.

Francisco stepped out of the shadows. He was holding the dragon-painted crossbow from Arkwright's artifact collection. Shit. I'd lost track of Francisco in the pandemonium. He must have snuck away as soon as Philip showed up, then waited for the right moment to attack.

This wasn't good. The shape inside the pillar of light was solidifying. Behemoth was almost here. Gabrielle and Bethany had their hands full with the demons. Philip was down. I turned to Isaac.

"Go," he croaked hoarsely. "I'll be all right. Kill Arkwright. It's the only way to end this."

He didn't have to tell me twice. I stuffed the hilt of the fire sword into my pocket and started running. I kept to the shadows, moving unseen along one side of the flight deck. Unfortunately, I was on the ship's port side, and the island where Arkwright had taken refuge was on the starboard side. Between us was an army of lesser demons. At some point I was going to have to cross the deck in the open.

As I grew closer, I heard Francisco call to Philip, "I told you we weren't finished, vampire! It's time to settle up!"

Philip stood up between the fighter jets, patting out tiny, smoldering patches of fire on his clothes. He tossed the smoking remains of his coat to the floor. The right half of his shirt, including the sleeve, had been entirely burned away. The skin beneath it was streaked with ash but otherwise appeared unharmed. I knew vampire flesh was a lot stronger than human flesh—I'd seen swords break rather than cut him—but I was still impressed.

"You've got seriously bad timing, asshole," Philip said.

Francisco sneered at him. "You humiliated me, vampire. In front of my employer. In front of my partner. I can't let that stand. You made me look like a bitch."

"If the shoe fits," Philip said.

Francisco leveled the crossbow at him. The bow pulled back on its own, cocking itself. A fiery bolt materialized within it. Francisco pulled the trigger, and the bolt flew right for Philip. But the vampire was gone before it hit him, striking the empty steel deck instead. The bolt exploded into a pool of flame that spread much too fast for the fire to be anything but magical. It didn't seem to need any accelerant or fuel.

I ducked behind a fighter jet for cover. Philip was a blur streaking across the deck toward Francisco. The baby-faced thug panicked, desperately loosing bolt after bolt but missing Philip each time. The bolts lit fires all over the deck and on several of the aircraft. We were lucky their gas tanks had been emptied long ago.

Philip barreled into Francisco without slowing down. The two of them rolled and skidded across the flight deck. They disappeared under the canvas wall of the huge aircraft restoration tent at the foot of the island.

Now was my chance. I bolted across the flight deck toward the island, already thinking about what to do when I got to vulture's row at the top. My Plan B.

I was only halfway across the deck when the aircraft carrier tipped suddenly beneath my feet. The bow lifted into the air above Twelfth Avenue, while the stern sank toward the river's waterline. The chains holding some of the aircraft in place snapped. Jets and helicopters, some still burning from the crossbow bolts, slid haphazardly across the deck. Some tumbled off the side and splashed into the water below. I dropped to the floor and lay spread-eagled on my stomach, trying to not slide off the ship, too. I glanced over to see if Isaac was okay. The fighter jet was still chained to the deck, though it had slid out of place. Isaac had moved to the railing along the deck's edge and was holding on for dear life with his good arm.

The ship leveled out again. The bow came crashing down, splashing into the river and sending an enormous wave across Twelfth Avenue. Cars screeched and honked. Pedestrians screamed in alarm. Damn. The cops would be coming now. Probably EMTs, too. The last thing we needed were more people in the line of fire.

I got back to my feet and saw Bethany and Gabrielle had recovered their balance, too. They stared past me, openmouthed, to the stern of the ship. The remaining lesser demons had stopped fighting and were staring, too. I heard something breathe at my back. A blast of hot air hit me. Something was behind me. Something whose sudden, extra weight had caused the ship to tip off-balance momentarily. I turned slowly.

The rift still burned brightly in the sky, but the colossal pillar of light was gone. In its place stood a creature that towered seventy feet above me. Thick, ropy muscles flexed beneath an intricately patterned, purple-and-black hide. His bare torso, arms, and bald, horned head were vaguely humanlike, but from the waist down he resembled a centipede. Six rounded, armored segments stretched behind him, each sporting two pointed, articulated legs. He balled his hands into fists, threw back his head, and let out a terrifying, bestial roar.

The lesser demons gibbered in terror. Ignoring Bethany and Gabrielle, they ran for the stairs, retreating up the island to vulture's row. They knew a greater demon when they saw one.

I stared up at Behemoth, brother of Nahash-Dred, Lord of Ruination. I didn't have Nightclaw. I didn't have the Codex Goetia. I didn't know any binding or banishing spells.

There was no Plan B for this.

# Thirty-Nine

Behemoth's eyes were filled with fury. He extended one enormous hand above me, palm down. Suddenly, it was like the world had turned upside down, as if gravity had changed direction. I fell upward off the flight deck toward Behemoth's hand. Bethany and Gabrielle watched in horror from the deck, unaffected by the shift in gravity. It was only me. Behemoth had trapped me in some kind of a gravity field. I tumbled upward toward his enormous hand. His fingers looked as thick as tree trunks, capable of crushing me to dust. But then Behemoth hesitated. My upward fall stopped. I floated in the air before him like a fly caught in amber. He studied me closely, and a change came over his face. He lowered me back to the flight deck and released me from the gravity field.

I didn't understand. I stood rooted in place, not taking my eyes off the towering demon. Behemoth watched me with just as much interest. I'd been given a chance to run, but I didn't move. It wasn't just fear that kept me there. It was curiosity. Behemoth had spared me for a reason. I wanted to know why.

The silence was shattered by Francisco bursting out of the aircraft restoration tent. His clothes were on fire. He ran screaming across the flight deck. Behemoth let loose another deafening roar and extended his hand again. Francisco, caught in a gravity field, was lifted off the deck and into the air. He floated before Behemoth, screaming and burning. Behemoth closed his empty hand into a fist. In the air before him, Francisco's body crushed in on itself. The flames extinguished instantly. The screams stopped. I heard Francisco's bones snap as his body compressed down to a small, lumpy object. Then Behemoth released it from the gravity field, and what was left of Francisco fell to the deck in front of me. An unrecognizable mass of bone and tissue, it looked like something that had come out of a car crusher in a junkyard.

Jesus. I tried to swallow, but my throat was too tight.

Philip charged out of the tent with Francisco's crossbow, unloading fiery bolts at Behemoth. The demon swatted at them, but the tactic backfired. They exploded on impact, their magical fire spreading over Behemoth's hands and arms.

The sight of this titanic demon half on fire was finally enough to get my legs moving. I ran over to Bethany and Gabrielle.

"Are you all right?" Bethany asked me. The sword blade retracted into her bracelet.

"I'm fine," I said. "Behemoth let me go. I don't know why."

I looked back. Behemoth didn't seem bothered by the fire from the crossbow bolts. He didn't appear to be in pain, and the flames died out quickly on his hide. Philip loosed more bolts to keep the demon distracted. But damn it, why wasn't he using Nightclaw? The dagger could end this now.

"Where's Isaac?" Gabrielle asked.

"Right here," the mage said, limping toward us. Bethany and Gabrielle saw he was missing a hand and ran over to him. "It was the infection," he told them. "I didn't have a choice."

"But how . . . ?" Gabrielle demanded.

"There's no time to explain," he said. "Listen to me. We can't let Behemoth off this ship. If he gets out into the city, it'll be catastrophic."

Behemoth let loose a deafening roar then. He pushed out one massive hand, and Philip, dozens of feet away, was repelled backward by a gravity field. He soared through the air, slammed into the side of the island, and then slid down to the flight deck. We ran over and found him slumped against the island wall. He was conscious and wasn't bleeding. No bones appeared to be broken. If he'd been human, he would have been killed by the impact. Being a vampire, he was just a little banged up. The crossbow wasn't as fortunate. It lay in a broken heap beside him.

"Son of a bitch can manipulate gravity," Philip growled, straightening his mirrored sunglasses.

"Sorry, I should have warned you," I said. I reached down to help him up.

He waved me off and stood on his own. "I'm fine."

"Where's Nightclaw?" Isaac asked. "We have to put Behemoth down before this goes any further."

"Damned if I know," Philip said. "I dropped Nightclaw when Francisco attacked me. I have no idea where it is now."

"We have to find it," Bethany said. "We can't kill Behemoth without it."

Philip glared at her. "Thank you, Captain Obvious."

"Can that thing even *be* killed?" I asked.

"*The Book of Eibon* says demons can die, just like everyone else," Gabrielle said. She glanced at me. "Present company excluded. But yes, we can kill Behemoth with Nightclaw if we can get close enough. I'm sure of it."

From vulture's row atop the island, Arkwright shouted something. It wasn't English, but whatever language it was, Behemoth understood it. The demon started moving toward the island, his huge centipede legs clanking loudly on the steel deck. We ran away from the island as Behemoth stamped toward us. A red-and-white F-14 Tomcat had come loose and rolled into the center of the flight deck. We ducked behind it and watched Arkwright hold the Codex Goetia before him like a shield. A bright light flickered from it, strobing in Behemoth's eye. Arkwright began chanting.

"It's the binding spell," Bethany said. "If it works, Behemoth will be under his complete control."

"And if he messes it up like last time?" I asked.

"Then Behemoth will kill us all," she said. "Six of one, half a dozen of the other."

I needed the binding spell to work. Then all I had to do was kill Arkwright and Behemoth would be sent back to his own dimension. Two birds, one stone. Except getting to Arkwright wasn't going to be easy. In the meantime, we still had to deal with Behemoth.

We needed Nightclaw. But the dagger was out there on the flight deck somewhere, hidden among the bodies and the various aircraft that had slid out of place. I scanned the deck. Small fires burned everywhere, sending light into the shadows, but I couldn't see Nightclaw.

"Isaac or Gabrielle, do either of you have a spell that can, I don't know, teleport Nightclaw over to us?" I asked.

Isaac shook his head. "It doesn't work like that. At the very least, I would need a clear line of sight to do something like that."

"I might get a better view from the air," Gabrielle said.

"Forget it," Isaac said. "I don't want you flying anywhere near Behemoth. You saw what he did to Francisco."

Gabrielle rolled her eyes. "How much more do you need to see before you get it, Isaac? I can take care of myself."

Philip turned to her. "You're carrying magic." It wasn't a question.

"Figured that out on your own, did you?" Gabrielle said. "Don't tell me you've got a problem with it, too."

"Not yet," he said.

"Good enough." She glared pointedly at Isaac. "I've already got one mother who worries about me, I don't need more."

I continued scanning the deck around us. Nothing moved in the flickering light of the fires. Nothing, and no one.

"Nahash-Dred is here somewhere," I said. "Arkwright said he was waiting, but I don't think that's what he's doing at all. I think he's hiding. I don't think he wants any of this."

"You can't know that for sure," Bethany said.

"If he doesn't want this, why isn't he doing something to stop it?" Philip demanded. "He's a greater demon, too, just like his brother. He could probably stop Behemoth in the blink of an eye."

I shrugged. "I don't know. Maybe he knows it's a trap. Maybe he knows if he does anything, Arkwright will bind him."

"Then he's a coward," Philip said.

I couldn't argue. For all I knew, Nahash-Dred was long gone. And yet, somehow I sensed he wasn't. He was still here, somewhere. I was certain.

The sound of helicopter blades chopping the air caught our attention. An NYPD helicopter came flying upriver toward the ship. Its powerful spotlight snapped on and swept the area. It found Behemoth and stayed on him. At the same time, another chopper came from the New Jersey side of the river. This one wasn't the police. It was a news helicopter with the number 7 and the words EYEWITNESS NEWS painted on the cabin. It switched on its own spotlight and hit Behemoth with it.

Distracted by the bright lights, Behemoth turned away from Arkwright and the binding spell. He shielded his eyes with one massive arm and roared angrily at the helicopters.

Shit. The tidal wave that had hit Twelfth Avenue had brought both the police and the media. They had no idea what they were dealing with.

I jumped up, waving my arms. "Get out of here! Get the hell out of here!" I shouted.

It was already too late. Behemoth gestured, and the NYPD chopper stopped abruptly in midair, as if it had struck an invisible wall. The rotor blades bent and snapped. Then Behemoth crushed the helicopter just as he'd crushed Francisco. The demon sent it hurtling over the aircraft carrier. I ducked down as it passed overhead. The chopper crashed into the pedestrian bridge that spanned Twelfth Avenue and exploded. Fiery debris rained into the street below. Amid the screams, screeching tires, and crunching metal of panicked collisions, the pedestrian bridge itself began to crumble and fall.

Behemoth turned his attention to the news chopper next. It was already retreating, but it didn't get far before Behemoth caught it in a gravity field. He crumpled it, too, and sent it soaring toward the city. It struck the corner of a multilevel storage facility on the other side of Twelfth Avenue, exploding and knocking great chunks of glass and concrete from the building. More screams, more screeching tires. The streets glowed with fire.

Isaac was wrong. He'd warned us it would be catastrophic if Behemoth got off the ship. But Behemoth didn't *need* to get off the ship to show us exactly what being Lord of Ruination meant.

"We need a plan, and we need it fast," Bethany said.

"Did the binding spell work, or did the helicopters interrupt it?" I asked.

"I don't know," Bethany said. "We have to assume it worked."

I looked up to the top of the island, where Arkwright stood on vulture's row. If the binding spell worked, I knew what I had to do.

Behemoth swept one arm before him. The F-14 Tomcat we were hiding behind was knocked clear off the ship by a gravity field, falling off the port side and crashing onto the cement pier below. It left us out in the open and vulnerable. Hanging back and playing defense was no longer an option. Gabrielle and Philip attacked the demon first. She struck from the air, pounding Behemoth with shock waves. Philip attacked from the ground, using his immense speed to land blow after blow on the demon's lower, centipedelike segments. Together they tried to drive Behemoth backward, off the ship and into the water.

Bethany stayed behind to protect Isaac, who was still too weak and too drained to fight. I ran for the stairs on the side of the island. I sprinted up them, the fire sword blazing in one hand. There were probably still fifteen to twenty lesser demons standing between me and Arkwright. They might be frightened of Behemoth, but they still served their master. They would fight to protect him. As if on cue, I heard the clatter of lesser demons' feet as they raced down the steps toward me. There was no way I would be able to fight my way through all of them, but I didn't need to. All I needed was for them to capture me and bring me to Arkwright. All I needed was to get close.

The demons were faster than I was. I'd only climbed as high as the flag bridge on the first level of the island when two of them reached me. I swung the fire sword right for their eyes. The demons parried and fought viciously. With unbelievable speed and strength, they beat me back. These demons were stronger than the ones I'd fought at Bethesda Fountain. I wondered if being this close to the doorway between dimensions was somehow feeding their strength.

The demons forced me back up against the railing. They both brought their swords down upon me simultaneously. Holding the fire sword horizontally, I managed to block their attack. But they kept pressing forward, their combined strength driving the fire sword closer to my own throat. I strained my arms, trying to push back, but I was outnumbered. In a few seconds, the fire sword would cut into my neck.

I gave one final shove against their blades and threw myself backward over the railing. Luckily, I hadn't climbed that high. When I landed on the deck I wasn't in any danger of smashing my head open. My ankle was another matter. I landed wrong, twisting it. My ankle didn't break, but it hurt like hell.

From the landing above, the lesser demons laughed at me. Apparently assholes existed among demonkind, too.

Behemoth's angry roar caught my attention. I turned to see Gabrielle pummeling him with shock waves. She managed to knock him back a step, but the demon seemed more annoyed than injured. He extended a hand toward her. She tried to fly away, but it was too late. Behemoth caught her in the same gravity field he'd used to crush the others.

# Forty

Hanging in midair, Gabrielle struggled against Behemoth's gravity field, but she couldn't move. I jumped to my feet—then fell again. Damn. My ankle was weaker than I thought.

Across the flight deck, Philip sprang into action. He grabbed the wing of a fighter jet near him and pulled, gritting his teeth with the immense effort. A jagged chunk of metal tore off the wing. He hurled it at Behemoth. The colossal demon didn't see it coming until it struck him in the face. He reeled back with a roar, breaking his concentration and freeing Gabrielle from the gravity field.

A line of oily red blood appeared on Behemoth's cheek where the sharp metal had cut him. I was surprised that anything could make him bleed. But it gave me hope that maybe we could stop him after all.

Gabrielle flew away quickly as Behemoth turned his fury on Philip. He pointed at the vampire, and Philip fell to the flight deck, unable to move. Behemoth lifted one massive centipede leg and slammed it down on Philip's stomach. Philip cried out in pain, but the appendage didn't go through him. Apparently Behemoth was more interested in crushing him to death than impaling him.

I got to my feet again. My twisted ankle screamed at me, but I forced myself to ignore it. I hobble-ran across the deck toward Philip. I didn't have a plan. All I had was the fire sword, which I was pretty sure would be useless against Behemoth, like trying to stop a rampaging bull with a match. I had no idea what I would do once I got there.

But Behemoth didn't let me come any closer. One of his immense centipede legs kicked out, knocking me to the floor. I skidded across the deck portside, stopping between two fighter jets. Wincing in pain, I turned onto my stomach and tried to push myself up. My ankle had other ideas. Unable to get up, I looked back at Philip, hoping he was still alive.

He was. Philip dug his fingers into the hard cartilage of Behemoth's centipede leg. He grunted with effort, muscles and veins bulging beneath his skin. Then, with a loud *crack,* the leg broke, its tip jerking suddenly at an unnatural angle. Behemoth roared in pain, releasing Philip. The vampire ran away in a blur.

I sank back down to the deck. Something under one of the fighter jets caught my eye. It was a lump of burnt cloth, the charred remains of Philip's coat. Next to it was Nightclaw. This was where Philip had dropped the dagger. I began pulling myself toward it—

Something grabbed me from behind and dragged me away from Nightclaw. The next thing I knew, I was rising into the air in a gravity field. Apparently Behemoth was no longer interested in sparing my life. Instead, the demon hurled me through the air toward the side of the island, just as he'd done to Philip. But unlike Philip, I wasn't a vampire. I wouldn't survive a high-velocity collision with a solid steel wall. I braced myself for the impact and hoped the others knew enough to stay away from me when I died.

Gabrielle caught me in midair. My momentum knocked her backward. I held on tight as she regained control and flew me to the opposite end of the ship from Behemoth. The others had already gathered there. She set me down safely.

"Thanks," I said.

Isaac was holding onto Philip for support. He looked worse than before. He'd torn a piece of cloth off his shirt and tied it around the stump of his arm in a makeshift bandage. He was as pale as paper. It wasn't blood loss. The fire sword had cauterized the wound. But Isaac had been fighting off shock for as long as he could, and now it looked like the shock was gaining ground. A stiff breeze could have knocked him down.

"We have to . . . stop Behemoth," Isaac said.

"I found Nightclaw," I said, "but I didn't get a chance to take it. It's still there, under those jets." I pointed.

"How the hell do we get to it?" Bethany asked.

"A diversion," I said. "Gabrielle and Philip can keep Behemoth distracted while you and I—"

"I'm not going anywhere," Philip interrupted. "I'm staying with Isaac."

"No," Isaac said. "You have to. They—they need . . ." He started coughing and hung weakly against Philip.

Philip helped him upright again. "Like I said, I'm not going anywhere. I mean it this time."

"Let Philip stay. I can distract Behemoth on my own," Gabrielle said.

I nodded. Gabrielle took to the air again. Bethany and I started running for the dagger. We didn't get far before Behemoth did something that stopped us in our tracks. Something that told me we couldn't win. That, in fact, we'd already lost.

The giant demon raised his hands over his head, gripped together in a ball. Then he slowly pulled them apart. Something appeared between them, growing larger as he spread his hands.

Gabrielle landed next to me, gaping at it. "My God, is that . . . ?"

I could only nod dumbly. We'd made a terrible mistake. Arkwright told us Behemoth had his own way of tearing the world apart. We should have listened. Behemoth could manipulate gravity. But gravity could do more than crush or repel. It could do more than destroy. It could create things, too. One thing in particular. One terrible, unstoppable thing.

The object growing between Behemoth's hands was a black hole.

Light and dust swirled around it, falling toward it, stretching, fading. The air seemed to bend and distort as it was sucked inside, creating a vacuum that sucked us forward. As it picked up speed and power, Bethany, Gabrielle, and I were pulled off our feet and dragged. A piece of metal debris skittered across the deck, jumped into the air, and soared directly into the black hole. We would follow shortly. That was how black holes worked. They ate everything around them, until there was nothing left.

With one hand, I managed to grab the chain mooring one of the remaining fighter jets in place. With the other I caught Bethany by the wrist. Gabrielle slid past us, but Bethany grabbed her with her free hand. Together, the three of us held on, a human paper chain. But I didn't know how long I could do this. My shoulders were being pulled in two different directions. Already they felt like they were being yanked out of their sockets.

At the top of the island, Arkwright held onto the railing around vulture's row and laughed with sheer, spiteful joy. The lesser demons held on, too, but three of them were pulled off. They flailed through the air toward the black hole, their screams cutting off instantly as they disappeared into it.

Over the howling wind and clatter of debris I heard the sound of wheels. An immense black shape rolled forward along the flight deck. A huge A-12 Blackbird stealth aircraft had been caught in the black hole's gravitational pull, dragging its broken mooring chain behind it. The Blackbird tipped up, then tore through the air. As it approached the much smaller black hole, the Blackbird seemed to stretch out, pulled into the center, and then, without a sound, it was gone. Just gone. Swallowed whole.

All the while, Behemoth stood directly beneath the black hole that grew between his spreading hands, unaffected by its gravitational pull. Maybe that was part of the demon's magic.

The chain I was holding onto didn't break, but the jet it was mooring began to slide. Its rear section swung around one hundred and eighty degrees to face the black hole. The chain twisted in my hands, grinding the skin of my palm. I forced myself to ignore the pain and not to let go. Overhead, more debris rocketed past us into the black hole. The stars in the sky, the bright windows of the New Jersey skyline across the river, even the *Intrepid* itself, they all began to look distorted as the black hole pulled in more and more light.

This was it. This was what the oracles had foreseen that sent them running. This was what Biddy, in his madness, had believed the trembler could protect him from if he fed it enough women. This was what had sent countless supernatural entities fleeing to the Nethercity. This was the end.

The gravitational pull lifted Bethany and Gabrielle off the deck. The only thing that kept me from joining them was my grip on the chain. The pain in my shoulders extended all the way down my arms, but I held onto Bethany's wrist as tightly as I could. Our eyes met. A thousand unspoken regrets passed between us. We'd wasted so much time.

"I can't hold on!" she shouted over the wind.

"You have to!" I squeezed her wrist tighter. "Bethany, you have to!"

"It's too strong! It's pulling me apart!"

I tried to pull her back toward me, but I couldn't. My arm felt like it was on fire. She was right, it was too strong. Her wrist started to slip out of my fingers.

"Trent!" she shouted.

"Bethany, hold on!"

From Bethany's other side, Gabrielle shouted, "Let go, Trent! You have to let go, or you'll die, too! It'll tear you to pieces!"

"No!" I tried to pull them back again. The muscles in my arms and shoulders burned with pain. I ignored it, squeezing my eyes shut and pulling with everything I had. I didn't care if it tore me to shreds. I didn't care if I died and never came back. I refused to let go. I refused to let the black hole take them. I'd already lost Jordana because I couldn't hold on. I wasn't going to let it happen again.

"Trent." It was Bethany's voice. She sounded remarkably calm. I opened my eyes. She was there in front of me, off the ground, her hair flying all around her face, her bright blue eyes focused on me. Tears ran down her cheeks. "She's right. You have to let go. Just let go."

I shook my head. Now there were tears on my face, too.

"It's okay," she said. "It's not your fault, Trent. Please don't ever think this was your fault. You tried. But you have to get away, so you can stop Behemoth before more people die. You can't do that if you don't let go. And then it will all be for nothing."

"No!" I shouted, shaking my head again. But I could already feel her small hand start to slip through mine. "Bethany, hold on! Please! Bethany, I love—"

And then she was torn away from me, she and Gabrielle both, and there was nothing in my hand but the rushing wind.

# Forty-One

It was Isaac who saved their lives. In the end, it was Isaac who saved everyone.

Behemoth roared suddenly in pain and anger. The intense gravitational pull of the black hole stopped. Debris fell out of the sky all around me. So did Bethany and Gabrielle. They tumbled out of the air just a few yards from where the black hole had been.

I blinked in surprise. The black hole was gone. What happened?

I let go of the chain and stood up. At the ship's stern, Behemoth swayed back and forth like he was drunk. I didn't understand until I saw Isaac and Philip. Philip was holding onto the railing at the edge of the flight deck with one hand, and with the other he was holding Isaac by the leg. The mage was right behind Behemoth, his hand wrapped around Nightclaw's hilt. The dagger's blade was sunk deep through the armor of the demon's hindmost centipede segment.

Thick black veins spiderwebbed out from the stab wound. Behemoth teetered precariously on the edge of the *Intrepid,* then fell backward into the river with an enormous splash. A huge wave washed over the deck. Philip pulled Isaac back, still holding tight to the railing so they wouldn't be swept off the ship.

I started running toward Bethany and Gabrielle, ignoring the pain in my ankle, my shoulders, everywhere. The two of them were sore and sopping wet from the wave, but they were alive. I slid to a stop and knelt down over Bethany.

"You're alive!" I shouted.

She smiled up at me. "Now who's Captain Obvious?"

She sat up. I hugged her tight. Her wet clothes soaked into mine, but I didn't care. "I thought I lost you again. Don't scare me like that."

Hugging her was impulsive, spontaneous. I did it without thinking. It surprised me when she hugged me back. I didn't expect her to, but suddenly her arms were tight around me. She was more shaken by her brush with death than she was willing to say, but the way she trembled and held onto me couldn't mask it.

Gabrielle tapped me on the shoulder. "What am I, chopped liver?"

Bethany and I laughed, and we hugged her, too. I helped them both to their feet.

Philip helped Isaac walk over to us. Both of them were sopping wet, but Isaac looked dangerously pale. He blinked rapidly, like he was having trouble keeping his eyes open.

"Something is wrong," Isaac said. "Behemoth's body hasn't surfaced."

"He's dead, he has to be," I said. "Nightclaw can kill anything. You said so."

Isaac nodded. "I know, but something's . . . not right . . ."

He slumped against Philip then, finally passing out after fighting to stay conscious for so long. Philip caught him. He tried to wake Isaac, but the mage was unresponsive.

"Is he all right?" Bethany asked.

Philip scooped Isaac up in both arms. "He will be. In the meantime, Bethany, Gabrielle, spread out and keep an eye on the water. I won't believe Behemoth is dead until I see his body come up."

"What about me?" I asked.

"I'm told you have a plan to take out Arkwright," Philip said. "Make it happen."

I looked up at vulture's row. My hands curled into fists. Finally.

Bethany touched my arm, bringing my attention back to her. "Be careful. This plan of yours is dangerous."

"Aren't I always careful?" I asked.

She arched an eyebrow. "Don't make me answer that."

I left them and ran up the steps of the island. The pain in my ankle was forgotten as I focused on Arkwright. No demons came down to greet me this time. The stairway ended on the second level. I was forced to run through the narrow hallways and cramped rooms of the navigation bridge, past banks of old, brass equipment and through small, oval doorways, before I could continue climbing to the top. Arkwright had left a trail of smashed open doors and gates for me to follow. The trail led me to a rusty ladder, and at the top, vulture's row.

The demons were waiting for me there. As soon as I reached the top of the ladder, they swarmed me. I didn't even have time to light up the fire sword. They pulled me off the ladder and pushed me down onto my knees. I felt a sword at the back of my neck.

Then I waited for Arkwright. I knew his type. He wouldn't let them kill me. Not before he had the chance to spit in my face first.

The demon lifted its sword, preparing to chop my head off.

Come on, Arkwright . . .

"Wait!" Arkwright's voice boomed. "Not yet! Bring him here!"

I smiled to myself. The demons hauled me to my feet and dragged me before him. They threw me to my knees again and held me there.

"I take it you've come to gloat," Arkwright snarled.

I shrugged. "Gloating is more *your* style. Although, it looks like your plan isn't going very well. Behemoth was a bust."

"It's not over." He couldn't hide the angry desperation in his voice. He shook the Codex Goetia in his hand. "I still have the only thing that matters. The Codex names almost a thousand other demons I can summon tonight. I don't need Behemoth to end the world. I don't even need Nahash-Dred. *This* is all I need. I can bring *all* of demonkind here!" He smiled at me, but it was a vicious smile. "Jordana did her job very well, leading me to it."

"Jordana's dead," I told him.

Arkwright shrugged, unperturbed. "She served her purpose."

That son of a bitch. If it weren't for the lesser demons all around me, I would have throttled him until I saw the life drain out of his eyes.

"You lied to her," I said, seething. "You infected her. You turned her into a killer."

"She didn't take much convincing. She took the magic into herself willingly."

"Because she trusted you," I said. "You were the only family she had left."

"Ah yes, Jordana's family. Such a shame what happened to them," Arkwright said. "Her brother Pete was a smart man. He began piecing together my past before anyone else. Unfortunately, he started asking uncomfortable questions, so he had to be dealt with. I cut his throat in an alley downtown. It was an inelegant solution, but I was pressed for time. I thought I hid my tracks well. I even took Pete's wallet so it looked like a common robbery gone wrong. But I suppose I didn't do as good a job as I thought. Pete and Jordana's mother, my wife at the time, grew suspicious. The insufferable cow started poking into his death. She got much too close to the truth for my liking."

"So one night, in Aspen, you summoned a lesser demon to kill her," I said. "Probably to kill Jordana, too. What happened? Why did you call it off?"

"So Jordana told you about Aspen, eh? What she saw there? You're right, I summoned the demon, and I called it off. It would have been too public and gruesome a death to avoid a police investigation." Arkwright grinned cruelly. "There were better ways to silence my wife's suspicions. A quick and extremely painful wasting spell took care of everything. The doctors didn't stand a chance of figuring it out in time to save the poor woman."

I stared at Arkwright in horror. "You killed them both. Jordana's brother. Her mother. You killed Jordana's whole family, and she never knew."

He was responsible for Jordana taking her own life, too. His evil had destroyed an entire family. Arkwright was no better than the predator Philip had been when he wiped out an entire bloodline, albeit with one big difference. Philip was trying to make up for what he'd done. Arkwright hadn't changed at all in the fourteen years since he first tried to end the world. If anything, he'd become worse.

"You sick bastard," I spat. "All Jordana wanted to do was hold onto what was left of her family. You. All she wanted to do was make you happy."

Arkwright grinned. "And I assure you, after her mind was infected, she did. In so many ways."

I struggled like an animal against the demons holding me. I wanted to tear Arkwright to pieces with my bare hands.

"You have no idea how disappointed I am in you, *Trent*," he said, spitting my name like it was a joke. "That you would fall for a ruse that simple. That you would actually care about a pathetic half-succubus with daddy issues."

My hands closed into fists so tight I thought the skin of my knuckles would split.

"But most of all," he said, "I'm disappointed that you don't remember me. Or why you were in the sanctum the night Nahash-Dred was summoned. It's like a riddle, isn't it? The world's simplest riddle, and yet you can't answer it because you *forgot*."

"Why don't you tell me, then?" I said through gritted teeth.

He shook his head in frustration. "It would be pointless. You have to figure it out for yourself. You have to remember. It only works if you *remember*."

"*What* only works?" I demanded. "You're not making sense—"

Arkwright silenced me with a punch to the face. I spat blood onto the floor, my jaw thundering with pain.

"Who are you? What is the *point* of you?" Arkwright raged. "If I could beat the memories back into you, I would, but you have to remember on your own!"

I glared up at him. "I knew it was a long shot, but I thought maybe you would tell me. If you're not going to, I don't see why I should wait any longer."

Arkwright laughed derisively. "Wait any longer for what?"

"Apparently, you have the same problem I do, Arkwright," I said. "You forgot something from that night, too."

"And what would that be?" he scoffed.

"Your mistakes," I said. "The other demons you accidentally summoned, because you and your brethren were too stupid to summon Nahash-Dred properly."

Arkwright chuckled. "Too stupid? Nice try, but you're not going to get under my skin that easily. And who cares about the other demons? They're long dead by now."

"Not all of them," I said.

I whistled. A dark shape detached itself from the antenna array where it had been waiting, unseen. My Plan B dropped down and landed on Arkwright's back, knocking him to the floor. Around us, the lesser demons gibbered and shifted their weight nervously, unsure what to do. Like before, they knew a greater demon when they saw one.

"Erickson Arkwright, meet the Mad Affliction," I said. "He's got a bone to pick with you."

The Mad Affliction wrapped his long fingers around the top of Arkwright's head. His enormous, saucer eyes sparkled with delight. "There is so much madness inside his mind already. So much raw clay I can mold."

Arkwright trembled beneath him. "Get it off of me! Get it off!"

But though the lesser demons continued to hold me where I knelt, they were too frightened of the Mad Affliction to come to Arkwright's rescue.

"You see, the Mad Affliction and I have a deal," I continued. "He helps me, and I send him home."

"You idiot!" Arkwright yelled. "Do you really think that's why he's obeying you—?"

The Mad Affliction slammed Arkwright's face down against the floor, cutting him off and bloodying the man's nose.

I looked at the Mad Affliction. "What does he mean?"

"Nothing. His words are trickery, that is all. Do not listen." The Mad Affliction ran his fingers down the length of Arkwright's skull. "Hold your peace, human, or I will make you pull out your own tongue. You think you know madness now? Believe me, you know only a taste."

"Wait! Please!" Arkwright cried, terrified.

The Mad Affliction leaned closer, his tumescent nose brushing Arkwright's ear and making the man shiver. "I can make you shit yourself and like it. I can bring you to the point where you will *live* to shit yourself. Or I can do worse. Much, much worse."

"Wait!" Arkwright pleaded, looking at me. "If anything happens to me, you won't know the answer! You—you won't know why you were in the sanctum that night! And that means you won't know who you are!"

"I already figured out the answer to your riddle, Arkwright," I said. "I didn't get it at first because it took me a while to understand the question. But I get it now. I know who else was there the night you summoned Nahash-Dred. But you're wrong. That's not me."

"Are you sure?" Arkwright asked. "Tell me, what happened when you touched the lock on the Mad Affliction's cage?"

The Mad Affliction slammed Arkwright's face into the floor again. He yanked the man's head back up. Arkwright looked dazed. Blood streamed from his broken nose, and from the corner of his mouth.

I looked into Arkwright's glazed eyes. "I'm going to let you in on a little secret, Arkwright. The only reason my friends agreed to let the Mad Affliction out of his cage—the only reason they let him be a part of this at all—is because I told them he could get to you when no one else could. I told them how much he wanted revenge. But when we got to the sanctum, they waited in the car and I went in alone. I freed him from the cage you left him in. Then we had a little talk. We came to an understanding about the real reason I wanted him here. The reason my friends will never know."

The Mad Affliction ran one finger through the blood on Arkwright's face, then licked it. His eyes rolled back in his head ecstatically. "Oh, my stomach is a yawning chasm waiting to be filled. I can hold off no longer. Please tell me I get to eat him now."

Terror made Arkwright's glazed eyes sharpen again. "What?"

"Sorry, I forgot to mention," I said. "I didn't just promise him revenge. The Mad Affliction was starving to death when I found him. I also promised him a meal."

"No, you—you wouldn't! You can't just let this—this *thing* eat me alive!"

"That's the secret I wanted to let you in on, Arkwright," I said. "I would, and I can. You see, up until now I thought you should die as painfully as Jordana did. Up until now, I thought that you didn't deserve mercy."

"And—and now?" he asked.

"Now I *know* you don't," I said. I nodded at the Mad Affliction. "Bon appétit."

The Mad Affliction was barely able to contain his joy. His face split into a wide, toothy smile. Then he bit a chunk of flesh out of Arkwright's shoulder. The lesser demons around us chittered fearfully.

Arkwright screamed as blood from the wound spilled across his coat. He glared at me, his face twisted in pain and rage. "Killing me won't stop what I've already set in motion. It won't change anything."

"That's not why I'm doing it," I said.

The Mad Affliction stretched out his wings and tented them over himself and Arkwright. The nervous chitters from the lesser demons grew louder. I couldn't see what was happening under the Mad Affliction's wings, but there was something deeply satisfying about the terrible screams and the sound of tearing flesh and gnashing teeth. Each of Arkwright's screams felt like retribution for what he'd done to Jordana. Each scream felt like vengeance for the lives he'd taken—Jordana's brother, her mother, Yrouel, the *Intrepid* guards down below, the innocent bystanders Behemoth had killed tonight, the real Clarence Bergeron, and who knew how many countless others he'd killed along the way.

Was Calliope among them? I still had my doubts.

Arkwright's screams didn't last long. Not as long as I would have liked, anyway. But even after they stopped, the sound of eating continued. The lesser demons all around me wavered like heat mirages and then vanished. Erickson Arkwright was dead. And this time, he would stay dead.

I got to my feet again. When the Mad Affliction was finished with his meal, he folded his wings back and wiped a hand across his bloodstained mouth. I looked at the foul, bloody mess he crouched over, the bones and gristle that were all that remained of Arkwright. The son of a bitch had gotten what he deserved. I pulled the Codex Goetia out of what had once been his hand and put it in the inside pocket of my trench coat.

The Mad Affliction licked the blood off his claws and looked over the railing at the flight deck below. Gabrielle and Bethany were still watching the water for signs of Behemoth. Philip was off to one side, tending to the unconscious Isaac.

"I thank you for the meal, but after such a long fast I am barely sated," the Mad Affliction said. "Perhaps you will allow me dessert? The vampire looks particularly tasty. His kind always tastes of spice and smoke."

"That wasn't part of the deal," I said.

The Mad Affliction nodded, disappointed but understanding. He turned back to me. "Where I come from, there are those who are loyal to Behemoth, and those who are loyal to his brother Nahash-Dred. I am loyal to Nahash-Dred. If Behemoth is dead, you have made my lord the crown prince, the next in line for Leviathan's throne. I suppose gratitude is in order for that as well."

"Arkwright said Nahash-Dred was nearby," I said. "Is that true?"

The Mad Affliction paused a moment, then nodded.

"Where is he?" I asked.

"Close," the Mad Affliction said. "Closer than you think. I told you I would not recognize him if I saw him in another form. That is not entirely true. But my lord has hidden himself for a reason. Perhaps we should let that stand."

"Just tell me if he's a threat," I said. "If he's not, if he just wants to be left alone, then I've got no beef with him. But if he's a threat, I need to know."

The Mad Affliction thought a moment. "Is a tiger dangerous even if it does not wish to be a tiger anymore? It still has claws, it still has teeth. Its nature is tiger even if it wishes to be something else. And so it is with my lord. One day soon, I fear he will have to choose which to embrace: his true nature, or the life he has chosen in its place. No one can have both for long. Not even the Destroyer of Worlds."

I knew the feeling. Once again, unexpectedly, I found myself sympathizing with Nahash-Dred. His experiences and mine didn't seem so far off. But then another feeling came over me. A terrible, sinking feeling.

*What happened when you touched the lock on the Mad Affliction's cage?*

"Nahash-Dred isn't the cloaked man," I said.

"No. That is not the form he has taken."

I swallowed through a tight and dry throat. "When Arkwright said my promise to send you home wasn't why you were obeying me, what did he mean?"

The Mad Affliction looked at me with an expression that seemed almost tender coming from a demon. He held out one clawed hand. "Goodbye, my friend. Until we meet again."

I took his hand. It was bigger than mine, the skin as rough as stone where it wasn't slick with Arkwright's blood.

"Goodbye, Mad Affliction. But we won't meet again."

"I think we will," he said. "When you have made your choice."

The Mad Affliction flew up into the sky. I watched him go, flapping steadily toward the glowing rift in the sky, a silhouette against the bright light.

I looked down at my hand. There on my palm, under streaks of dirt and demon eye goo and Arkwright's blood, was a fading red burn mark in the shape of a pentagram. It didn't hurt anymore, not like it had when I first got it. The pentagram had been etched into the padlock on the Mad Affliction's cage. It was why the demon couldn't break the lock himself. It burned him whenever he touched it. When I went to free him, it had burned me, too. In the end, I'd had to break the padlock with the butt of my gun.

Who else had been there the night nearly fourteen years ago when Arkwright's doomsday cult summoned Nahash-Dred? I knew the answer. There was only one person it *could* be.

A wise man once said that when confronted with a mystery, the easiest and least complicated solution was usually the right one.

I turned around and went back down the island toward the flight deck. Passing through the navigation bridge again, the interior of the ship felt vast and silent and empty. I felt the eyes of thousands of ghosts upon me, all of them dead before their time. Had they always been watching me? God knew they had reason to.

Bethany met me at the bottom of the steps. "Are you okay?"

I nodded.

She looked up and saw the Mad Affliction flying toward the rift. He grew smaller and smaller as he approached the light. And then he was gone, back on his own side of the doorway.

"I take it the plan worked?" she asked.

"Arkwright is dead," I said.

She turned back to me and studied my face. "Are you sure you're okay?" She put her hand on mine. I looked down at it, then back up at her.

"I think so," I said.

"You said 'I love,'" she said.

"I . . . what?"

She brushed the wet hair out of her face. "Before, when the black hole was open, you said 'I love,' but you never finished the sentence. What were you going to say?"

I studied her face. Her sky blue eyes sparkled like diamonds. She already knew what the rest of that sentence was. I could see it in her eyes. She just wanted me to say it out loud.

And I wanted to. Christ, how I wanted to. But how could I, now that I knew the truth? How could she ever trust me if *she* knew?

We were interrupted by Gabrielle. "Trent, are you all right?"

"It's over," I said. I opened my trench coat and showed them both the Codex Goetia in the interior pocket. "Short of breaking it into fragments and hiding them again, I think Isaac's vault is the safest place for it. How's he doing?"

"I think he'll be okay. Philip's looking after him," Gabrielle said.

On the other side of the deck, Isaac was lying unconscious on the floor with his rolled-up duster under his head. Philip crouched over him.

"I swear, those two should just get a room already," Gabrielle muttered. "How did it go with Arkwright?"

"He's dead," I told her, "and the Mad Affliction has gone home."

She nodded. "I'm glad it worked out. Involving another demon in the plan was pretty damn risky. The Mad Affliction could have turned on you up there."

Somehow, I doubted he would have.

Bethany looked up at the sky again. "Uh, guys? If Arkwright and Behemoth are both dead, why is the doorway still open?"

I looked up at the brightly glowing rift in the sky. Strange. I'd figured it would take time for the doorway to close all the way after Arkwright's death, which was how I knew the Mad Affliction would have time to fly home. But the rift hadn't gotten any smaller. Something was keeping it open.

Two colossal hands appeared on the side of the deck. The railing crumpled under Behemoth's immense weight as the demon pulled himself up. River water poured off his titanic form.

I stared at Behemoth in horror. It was impossible. How had he survived being stabbed with Nightclaw? Then I saw his lower, centipedelike body now had only five armored segments instead of six. His hindmost segment, where Isaac had stabbed him, was gone. Behemoth had shed it before Nightclaw's deadly magic had spread to the rest of him, like a lizard dropping its tail.

Behemoth reared up, towering above us. He bellowed a roar that was both angry and triumphant. In that moment, two things became horribly clear. The first was that Arkwright hadn't completed his binding spell after all. If he had, Behemoth would have returned to his dimension the moment Arkwright died. The second was that the doorway between worlds was still open because Behemoth, Lord of Ruination, crown prince of all demonkind, *wanted* it open.

# Forty-Two

Behemoth hit us with a gravity field before we could react, sending us flying in different directions. I landed on my back halfway down the flight deck. When I tried to get back up, I couldn't. Even turning my head took immense effort. I managed it just enough to see the others pinned to the deck, too.

Behemoth went for Gabrielle first. She was closest to him, slumped against the base of the island. She tried desperately to stand, pushing with her hands against the wall behind her and with her feet against the floor. It was no use. She couldn't move. Behemoth approached her, his five pairs of centipede legs thumping on the flight deck.

I tried to push myself up, but I was stuck like a subway rat in a glue trap. As much as I labored and strained, all I could do was watch in horror as Behemoth extended one hand toward Gabrielle, preparing to crush her in another gravity field.

Thornton stepped between them, his wolf form translucent and glowing like a star.

Gabrielle's eyes widened in astonishment at the sight of him. Apparently, I wasn't the only one who could see him. Thornton looked up at Behemoth, his lip curling in a snarl. Behemoth reeled back. The demon looked almost afraid.

His hold on us broke. I sprang to my feet and ran toward the others, ignoring the sharp pain in my ankle. I reached Bethany first. She was just getting to her feet, staring incredulously at Thornton. The wolf advanced on Behemoth. The demon inched backward, away from him. Gabrielle stayed where she was, staring at Thornton.

"Do you see him, too?" Bethany whispered to me in awe.

"I see him," I said.

I took her hand and started running again, this time toward Philip. The vampire crouched protectively over Isaac's fallen form, staring at the ghost wolf in amazement.

"It's Thornton, isn't it?" Philip said. "Somehow I knew we hadn't seen the last of that hairy son of a bitch. But what's he doing here? *How* is he here?"

"He had to have help," Bethany said. "Someone on the other side. Someone powerful enough to help him cross back."

She didn't know who it was, but I had a few ideas. Ingrid Bannion, Willem Van Lente, even Morbius sprang to mind. Any one of them could have helped send Thornton back. But why? What was he doing here, besides saving our asses?

Gabrielle finally moved. She crawled on her hands and knees toward Thornton. She reached for him. Her fingers grazed the aureole of Thornton's glow—and then passed right through him. Dejected, she moaned, her shoulders slumping.

Thornton turned to her. The moment he broke eye contact with Behemoth, the demon attacked. The tall, metal island above Gabrielle bent, warped, and started to fall. She leapt to her feet and ran as the antenna array and radar dishes crashed to the deck. I couldn't see Thornton anywhere in the collapse. Apparently Behemoth couldn't, either. No longer interested in us, the demon began poking through the wreckage, searching for the ghost wolf.

Gabrielle reached us and stopped to catch her breath. "It's Thornton! He's here, he came . . ."

She couldn't finish. Every emotion she'd forced down into her gut, every emotion she hadn't let herself feel since starting her quest for vengeance came bursting through the dam. Overwhelmed from the force of it, she broke down and sobbed. Bethany put her hand on Gabrielle's arm. Gabrielle pulled Bethany to her and cried into her shoulder.

Across the deck, Behemoth lifted the crumpled radar dish and tossed it aside with a loud crash.

"Philip, take Isaac and get back," I said. "It's not safe here."

Philip scooped up Isaac's unconscious body. "What about you?"

I pulled the Codex Goetia out of my coat. "This thing is supposed to be the big demon-controlling artifact, right? I'm going to see if it lives up to its reputation. Now move."

Philip carried Isaac to the far end of the ship, overlooking Twelfth Avenue. I studied the etchings and designs on the face of the Codex. I wished I knew what the hell I was looking at. I couldn't read the words written on it. I couldn't make heads or tails of the concentric shapes on it, either. A circle, a heptagon, a seven-pointed star, a smaller heptagon, and a pentagram. What did it mean? What the hell did any of it mean?

Behemoth continued poking through the wreckage. It wouldn't be long before he turned his attention to us again.

"Trent, hurry," Bethany said.

"How do you work this damn thing?" I demanded.

"We don't have time to figure it out," Bethany said. "We have to try something else."

"What else is there?" I asked. "Even Nightclaw failed. The Codex is all we have left."

Unable to find Thornton in the debris, Behemoth turned back to us and roared angrily. Time was up. I would have to wing it. I held up the Codex, pointing it at Behemoth. I hoped it would know what to do on its own. It didn't. Nothing happened. Like Erickson Arkwright, I didn't know how to use the Codex. And like him, I was going to get everyone killed because of it.

The Codex was pulled out of my grasp to fly through the air into Behemoth's waiting palm. He closed his hand into a tight, crushing fist. When he opened it again, tiny, broken pieces of metal rained down to the deck. Damn. There was no way anyone could put those pieces back together again. The Codex Goetia was gone. Destroyed. There was no way to bind Behemoth now. No way to banish him back to his dimension.

"Shit," I said. "Run."

We ran to the far end of the ship, where Philip was waiting with Isaac's prone form. "I take it the Codex didn't work out?" Philip asked.

"Didn't stand a chance," I said.

"It's just as well," he said, picking up a lesser demon's fallen sword off the deck. "That wouldn't have been as much fun anyway. Keep an eye on Isaac. He's out cold, but he's stable."

"What are you going to do?" Bethany asked.

"This," Philip said. He blurred across the deck toward Behemoth. But even at that speed, Behemoth stopped him with a gesture. With another, Philip was blown clear off the ship and into the Hudson River.

By now, it was clear Behemoth had had enough of us. He brought his hands together over his head. A new, tiny black hole began to form between them. Behemoth glared down at us. He knew there was nothing we could do to stop him now. Bethany and Gabrielle knew it, too. I could see it in their faces. They knew this time the black hole would grow bigger and bigger, unchecked until it tore the world to pieces. They knew this time they wouldn't be able to stop it.

The pentagram-shaped burn in my palm began to ache again. I looked at it, swollen and red on my skin. Then I remembered the pentagram at the center of the Codex Goetia, and an idea formed in my head.

There was still one final chance to stop Behemoth. Something only I could do.

There was more than one way to bind a demon.

Normally this was something I would have asked Isaac to help me with, but the mage was unconscious. Gabrielle, however, was not. She wasn't as adept at magic as Isaac was, but she was all I had. I told her what I had in mind.

"We can't banish him without the Codex, but we can snare him," I explained. "All we need is a pentagram. A big one. It won't kill him, but it'll keep him trapped."

"How big does it need to be?" she asked.

"As big as you can make it," I said.

"Give me the fire sword," she said.

I handed her the hilt. She lit it up and threw it with all her might, shouting a spell. The fire sword stayed lit and flew like a torpedo down the length of the flight deck. Then it swerved, circling around Behemoth. Its blade pointed down to the floor, tracing fire in its path. Like the crossbow bolts, this fire was magical. It didn't require fuel to catch. The sword drew a burning circle around the demon, then zipped quickly back and forth under him until it had formed a burning Five-Pointed Star within the circle. Then the fire sword extinguished and dropped to the floor.

The entire aft section of the ship had become one giant pentagram of fire. The flames leapt into the air, growing taller, shooting upward to form a curtain around Behemoth. It had all happened too fast for the demon to stop it. Now he found himself trapped. He screamed in agony, but not from the flames. It was the pentagram itself that was burning him. The black hole forming above him collapsed in on itself like a closing iris.

Gabrielle and Bethany let out a loud cheer of relief. But it wasn't over. Not yet. Behemoth was trapped, but he wasn't dead. He was still dangerous. As if to show us just how dangerous, the aircraft carrier began to rise up out of the water and into the air. The ship tilted suddenly to one side as the thick, woven anchoring lines fastening the *Intrepid* to the pier went taut. Some of them snapped, others pulled their mooring posts right out of the cement, and the ship leveled off, continuing to rise. Behemoth wanted us dead. He would do whatever it took, even if it meant levitating the whole damn ship so high we suffocated from lack of oxygen, or dropping us so that we were crushed on impact.

"The only way this is going to end is if Behemoth dies," I said.

"How?" Bethany demanded. "We don't have Nightclaw anymore."

"I know a way," I said. "There's something I can do. But only me."

"No," Isaac interrupted. He was awake again. He wrapped his good arm around the railing and pulled himself up to his feet. Some color had returned to his face, but he still looked the worse for wear. His voice was scratchy and hoarse. "I'm not going to let you sacrifice your life so you can take Behemoth's. You lost control when you tried that with Stryge, remember? His power was so immense it overwhelmed you. You wound up nearly killing the rest of us. What do you think is going to happen if you absorb the life force of a greater demon?"

Isaac was wrong. It wasn't Stryge's power. Reve Azrael had told me the truth. I knew that now. The power was mine. It had been mine all along.

"Dying isn't what I have in mind this time," I said. "But we're out of options, Isaac. There's only one way to stop Behemoth. Trust me. I know what I'm doing."

Isaac took a deep breath, then nodded. "Just be careful."

I turned to go, but Bethany stopped me. "Trent, wait. If it doesn't work . . ."

"It'll work," I said. "It has to."

The ship continued its slow rise into the air above the Hudson River. Bethany grabbed the lapels of my trench coat, pulled herself up onto her toes, and kissed me. For a moment, everything stopped. I wanted it to stay like that forever. It didn't. It never does. When she pulled away, I stared at her in surprise.

"I know what the rest of the sentence was," she said. "But how about when this is over, you can tell me if I'm right?"

I touched my forehead to hers. It sounded wonderful. It sounded like everything I'd ever wanted. But I knew when this was over I would have to tell her the truth about me, and that would change everything.

I turned away from her so she wouldn't see the anguish in my face. I walked toward the enormous fire raging on the other end of the aircraft carrier, and the bellowing demon that waited for me within it. As I drew closer, Thornton appeared before me. His lips pulled back in a snarl. His hackles rose. Was he mad at me about something? I was confused, but I ignored him and kept walking toward the fire. I couldn't let myself be distracted now. Thornton leapt at me. His translucent, glowing form passed through me. There was no vision this time. Instead, I only felt the hot blast of an urgent word slamming into me.

*STOP!*

Why did Thornton want me to stop? Did he think the fire would burn me? Did he think Behemoth would kill me? I was worried about those things, too, but I kept walking. I didn't have a choice. There was no other way out of this.

My vision shifted as I approached the curtain of fire. It wasn't involuntary. This time it happened because I *wanted* it to. For the first time, I was in control of it. I knew why. I'd accepted it as part of me. I'd accepted the power as mine. In front of me, the curtain of fire became a wall of jumping, swirling, blazing atoms like tiny exploding suns that gave off ripples of streaming, red heat. I performed a simple rearrangement, and the curtain opened for me. I passed through, into the pentagram. The burning circle closed up behind me.

And then we were alone, just Behemoth and me.

# Forty-Three

It was unbelievably hot inside the curtain of fire. On either side of me were two angled, flaming lines of the burning pentagram. Sweat squeezed out of every pore in my body. Within seconds, my clothes were soaked.

Behemoth towered before me, roaring in pain. The pentagram was burning him in a way that the flames couldn't. It was a pain beyond physical agony. I knew because I felt it, too, being inside the pentagram. It took everything I had not to roar in pain with him. Slowly, Behemoth became aware of my presence. His expression changed as he looked down at me, just as it had the first time he saw me. Except now I understood why. He recognized me.

Inside Behemoth were atoms the likes of which I'd never seen before. They were big and angular and ringed. The atoms of his dimension, not ours. Instead of being bound together by the silken threads, they were interlocked by long, curling, leathery tendrils.

But the strangeness of Behemoth's atoms didn't matter. I could still manipulate them. With no more than a thought, I rearranged them—mixed them, swapped them, pulled them apart. Behemoth screamed in agony. But even though Behemoth wouldn't have hesitated to kill everyone I cared about, I felt no satisfaction in this. No sense of triumph. Because killing Behemoth this way told me without question who I was. It showed me my true nature and forced me to embrace it.

Behemoth screamed and screamed.

I put him out like a dying star.

Behemoth fell to the deck with a heavy thump. My stomach lurched as the *Intrepid* dropped back into the river. It hadn't lifted very high, thankfully, but it splashed down hard. The ship rocked violently. I fell to the deck. I was lucky I didn't break any bones or get thrown into the fire. I couldn't see them through the flames, but I heard tidal waves crash all around us—onto the cement pier, onto Twelfth Avenue, into the river. I got to my feet again as the ship found its equilibrium.

Behemoth was still alive, but dying. I could hear his heart beating in the massive cavern of his chest, slowing with each thunderous stroke. He'd fallen with his head right beside me. His gigantic eyes were already glazing over as they fixed on me.

And then he spoke.

"There are more coming through the doorway behind me, brother."

"Don't," I said. I shook my head, fighting back tears of anguish. "Don't call me that."

"The Selenian Legion," Behemoth continued. His breath rattled in his chest. Blood dripped from his mouth. "My personal guard. I have thrown open the gates of Nimon and freed them from Tellenor, where you imprisoned them so long ago."

I looked up at the rift in the sky.

"You are too late," Behemoth said. "The doorway cannot be closed. I have seen to that. When the Selenian Legion finds you, my brother, they will take their vengeance upon you."

I shook my head. "Stop calling me that."

"Why do you continue to wear the face of these ridiculous creatures?" Behemoth asked. "You should have destroyed them when you had the chance. Or was this your plan all along? Was this how you plotted to steal Father's throne from me? Well played, brother. Such cold-minded treachery. You are indeed our father's son. I think he must have foreseen this day when he named you. Even when you were a child, he knew of your temper and the havoc that spread in your wake. It is why he named you Nahash-Dred. In the old tongue, it means the Storm Without End."

The Storm Without End. The Immortal Storm. Suddenly it all made sense. A bitter, terrible sense.

Tears streamed down my cheeks. "No, no, this isn't me . . ." But it was pointless. I knew Behemoth was telling the truth. Deep down, I knew. I'd known since I figured out Arkwright's riddle.

Who else besides the cult had been there the night Nahash-Dred was summoned? It was a trick question. The answer was right there in the wording. The night Nahash-Dred was summoned . . . Nahash-Dred was there.

The Destroyer of Worlds. He Who Puts Out the Stars. The Burning Hand.

The Wearer of Many Faces.

The clues had been right in front of me, but I'd refused to see them. Before she died, Ingrid had seen something in my aura that terrified her, something that wasn't human. The oracles had called me a mighty warrior in the guise of a man, a man who wasn't a man. They said that as long as I walked upon this world, I was a danger to everyone. Erickson Arkwright had recognized me because he'd seen the human form Nahash-Dred had taken upon leaving the sanctum. *My* form. And then there were the sarcophagi where Nahash-Dred had hidden the three fragments of the Codex Goetia. Each time they pricked my finger, they hadn't been taking a sacrifice. They'd been taking a blood test. Because only my blood could open them. My fingerprints, my retinas, every physical feature that could be used for identification could change as easily as my face. But my blood would stay the same. My blood was the key.

The Guardians had warned me that Nahash-Dred would be revealed tonight. They'd asked me if I was prepared for it. Like a fool, I'd said yes.

I thought of all those pictures of ruined civilizations. Of the enormous, terrible creature towering above the trees in the film from 1950s Africa. Me. It was me.

"I don't remember," I told Behemoth. "I don't remember any of it. Why can't I remember?"

But Behemoth was already dead. His eyes stared sightlessly at me. This was the moment Arkwright would have bound me, I realized. In order to kill Behemoth, I'd had to embrace the truth about myself. I'd had to accept who I was. If Arkwright were still alive, he would have taken the opportunity to bind me with the Codex Goetia. He would have forced me to destroy the world for him. To kill everyone I cared about. He was right, it would have been the perfect revenge.

I touched Behemoth's cheek. His skin was tough and leathery and warm—from the fire, not from life. The atoms inside him hung cold and still. My brother. I'd killed my own brother. Another victim of Nahash-Dred, like the thousands of ghosts I'd imagined watching me earlier. Or maybe I hadn't imagined them. Maybe they really were watching, waiting to avenge what I'd done to them. Wasn't that what I deserved? With all the blood on my hands, didn't I deserve to die, too?

Except . . . I couldn't.

There was no doubt who I was anymore. I was Nahash-Dred, a shape-shifting demon who had lost his memories and gotten stuck in the shape of a man. I looked at Behemoth, lying dead before me. Demons could die. *The Book of Eibon* said they could die. Behemoth *did* die. So why couldn't I?

I'd peeled back one mystery only to find more waiting, unanswered.

I extinguished the fires of the pentagram, mentally putting out each of its burning atoms. With the pentagram gone, the pain left me, too. I let my vision return to normal. I stood on the scorched flight deck of the half-destroyed *Intrepid* amid the ruins of its antique aircraft collection, next to the dead body of a gigantic greater demon who used to be my brother. Just another day on the job. I didn't know whether to laugh or cry.

Bethany came running up to me and jumped into my arms. She didn't say anything. She didn't have to. She kissed me again, but all I could think about was the shame of who I was, and the horror she would feel when I told her. I gently lowered her back down to her feet. I didn't want to tell her. I never wanted to tell her.

"Are you okay?" she asked.

"I am now," I said.

She looked at Behemoth's body within the charred remains of the pentagram. "What happened in there?"

"I took his insides apart," I said. "The same way I took apart Arkwright's library. It was the only way to stop him."

Gabrielle came up then, helping to support a woozy-looking Isaac. "Was that Thornton I saw?" she asked.

"Yes," I said. "He tried to stop me from going inside the pentagram. I don't know why. Maybe he was trying to protect me. Where is he now?"

"He's gone. Again," she said sadly. "He keeps . . . not staying."

Philip's booming voice came from one side of the ship. "Looks like I missed the party."

Soaking wet, he pulled himself over the railing and onto the flight deck. His torn, sopping clothes trailed river water behind him as he walked over to us. Yet somehow his mirrored shades were still perched over his eyes. They weren't even scratched.

"Heads up," Philip said. "This isn't over yet. Shit's about to get a hundred times crazier."

"What do you mean?" I asked.

"I don't know what's going on, but there's about a hundred revenants standing at the bottom of the river," he said. "They're not doing anything. They're just standing there, like they're waiting."

Revenants? I ran to the railing and looked down at the water lapping at the hull below. I couldn't see anything in the river, it was too dark. But if there were revenants down there, it could only mean one thing. Reve Azrael was still alive. She'd survived the fire. Damn it, would I never be free of her? What did she want? Why send her revenants here?

I stiffened as the answer came to me. Oh, God. Thornton had tried to warn me. It was why he'd wanted me to stop. It wasn't because he thought I was in danger. It was because he knew what would happen if I killed Behemoth.

I started running back toward the others. "Get away from him! Get away from the body!"

But it was already too late. Behemoth's enormous pupils filled with red light. The dead demon stood, rising onto his enormous centipede legs. Bethany and the others scattered, running past me. I stayed where I was. I knew what Reve Azrael wanted. Me.

"At last," she said through Behemoth's mouth. "A body worthy of me. Thank you, little fly. I knew I could count on you."

"You survived," I said.

"Barely," she replied. "You could call that pathetic, half-burnt *thing* in my lair alive if you choose, but as a body it is useless. It always was. As you can see, I have a better one now. Stronger. Brimming with power. Such unimaginable power."

She extended one hand. Caught in a gravity field, I began to float off the deck. I didn't bother struggling. I knew I couldn't fight Behemoth's power. *Her* power, now. She lifted me until I floated before her.

"This is a thousand times better than Stryge's power would have been," she said. "And I owe it all to you. You are so easy to manipulate. All I had to do was leave a message to get your attention."

"What message?"

"The woman you rescued from the lunatic in the park," she said.

"Calliope?" I went cold. A pit opened in my stomach. "*You* killed her. *You* gutted her and nailed her up like that."

"I suppose I have always had a flair for the dramatic," she said. "When my revenants and I broke into her attic and entered her home, she surprised us on the stairs. I cast a quick spell. I meant only to incapacitate her. I wanted to enjoy her suffering before killing her, you see, but the wretched woman fell back and struck her head on the steps. There was so much blood. She was dead before she even knew what hit her. I found her death much too quick for my liking, and hardly enough of a spectacle to get your attention. So I took over her dead body and . . . played with it awhile. A woman has to have her fun, don't you think? And this was very, very fun. With a knife, I made it cut itself open and play with its own innards. Then, when I grew tired of it, I had my revenants nail the body to the ceiling."

Now I understood why there'd been such an excessive amount of blood on Calliope's hands. Except for a bare, rectangular patch on her right palm. The size and shape of a knife's handle.

"I am disappointed you did not recognize my message to you," Reve Azrael said. "I stretched out her innards to make her look like a fly caught in a spider's web, just for you. You *are* my little fly, are you not?"

I felt sick. Calliope wasn't dead because she'd gotten too close to Arkwright's secret. She was dead because of me. Because Reve Azrael wanted to send a message. She must have been spying on me the night I brought Calliope home. The guilt sat like a stone in my chest.

"She had nothing to do with you and me," I said. "She didn't deserve that."

Reve Azrael cocked Behemoth's head at me. "What does deserving have to do with it? I wanted her to die, and so I made her die. Her death led you where I needed you to go. It led you to this very spot. Led both of us to this moment, where I would have a body worthy of my ambitions, and you would discover the truth of who you are."

"So you knew," I said. "You knew who I was all along."

"From the moment of your first death, I knew," she said. "I know all who cross the dark. Though why you refuse to stay dead remains a mystery to me. You confound me and fascinate me in equal measure. That is why even though I have the power to crush you with a thought, or release you from gravity's pull to float up into the cold, airless wastes, I know you would only continue to plague me."

Bethany's voice came from below. "Put him down."

I looked down. She was standing beneath us. The sword blade sprang out of her bracelet like a warning.

Reve Azrael laughed. "Ah. The tiny woman. She is never far from you, is she? Shall I make you watch as I crush her bones to dust? Would that be fitting enough punishment for everything you have done to me? The pain you have caused me?"

"You're going to have to get through the rest of us first," Isaac said.

I looked down again. They were all there—Isaac, Philip, Gabrielle, and Bethany. They'd come back for me. They shouldn't have.

"Go!" I shouted down to them. "Get out of here while you can!"

"We're not going anywhere," Bethany said. "Not without you."

"Let Trent go," Isaac said. "We defeated Behemoth once. We can defeat him again."

Reve Azrael looked at me, amused. "He called you Trent. They do not know, do they? You have not told them."

I didn't answer.

"Surely they have the right to know for whom they are risking their lives?" she said.

"Trent, what is she talking about?" Isaac asked.

"Don't," I begged Reve Azrael. "I'll do whatever you want, just don't."

The dead demon's face split into a wide smile. Reve Azrael laughed and released me. I dropped to the deck. My ankle flared with pain. I collapsed onto my side. Bethany rushed over to me, the blade retracting into her bracelet. She knelt down and cradled me against her knees.

"Are you okay?" she asked.

"Go," I said, tears squeezing out of my eyes. "Get away from here."

"I am talking about his true name, mage," Reve Azrael answered Isaac. "He has not told you his true name."

Bethany glared angrily up at her. "He doesn't know his name, you know that!"

"He knows it now," Reve Azrael said. "Behold the demon. Behold Nahash-Dred in the form he took in which to hide. The form he took so he could forget."

I could feel their eyes on me. Staring at me. Wondering how this could be true.

I lifted myself off Bethany's legs and onto my knees. "I didn't know," I said, looking at each of them. "Please, you've got to believe me. I didn't know until now."

"This was not how I wanted you to find out, little fly," Reve Azrael said. "Not at first. But I promised you your defiance would not go unpunished, remember? I cannot kill you, we both know that. But I can destroy you. I can crush your spirit. And how better than with the truth you have been looking so hard for?"

"I didn't know," I repeated, looking up at Isaac. He, Philip, and Gabrielle stared at me, agape. I turned to Bethany. Reached out for her. "Please . . ."

She backed away in fear and confusion. If I could have willed myself dead, I would have done it in that moment. But then she paused. Collected herself. She took a step toward me—and another, quicker, and then she had her arms around me. She helped me to my feet. I held her close.

"I'm sorry, I'm sorry," I repeated.

"You don't have to be," she said, her voice breaking. "I told you before, it doesn't matter who you used to be. All that matters is who you are now. We all have choices to make. We all have to decide who we want to be. But that comes from inside, not from anyone else."

"How touching," Reve Azrael said. "A shame time is about to run out. Do you remember what Behemoth told you, little fly, right before he died? The memory is still fresh in this body's mind."

The sky flashed then, brightly and repeatedly, but it wasn't lightning. Balls of fire fell out of the rift like comets. They splashed down into the Hudson River, rocking the boat with their waves.

"The Selenian Legion," Reve Azrael said. "Behemoth's personal guard. A force so destructive, so unrelenting that Behemoth's enemies, including you, imprisoned them out of terror. They are the demons that even demons fear, and they obey only Behemoth. To them, I *am* Behemoth. When they look upon me, they will see their master, and they will obey me. Only me."

Where each of the comets had splashed down, a gigantic shape burst up from the water. There were seven of them in all, each as tall as Behemoth. Their charcoal-black bodies looked more like stone than flesh, run through with glowing veins of fire. Enormous, bull-like horns crowned their foreheads. Slabs of iron had been bolted over their eyes, and huge iron collars circled their necks. They wore iron manacles on their wrists, from which dangled the broken ends of huge, iron chains.

"Run, little fly," Reve Azrael said.

We backed away from her. When her army of revenants started to climb out of the water and onto the ship, we broke into a run. My ankle slowed me down, but Bethany held onto me, pulling me along.

"Run!" Reve Azrael called after us.

The seven demons of the Selenian Legion threw back their enormous, horned heads and bellowed. They waded toward the *Intrepid,* their colossal legs churning up waves that rocked the ship. Isaac lost his footing and fell. The Guardians' scroll fell out of the inside pocket of his duster. It rolled across the floor and into one of the small fires still burning on the deck. The old, crisp parchment caught fire immediately, its ashes blowing away on the wind, just like the Guardian of Time had said it would.

Philip and Gabrielle helped Isaac to his feet. We kept moving as the Selenian Legion waded closer to the ship. Their stony bodies burned. Their immense horns seemed to scrape the sky.

"Run far and run fast," Reve Azrael shouted after us. "Because this city, this *world,* is mine!"

# Forty-Four

I tried to save the world. I tried, and I failed.

I was wrong about the horrors the oracles foresaw. I was wrong about what Calliope and the others knew was coming. It wasn't Nahash-Dred. It wasn't even Behemoth. It was Reve Azrael and the Selenian Legion. The city would crumble. Countless people would die. It was what some had seen and others sensed. It was why they ran. It was what Calliope had tried to stop, before Reve Azrael killed her. For nothing. For me.

And it was why *we* ran. With the Selenian Legion wading closer at our backs, we ran off the wreckage of the USS *Intrepid*. Already the towering demons were kicking up waves that crashed across the piers and onto Twelfth Avenue. Or what was left of Twelfth Avenue. The rubble from the destroyed overpass and the damaged storage facility had fallen to the street. Our Escalade lay somewhere beneath mounds of debris. Other cars did, too. And people. Pedestrians, drivers, the police and EMTs who had responded to the catastrophe. All of them killed by Behemoth.

Something stirred in the rubble. A block of concrete fell away from a crushed police car, and a uniformed officer pulled himself out. He straightened, standing on a hill of debris. Blood soaked his clothing and his face. One side of his body had been mashed to a pulp. A bright red glow emanated from his eyes.

"Run, rabbits," Reve Azrael said through the dead officer's mouth. "Run!"

More rubble shifted. Dozens of red-glowing eyes opened beneath the concrete and twisted rebar. More maimed, blood-soaked revenants pulled free of the ruins. I kept running, taking a moment to glance back at the

*Intrepid*. On the ruined flight deck, Reve Azrael in Behemoth's body gathered the Selenian Legion to her. Below, revenants climbed out of the Hudson River and onto shore.

We scrambled over the chunks of concrete and twisted scraps of metal in our path, but it felt futile. We didn't have a car. We had no place to go. We'd never reach Citadel before we were overtaken.

"Look!" Gabrielle shouted, pointing.

It was Thornton. The glowing ghost wolf stood atop a mound of rubble, watching us.

"He wants us to follow him," Gabrielle said.

"How do you know?" Isaac asked as Philip helped him over the debris.

Gabrielle knit her brow. "I—I can hear him in my head."

"It's your gift," Isaac said. "Your ability to read minds. Somehow, he's using the connection between you to tap into it."

"I don't care how he's doing it," Gabrielle said, her eyes tearing up. "I'm just glad to hear his voice again."

We followed Thornton up Twelfth Avenue, away from the *Intrepid*. Slowly I began to recognize the neighborhood. I realized then where he was taking us. The only safe place left in New York City.

I heard screams behind us. The screeching of tires, the blasts of car horns. The unmistakable rumble of a building collapsing. I turned around in time to see the brown, brick UPS building across from the *Intrepid* fall over. The Selenian Legion had come ashore.

Bethany grabbed my hand. "We have to keep moving!"

I stared at the devastation unfolding behind us. Towering, horned shapes moved against the skyline. Another building collapsed into a cloud of dust and debris. More screams. I went cold. There was no one to help them. There was no one to stop this.

Bethany pulled me forward. "Trent, we have to go! There's nothing we can do!"

I ran with her to catch up to the others. She was right. There was nothing we could do. But what if there was something *I* could do?

A squad of police cars raced past us down Twelfth Avenue, their sirens screaming. Behind them came fire trucks and ambulances, and then the news vans. Police choppers zoomed overhead. I wanted to tell them all to turn around. They didn't stand a chance. They were rushing to their deaths. But they flew past me too quickly, and there was no way to reach them.

Isaac was feeling strong enough to walk on his own, so Philip let go of him. The mage didn't fall. He had regained at least some of his strength. I broke away from Bethany and pulled Philip aside, out of earshot of the others. I asked him for two favors. The first was to go back to Citadel to pick up a couple of important items. Knowing how fast he could move, he was the only one who could do it safely. The second favor was much more dangerous, but again, he was the only one I could ask. He agreed to both without hesitation. He ran off in a blur. I rejoined the others and continued up Twelfth Avenue with them. When they asked me where Philip had gone, I told them he would be right back.

A few minutes later, we reached the hollow ruins of an old apartment building across from De Witt Clinton Park. I remembered this place. Thornton led us into the overgrown field behind it. A metal door sat in the ground. The wolf passed through it and disappeared. Gabrielle didn't need to translate that one for us. Thornton wanted us to follow him down to Tsotha Zin, the Nethercity.

I pulled open the door for the others and held it as they climbed down into the darkness. Gabrielle went first. Isaac followed, maneuvering himself slowly down the rungs of the ladder with his one hand. Bethany went next. I was about to go in last when I saw a shape watching us from the shadows of the overgrown field.

It was the cloaked man. The crow perched on his shoulder cocked its head at me.

Fuck this guy. I wanted answers and I wanted them now. I stormed over to him. The cloaked man waited for me. A grin grew on his pale lips beneath the black hood.

"Who are you?" I demanded. "What do you want from me?"

"You have paved the way," he said. "It has begun."

"You knew this would happen?"

He didn't answer. Of course he knew. He'd shown me the future. He'd shown me what I had inadvertently set in motion tonight by killing Behemoth. I felt a growing urge to punch him in the face, but I resisted it. He knew something, and I wanted to know what it was.

"What's begun?" I asked. "What have I paved the way for?"

"The return of the true masters," he said. "And the end of everything."

I grabbed his hood and yanked it down. His white skin was veined with black all the way to the top of his bald head. He had dark, empty holes where his eyes should be. Eyes that were on the backs of his hands instead. He laughed and laughed.

Bethany called my name. I turned around. She was poking her head out of the doorway in the ground. "Are you coming?"

I turned back to the cloaked man. He was gone.

The end of everything. Just like they'd always said. The Immortal Storm would bring about the end of everything.

I climbed down the ladder after Bethany. I left the door open for Philip. I hoped he wouldn't be too much longer.

Bethany waited for me at the bottom of the steps. "What were you doing up there?"

I looked back up at the open doorway far above us. "Did you see him?"

"See who?" she asked. "All I saw was you."

"The cloaked man came back," I said. "He told me it was the end of everything. Then he was gone. Who is he? Why does he keep showing up?"

"I don't know, but we need to find the others. Come on." She took my hand and pulled me into the sewer tunnels.

We caught up to them as Thornton led the way through the tunnels. I knew now why he'd come back. Why he'd been following me all this time. To stop me from making a crucial mistake. But it hadn't worked. I'd killed Behemoth. Just like the cloaked man said, I'd paved the way for Reve Azrael to take control of his body and the Selenian Legion. I'd paved the way for the end of everything.

Deep in the lower levels of the sewer system, the secret doors that led to Tsotha Zin were already open. Eventually, we came to the ice bridge that was the entrance to the Nethercity. My breath clouded in front of me. I gathered my trench coat around me to keep out the chill. In the distance an impossible, snow-capped mountain range sat far below the streets of New York City.

Gregor was waiting for us by the bridge. His massive, reptilian head emerged half-shrouded from the mists below. The cold, white fires of his eyes burned from within his stone-gray scales.

"There is little time left," the dragon said. "Tsotha Zin is already swollen with refugees. We have opened our doors to more topsiders than I ever imagined. Were you not Thornton's friends, I would have turned you away."

It occurred to me this was where Thornton had disappeared to. After he warned me to stop and I didn't, he knew what would happen. He'd come here to make preparations. His own Plan B. How many times did I owe my hide to that crazy, dead werewolf? I'd lost count already.

An open iron door waited in the rock wall on the other side of the bridge. Thornton sat on his haunches in front of it. Gabrielle crouched down beside him. Thornton tipped his head toward her. She did the same. Their foreheads passed right through each other, but Gabrielle laughed as tears streamed down her cheeks.

"I can hear you," she murmured. "Oh God, I missed your voice. I missed you so much."

Philip came running onto the bridge to join us. He was wearing a new shirt and coat, and was holding one of the items I'd sent him to Citadel for. Kali, secure inside her carry case. The cat was wide-eyed with fear, mewling and pressing herself against the back wall of the case. Philip was sopping wet, but he spoke before I could ask him why.

"It's a shit show up there," he said. "They've moved inland from the Hudson River. They're already in Hell's Kitchen, destroying everything they come across. I saw whole apartment buildings come down. There are bodies in the street, but they don't stay down long. Reve Azrael is reanimating them. People are trying to get away, but if the demons don't get them the revenants do. It's bedlam."

"I always knew this day would come," Gregor said. "I always knew the darkness on the surface would grow too strong to be contained. I warned you topsiders of this many, many times, and yet you chose to continue living on the surface. If only you had come down to Tsotha Zin long ago, as so many others did." He swung his massive, horn-crowned head toward the door. "I must close the door soon. When I do, it will remain closed. Enter now, and be quick. There is nothing we can do but wait out this madness, and try to survive until it is over."

"You're wrong. There *is* something," I said. Bethany was pulling me toward the door, but I stopped her. "I can't go with you."

"What?" she demanded. There was panic in her eyes.

"Someone has to try to stop this," I said.

"But you can't—"

"Think about it," I said. "They're demons. Apparently I am, too. No one else can stop them."

She shook her head. "Trent, no, it's too dangerous."

"If you're going, you're not going alone," Isaac interjected. "I'm coming with you."

I looked at him. He was pale and stooped, drained and exhausted. I wouldn't be surprised if he was still partially in shock. He wouldn't be any use like this. He'd only get himself killed.

"Forget it, Isaac," I said. "You're needed here. So are you, Bethany."

She shook her head again, harder this time. "I won't stay if you're not staying."

"You have to. I can't do this if I don't know you're safe."

"I can't stay here if I don't know *you're* safe," she insisted.

"I will be. I'm taking a bodyguard." I turned to Philip. "I know you already said yes, but I have to ask again. Are you sure you're up for this?"

"Damn straight." The vampire turned to Isaac. "As long as it's okay with you, old man. It's you I've pledged service to, not Trent. If you say the word, I'll stay with you."

Isaac nodded. "Go. If anyone can help keep Trent safe, it's you. After all, you've done it for me all these years."

"I won't let you down, old man," Philip said. He pointed at Bethany and Gabrielle. "I'm leaving him in your care. If anything happens to him, you'll have to answer to me." He pointed at Thornton. "You too, fuzz face. Just because you're dead doesn't mean I can't fuck you up."

Thornton dipped his head in a nod. Then he turned around and loped through the open doorway.

"Good luck, you two. Watch your backs out there," Gabrielle said. She hugged us, took Kali's carry case, and followed her fiancé through the door.

"There are no phones or e-mail down here," Isaac said. "If you two are going back topside, you'll be completely on your own."

"I know," I said.

"If it doesn't work," Isaac said, "if you can't stop them, come back."

"If we can't stop them," I said, "there won't be anything to come back to."

Isaac nodded solemnly. He shook my hand, then went to Philip.

"And you," he said. "What can I say? You've come such a long way, Philip. The things you did in the past, the things you've tried to make up for . . ." He paused, his eyes growing teary. "Your bravery, your integrity, and yes, your *goodness* have made me proud."

Philip frowned. "Cool it, old man. I've got a reputation to uphold."

Isaac held out his hand. Philip shook it. They grasped hands for a long moment. Then Isaac let go and walked through the door.

Bethany looked up at me. Her eyes were full of things she wanted to say, all fighting to come out first. Finally, she said, "Be careful."

"Don't worry about me," I said. "If there's one thing I'm good at, it's not dying. For long."

She threw her arms around me and hugged me tight. I hesitated to return the hug.

"You know who I am now," I said. "*What* I am."

"I don't care." She pulled my face down to hers and kissed me. "You're Trent. You've always been Trent to me. Any other name, any other life you had, they don't matter to me. *You* matter."

"You're not scared of me?" I asked.

She smirked. "How could I be scared of you? You can't even beat me at gin rummy."

I laughed and kissed her again.

The booming sound of an explosion from far above interrupted us. Dust and pebbles rained down onto the ice bridge.

"They are close," Gregor said. "I must close the door now."

"Trent," Bethany said.

"I'll come back for you," I said.

We kissed again, one last time, and then Isaac and Gabrielle came back out and pulled her away from me. Pulled her through the doorway. She called my name one more time. The iron door slammed shut, cutting her off. I went to the door and put my hand on the cold metal. I hoped she would be safe here. I would do everything I could to make sure she was. To make sure they all were.

"If you are going topside, you must go now," Gregor said. "I will seal the doorways behind you. Good luck. I pray you succeed. But if you do not, then I pray your deaths are quick and without pain." With that cheery farewell, the dragon sank back down into mists.

Philip looked at me. "You really think we can do this alone? You saw those demons. They're as big as redwoods."

"We won't be alone," I said. "Did you bring the other thing I asked you to?"

He nodded. "It was right where you said it would be. Under your mattress. You might want to come up with a new hiding place one of these days."

"It's an old habit," I said.

Philip took the object out of his pocket and put it in my hand. It was a carved bone whistle the gargoyles had given me.

*Use this should you ever have need of us, and no matter where we are, we will come.*

"There's just one more thing," Philip said. He reached into his soaking wet coat and pulled out Nightclaw, wrapped in its black velvet cloth. "I had to go back in the Hudson for it, but it was just where we left it, sticking out of Behemoth's ditched hindquarters. One blow from this dagger will end any demon that tries to mess with our shit." He looked at me pointedly. "*Any* demon. You understand me? You start reverting back to your old ways, I won't think twice about cutting you. And don't go thinking this is something you can come back from, either. This is Nightclaw. The Guardians forged it to kill the Voyavold. If I cut you with it, you'll stay dead. So you make sure to keep that demon shit in check."

"Fair enough." I took a deep breath. "Are you ready for this?"

"To watch a demon fight other demons? I wouldn't miss it for the world," he said.

A demon fighting other demons. It reminded me of something Crixton said. *Demonwar is coming.* I didn't know what he meant until now.

Another crash sounded above us. More dirt and stone rained down onto the bridge.

"Going back up there is suicide," Philip said. "But I suppose we all have to die sometime."

"I suppose we do," I said.

We left the ice bridge, retracing our steps back through the tunnels toward a dark and dying city.